A CROWN
This
COLD
and
HEAVY

STACIA STARK

If you can force your heart and nerve and sinew
To serve your turn long after they are gone,
And so hold on when there is nothing in you
Except the Will which says to them: 'Hold on!'

— Rudyard Kipling

1

PRISCA

Click.
Click.
Click.

The sound scratched at my senses. My eyelids were so heavy, it took everything in me to open them even to slits.

Sunlight stabbed into my eyes, and I instantly slammed them closed. But I'd gotten a glimpse.

A carriage.

I was in a carriage. Moving. I tensed my hands. Tied. My mind whirled. What was I doing—

Lorian.

Demos.

Asinia.

Oh gods. *Cavis.*

The web on his face. The web that meant he was one of the human king's spiders. Those who were often planted in foreign courts as children.

Lorian's words drifted into my mind.

"Cavis was from Jadynmire. One of Galon's men found him wandering

alone and barefoot in the forest. He was the only survivor."

He'd only reached six winters. And Regner had already gotten to him, twisted his mind, used his filthy magic to plant a seed in Cavis that he could use at any time.

Fury blazed through me. And this time, I managed to keep my eyes open.

They met bright-blue eyes. Eyes that laughed at me.

I knew those eyes.

The man smiled at me, and I went still in the way of prey. His smile widened.

"I'm not exactly sure how you've woken so soon," he said. "But it's rather impressive."

I kept my expression blank. Dark hair, wide shoulders, and those amused blue eyes. I'd met him at an inn soon after Lorian and I had docked in Gromalia. I'd been consumed with bitter jealousy as Lorian spoke to a beautiful fae woman, and this man had approached me.

"You're far too beautiful to be frowning into the flames."

How long had he been following us? Who was he? And how quickly could I slit his throat and jump from this carriage?

His mouth twitched. "You're sitting there, half drugged, clamped in fae iron, yet you're actively planning my murder, aren't you?"

Ignoring him, I turned my attention to the other man in the carriage. The one I hadn't yet been able to look at.

Cavis stared straight ahead, as if he wasn't present.

Blood slipped from his nose in a steady drip. Dread coiled in my stomach, my throat clamped shut, and the world spun around me. Cavis had done everything he could to let Lorian kill him before he took me. Now…he looked like he was gone.

"What did you do to him?"

The man tutted. "That's from fighting the compulsion, I'm afraid. Regner will be *very* interested to see this."

My breath shuddered from my lungs. It might not look like it, but Cavis was still fighting. Looking at him was agonizing, and the man who'd put me in this carriage was obviously enjoying my pain. I turned my gaze back to him.

"What exactly do you want from me?"

"Perhaps I'm interested to see who the hybrid heir is when she's not clamped to the side of that fae bastard."

I gave him a pitying look. "If you think he'd beat you in a fight, just say that. This is unnecessary."

His smile was cold. "Let me guess. You think he's coming for you."

I knew he was.

He angled his head. "Do you truly believe we didn't have something special waiting for the Bloodthirsty Prince, your brother, and anyone else stupid enough to travel with you? They're not going to rescue you. By now, they're all dead. So I suggest you begin learning how to cooperate if you want to save yourself some pain."

My stomach clenched, and I clamped down on the urge to heave. It was a lie. They weren't dead. I would know, deep in my bones, if they were. I would feel it. He was trying to get under my skin.

"Don't believe me?" He shook his head. "You will."

His fist flew toward my temple, and the world turned black.

LORIAN

The creature smashed through the labyrinth walls, tossing stone and fae iron aside as if they were nothing.

Four colossal legs, gnarled and twisted—the bark-like skin resembling ancient tree trunks. Those legs ended in wickedly curved talons that gleamed in the light orbs.

Asinia ducked, narrowly missing a rock to the side of her head. A rock the creature had kicked at her.

That told me it had some level of intelligence.

"Watch for the traps!" Demos roared as we sprinted toward the entrance.

"It's almost on us," Asinia panted. She tripped, and Demos caught her arm, pulling her faster.

I brought up the rear, guarding their backs. The creature's fetid breath dampened the air, and I cursed. "We need to make a stand."

Demos darted around another rock. "We need to get closer to the entrance first."

He didn't say the words we were all thinking. With the way the creature's vicious horns were slamming into the roof of the caves, they could crumble at any moment.

We'd spent two days down here, moving as quickly as we could. Regner had arranged for the creature to find us at the worst possible time—when we were running out of food, water, and patience.

I risked a glance over my shoulder, aiming my power in a thin bolt toward its feet. I had so little left, I was almost completely drained. Useless.

The creature roared, falling back. But not before I caught another glimpse of it.

It looked like something out of my worst nightmares.

My worst nightmares *before* I'd met Prisca. Now, the slobbering beast behind us was nothing compared to the knowledge that she was gone.

That she had been *taken*.

Right in front of me.

Demos wore her hourglass around his neck. And he was moving faster, while my own steps slowed.

The hourglass was countering the fae iron. Because it recognized his blood.

"Use your power," I snarled.

"I am. My power is telling us to fucking run."

I didn't even have the energy to curse. Asinia launched herself over one of the traps, and I followed, sending another bolt over my shoulder.

The creature snarled.

Prisca had already lost too many people. Of the three

of us, I had the best odds of survival. "I'm going to distract it." I lunged over one of the traps. "Get out of here."

"Not happening," Demos snarled back, ducking beneath the low ceiling of the next cavern. "Prisca needs you. You're our best chance to get her back."

I didn't bother arguing. He was as stubborn as his sister, and it would just waste time. Silver flashed on one of the walls, catching my attention. I recognized these caverns. We'd hidden a few dead bodies around here somewhere. "Where are the guards we killed?"

Behind us, the creature roared. Asinia let out a choked sound that might've been a laugh. "Something tells me the monster set off one of the traps. Hopefully that distracts it for a while."

"The bodies are three caverns to our left," Demos said. "I think."

"I have an idea."

MADÎNIA

"Do you need anything else?"

I smiled at the innkeeper's wife. "No thank you. I'm going to rest."

"Well, be sure to lock your door."

I kept the smile on my face, nodding as I closed the

door. I'd need to find new accommodations soon. This woman was far too nosy.

Her insistence on making sure meals were delivered to my rooms had made it much too difficult to eavesdrop on drunk patrons. I ground my teeth. Eavesdropping was my best chance at finding the smallest seed of information about Jamic's whereabouts. If we could find Regner's false son, we could prevent the human king from reinforcing his barrier.

I needed *something*. A direction. A whisper about guards gathering somewhere remote. A sighting of one of Regner's generals in a place he shouldn't be.

Instead, drunk travelers had spoken of strange creatures being bred near various mountains, of wards in unlikely places, of armies gathered in the ashes of several northern villages.

So I traveled through Eprotha in the guise of a rich widow, listening for anything we could use.

I traveled alone. I ate alone. I slept alone.

And it was glorious.

There was no one to look at me with censure in their eyes. No one to demand *obedience*. No one to stare at me as if *I* were the great betrayer.

Father's ashen face flashed through my mind.

"How? Gods, how? How did I miss such a thing?"

And then, to learn he knew I wasn't corrupt. Knew my magic wasn't a rejection of the gods but was instead from my mother's bloodline…

Prisca had made my father admit to being weak. And

a hypocrite. At the time, I'd wanted to slap her. Now, I recognized it for the gift it was.

Because I didn't have either the time or the inclination to mourn a weak hypocrite.

Striding to the window, I threw it open, gazing down into the bustling street. I'd made it to a fishing village north of Thobirea. An area of the kingdom I'd never been to before. I wanted to be out, roaming the city like a stray cat, soaking up everything I could. Unfortunately, I had to be careful not to draw attention from the guards. The priestesses. Even with the wash of blue on my temple declaring me *legal*.

A knock sounded on my door. The innkeeper's wife. Again. My skin burned at her intrusiveness, but I pasted on a smile and crossed the room.

The boy who blinked at me was unfamiliar. He was also dressed in Regner's colors. I went still, summoning my fire until my hand heated—the warmth a comfort.

"Are you Madinia Farrow?"

My hand heated further, and he swallowed as if he knew just how close to the edge I leaned.

One second to kill the messenger, another three to drag his body inside. My bag was packed, and I'd already climbed from the window my first night here to ensure I'd never be trapped.

"Message from Her Majesty," he said, slowly holding it out.

My heart stopped and then restarted again, pounding double time. How exactly had that bitch found me? I wasn't even due to cross into Eprotha until three days from now.

I'd found a woman who'd helped me dye my hair the moment I'd left the fae lands, and it was now a dark brown. I kept to myself and had sent no messages except to let Prisca know where I was.

The safest approach would be my first plan. And yet, my hand rose as if on its own, plucked the message from his hand, and left a coin.

My curiosity would always be my downfall.

"Go," I said.

He went.

Turning, I moved back to the window, watching as he left the boarding house, glancing over his shoulder. No one followed him.

I opened the message.

Madinia,

A clever woman would notice Gromalian forces gathering in the eastern sector of Thobirea.

You always were far too clever for your own good.

No signature, but that wasn't surprising. Besides, I'd recognize Regner's queen's handwriting anywhere.

The question? Was she leading us into a trap?

I'd seen Kaliera commit a number of atrocities over the years. This could be her attempt to regain trust with Regner. He would enjoy sentencing me. And he'd certainly enjoy watching Prisca burn.

My mind provided me with an image of my father's head hitting the ground. Directly before the rest of his body. I fisted my hand, crumpling the letter.

Before we'd left the camp, Lorian had given us all fae-bred pigeons to ensure we could communicate.

But…Prisca needed to find the hourglass. Tibris wasn't an option either. He'd left to negotiate with Gromalian rebels, and the last I'd heard, Demos had gone with Prisca. Besides, Demos was an inflexible bastard.

Vicer would be deep in Eprotha by now, attempting to convince the hybrids to travel south to the fae lands. But…he might have people on the ground. If he didn't, he could probably put a team together.

Scrawling a quick note of my own, I took my pigeon out of her cage. I didn't understand how the birds knew which of us to travel to, but Lorian had simply told us to clearly state the name of the person we wanted to contact.

"Take this to Vicer," I said.

2

PRISCA

Pain.

Awareness came hand in hand with the pain that exploded behind my closed eyelids. With a strangled gasp, I managed to curl to the side.

"She's awake."

"I told you she'd wake up."

"She could still die. He hit her too hard."

I barely suppressed the moan that wanted to escape. The air had been stolen from my lungs. My eyes burned, and I sucked in an unsteady breath.

Demos had once told me the first rule of being a prisoner—you cry, and you're done.

But gods, it hurt. And beneath the pain was a blind terror I'd never felt before.

I swallowed down the lump in my throat, took a deep breath, and attempted to push the hair off my face. My hands didn't move.

Fae iron. Claustrophobia bit at me

with sharp teeth. No wonder it felt as if I were suffocating. The manacles were constructed from dark iron, the surface pitted and scarred. They were heavy enough that it was difficult to lift my hands, the chain between them short.

I scanned my surroundings. My cell was dim, lit only by a light orb floating in the corridor across from the bars encaging me.

The cell was perhaps seven footspans wide and nine footspans long, the stone floor and three of the walls cracked and damp. One corner held a bucket of water, the other an empty bucket I refused to think about. A wall of bars separated me from what seemed to be a long corridor, and the guard dressed in Eprothan colors leaning against those bars.

My heart tripped, and I took another deep breath. And then another. Slowly, I sat up, the room dancing. My gaze managed to lock on the face pressed to the bars. Clean-shaven, red hair, missing several teeth.

This wasn't the dungeon beneath Regner's castle. So, where was I? How long had it been since I was taken?

The guard grinned at me. I stared back at him until the smile dropped from his face.

"You don't look like much, Hybrid Heir."

Ignoring that, I checked the rest of my body. I had a bruised elbow, my muscles ached, and my head felt as if someone had stabbed me in the temple. But I was alive.

Where was Cavis?

The guard stepped back, already bored. Were there cells next to mine? I couldn't hear any other prisoners, but the guard had moved to my left, out of sight. He muttered to the other man—likely the first guard I'd heard speak.

Giving in to the dizziness, I lay back on the floor.

Cavis appeared in my mind, that web covering one side of his face. The shock and horror in his eyes when he'd realized he was acting against his own free will.

Lorian, Demos, and Asinia had to be alive. I refused to even consider the alternative.

But they were expecting me to stay alive too. I wouldn't let them down.

"I once told you that until you faced up to the reality of your life, you would continue to be a victim to it. And my reality is this—I'm in love with you."

I hadn't said it back. I'd felt the words deep in my soul, and I hadn't told him. If I died here, Lorian would never know how I felt.

I'm in love with you too.

LORIAN

The creature snorted in the distance, heading straight for the bodies. Demos had dragged them into one of the main caverns, ordering Asinia to hide and wait. Her crossbow wasn't ideal for fighting in close quarters, but she was hidden in the cavern across from me now, crouched down and peering around the rock.

Demos cursed as he got into position. Despite his dark mood, he'd agreed my plan was strategically sound, suggesting only minimal changes.

I pulled my knife. The blade was long, light, and would let me thrust and cut as needed. It was as familiar in my hand as if it were merely an extension of my limb, and yet never had it been so important.

Every minute we spent in these fucking caverns was another minute Prisca was alone and in danger.

Demos cursed again.

I aimed a glower his way. "Perhaps you should speak a little louder. The creature might not have heard you yet."

He let out a garbled string of insults that would have made me smirk under any other circumstances. Then he fell silent. Across the cavern, Asinia tucked herself farther around the corner, until the tip of her arrow was all I could see.

The creature let out a sudden roar. We'd managed to remember where the traps were located, and while some of them had been disarmed by Regner's guards, there were plenty that the beast continued to stumble into. Hopefully it would be weakened by the time it reached us.

Although, from the enraged growls coming closer, that was unlikely.

Another roar, and now I could smell the sickening scent of its breath—a cross between mold and carrion. Asinia let out a choked sound and immediately fell silent.

This would be the most dangerous part. The creature had been tracking us, but it was difficult to know just how sharp its sense of smell was. The bodies we'd found were now sprawled just ten footspans away. I breathed through my mouth, squinting in the dim light as the creature drew closer.

Those tree-trunk legs were powered by a huge mass of corded muscle and thick hide. Spikes arced over its broad back, perhaps a footspan apart. Fuck.

Two long horns jutted from its head above glaring yellow eyes, burning with crazed hunger. It caught sight of the bodies and roared again, its gaping maw stretching wide, revealing rows of serrated teeth.

One of Asinia's bolts flew through the air, wedging itself into the creature's flank. It snarled, but the arrow had barely even pierced its bark-like skin. The creature ignored it and slowed, trotting toward the bodies.

Not ideal. But my fae-made dagger was more likely to be able to penetrate its skin.

Stepping out from my hiding spot, I slashed my knife across its neck. Blood sprayed, but the creature kept moving, barreling into me. My back slammed against the cave floor, the air driven from my lungs. I lifted my knees to my chest, protecting my body from its gaping mouth and long, sharp teeth.

Asinia fired again, this time hitting below its neck, where the skin was thinner. Her bolt stuck in its throat, and its next roar was one of pain. It lowered its head, snapping its teeth at me and bathing my face in its hot, rancid breath.

I drove my knife up beneath its chin. Blood poured,

drenching my face.

Demos dropped onto its back. He'd managed to slide neatly between the spikes, right behind its head, and he slashed his sword into the side of his neck, slicing flesh and muscle.

I wedged my knife deeper, driving it up, until I caught a glimpse of it in the creature's mouth. Above me, Demos sliced, his teeth bared as he held on to one of those horns, and the creature tossed its head in an attempt to throw him off.

Asinia darted forward.

"Don't," Demos snarled.

She ignored him, nimbly dancing around the creature's huge legs and shoving her own knife into its belly.

The sound it made was terrible.

Asinia ripped the knife through its vulnerable skin, gagging at the ropes of intestines that slipped out. She'd mortally wounded it. Impressive.

The creature lashed out with a leg, slamming it into her chest.

She flew across the cavern, hit a wall, and slumped to the ground.

"Sin!" Demos roared.

"Keep slicing," I ground out, yanking on my knife until the creature let out another snarl. It was fighting to get away now, attempting to rip itself free from my knife in its mouth. Demos continued to cut, but his knife had less effect, as if his blade were dulling against the creature's skin.

The beast dropped to one knee, and I rolled free, leaving my knife in its mouth.

Pulling my sword from its sheath, I slashed at the side of the creature's neck. It howled, and slumped, falling either unconscious or dead.

Fucking finally. I caught my breath as Demos leaped off its back, dropping to his knees next to Asinia.

"She's alive," he said, his voice tight. "But she's unconscious."

My eye twitched, and I pressed a finger to the muscle. Now we needed a healer. Demos was also wounded, although trying to hide it, and if Asinia was still limp, utterly defenseless, her head wound was serious.

Stalking over to her, I gently ran my thumb over the back of her head. The lump showed distinct swelling. Fuck.

My body would naturally begin healing as soon as we were out of these fucking caves. My plan had just changed. I'd get Demos and Asinia to a healer, and if they were unable to travel, I'd find Prisca alone.

I could feel her. She was still alive. But she was the single greatest threat to Regner. If I didn't get to her soon, she was dead.

Everything in me rebelled at the thought.

Demos hauled Asinia into his arms. I studied the blood matted in her hair. "We'll find her a healer," I told him. Just as long as we didn't run into any more of Regner's little surprises.

Demos just nodded. I gathered my weapons, and we continued our slow progress toward freedom.

THE QUEEN

The musicians were already playing when I entered the ballroom with my ladies. Gone were the days of the girls bickering with one another and flirting with rich, titled nobles. Now, they clung together like a flock of sheep surrounded by wolves.

Sabium lounged on his throne as the court bowed to me. Disgust tightened my throat. He looked in the peak of health, his eyes gleaming, cheeks flushed, as if he enjoyed nothing more than war. The court straightened, watching as I walked to my throne. This ball was about keeping up appearances and making it seem as if this kingdom—and this court—were untouchable.

Patriarch Rothnic Boria stood near the throne. He'd taken his son's death badly. Sabium had delighted in this, promising him his revenge—if he could use the brilliant mind that had created horseless carriages to create something far more…deadly.

Rothnic had agreed. Several of my spies had attempted to uncover exactly what he was working on, with no luck. The patriarch worked night and day, obsessed with obliterating Madinia.

If he ever got his hands on her, she would die screaming for mercy.

A calculated risk.

I sat, waving away a cup of wine. Sabium continued his conversation. He no longer even attempted to hide most of his plans from me.

I knew what that meant.

The moment he killed my son, he would kill me too. Why would he bother lowering his voice when I wouldn't be alive to tell anyone his secrets?

My heart pounded until I could hear it in my ears. I knew Sabium. And recently, he'd begun looking at me with the ghost of a smirk on his face, those dead eyes glinting with suppressed amusement. If everything went according to his plan, my life would be over in a matter of weeks, if not days.

"Tell me, Your Majesty, have you managed to find Caddaril the Cleaver?" Rothnic asked.

A muscle twitched in Sabium's cheek. No one else would have dared ask such a question, but Rothnic knew he was safe. At least for now.

Sabium had allowed his guards to arrest anyone suspected of being "corrupt". However, many of them used the opportunity to settle old scores. Caddaril's human son had been burned as a hybrid, and the crime lord had fanned the sparks of fury among the population. That fury had turned into riots, which had taken weeks to suppress. I'd hoped for even more unrest, but the residents of this city had grown fearful as Sabium's guards slaughtered those creating the most mayhem.

Sabium had invited the Cleaver for dinner. Caddaril had gone underground instead. Now, Sabium looked weak. But more importantly, the Cleaver wanted revenge.

"Not yet." Sabium kept his voice neutral and stretched out his legs. "However, it is only a matter of time. He will fall in line."

No, he wouldn't. Sabium had killed his only son. Once again, he was demonstrating that he had no idea how people reacted to such loss.

I allowed myself to fantasize about Caddaril taking Sabium by surprise one day. Driving a sword into the king's gut when he least expected it. Sabium was too well guarded—and warded—for that, of course, but the thought was as comforting as a hot fire on a frigid day.

A messenger approached Sabium's throne, bowing deeply. Sabium flicked his fingers, took the message, and scanned it.

Shock darted over his face, followed immediately by unmistakable triumph.

My mouth went dry, my stomach churning uneasily. Anything that Sabium looked that joyful about…

"I have something I need to attend to," he said. He wasn't speaking to me. No, he nodded at Rothnic, who bowed his head, his eyes glittering with curiosity.

Sabium got to his feet, ignoring the court as they bowed. He stalked from the room, and I swept my gaze over the courtiers. None of my spies was here. But I knew where one of them would be.

If I left now, so soon after Sabium, it would be noted. And I couldn't afford any hint of suspicion. So I waited, pasting a placid, bored expression on my face. I even allowed Rothnic to lead me onto the dance floor, my skin prickling in distaste the entire time.

"You seem distracted, Your Majesty."

"We're at war, Patriarch Boria. All of us are distracted."

"Hmm."

"If you'll excuse me," I said when the dance ended. "You know how these things drain me."

"Of course." His gaze met mine, and my pulse quickened. Rothnic had always been dangerous, but his son's death had unleashed something else in him. Something that wanted blood. He smiled and released me. "Goodnight, Your Majesty."

I scanned the room for my ladies. They were allowed to stay as long as they liked at these things, but all of them fell into formation, following me out the door as if I would protect them.

"Do you need anything, Your Majesty?"

"No. Goodnight, Lisveth."

She nodded, glancing at the others. They walked together up the stairs. The terror of this court had done what nothing else could have. They'd given up their petty jealousies and chosen to cling together for safety instead.

I found Nelia outside my rooms, pretending to examine a mirror in the corridor for smudges. She wore her usual heavy woolen dress, her shoulders rounded and bent. As the woman who oversaw every servant—from the stable hands to the kitchen workers—Neila had access to every inch of this castle, which made her an exceptional source of information.

"The servants you manage have been a disappointment," I snapped at her. "My own mirrors are covered in fingerprints."

Nelia's eyes met mine. Deep frown lines were etched between her brows, and she bowed her head. "Please allow me to take a look, Your Majesty. I will punish whoever is responsible."

I waved my hand, and she hurried forward, opening my door.

"I will check all of your mirrors personally," she announced loudly.

"Fine."

Nelia checked each room for anyone who might be lingering, while I stood in front of the fire. The weather was much milder than it had been, but I still preferred the warmth.

Finally, she stepped out, her face pale.

"The hybrid heir has been caught," she blurted, dropping her obsequious act. "She is being held in one of Regner's hidden dungeons."

A hole opened in the pit of my stomach. Without the heir alive, my son had no chance.

"He won't bring her here." I turned and faced the fire. "At least not until he's gotten everything he needs out of her."

"No, Your Majesty. He knows this castle is full of spies. And he won't risk someone setting her free."

I turned to face her. "Where is he keeping her?"

"I'm not sure."

I wasn't surprised. I'd known my husband had many dungeons scattered across this kingdom, and all I could do was narrow down the potential options until we had more information.

"What happened to the Bloodthirsty Prince?"

"I don't know, Your Majesty."

My hands fisted, and I reached for patience. "How many guards did Sabium take with him? How much food are they traveling with? Did any of them mention how many nights they were expecting to be away?"

She blinked. "I will find out."

I nodded. "Quickly."

She turned and strode from the room. I swiped a shaking hand over my face. If the hybrid heir was slaughtered before she managed to free my son, all of this was for nothing.

Sabium's face flashed in front of my eyes. The shocked pleasure. He'd laid all of his plans, hoping to capture her, and yet some part of him hadn't expected it to work.

Would Madinia trust me regarding the Gromalian hybrids? And if she did, would that trust make her believe me if I could discover the location of Sabium's dungeon? I was trapped here, unable to free the hybrid heir. But if

Madinia trusted me, there was a chance she could free her.

Depending on the location of the dungeon, it would take Sabium anywhere from hours to days to reach the heir. He might even lose control, kill her there, and bring her body back to be displayed on the city walls.

I couldn't let that happen.

At least, not yet.

3
PRISCA

ootsteps on stone. I roused myself enough to crack my eyes open as the man from the carriage appeared…*Eadric*. Gone was the feigned amusement he'd worn like a mask. Now, his expression was blank, eyes hard. My chest tightened. This didn't bode well for me.

He gestured to the red-haired guard without sparing him a look. The guard sneered at me as he unlocked my cell door and slipped the key back into his pocket. Another man followed Eadric into my cell. Shorter than me, skinny to the point of scrawny, he walked with quick steps, almost scurrying after Eadric. He kept his thinning hair long, and it parted as he walked, revealing a wide section of bald scalp.

The cell door slammed closed behind them, and the space seemed to shrink by several footspans.

A muscle twitched in Eadric's cheek. He was clenching his teeth now. I kept my back pressed against the wall and waited him out.

Two men joining an unarmed woman in a locked cell never ended well. At least, for the woman.

"It seems your brother has taken the hourglass," he told me.

My chest lightened, and I could suddenly take a full breath. If Demos had the hourglass and Eadric didn't know where he was, it meant they'd survived whatever Regner had lying in wait for them.

"That sounds like Demos," I said.

Eadric smiled coldly. "He shouldn't have been able to touch it. How about you tell me how he broke the ward?"

"I'm not telling you—"

He gestured to the man next to him, who raised his hand, opening a long, bloody cut down my bicep.

Pain erupted across my arm. I screamed, attempting to slap a hand over the wound, but the heavy chains made it impossible. He'd cut through my tunic with his power, slicing deep into muscle. Clenching my teeth, I sucked in a deep breath.

Eadric gestured again. The man nodded, and another deep slice opened along my left ankle. I hissed and Eadric studied me. His eyes lightened with amusement. "You just don't know when to yield, do you?"

"Torture me all you want," I said. "I won't give you anything."

"I had a feeling you'd say that."

I writhed as more cuts opened up all over my body. Warm blood slipped down my skin, the metallic scent making me dizzy. But I wouldn't scream again. And I certainly wouldn't tell this bastard anything.

Eadric angled close as I leaned against the wall, panting through the pain. "Soltor can cut you down to the bone," he told me conversationally. "Then he can close those wounds, and we can do this all over again. For days."

I clung to that last word. Days. Days meant that Regner still had to make his way here. Days meant that Cavis and I could escape before Regner arrived.

Eadric tutted. He must have signaled Soltor, because my skin began to weave together, the deep slices closing. It was agonizing, as if my wounds were being stitched one by one.

"Again," Eadric said.

Pain ripped through my body as it was flayed open again and again and again.

I closed my eyes, blocking out the pain, blocking out Eadric's voice, blocking out Soltor's panting breaths. Instead, I focused on Lorian. Asinia. Tibris, Demos. On Galon, Marth, Rythos, Madinia. And the hybrids, hidden across this continent, desperate for peace and safety.

"This can all end," Eadric said. "I'll take you out of this cell, order you a bath, and we can be discussing this over dinner like two rational people."

I snorted. Eadric caught my chin, and my eyes slammed open. My attempt to smash my hands into his face was thwarted by his other hand clutching the chain between my manacles.

"Let's try this," he said. "They have the hourglass. We have you. Where will they travel next?"

I laughed.

That muscle twitched in his cheek once more, and he tightened his hand on my chin, squeezing painfully.

"What's wrong?" I asked. "Worried Lorian will come for you? Because he *will*."

His mouth tightened, and he released my chin, gesturing to Soltor. Agony burrowed deep into my body, tearing through my defenses. The world turned white around me.

In the distance, someone roared in response. Cavis. Relief surged against the edges of my mind, and it was suddenly easier to breathe.

He was still alive.

Eadric turned to the blond guard. "Have our guest brought here."

My heart stuttered. "You son of a bitch."

He leaned close enough to murmur in my ear. "I will *break* you."

My head snapped up, slamming into his nose. Eadric stumbled back, cupping his nose as blood poured. Dizziness swept through me. With my current injuries, I probably shouldn't be using my head as a weapon.

Worth it.

The cell opened. "Healer?" the red-haired guard offered, dragging Cavis in front of him. Eadric ignored the guard, his gaze on Cavis.

I would have rather been ripped apart than watch

Cavis walk in here, his brow lowered in confusion. Our eyes met, and his eyes cleared. He recognized me.

"I've been watching you for some time," Eadric told me. "And my people listened to all kinds of rumors. Apparently, you're not just fucking the Bloodthirsty Prince. In fact, there are numerous witnesses who swear you've claimed all of them as your own."

It had been so long since that night at the inn. Since the first time I'd teased Lorian and the others. The first time I'd heard Lorian laugh. Eadric thought he could shame me, but the memory shored up my defenses.

Cavis met my eyes. He was back, mentally here once more. Neither of us said a word, but that look was enough. A strange calm settled over me.

"Let's try something else," Eadric said. "I'm going to ask each of you questions. And every time you don't answer, you'll watch your lover bleed."

I clamped down on a sob. Cavis hadn't talked. He was under the king's compulsion, and yet he hadn't said anything. It would be costing him.

"I don't even need Soltor's help," Eadric said. "Do you know what happens when one of the king's spiders manages to defy him?"

I stayed silent. Eadric smiled. "It's incredibly rare— and only possible because King Sabium isn't yet here to ask these questions himself. But each time your lover manages to fight the compulsion, parts of his brain bleed and die. At some point, there will be nothing left of him."

He wouldn't let Cavis get close to that point. Surely

Regner would kill Eadric if Cavis died before he got to interrogate him. After all, Cavis had been close to Lorian and Conreth for decades now—within the trusted inner circle. Still, how much damage could Cavis take and still be himself after? I didn't know much about the mysteries of the brain, but Tibris had once told me some of his theories regarding personality and memories stored in different parts of our minds.

Angling my head, I sneered at Eadric. "You need to bring someone else into this? What happened to breaking me?"

"I don't just mean physically. I'll break your mind. Break your spirit. It's the least you deserve."

"What did I ever do to you?"

Eadric frowned as if he didn't understand the question. But it was clear something about this was personal. I racked my brain, but I'd never seen him before that day at the inn with Lorian.

He gestured at Soltor. "Let's get started."

Soltor waved a hand. A long slice opened up right over my ribs, deep enough to reveal bone. My head spun, and I gagged. Eadric laughed.

Cavis lunged at Soltor. Eadric stopped laughing as Soltor backed up against the wall, flinching away from Cavis.

"Stop," Eadric ordered Cavis.

Cavis ignored him, blood pouring from his nose, his eyes.

"Cavis, *please* stop," I begged.

Eadric glanced at Soltor, and this time, he cut Cavis,

opening a long gash across his thigh. Cavis's leg went out from under him, and he smashed to the floor. The black web contrasted against the pale skin of his face, his dreamy eyes now glazed with pain and confusion. Heat coursed through my veins, as if my blood were simmering.

Soltor sliced along Cavis's cheek, tearing the web in two. His flesh hung torn, the white of his cheekbone stark against the blood.

What could I do? How could I end this? I was useless. Utterly useless. I strained against the manacles, searching for some glimmer of my power. I felt nothing. My eyes burned, my breaths coming faster and faster.

Eadric smiled at me, as if reading my mind. "Torture alone is boring," he said conversationally. "After all, there's only so much damage the body can take before it begins to shut down. That's why Soltor's power is so interesting. There's no limit to the pain you will suffer. The pain your lover will suffer. We will heal you again and again and again, and it will be your mind that breaks before your body. It's far more enjoyable that way."

He nodded at Soltor, and the skin began to knit together on Cavis's face. I kept my expression blank, hiding the relief that swept through me. Soltor let out a breath of his own, turning his attention to my wounds. But this time, they didn't heal all the way.

His power *wasn't* limitless.

My gaze met Cavis's. His eyes had cleared once more, and his calm, steady stare helped me rebuild my shaky defenses. We just had to hold on a little longer.

LORIAN

The forest was cool. Towering pines crowded close, branches intertwining to blot out the sky. Weak sunlight slid between the branches, creating dappled patterns on the lush ferns. I planted one foot in front of the other, footsteps muffled on the carpet of shed needles from those pines, my wounds slowly healing as I walked.

Demos and I had taken turns carrying Asinia until she'd woken a few minutes ago, insisting she could walk. Her movements were unsteady, and she weaved as she moved, her eyes unfocused. Since she'd just vomited, it likely wouldn't be long until she was being carried once more. But she was just as stubborn as Prisca.

My mate.

My gut twisted violently, as if an invisible hand had reached in and was squeezing my insides. Each day, the hollow in my chest grew deeper, the void threatening to swallow me whole. To be so far from her, to know she was in mortal danger… There was no greater torture. Perhaps this was my punishment for the blood on my hands after all these years.

The gods knew exactly where to strike. I would give *anything* to take her place.

Asinia muttered a curse as she tripped on a branch. Demos and I were silent. There were no words left to say. We'd sold our horses in the closest village before making our way into the caves, unwilling to risk the horses starving or being taken by our enemies if we found ourselves trapped in the caves. But the village of Hemiarath was still several hours away by foot.

"Hawk," Demos grunted. I turned to find him gazing up at the sky.

Aquilus dropped down, skimming the trees, until she landed on my shoulder. Relief trickled through me, like frigid water on a burn. I stroked her, and my mind cleared enough to focus.

"I'll send a message to Galon and the others," I said.

Asinia nodded, placing her hand on Demos's arm to keep her balance. Panic and helpless rage glimmered in Demos's eyes as they met mine. Yes, we needed a healer.

"They'll be watching for us in Hemiarath," Asinia said. "Regner will have spies there just in case we survived."

"I know." Thankfully, I had another option.

"We can't stop there. We have to keep moving. Pris—"

Demos slowly turned his head, and nothing human remained in his eyes. If I hadn't known for sure that he was a hybrid, I might have thought he was fae in human glamour. "We will stop in Hemiarath, and you will see a healer."

She hissed. "You're not in charge here. If we make

it into the village, only to be arrested by Regner's guards, who will find Prisca?"

"You're outvoted," I said mildly, leashing my temper as I dug deep into my pocket, finding a scrap of parchment, which I ripped in half.

"But—"

I raised my gaze, and she flinched. Demos went very still, slowly maneuvering her behind him. His eyes blazed with fury as they met mine.

"You should drink some water," Demos muttered, handing Asinia a waterskin. She stepped away from him, gulping it down, and I scrawled my messages.

One message to a fae woman who lived on the outskirts of Hemiarath. She wouldn't be pleased to hear from me. But she owed me.

The next message was to Galon. I couldn't tell him about Cavis. Not like this. But I told him of Prisca's kidnapping, writing to him in the fae language. We would spend one night just outside Hemiarath. And then I would begin questioning guards in every village and town in this kingdom until I learned where they were holding Prisca.

I stared into Aquilus's eyes. Tying the first message to her right leg, I tapped it. "Valdoria first," I said. She angled her head, and I tied the next message to her left leg. "And then Galon," I said.

It had been a long time since Aquilus had taken a message to Valdoria, so I gave her a moment to remember.

Then I tapped her right leg again. "Valdoria."

I tapped her other leg. "Galon."

She gently touched her beak to my cheek.

Good.

"How do you ensure the recipient of the first message doesn't read your message to Galon?" Demos asked.

"Fae-trained hawks are not only magically enhanced, but they are incredibly brutal. Aquilus is also resistant to other magic—a natural ward bred into the birds."

Aquilus launched from my shoulder, and we began walking once more. Galon, Rythos, and Marth would have left Quorith days ago. Hopefully, they had already made it back into Eprotha.

I would have to tell them about Cavis.

Cavis.

If Demos and Asinia hadn't witnessed it with their own eyes, I would have been convinced I was seeing things. But it was true.

Regner must have gotten to him when he was a child, before we took him in. If Cavis had known, he would have put himself down. He never would have started a family.

The agony in his eyes when he'd realized what was happening to him…

It was as if he'd been a puppet, each of his movements out of his control.

Prisca would fight for him. No matter what. She couldn't see that Cavis was no longer the friend she knew. But Cavis had known it. It was why he'd begged me to kill him. Bile burned up my throat. I'd failed.

And I'd failed to protect Prisca too.

Eventually, we stopped near a river, refilling our

waterskins. Demos removed his shirt, dunked it in water, and pressed it to Asinia's head as she sat by the river, her face deathly pale.

"They'll torture Prisca," she said.

"She has the disk," Demos said, his expression darker than I'd ever seen it. "She'll never allow herself to divulge hybrid secrets."

The disk. A fae creation that allowed a prisoner to take their own lives, perfectly suiting exactly this situation. They'd each hidden one on their bodies.

"No, she doesn't," I ground out. I'd taken Prisca's disk from her the moment I'd noticed it.

Asinia made it to her feet. "You selfish bastard."

"I will find her."

She opened her mouth, snapping it closed at whatever she saw on my face.

I made my vow to her, to Demos, to the gods themselves. "I will search every inch of this continent if that is what it takes. I will slaughter anyone who stands in my way. Prisca will live. I will make sure of it."

4

PRISCA

The torture continued for hours. When Soltor cut through Cavis's pointed ear, I came shamefully close to telling him anything he wanted to know. Instead, I gritted my teeth, well aware of what would happen if I broke. We would die anyway. And so would all our friends. Our family.

I barely suppressed my tears when Cavis lost that spark in his eyes, turning blank once more. I could take anything, any pain, but not this. Not the loss of Cavis while he was still standing in front of me.

When Cavis shut down, Eadric let out a string of curses. Cavis didn't seem to recognize pain in this form, which made that part easier.

I wouldn't tell Eadric a fucking thing.

Soltor's nose had begun bleeding as Eadric forced him to continue past the limit of his own power. I knew what that headache felt like. I hoped it thundered through him.

Finally, Eadric stalked out, followed by a stumbling Soltor.

"Don't get too comfortable," Eadric said over his shoulder. "We'll be back."

That was the true torture. Knowing, at any moment, it would begin again. Eadric smiled. He knew.

Cavis slumped against the wall, his eyes glassy. Crawling over to him, I reached for his hand. It was freezing.

My whole body trembled. My wounds were shallow enough that I wouldn't bleed to death, but the pain remained.

"Cavis? Can you hear me?"

He slowly turned his head, a hint of recognition entering his gaze. "Pris. You need to kill me. I can't do it myself. The compulsion won't allow it."

I snatched my hand away. Cavis caught it and squeezed.

"Cavis—"

"Listen to me. I know too much. I'm…remembering now. Regner waited all this time so I would have decades close to his enemies. So I would know the fae court. So I would understand Conreth's mind, predict Lorian's strategies. I know how our people respond to threats, and who will be used for each type of attack. I understand how each territory will vote, and who is likely to work with Conreth. If I live, Regner will learn all that information as well." Grief flickered across his face.

I shook my head. I wouldn't even entertain this.

"We're going to find a way to undo what he did to you," I said. "As soon as we get out of here, we'll travel back to Lorian and the others. We'll keep you somewhere you can be watched while we learn how to…"

"There's no fixing this. The longer I spend alive, the greater the threat I present to you, to Lorian, to everyone. I know how to break the fae wards at the hybrid camp. The camp where Sybella and Piperia are currently living."

My eyes stung. I heard what he was saying. But if we managed to get free of this place, he could be healed. I knew he could.

"Cavis."

"I've lived a beautiful life, Prisca. I may have lost parts of myself while I was too young to remember it, but in exchange, I found brothers whom I've fought back-to-back with for decades. I found Sybella. Piperia. I would die a hundred times to keep them safe."

My throat was so tight, it ached. "You deserve more time. Don't give up, Cavis. Please."

Cavis just squared his jaw.

I refused to accept this. *Refused.*

The manacles around my wrists seemed to tighten in response to my thoughts, and I studied the locks. Unfortunately, they'd confiscated my hairpins. I swept my gaze around the cell.

"The red-haired guard has the keys to our chains and the cell," I whispered to Cavis. "We'll need to work together."

The look he gave me was achingly gentle. "Tell

Sybella it was always her for me. From the moment I saw her. She knows it, but I want to remind her. Tell her…tell her every second of this was worth it for the time I got to have with her. And one day, when Piperia's old enough, tell her I helped in the war against Regner. Feel free to make my part larger than it was." His smile widened, even as his eyes glittered. "Every little girl should think her father was a hero."

My throat was so tight, I couldn't say a word. Cavis just continued talking.

"Look after Lorian. Hold him tight and savor every moment. He's been waiting a long time for you. And tell him and Galon and Marth and Rythos… Tell them that being their brother was the honor of my life. "

"I'm not talking about this."

Cavis let out a low laugh. "Don't lose that stubbornness, Pris. You'll need it. I remember now, you know. When I was a small boy. I remember my parents dying, and I remember running for safety. Someone hit me, lifted me into their arms, and I was taken to Regner. He was pleased to learn of my power. He said one day I'd tell him all the secrets I'd learned over my life. All the conversations I'd overheard in every language."

We were quiet after that. I refused to entertain the thought of him not walking out of here, and he seemed content to stare thoughtfully at the wall.

Eventually, I began to shiver. Cavis lifted his chained hands, and I shuffled until I was lying against his chest. "Don't give up," I begged.

"I'm not. But I need you to be prepared. If something happens to me, you get out."

"Stop," I insisted. "We'll get out. Or Lorian and the others will find us. It's going to be okay."

Cavis smiled. But he didn't agree. "Promise me, Pris. You get out, and you don't let them break you. You don't let *this* break you."

I stared into those dreamy eyes, unable to deny him this. "I promise."

MADÎNIA

The bitch wasn't lying.

Vicer had people stationed in Gromalia. Once he'd received my message, those people had warned the hybrid camp of the impending attack. The leaders immediately removed the young, sick, and elderly. Anyone who could fight lay in wait for the Gromalian king's men to arrive.

There were heavy losses on both sides. But eventually, the Gromalians were forced to flee. Without Kaliera's warning, it would have been a slaughter. Now, the Gromalian hybrids were moving down to the fae lands and would join the hybrids in the camp there.

What was Kaliera up to?

She did nothing out of the goodness of her heart. It

was debatable as to whether she even *had* a heart. I'd once seen her strike a servant because the tea she'd brought her was too cold.

Not to mention the way Kaliera had thrown that hybrid into Regner's dungeon—only for Regner to burn her with the dawn. Wila. That was her name. Prisca still carried that death with her.

So why would the queen warn us about the hybrid camp?

I leaned back in my seat and forced myself to concentrate on the voices around me. I was sitting in yet another tavern, this time in a boarding house on the outskirts of a small village. The location and size of the village meant there were no innkeepers prone to snooping—they were currently too busy dealing with travelers stumbling in after a long day on the road.

A group of drunk men laughed uproariously a few tables away. They'd been getting progressively louder for the past couple of hours as I nursed my wine.

But it wasn't them I was interested in.

No. I was interested in the two men sitting behind me, both of them wearing cloaks, their voices carefully hushed.

Those men wore fine boots and carried even finer weapons. Their cloaks were plain, unembellished, but I knew quality, and the wool was both warm and spelled to keep the rain from soaking through.

Both men were bearded, although one of them was much older—his hair and his beard streaked with gray.

When the other man lifted his cup to his mouth, both old scars and fresh cuts decorated his knuckles.

Mercenaries.

Gray cursed at something Scars had said, and Scars nodded sagely. "That's what I said."

I lowered my gaze, feeling one of them glance at me and away.

"From Mistrun, you said?"

"Yes. They said the village was completely slaughtered. No survivors."

I lifted my wine to my mouth in an attempt to hide any sign of a reaction. They were talking about Prisca's village. Before she'd left to search for her hourglass, she'd sent me a message letting me know exactly what had happened to the people who'd lived there. I wasn't sure what she'd needed from me—whether she wanted my pity or if she was merely informing me so I knew Regner would likely search for my own weaknesses. I had no weaknesses.

I hadn't replied. And Prisca hadn't sent any further messages.

I dared a quick glance at the men as Gray leaned across the table. "Who did it?"

"Scrolls were delivered to every village, town, and city in Eprotha. According to King Sabium, the hybrid heir and her friends were responsible for the massacre."

I ground my teeth at that, waiting for Gray to curse our names, to immediately vow retribution, to plan to hunt us. Instead, he…snorted.

"And he truly expects everyone to believe she killed her own people?"

"Not *her* people. They're humans. She's corrupt."

Gray leaned back in his seat. "I've seen too godsdamned much in the last few years to believe Sabium. And if you're honest, you have too."

A long silence followed his words. Finally, Scars sighed. "Doesn't matter what I believe. Sabium has begun recruitment. He's taking them from the villages first."

I closed my eyes. Of course he was. Prisca once told me about how all of the men in the villages were trained—allegedly in case the fae were ever to attack Eprotha. Regner had never been subtle, and this message was easy to understand. If you wanted to protect those you loved, you needed to go to war against the repugnant corrupt and the evil fae. Otherwise, your village could be next.

Prisca may be cunning, and she may have a unique understanding of people as individuals, but Regner had mastered the art of manipulating entire populations over centuries. He understood how to create fear. And he most certainly understood how people reacted when their loved ones were threatened.

Attacking Prisca's village hadn't just been a punishment or a taunt. In all Regner's years of ruling, he had never conscripted his people before. This would allow him to break that peace. To convince mothers to kiss their children and send them to die for him. To convince husbands to leave their wives and babies and swing their swords on the front lines against fae and hybrids.

Regner's armies were large. But he knew he would need greater numbers, particularly if we managed to convince the Gromalians to join us. And poor, uneducated villagers wouldn't want to leave their families behind and march toward the border—especially the northern villagers who were unlikely to see the realities of war.

The king's guards would force them to march. But those who were forced to go to war would never fight with the same fervor as those driven by genuine conviction.

For a king as far removed from his people as Regner, he understood them more than I'd expected. He'd made the threat of the fae and the hybrids personal. He'd made us dangerous to their lives. To their *families*.

How did we counter that? Sure, these mercenaries may know the truth, but that was because they were well traveled and had seen reality for themselves. How did we spread the knowledge?

And once the humans knew the truth, how did we return their power to them?

The men were still speaking. I'd missed whatever they had said next, and I forced myself to focus.

"Some of Sabium's ships were spotted moving south a few nights ago," Gray said. "I just heard it from a sailor while you were taking a piss."

The world seemed to dim at the edges.

It was too soon. We weren't *ready*.

Which was exactly why Regner was moving into position. He would ensure anyone who thought to ally with us learned of his fleet as it moved toward the Gromalian coast. It was also a warning to the Gromalian king, who must have agreed to allow that fleet into his waters.

We needed a fleet of our own. One that could rival the Eprothan and Gromalian fleets. But we also needed an army on the ground. My head spun at the implications. Regner was moving soldiers into position, while we were still scrambling to find allies.

I needed to get a message to Prisca. Now.

THE QUEEN

The flowers were suffering.

I'd spent years strolling through these gardens, admiring the colors, the scents, the soft petals, the resilience of the flowering buds.

On my worst days, the thought of checking on my roses was the only reason I had to summon myself from my bed. The gardens were ever-changing and yet comfortingly familiar, year after year after year.

My wispbloom roses, usually a dusky pink, were now spotted with brown in places, their petals curling at the edges. The lovely, if deadly, Nightmare roses should have been a vibrant crimson, their silver thorns as long as a man's thumb. Today, their blooms held a touch of rot, their scent not quite as enticing as usual.

Beyond my roses, the delphiniums—usually towering majestically—now leaned drunkenly against each other, the bright-blue flowers barely clinging to their stems.

Fury slithered through me like slow-acting poison. I kept walking.

To my right, the wall of wisteria had fewer blooms than ever before, their leaves beginning to yellow. The golden trumpet vine was being strangled by the untrimmed tendrils of that wisteria, just as I was strangled each day in this godsforsaken castle.

I had no doubt Sabium was behind this. Just more of his slow torture.

"Your Majesty?"

I slowly turned. My ladies each took a large step back, eyes glued to my face. They huddled behind Lisveth, as if her innocent demeanor and childlike disposition could protect them.

My mouth opened as if entirely on its own, poisonous words on the tip of my tongue.

Panting sounded to our left, and a castle messenger sprinted down the garden path. His eyes were wild, hunted, and I knew exactly why.

Madinia had paid attention to my message. Sabium's planned slaughter of the Gromalian hybrids hadn't been successful.

Since Sabium was currently traveling to wherever he had hidden the hybrid heir, it would be his generals who were dealing with the aftermath. Each of them would be fighting over who would send the message to their king. Who would be unlucky enough to draw his ire.

I held out my hand for the message, forcing my expression into its usual amused neutrality.

The note was from Tymedes. The general dared imagine he could summon me, as if he were in charge here?

I swept my gaze over my ladies. Thankfully, they were no longer cowering like idiots. "Organize a carriage. I wish to go to the market. Now."

Lisveth could move surprisingly quickly when she was appropriately motivated. Within minutes, we were seated in the carriage. No one spoke, leaving me to my own thoughts. What would be Sabium's next move? Would this drive a deeper wedge between him and the Gromalian king?

We made it as far as the castle gates before the carriage began to turn around.

"What is happening?" I demanded. Other than Sabium, I knew no one who would dare ignore my wishes this way.

"I'm not sure, Your Majesty," Alcandre said, her voice high and breathy. "Something must be wrong with the carriage."

Realization slammed into me, and my hands shook with barely suppressed rage. No, there was nothing wrong with the carriage.

"Out," I instructed when the carriage returned to the castle entrance.

My ladies filed out, hesitating as I stayed seated. I waved them away, and after a long moment of confusion, they finally trotted into the castle.

I sat, well aware of Tymedes's little game. He imagined he could call me to him as if I was a dog and he was my master. I answered to Sabium because he held my son's life in his cold hands. But I would never answer to his spineless general.

I watched the sun move above me, until I must have spent at least an hour in the carriage. It was becoming warmer, but this far north, it wouldn't be stifling for another month, and that heat would only last for a few weeks. Still, I smiled as a footman appeared, hesitating outside my carriage door.

"Do you need some help, Your Majesty?"

"No. I require water. And wine. Also, you will ask one of my ladies to step into my bedroom, where they will find my fan and the book on my bedside table. Bring them to me."

I spent the afternoon lounging in the carriage and pretending to read. I could practically feel Tymedes pacing in the castle as he attempted to wait me out. What he didn't realize was that with Sabium away, I had the freedom to make his life as difficult as possible.

By overriding my plans, he had brought this upon himself.

He would be sitting in that castle, teeth clenched as he attempted to find a way to make me go to him without either looking weak or crossing lines that would make

Sabium kill him. And as long as Tymedes was focused on his new war with me, his mind wouldn't be fully on the news he had received today.

The news he would have to communicate to the king.

And so I stared at the same page of my book, my mind creating and discarding plans. With Sabium currently away, this was my best chance to learn where he was going. But if my spies followed him, he would still have enough time to slaughter Nelayra—or *Prisca*, as she called herself—before I could warn Madinia of her friend's fate.

Sabium was far too cunning. I'd learned about many key locations over the years, but he had been careful with his dungeons. Likely, he'd kept the location of this particular dungeon up his sleeve for an important occasion.

Finally, when the sun was sinking in the sky, Tymedes strolled from the castle, his hands in his pockets, as if wholly unconcerned. But his eyes glittered with rage.

"Is there a reason you're spending the day in your carriage, Your Majesty?"

I let my gaze fall back to my book. "Perhaps it is the same reason you somehow summoned the audacity to take control of my carriage."

"You were needed."

"You do not instruct me," I said, turning the page of my book.

He climbed into the carriage. I raised my gaze, arranging my expression into faint annoyance.

"You know, Your Majesty, a curious man might wonder why your first response was to flee the vicinity when I received unwelcome news."

"You received unwelcome news? Why would I be aware of that? All I know is you overrode my carriage and greatly overstepped your role, General."

He bared his teeth, leaning forward into my space. Distantly, I was aware of my own personal guard surrounding the carriage. Tymedes likely imagined I was threatened by his posturing. But I was married to Sabium. When Sabium got this close to me, my blood turned to ice.

Tymedes lowered his voice to a hiss. "For years, I've watched you strut around this castle as if *you* were the true king. You wouldn't have noticed me as I worked my way up to the position I am in now. You're not known for paying attention to underlings."

I raised one eyebrow, but he kept speaking.

"And I asked myself why Sabium would have chosen a queen who isn't particularly well-liked by his people. Your family was noble, but not remarkably so. You're incredibly beautiful, but so are many women of your status." He smiled. "Then I realized it's because you are so pliant. You may wear that haughty mask, pretend to be as dangerous as a collared tiger, but in reality, you are a kitten who has been declawed. Cute, easily distracted, and remarkably stupid."

If I had respected Tymedes even the smallest amount, his words might have cut deep. But the truth was, they proved that I had been successful with my disguise. When I put my plans into place, Sabium would never see them coming.

Tymedes was clearly waiting for a response. Stretching out my legs, I repositioned my gown over them.

"Sixteen," I said mildly.

Confusion and irritation fought for dominance across Tymedes's face. Confusion won. "Excuse me?"

"Sixteen generals. That is how many men have been in your place since I married Sabium. All of them were in charge of the king's guard. Just as you are now."

He opened his mouth, and I merely held up a finger.

"Four were poisoned. You see, *they* were popular enough that Sabium couldn't outright order their deaths—he had to be subtle. And you can be sure His Majesty vowed to avenge them once they were buried. Three generals were victims of the battlefield. Five were publicly put to death for failing Sabium. Three died in skirmishes with the fae. And one had the unlucky task of telling his king that the hybrid queen had destroyed his capital city after Sabium attacked their kingdom." I pretended to wince. "*His* death lasted for days."

Tymedes's face had gone very pale. I gave him a sweet smile. "So, *General*, believe me when I tell you I care not for what you think of me. Unlike the sixteen before you, and the many who will come after you, I have lived in this castle for years, witness to its horrors but safe in the knowledge that Sabium needs me. When the day comes and he orders *your* death, I promise to act very shocked." I lowered my voice as if we were sharing secrets. "But we both know I will be celebrating."

A muscle twitched in his cheek. With a grim nod, he unfolded his body and left my carriage, stalking back into the castle.

I waited until he was gone, and then I shuffled over to the door, holding out my hand. One of my guards instantly appeared, helping me from the carriage.

"Thank you."

I took dinner in my rooms, then paced, waiting for Pelysian. When my eyes had grown heavy and I'd accepted that he wasn't coming, he strode into my room with lithe grace. His hair was ruffled, as if he had just shoved his hand through it, while his dark eyes remained as inscrutable as ever.

"Where were you?" I demanded.

"I heard of the hybrid heir's capture. I assumed you would want me to attempt to locate the prison."

My heart thudded. "Have you found it?"

"No, Your Majesty. But our spies are doing everything they can."

My hands were twisting together, and I forced them apart. "If she dies…"

"I know." He took a step closer. "There are only so many places that would make sense for it to be. It needs to be close enough to the caves that she could have been transported there quickly—without drawing attention— while far enough from the nearest village to avoid curious eyes. The guards would need to take her along quiet trails that are both wide enough for a carriage but quiet enough that sightings of the king's men won't spread across the area. We will find it, Your Majesty."

Pelysian had never disappointed me before. But the stakes had never been this high either.

"What can I do?"

He raised an eyebrow. "Stay calm, ensure Sabium does not suspect you."

The usual. I was so tired of playing my part.

Pelysian was still watching me closely, his expression thoughtful.

I waved a hand. "Clearly, you have something to say. Speak."

His mouth curved. "I heard about the…situation in your carriage," he said.

"And?"

"Do you believe it is wise to make an enemy of the man currently overseeing the king's guard?"

"*Currently* is the word to pay attention to in that sentence. Besides, if there is one thing I have learned, it's that it is better for a man to make you his enemy than for him to believe you are helpless. Men respect their enemies, but they prey on the weak."

"I'm not sure he is an enemy you wish to make."

I ignored that. "Tell me, what do you know of the pirate queen?"

His gaze turned intent. "I'm unsure what you mean."

"Sabium ordered her death months ago. And yet she

lives. I want to know how, and if she would ally with us."

His eyes sharpened further, and he leaned forward. "The pirate queen is unpredictable. What exactly did Sabium say?"

I felt my brows lower and forced my expression to return to neutral once more. For reasons I couldn't quite explain, I was annoyed at the interest flickering in his gaze when I mentioned Daharak Rostamir. "He wants her fleet. Tymedes has been attempting to kill her for some time and yet can't seem to make it happen." I allowed myself a smirk. "If *I* had attempted it—"

"I warn you against finishing that thought, Your Majesty," Pelysian said.

The threat in his voice was clear, and I slowly got to my feet. "And why is that?"

He held out his hand, and one of the old scars on his palm began to fade before my eyes. I'd heard rumors of what that disappearing mark might represent. A fae blood vow. The hair on the back of my neck stood up.

"What—"

"I won't hurt you," Pelysian said. "Unless you threaten the pirate queen."

"And why would you care if I threatened her?"

He sighed. "Because she is my sister."

My mind whirled, a thousand memories of meeting with him behind closed doors over the years. I'd thought he was one of the few people I could trust. Had all of it been to set me up for Daharak Rostamir's plans?

Darting toward the door, I opened my mouth to

scream for my guards. Pelysian crossed the room in a flash, clamping his hand over my mouth. My back hit the wall with a thump. His hand was very warm on my face. This was the first time he'd ever touched me.

"Shh," he said. "I understand the instinct, but if I were to be found, *all* of our secrets would come to light."

I narrowed my eyes in a silent order to explain.

He sighed, his huge palm still covering my mouth.

"The blood vow prevented me from admitting my relationship with Daharak unless two conditions were met—her life was in danger, and there was a way for me to help. I haven't spoken to my sister for years, but she knows if she were to be targeted, I would attempt to save her life. May I lift my hand, Your Majesty?"

I nodded. It wasn't like me to react so impulsively. If the guards had discovered him here, he would have been tortured—and I would have been the one to pay for it. Slowly, Pelysian uncovered my mouth. We watched each other in silence.

"I'm glad you told me," he said. "I will find a way to warn Daharak of Sabium's renewed interest. My sister can be…rabid when it comes to those who attempt to take her fleet, and she has long been making fools of the kings on this continent."

My mind raced at this new information. "Would she ally with me?"

Pelysian smirked. "You would find my sister to be a difficult woman to manipulate, Your Majesty."

I waved that away. The hybrid heir's plan was

laughably simple—likely because she had so few choices. She needed Daharak Rostamir's fleet. But if there was one thing I knew about the pirate queen, it was that her loyalty could be bought. Rostamir might ally with Prisca—but eventually, I would convince her to betray her.

After all, this little conversation had proven one thing: I had something that the pirate queen considered precious, even if she had attempted to conceal his existence.

Her brother.

5

LORIAN

By the time we made it to Valdoria's, it felt as if we had been traveling for weeks—each second stretching longer than the last.

I studied her house. Clearly, Valdoria had made herself at home—despite her preference for the fae lands. Ivy climbed the stone walls of her cottage, and she'd planted roses along the worn stone path. She'd settled in an ideal location for fae who needed a meal, a night of rest, or a healer. When Conreth had asked for someone to live here, far from the fae lands, she'd volunteered, leaping at the chance to help our people in her own way.

"Where exactly is it?" Demos asked.

Anyone who didn't know the exact location of this cottage would find that Valdoria's wards urged them to keep walking. Her home would appear to be nothing more than a dilapidated one-room shack on the outskirts of Hemiarath.

Asinia had fallen unconscious shortly after we'd left the riverbank. And she hadn't woken again. Demos and I had taken turns carrying her, but she was worryingly pale. Somewhere along the way, I'd gotten used to her chatter, and it was too quiet without her continual opinions on our surroundings.

I would stay for one night, long enough for us all to rest and eat, and for a healer to attend to Asinia. Then I would leave and continue my search. If Demos and Asinia weren't able to travel, they could wait and leave at a later time.

I knocked, and the door swung open immediately.

The last time I'd seen Valdoria was in a Gromalian inn, shortly after disembarking the merchant vessel we'd taken from Eprotha to Gromalia. When Prisca's mood had become darker that day, it had taken me a while to understand what was happening. The moment I'd realized she was jealous of Valdoria...I'd ached to drag my wildcat to me and make her accept whatever it was she'd felt.

I wasn't a man who was used to regret, and yet now, I regretted every single moment I hadn't been honest with Prisca. Every time I hadn't told her exactly how I felt.

So much wasted time.

Demos swept his gaze over her disinterestedly, and Valdoria's mouth curved. Her hair fell in long waves to the small of her back, and she wore a simple dress with a white apron tied around her waist.

I met her eyes. She was objectively beautiful. We'd

had one night together, decades ago, before I'd realized I would be forced to deal with her again and again as my brother put people into place throughout Eprotha and Gromalia. She'd shrugged off my rejection with the ease of a woman who knew she had no shortage of men vying for her attention.

Demos tensed as we stepped inside the cottage and Valdoria's wards adjusted, revealing the spacious living area, pots of flowers sitting on almost every available surface. A rich, savory scent twined toward us. Valdoria had clearly been cooking. To our left, a set of stairs led up to the second floor.

I took a single step, and my instincts prickled. Someone else was in this house.

"A healer," Valdoria assured me, casting me a long look. Finally, she gestured to our right. "Through here."

She opened wide double doors, revealing a small room. A fae man sat near the window, body still, hands open, revealing himself to be weaponless.

My temper was likely putting everyone on edge, and I fought to leash it. Nodding at the healer, I stepped away as Demos placed Asinia on one of three narrow beds.

"This is Jyris," Valdoria said. "He is the best healer I know."

Demos's expression was tight as the healer got to his feet. He leaned against the wall and watched Jyris's every move.

"We will need quiet and privacy," Jyris murmured, glancing at both Demos and me.

Demos showed him his teeth, his body bristling with restrained fury.

I met the healer's eyes. "He stays."

Jyris sighed, but after a long moment, he nodded.

I followed Valdoria back into her main room.

One wall was made entirely of bookshelves, and my memory threw me back to Regner's castle. To sneaking beneath the human king's rooms with Prisca, as I forced her to eke out every last spark of her power for my own use.

She'd been tired. She'd told me she had been using her power all night. I'd merely given her a scrap of my shirt to stanch the blood dripping from her nose, some feral part of me pleased that she would be forced to breathe in my scent.

I didn't regret it. Didn't regret pushing her to dig deeper into her power. But I did regret scaring her. I regretted pushing any hint of emotion away. Pushing *her* away.

The cold lump I called a heart had already begun beating once more at that point. Not that I would have admitted it. Occasionally, when we'd fought or we'd kissed or she'd smiled, that heart had ached as if it was coming back to life. And I'd wished I could rip it from my chest.

"Lorian," Valdoria said, in a tone that made it clear she'd been attempting to get my attention for some time. I'd been staring at her front door, as if expecting Prisca to walk in at any moment.

"She must be an incredible woman," Valdoria said.

"Prisca is my mate."

Valdoria stared at me. "If this is what mating does to a fae, perhaps it is better to avoid such a thing."

My head pounded. I rubbed at my temple. I'd lost track of the last time we'd eaten. I'd kept watch most nights, unable to sleep anyway, but my body was now making its needs known.

Valdoria was still watching me expectantly.

"Falling in love with Prisca was the most inconvenient thing to ever happen to me. And if I had never met her, I would have lived a long, empty life."

Her eyes widened, giving her an innocent, startled look. I almost smiled. I'd once seen this woman gut a fae who had betrayed us to the humans. She wielded her face the way others wielded their weapons.

After a long moment, her expression cleared, and she nodded.

"Regner has a regiment a few hours' walk from here. If you take one of my horses, you can reach it quickly."

Satisfaction curled through my gut. Regner's regiments were made up of between four and six battalions. Each battalion would have anywhere from 300 to 500 men. I would need to be prepared for anywhere from 1200 to 3000 soldiers, all of them armed with fae iron.

I smiled, my mind providing me with the scent of blood, the sound of screams. It had taken everything in me to behave as normally as possible up until now. But there was a chance one of those soldiers knew where Prisca was…

"Lorian?"

I forced my mind back to our conversation. "Regner is moving his people into position."

She nodded. "They've cleared several thousand footspans of trees and have made their camp away from the main roads and any trails. But they're not being particularly quiet about it."

They wouldn't need to be. Any humans who learned of their location were likely more than happy the soldiers were there, protecting them from the wicked, vicious fae.

"Your power?"

"Back in full." I didn't tell her about the fae fire. I hadn't told anyone yet. Prisca had wanted to talk about it, and then we had learned of the attack on her village, we'd gone after the hourglass, and she'd been taken.

It was unusual for a fae of my age to deepen their power. Practically unheard of for us to gain a completely new gift. And never had I heard of someone wielding fae fire.

I'd attempted to bring that power to the surface a few times, and yet I hadn't achieved my goal. I could only feel it bubbling beneath my skin when I thought of Prisca in danger. And even then, I suspected I could only control it when there was a direct threat to her life.

The rest of my power had slowly returned once I'd healed from the caves, and now I had to actively clamp down on that power. It felt alive. As if it wanted to destroy and burn and kill. Since I wanted the same things, it was particularly difficult to keep it contained.

"Going alone is suicide," Valdoria said. "Even for the Bloodthirsty Prince."

I felt my mouth curve, imagining Prisca's reaction to hearing Valdoria call me that name. Valdoria frowned at me, clearly confused.

I glanced toward the spare room. "Give them something to eat. Keep them contained. If they ask where I am, tell them I'm on watch outside." Usually, Demos would be paying careful attention, but his focus was split at this very moment.

"And if they figure out where you've gone and attempt to follow you?"

"They won't." Asinia would need everything the healer had. She wouldn't be going anywhere, which meant neither would Demos. Part of it was his commitment to Prisca and making sure her best friend stayed breathing. But that wasn't all of it—despite the way he was lying to himself.

"You should eat something," Valdoria said. "Rest a little first."

"No."

Since Prisca had been taken, I'd spent every moment desperate to *do* something. Despite my exhaustion, energy surged through my body at the thought.

My footsteps were silent as I made my way out of the house, across the sliver of grass and to Valdoria's small stables. She had three horses, and I took the largest, a mare who tossed her head, clearly eager to stretch her legs.

I saddled her, led her out, and met Valdoria, who handed me a fresh waterskin and a canvas sack packed with bread and cheese.

"Thank you."

"Be careful."

I nodded, nudged the horse, and we made our way back toward the main trail.

The mare had a smooth gallop, and I let her run. The trail was wide enough for two horses to travel side by side, and any horse Valdoria owned would be clever enough to avoid stepping in a rabbit hole and breaking a leg.

In the silence of the night, with no one poking at me to discuss plans, I was left to my own thoughts.

And they tore through me.

When we found Cavis…we would take him back to the fae lands where he could be safe and where we could monitor him carefully. Somehow, I'd find that fucking book Regner had used to create his spiders. And I would figure out a way to undo his dark magic.

When Cavis was finally free of Regner's spells…it was time for him to live his life with his family. No longer would I drag him across this continent, watching as his gaze turned dark with longing when he thought of them. At least one of us deserved to have a normal life. And Cavis had always wished for that normalcy, even as he'd fought with everything in him to help our people.

My gut clenched at the memory of that web on his

face. The horror in his eyes. I would have killed him in that moment, as he'd wanted. As *I* would have wanted if I were in his position. But Prisca was right. We would find a way to give him back his life.

I had spent my life doing the kinds of things that would make Prisca sick if I told her each one of them. She knew some of it—knew, and somehow had accepted me anyway. She believed it was Conreth who was at fault.

The truth was, I'd been fighting the monster inside me since the moment I'd crawled out from beneath that kitchen table, sure I would see my father, and met my brother's eyes instead.

No one made it through life without being made to pay for their worst choices. If the gods really did have a hand in our lives, they had waited patiently—until I had something I couldn't bear to lose. And then they had struck.

Finally, my senses pricked, and I slowed her to a walk, feeling eyes on me. I caught the gleam of a trowth stone, emerald green in the darkness. One of the sentries was about to warn his superiors of a fae approaching.

I dispatched the sentries from afar, spinning my power through the forest. Sentries wouldn't have the information I needed.

The generals would be in their own tents, helpfully marked by their much larger size and the extra guards stationed outside.

My power groaned within me, urging me to burn the entire regiment to ash. If I gave in to the lightning that cracked deep beneath my shields, thousands would die.

If that would lead me closer to finding Prisca, I might consider it. But disregarding the fact that she would be devastated to learn what I had done...

If I killed everyone, there would be no one left to question.

Tying my horse to a tree, I drew my sword. My fae senses gave me the advantage in these situations, regardless of how many men they had. I'd shifted back to my fae form, and my ears caught every snap of a twig, every whispered word, every small movement. A few hundred footspans to my right, a couple of soldiers were walking toward one of the tents, mumbling about one of their superiors.

I melted through the forest, easily finding the tents that would house the most important generals.

The sound of laughter spilled into the night, and I flexed my hand around my sword.

I stepped out of the forest, stalked toward the tent, and speared my lightning through every soldier who stepped between my body and the generals in that tent.

The laughter turned to screams.

I smiled.

PRISCA

It began again. And again. Eadric would leave us for a few hours, allowing enough of Soltor's power to regenerate. Then he would return. I lost all sense of time. I lost all sense of *myself*. The only thing anchoring me to the world was Cavis and the deep brown of his eyes as they met mine, urging me to hold on.

I *would* hold on. We would get out of this place. This would all end. I just had to keep going.

"I'm tired of this," Eadric said finally.

"Go…take…a…nap." I lay curled on the stone floor in a fetal position, shuddering with agony.

Eadric kicked out, slamming his foot into my gut.

I couldn't breathe.

Cavis roared. And I could hear the helplessness. The *powerlessness*. He was fae. A warrior. And Lorian had once muttered about Cavis's obsession with protecting those weaker than him.

The moment was spiraling out of control. I opened my mouth, but Eadric kicked me again, this time right beneath my ribs. My breath puffed out of my lungs again in a strangled groan.

When I could focus again, Eadric was pointing at Cavis. "Hurt him," he snapped. "Hurt him so badly, she has no choice but to tell us what we want to know."

It would work. I knew it would work. By now, Eadric

knew it too. And his eyes burned with sick delight.

If it were just me here, I could hold on for days. Weeks. But seeing Cavis in this amount of pain, seeing him fighting back...the confusion that kept turning his gaze distant as his brain bled, the manacles preventing him from healing...

There was no torture that could be worse than this.

Rolling, I made it to my knees. There had to be something I could give Eadric. Something that would keep him busy, buy us a little time while he had his people investigate it.

"They would go to Duskmire."

Eadric angled his head. "Why?" The word was flat, suspicious.

"We know it's one of Regner's iron mines. If I were ever taken, Regner's attention would be on me. Lorian promised me he would go. Take advantage of the distraction and wipe out one of Regner's main sources of fae iron."

I'd expected Eadric to walk to the cell door. To tell one of his men to look into it.

Instead, he laughed.

My blood froze in my veins.

"Do you know what makes me particularly helpful in these situations?" Eadric hissed. He stepped closer, ignoring Cavis and Soltor.

Every moment he was speaking was a moment we weren't being tortured. Perhaps I could keep him engaged for just a little longer. Every second counted.

"I'm a truth-seeker," he said.

I felt the remaining blood drain from my face, and the cell seemed to dance around me. Eadric leaned down and caught my chin, careful not to get close enough for me to strike out with my forehead. He'd learned that lesson.

"I don't like it when my time is wasted. So that little lie is going to cost you."

The dim light flashed off his blade as he brought it toward my face. "An eye, I think," he said. "Perhaps a fae healer would be able to help you regrow it if one got to you in time. But I don't think that's in your future, do you?"

This was it. This was the moment I would break. I could feel it inching toward me, just as Eadric grinned, bringing his knife closer. I kicked out, but he'd pinned me against the wall, his body heavy against mine. I was bleeding and weak, chained, and completely, utterly helpless.

"Stop," Eadric said, not taking his eyes off me. Behind him, Cavis had stepped toward us. Blood poured from his nose.

Cavis paused. And then he moved once more.

Eadric glanced over his shoulder at Soltor, who backed against the stone wall and opened up a long gash along Cavis's throat. But it was shallow. This was taking a toll on him as well.

Cavis took another step, and it was my turn to choke out a plea.

"Cavis, stop. Please!"

His eyes found mine, sharp and clear and resolved. My entire body seized, a scream catching in my throat as my instincts roared at me.

He gave me a surprisingly sweet smile. My lungs locked up.

"No. No, no, no, no, no, no!"

Eadric let out a displeased growl and spun. I slid along the wall, as far from him as possible.

He ignored me, leveling Cavis with a sneer. "Stop. Moving."

Blood slid from Cavis's eyes now. From his ears.

"Cavis, stop," I said. "Please. For me."

Nothing. I tried again. "For Sybella. For Piperia, Cavis. For your daughter!"

At that, his eyes met mine. And softened. "Tell them I love them, Prisca."

I stumbled toward him, but it was too late. He was lunging, swinging his mangled hands at Eadric.

Fear flickered over Eadric's face. And despite my terror, I reveled in it.

"Soltor," Eadric hissed.

Soltor was busy opening up deep slices along every inch of Cavis's body. I slid behind Cavis and launched myself at Soltor. His attention turned to me, slicing me from throat to waist. I screamed as my skin split open, and I swung, using my manacled hands like Cavis had, slamming them toward Soltor's face.

Pain exploded through my head, and I fell backward. Eadric had grabbed my hair, and he pulled me toward him.

But I was feral now, and I lashed out, aiming at his groin.

"If you're going to act like an animal," he grunted as he shifted and I hit his thigh. "You'll be treated like one." He used his hold on my hair like a leash, dropping me to my knees. I was still screaming, roaring, and Cavis...

His eyes were blank once more. And he was staring straight ahead, gaze distant. My chest tightened. It was better this way. He couldn't feel what was happening.

But now I was all alone.

"That's better," Eadric said, satisfied. He grabbed my face with his huge hand, fingers digging in on either side, holding me still. "Let's get back to work."

He leaned over me.

Movement.

Soltor let out a choked warning, and Eadric turned, just in time for Cavis to barrel into him. There was no life left in Cavis's eyes. He was there, but no longer there. It was as if his body was functioning without his knowledge now. He slammed his fist into Eadric's cheekbone, and I scrambled away, using the wall to get to my feet.

Soltor lifted his hand, and I leaped at him once more, blood dripping down my chest from the wound he'd just opened.

Cavis made a sound. Somehow, I heard it over Soltor's snarled warning, my own desperate screams. And I knew.

I whirled. Eadric stood over him, his knife buried in Cavis's heart.

Cavis's eyes met mine, soft and dreamy once more.

Those eyes were locked with mine as the life drained from them.

I screamed and screamed. The horror was torn from my lungs, burning up my throat.

Next to Cavis, Eadric stared at his own hand, as if the realization of what he'd just done was only now occurring to him.

Soltor looked mildly uncomfortable. I met his eyes, swallowing a hiccup.

"Dead," I choked. "You're dead. I'm going to kill you. But first, I'm going to kill everyone you love."

The color drained from Soltor's face. He believed me. Good.

Eadric recovered, strode over to me, and slapped me across the face. I just laughed at him, the sound high and thready. "And *you*." I laughed some more. "You're just going to *wish* you were dead."

At this very moment, I had so few things left to live for. But I wanted to see him die. And first, he would suffer.

"Interesting threats for someone wrapped in chains in a human king's dungeon." Eadric smiled, obviously recovered from the shock of his own actions. His hand shot out, clamping around my throat, and I sucked in a breath through my nose. I kicked, and he merely dodged my feet, leaning down closer until he was breathing in my ear. "Zathrian sends his regards."

He let my throat go, and I coughed.

Ringing sounded in my ears. My whole body turned numb.

Zathrian.

Eadric was working for my cousin. Did Regner know? Or was Eadric one of Zathrian's plants?

I should have killed Zathrian. Should have made it a priority when I'd learned he'd gotten to the elders before I could. And that he was trying to take my crown.

If I had, Cavis might be alive.

The agony of it was eating through my body. Through my soul.

Eadric smiled, clearly enjoying himself. With a gesture to Soltor, they both stalked out.

Crawling over to Cavis, I curled up against him and screamed my rage.

THE QUEEN

Only two people had access to Sabium's private graveyard. Sabium, so he could continue adding to his morbid collection, and me, so I could bear grim witness to my inevitable end.

I'd only visited it a few times. The first was the day Sabium had freed me from his dungeon—after I'd finally pretended to accept my fate. He'd had his guards lead me to the entrance before roughly grabbing my arm and pulling me through his ward.

"You can be buried here at any time," he'd said. "No one will mourn you. No one will ever know why you disappeared. If you don't comply, perhaps I will make you choose your own grave. Then I'll make you lie in it, awake and aware, before I bury you."

The threat had chilled me. And the thought of being buried alive—directly after choosing my resting place… it had driven almost all of the fight from me.

Today, I stalked toward the graveyard. My thoughts were so heavy, it took me a moment to realize someone had stepped into my path. I froze, barely preventing myself from slamming into a male body.

Tymedes glowered down at me. "Your Majesty."

"General."

"A strange thing has happened."

I raised one eyebrow. His gaze was pinned to my face, no doubt noting my every expression.

"Yes?"

Fury burned in his eyes. "Eryndan fell in line with His Majesty's plans and finally ambushed the hybrid camp."

"I have things to do, General. If you have a point, please make it."

"The hybrids were somehow warned about the attack."

I kept my expression cool, disinterested. A flush began to crawl up his neck.

"Only a few people knew of these plans," he hissed.

"You were one of them."

I narrowed my eyes. "Are you accusing me of treason, General?"

He paused briefly, as if the full weight of his accusation hadn't occurred to him until right at that moment.

"I would like to know who you told."

"Who I told what?"

"Who you told about the planned attack!"

I let out a gusty sigh. "You think *I'm* responsible for this? The Eprothan queen? Are you mad?" My laugh dripped with disdain. "If you believe such a thing, take this accusation to the king, and let us see what he thinks about you pinning your failures on his wife."

I kept my expression scornful as Tymedes stared at me. Cold sweat dripped down my back. If he did take it to Sabium, and Sabium decided to look closer…if Sabium used his truth-seekers…

I forced my lips to curve. The tiniest hint of uncertainty slid through his eyes.

This was the biggest risk I'd taken. I'd known it had to be done. The hybrid heir would never have trusted me otherwise, and I needed her and her allies to trust me so I could save my son.

After so many years of passivity, finally taking action had been glorious. It had felt as if I was finally unleashed. Yet perhaps I had acted too impulsively.

"My apologies, Your Majesty," Tymedes said finally, bowing his head.

"Lower."

He stiffened, likely fantasizing about pulling his sword and running me through. But after a long moment, he bowed lower.

I didn't know why I was so determined to wield what little power I had in such a way. Why I would risk alienating the very people who could lead to my downfall. It was a compulsion I could never quite manage to suppress.

Tymedes backed away, stalking toward the castle without another word. I continued walking around the back of the sanctuary, ignoring the priestess as she walked nearby with her nose in the air, blue robes swirling around her feet.

My power was unremarkable, but it was useful for times such as this, whispering the locations of anyone nearby and making my own presence difficult to notice. It wasn't strong—Regner had once called my power a "weak breeze." And it wasn't passive—I had to be concentrating deeply in order to use it. But it had saved me more than once. I let it trickle free, checking for any signs of people near the graveyard.

The ward allowed me entry, and I pushed open the wooden door.

The graveyard was little more than a patch of dirt and grass, enclosed by stone to protect it from prying eyes.

No markers, no headstones, no way to know exactly where each of Sabium's dead queens lay.

Had any of them known just how much of a monster

he was? Had they attempted to protect the babies thrust upon them as I had?

If they *had* tried, then they had failed. None of their sons were here. No, they were all lost to the sea, their throats slit, their power drained. And the women who'd come before me were buried beneath my feet.

I stepped farther into the enclosed graveyard.

It wasn't difficult to imagine those queens standing next to me, invisible as they screamed their vengeance.

"I'll make him pay," I vowed. The words settled within me, deep in my chest.

I would not fail. I would do whatever it took to make sure Sabium died.

If one of those women had seen the predator Sabium had been and refused to be its prey, I would not have ended up here. I would never have married Sabium...*Regner.* I could have had a happy marriage filled with children and laughter.

Forcing myself to push those thoughts out of my head, I focused on my reality.

I would be the queen who *lived.*

I had sacrificed my daughter for this. I would never feel her kick. Would never kiss her tiny toes or search her features for traces of my own. I would never know if she would have had my eyes or if she might have had more power than me.

She had never even existed. Would never exist. Yet some days, the loss of her seemed inconceivable. All that potential. Snuffed out.

I pushed the thought of her away. My son would take the throne, and we would tell our story. Oh, we would never let the population know Jamic wasn't Sabium's son, of course. The people were far too concerned about bloodlines for that. But we would make it clear that Sabium's evil was the reason so many of them had died. It was the reason the hybrids and fae wanted us dead.

Perhaps I would allow the hybrid heir to live for a few years. She could retire to her own continent and *stay* there, and we would enjoy peace. When I finally arranged for her death, I would ensure it seemed accidental. Or…I would make it look as if the fae king had ordered her death in retaliation against his brother.

The Bloodthirsty Prince would go to war. My kingdom would shut its borders, and the fae and hybrids would destroy one another. When it was all done, I would pick up the pieces, graciously allowing their people to settle in my lands.

Unlike Sabium, who was little more than a figurehead to his people, *I* would be known as the queen who suffered through an insane king, raised her son to be a selfless ruler, and prioritized her people.

I would be powerful. I would be generous. I would be loved. No—I would be *adored*.

Adoration surpassed mere love. With love came the expectation of reciprocation—people who loved expected to be loved back after all. But *adoration* assumed such a thing was impossible—since the focus of that adoration was on an untouchable pedestal, entirely out of reach.

And the higher a monarch rose beyond their subjects' grasp, the brighter they shone.

I took a deep breath, scanning the graveyard for the final time. Sabium would know I'd been here. Perhaps he would taunt me about it. But I'd needed to see the fate that awaited me if I was unsuccessful. I'd needed to remind myself that if I failed…I would be buried in an unmarked grave, my son lost to the sea.

I rolled my shoulders, lifted my head, and left the graveyard behind me. I would never return.

The castle was quiet as I made my way back toward my rooms. Waving Lisveth away, I entered my rooms to find Pelysian waiting. Something had changed between us now that I knew he was related to the pirate queen. It was as if before this, he had merely been a blank slate I could write my plans across. Now that I was learning just how much power he could wield if he chose to…he somehow seemed more alive.

"It's dangerous for you to be in here alone," I warned. I wasn't afraid of him finding my secrets. *He* was my biggest secret in this castle.

Pelysian smiled. His expression was animated, his eyes bright. My heart stopped, and I knew what he was going to say before the words spilled from his mouth.

"I've found the hybrid heir."

6

ASINIA

There was something incredibly undignified about being hauled around unconscious by two men. Even if one of them was your best friend's lover and the other was her long-lost brother.

I'd woken moments ago, my head pounding, my eyes watering as I forced them open. My gaze found Demos, pacing like a caged animal as he snarled at someone. Someone with a low, patient voice.

"She will wake when she wakes. Head injuries are immensely taxing on the body, and she will need plenty of rest. She should sleep for a few days."

"She won't," Demos muttered darkly, and I almost smiled.

The man sighed. "In that case, you will have to ensure she spends much of her time resting while you travel. Try to keep her in the shade and hydrated whenever possible. I will give her a tonic to take with her. But I must make it clear—if she travels in this condition, it is against my advice."

Demos was silent for long enough that I could practically feel him considering ways to keep me flat on my back while he went looking for Prisca without me. My jaw suddenly hurt, and I realized I was clenching my teeth.

Pushing against the soft mattress, I attempted to sit up. Stars burst behind my eyes, and I gasped at the pain. Somehow, my head seemed to hurt *worse* than before. What kind of healer was this man?

"Ah, she's awake," he said, stepping toward me. His face was weathered, his hands gnarled, his eyes kind.

Demos was instantly next to me. "Don't move."

Within a moment, he seemed to understand I was planning to ignore that order, because he cursed, locating a few pillows, which he unceremoniously shoved beneath my head and shoulders.

"Where are we?"

"Just outside of Hemiarath."

I studied the room. I was cocooned in a patchwork quilt, its fabric soft from years of use. The bedroom was cozy, inviting. Fresh wild flowers were placed in a squat vase on the nightstand, while two other beds with quilts were pressed against the opposite wall, dotted with embroidered pillows.

The vaulted ceiling and exposed roof beams added to the airy feel of the room, while the rug looked as if it had been handmade.

I attempted to sit up farther, giving up when it drove another shard of agony into my brain.

"Where's Lorian?"

Demos's eyes hardened. "He disappeared at some point, while I was busy ensuring you kept breathing."

I narrowed my eyes at him. "My apologies for the inconvenience."

A hint of humor flickered through those amber eyes. "Apology accepted."

The healer handed me a cup of water. "My name is Jyris. Can you tell me your name?"

"Asinia."

"And where are you from, Asinia?"

Demos went very still, his gaze landing on the healer.

Jyris sighed. "Memory loss is common with head injuries. If you don't wish to tell me where you're from, please tell me if you remember what you did today."

I cleared my throat and sipped at the water. "Uh, we were traveling. From the caves."

Jyris glanced at Demos, who nodded.

"And how old are you?"

Demos's eyes turned flat. He loomed next to Jyris, his body language making it clear he wasn't happy with this line of questioning. I couldn't detect any threat from Jyris, but Demos usually preferred to ere on the side of caution.

Jyris sighed once more. "Believe me, I have no desire to risk annoying the Bloodthirsty Prince."

"Don't call him that," I said automatically. Prisca had made it clear she didn't like it, and I couldn't exactly blame her. Demos sent me an amused look, and I couldn't help but smile at him. The moment stretched, and I returned my attention to Jyris.

"Tell me this, then," Jyris said, picking up my arm. "Do you remember how you got this scar?"

The scar encircled my wrist, and my blood went cold. But I forced myself to answer. "I was in chains. When I was healed, there were other, more important wounds to treat. So my wrists scarred."

Pity tightened Jyris's expression. "I'm sorry to hear that. It appears as if your memories are just fine, but you should let me know if you notice anything unusual. I'm going to give you a tonic, and then I want you to rest. You had bleeding between your skull and the outer layer of your brain. You're very, very lucky you survived."

I stared at him. I'd known I was hurt, of course. But I hadn't realized just how close I had come to not waking up. It seemed almost offensive, that I could have died without even knowing death was coming for me.

But the worst part was...once again, I'd been a victim. I'd had no way to protect myself and, instead, had been entirely reliant on Demos and Lorian hauling me around like a corpse. I was so tired of that being my story. And it was time to do something about it.

Demos turned and stalked away. Since he was often in a terrible mood around me, I wasn't exactly surprised.

"I need to be on my feet in the morning," I said. "Can you make that happen?"

Jyris's mouth thinned. "Against my own instincts, yes. But only if you agree to certain stipulations."

It was that, or Demos and Lorian would find some way to leave me here. And it was my turn to help Prisca.

"I'll agree."

"Fine."

LORIAN

The instant my foot crossed the threshold of Valdoria's cottage, Demos met me, shoving me against the wall with a snarl.

"What. Did. You. Do?"

I twisted, shoving him away. The fact that I hadn't felt his presence suggested I desperately needed sleep.

Valdoria stepped into the room and swept her gaze over me, pausing at the blood coating my tunic, dry and sticky on my skin. "Regner moved a regiment into place a few hours from here. Lorian went to ask them some questions," she said.

Demos's eyes narrowed. "You think Regner's not going to respond to that? He'll respond with a strike against the hybrids or any fae stupid enough to be in his vicinity."

"I don't care." The rest of the world could fucking burn.

Demos shoved me. Sparks began to rise off my skin, and I tamped down my power. If I killed Prisca's brother,

I would lose her for good.

"You don't *care*? Your actions are risking innocent lives. You think Prisca would want this?"

Just her name was enough to make me want to lash out like a wounded animal.

It was my turn to shove him. And he flew against the wall, hitting it with a thud.

"Stop this," Valdoria snapped.

I kept my gaze on Demos. "Prisca isn't here. Because you were too busy worrying about the fucking hourglass to strategize, and I was too slow to get to her."

The color drained from Demos's face. "She wanted me to take that hourglass."

"And now we have it, and Prisca is probably wishing she were dead."

Demos let out a humorless laugh. "Yes. *Wishing* she were dead. Likely craving it with everything in her. But instead, she'll be forced to betray the people she loves, because you couldn't stand the thought of her being able to *choose* her end when the time came."

"*Prisca will never end her life,*" I snarled.

Demos bared his teeth, stepping close enough that I could see him wrestling with the urge to reach for his sword. "Do you think I want to lose her? You may not know this, *Your Highness*, but some things are worse than death."

The door flew open. Asinia stood, swaying on her feet. At least she was up and moving, although she was clearly nowhere near fully recovered.

Demos leaped toward her, but she held up a hand.

"What happened?"

No one spoke. She turned her attention back to Demos. "Please tell me you're not poking at the unstable, murderous fae prince."

I narrowed my eyes at her.

Demos just growled. "He slaughtered an entire godsdamned regiment."

Asinia turned to me. "Did you learn anything?"

Valdoria snorted.

Demos threw up his hands. "How am *I* suddenly the voice of reason here?"

I spoke through gritted teeth. "First, I didn't slaughter the *entire* regiment. Just the generals and a few sentries."

And anyone else who had gotten in my way. A few hundred soldiers, at most. If they'd expected it, they would have met me with fae iron, but by the time I'd learned everything I needed, anyone responsible for giving those orders was already dead.

"They didn't know where Prisca would have been taken." And by the end, they would have told me anything to make me stop. "But there are other generals." I'd failed Prisca again tonight. But I wouldn't stop until she was freed.

"There will be consequences for this," Asinia said. Since it looked like she was barely keeping her feet, I stalked over and took her arm, guiding her to sit on the edge of Valdoria's sofa. The worst of my fury had drained, and I dropped into one of the stuffed armchairs as Demos paced.

Finally, he heaved a sigh. "If you can't control your murderous urges, then we use them." He rubbed a hand over his face. "We hit where they least expect it. Create enough fear and confusion that we rip into their morale before they meet us on the battlefield. Whenever we attack, we make sure at least a few of them hear us describe exactly how we knew to find them."

Asinia grinned. "Because the last men we tortured *told us* where to find them. Perhaps they did it easily, desperate to turn our attention elsewhere."

Demos nodded. "Any battalions Regner is moving down here are likely soldiers who will be ordered to fight next to one another. If we're going to risk attacking them, we use the opportunity to sow confusion and discord."

He glanced at me, and I nodded. It was a good plan.

"If that's settled, I'm going back to bed," Asinia said, getting to her feet. "Goodnight."

When she'd wandered away, Demos took her seat, leaning forward and leveling me with a hard stare. His amber eyes were so like Prisca's, my mood darkened further.

"I know Prisca is your mate," he said.

"What makes you think that?"

"Don't play with me."

I shrugged, aware it would irritate him. To his credit, he kept his face blank. I knew him well enough to know he'd decided to give me a brotherly warning. Since— against my will—I was beginning to like him, I would allow him to talk. For now.

He tapped his fingers against his knee, his expression thoughtful. "I know you're in love with Prisca. And I've heard enough about the fae and their mates to know what *that* means too. I know you're dealing with…impulses."

I stared at Prisca's brother and had the strangest urge to laugh.

"Impulses?"

He pinned me with a glare. "The kind of impulses I don't need to linger on when it comes to you and my sister."

I sighed. "The *impulses* are…difficult. But I learned she was my mate long after some part of me had accepted I needed her." If Demos thought it was just my fae blood tying me to Prisca, he might be tempted to dismiss it.

"You're saying the mating doesn't matter?"

"Oh, it matters. The fae are violent, territorial, and possessive. I've never battled with my instincts like this before."

He was still watching me, and I met his gaze. "I didn't need anything before Prisca. I wanted peace on this continent. I wanted our people to be safe. I wanted Regner dead. But I didn't need anything for myself. I didn't know I *could* have anything myself. And then I met her, and for the first time in my long life, I *needed*."

I didn't know why I was opening myself up like this. Especially to Demos, of all people. Perhaps it was just exhaustion, Even *my* body was finding it difficult to go this long without sleep.

Demos was silent for a long moment. "You'll put yourself between Prisca and anyone who wants to hurt her without hesitation, every time. That's all I need to know."

It should have been enough. I didn't need *friendship* with Prisca's brothers. Especially not this one. But I found myself grinding my teeth anyway.

"You would likely have preferred someone like Thol for her." I managed to keep my voice carefully neutral, shoving the bitterness down where it ate away at my ability to reason.

The other man was dead. We hadn't yet been able to remove his body from those caves to give him the burial he deserved. And yet some part of me was still deeply affronted at the knowledge that Prisca had once wished for a life with him.

Demos leaned back, angling his head. "You know, I talked to Tibris about Thol when he arrived at that inn. Tibris said Thol once told him he was going to marry Prisca. And yet he would have killed her for what happened in that village—without proof she was truly at fault. You would never have considered such a thing. In his place, you would have hunted her so you could protect her.

"If Prisca *had* been responsible for such slaughter, you would have prioritized her over anyone else. Even if she had been the one to kill all those people herself, you would have refused to allow anyone to punish her."

I wished I could argue with him. Could pretend I lived by a more stringent code of ethics. But my moral compass had always been broken—especially when it came to my wildcat. Demos was right. No matter what Prisca did—even if she was to truly become a monster—I would be by her side. If she ever lost the part of her that could reason, I would hide her away and guard her for the rest of my life.

Even if it meant losing everything else.

Demos nodded at whatever he saw on my face. "Thol's problem was that he could never love her enough. Your problem is the opposite. You may just love her too much. Since I don't believe my sister will ever become a threat to innocents, I prefer your unhinged kind of love. But if I ever think you're likely to corrupt her, I will find a way to end you."

PRISCA

In the dimly lit confines of my cell, all sound had disappeared, until I could no longer hear the guards' footsteps. My limbs tingled, as if they, too, were fading away.

Something had cracked open inside my chest—a part of me sucked into a void, now irretrievably lost.

Cavis's eyes meeting mine. No fear for himself. No, he'd been terrified for me. The rest had been fury and a hint of relief.

I was haunted by death.

My parents, Mama, Wila, all of the villagers, my neighbors, Thol, *Cavis*.

Reality sank into me, draining the strength from my muscles.

I wasn't getting out of this cell.

Cavis was gone, and when Regner arrived, I would die too—likely in a particularly gruesome, public manner.

Perhaps I would do more for my people in death than I'd ever done for them alive. At least if I died, they might rally behind my empty throne.

The thought chilled me. I didn't want to die. But my mind provided me with the sight of my village on that last day before I'd left. Only, instead of children playing in the village square, they were buried in a mass grave near the forest. Herica's bakery was splattered with blood, my friend's last moments nothing but terror. Abus, Natan, Chista, even Kreilor. None of them had deserved to die. All of them were gone.

I lifted my hand, examining the space where Thol's blood vow had sat. The line had disappeared with his death. Now, I was down to just two. Lorian's vow to me, and my vow to the pirate queen.

If I lived…if I somehow made it out of this cell…I would have to tell Lorian, would have to tell *Sybella* that Cavis was never coming home. Cavis, who should have stayed at camp with his family where he was safe and who'd, instead, followed me.

The wounds Soltor had opened mustn't have healed after all. Because I was bleeding out. And the thought of not waking up…

For the first time, death seemed like a mercy.

What was the point of it all? Regner had been spreading his poison and slaughtering our people for centuries. He always seemed one step ahead of us. We would die. Over and over again, we would die. Dying early in this war might be a blessing. At least this way, I wouldn't have to watch my friends and family be slaughtered one by one.

I wouldn't get to see Lorian again. Would never look into those wild green eyes. Would never feel his hands on my skin or simply breathe in the scent of him.

I would never see my brothers. Would never get to see the kind of men they would become years from now. They might draw closer to each other after this. Already, I'd caught glimpses of moments when they were almost… friends. Or, this might just kill any kind of relationship between them.

Asinia…she was one of the strongest people I knew, and yet this might break her. She was still mourning her mother. Still cried at night. I knew because in the mornings, her face was puffy. Unlike me, she was working through her grief instead of attempting to pretend it didn't exist.

And Telean. I had represented her hope. She'd once told me that she saw so much of my mother in me, it both hurt and helped. My aunt was so fierce, so determined to save our people, and she'd believed in me. Truly, down to her bones, believed I could do it.

Had I told them I loved them? Did they know?

Rythos, Galon, Marth…it was strange how quickly they'd begun to feel like family. As if they'd always been there waiting and we were always supposed to find each other.

I let my gaze drift to Cavis. His face was so still. Almost peaceful. I'd closed his eyes, and the web had faded from his skin—as if now that he was dead, his purpose was complete.

He was supposed to make it. He was supposed to go home to his wife and daughter.

I shuddered. My eyes burned with the need to cry. Sobs had collected in my throat, my lungs tight. But I'd suppressed it for so long… I *couldn't* cry now. My body had turned numb.

"Eat, bitch," one of the guards laughed, shoving the tray beneath the bars. A small cup of water, a few pieces of chicken still on the bone, and a half-rotten apple.

Ignoring them, I turned away.

"Promise me, Pris. You get out, and you don't let them break you. You don't let this *break you."*

I'd promised. I'd promised, and the thought of that promise hurt so much, I would have given anything to make it all end.

For the first time in a long time, I loathed Lorian. I hated that he'd taken that disk from me. That he'd refused to allow me the *choice.*

My head felt as if it were floating above the rest of

my body. As if I were staring down at it from the stone ceiling.

And yet, Lorian's voice cut through the dull whine in my ears.

"When it comes to your survival, you cheat. You cheat and you lie. You fight dirty. And you do whatever else it takes to stay alive."

I could practically hear him snarling at me, urging me to *think*. To plan.

"What have I told you, Prisca? You never give up. Not you."

Attempting to block him out, attempting to ignore the memory of Cavis's steady gaze, urging me to keep my promise, I closed my eyes.

In the end, it wasn't Lorian's voice in my head that made me open them once more. It wasn't the will to survive burning through me.

No, that fire was little more than a spark.

I needed something far more important than survival.

I needed *vengeance*.

My gaze fell to the manacles keeping me confined. Each cuff was a single piece of metal encircling my wrist, fastened together by a crude hinge on one side. The lock was a simple keyhole, the wear on the keyhole…

I was guessing the internal mechanisms of these locks were just as old and worn.

Shuffling close to the bars of my cell, I picked up the chicken. Slowly, carefully, I began peeling off the meat.

Eating seemed like a commitment to survival I

wasn't sure I could stand behind, but I had to eat some of the chicken or it would be suspicious. Forcing it in my mouth was one of the hardest things I'd ever done. I didn't want to eat. I didn't want to do anything except curl up in this cell and be left alone.

I gagged.

"You don't let this break you."

Time dragged on. But I'd meant what I'd said. Soltor and Eadric were going to die slowly and painfully.

And Regner?

He was going to suffer before he died.

I lost myself in thoughts of what I was going to do to all of the men who had caused such horror. The ways I was going to make them *beg*.

When all the chicken meat had been removed, I studied the bones—the discarded bits of calcium and marrow my only hope of freedom. After long moments of deliberation, I chose the sturdiest bone, its smooth surface slick with residual grease. The next bone was more difficult. It needed to be thinner, more flexible, but unlikely to snap. I pressed my finger against the most likely choice, breaking it from the others and tucking it into my boot.

Examining the walls, I traced a finger over the rough-hewn stone.

I curled my body into the wall, as if I was sleeping. Raising my chained hands, I pressed the larger bone to the abrasive surface. Gently, carefully, I scraped the bone against the wall.

Footsteps sounded, and I hid the bone up the sleeve of my tunic, closing my eyes. The footsteps slowed, then sped up once more.

It was painstaking work, each scrape of bone against stone echoing in the dank cell. Sweat broke out across my neck each time a guard walked past. My muscles screamed in protest at my position, my wrists burning in the heavy chains.

But each pass of the bone along the stone meant I was one moment closer to vengeance.

So I lay still. And I scraped.

MADÎNIA

A few days after the first note, I was almost unsurprised when the queen's messenger found me once more, despite the fact that I'd chosen a new inn, painstakingly covering my tracks.

How was she doing this?

Handing the messenger a coin, I plucked the note from his hand, not bothering to ask him how he'd found me. Unless he was an idiot, he would be far more afraid of the queen than he was of me.

It was a good choice to trust me. Now take that pride

*of yours and bury it long enough to trust me again. The
sixth has been taken. Her life-span grows shorter each
day. Find her near poison's homeland.*

The sixth.

What did she—

The only sixth she could be talking about was her
sixth lady. Prisca had taken that spot.

My entire body seized.

If Prisca had truly been taken...

Lorian must be dead or dying. He wouldn't have
allowed her to be taken otherwise. The fae was like a
rabid wolf when it came to her.

Poison's homeland.

I stared at the note some more.

Poison's homeland.

The reference escaped me.

I could almost hear the bitch queen in my head,
tutting at my stupidity.

Clearly, she thought it was somewhere I would
recognize.

My hands shook, and I gripped the note tighter,
careful not to tear the parchment.

Perhaps Kaliera had used her first message to ensure
we would trust her. So we would descend on *poison's
homeland* and die directly after.

Prisca was annoyingly idealistic, overprotective of
her family and friends to the point that she was clearly
battling some inner demon. Not to mention, she was

stupidly self-sacrificing. The chances of her making it through this war alive were low, while the chances of her making it through undamaged were much, much lower.

But…

She'd saved my life in that castle.

In a choice I'd never have been able to take back, I'd attempted to set myself on fire. Remembering that moment now, I found it difficult to understand what I'd been thinking. I *hadn't* been thinking. But I'd seen no way out. And if I was going to burn, it would be by my own hand.

Still, when I'd asked Prisca to leave the camp—and oh, how the fact that I'd needed to *ask* had chafed—she hadn't hesitated.

"You're clever, vicious, and you were one of the queen's ladies for years. I'd be a fool not to use you."

Our eyes had met, and I'd understood. Prisca had known that if I'd stayed just a few more days in that tent, something in me would have shriveled up and died.

So she'd gotten me out.

And now she was the one who was trapped, and at risk of truly dying within days, if not hours.

"Fuck," I hissed.

All I wanted was to be left alone. And now, I was going to have to decipher the queen's fucking riddle and find a way to save the hybrid heir.

Before she was slaughtered by the same man who'd killed my father.

7

ASINIA

The next morning, we left as soon as the sun rose, moving north. We traveled quickly, pushing the horses and ourselves, and only resting when necessary. Fatigue weighed on me constantly. My muscles, my bones, my joints… my entire body hurt. But I rested when I could, and I fell exhausted onto my blankets as soon as the sun fell each night.

We were always up and moving as soon as dawn lightened the sky.

None of us spoke more than necessary. Lorian bristled with unspent power—all while emanating a deep rage that kept all of us on edge.

Tonight, he'd disappeared somewhere, likely to see if the rumors of another regiment close by were true. Demos was seeing to the horses, while I unpacked our meager food supplies.

That was as much as I was allowed to help when it came to setting up our camp each night. I hadn't bothered to argue. My injury had cost us too much time already.

So I sat on the log Demos had pulled near our fire and *willed* Prisca to stay alive.

I'd once thought that if you hoped and wished and worked hard enough, you could achieve almost any dream. My mother had said that over and over while I was growing up. When I learned what I was—and that my mother might have either known or even been a hybrid herself—I'd caught myself hoping my father was the hybrid, the man who'd left my mother when I was just months old.

At least then, my mother wouldn't have purposefully kept me in the dark.

My dream had once been to travel to the city and work as a seamstress for the queen. I would dress all the most important people, working with the kinds of fabrics I'd only dreamed of. My designs would set trends as nobles noticed what I could do. I wanted to be wealthy. I wanted to be respected. I wanted to be *someone*.

Now, my heart ached for just one more quiet morning with my mother in our tiny home, the comforting scents of woodsmoke, dried herbs, and fabric surrounding us.

Our home had never been large, but the rolls of silk and cotton, stacks of wool, and the worktable had kept my imagination alive—the myriad of colors and textures representing so much *possibility*.

"What are you thinking?"

I jolted, meeting Demos's amber eyes. "Just… remembering. Life in my village. With my mother. I'm wondering what she'd think of me now. Sometimes I'm worried that I'm forgetting her. What her laugh sounded like. How she smelled."

Demos finished brushing my horse and wandered over to the fire, hands in his pockets. He was so…male. He took up space wherever he was, drawing gazes, speculation, and especially feminine interest.

I didn't understand how his body had gained so much muscle so quickly. It was as if it had remembered who he'd obviously been before his imprisonment and reverted to that same form overnight. His shirt molded to his chest, his biceps, and especially his shoulders. Every few weeks, he was forced to buy new shirts or risk splitting them at the seams.

He met my eyes. "Her laugh was surprisingly high and loud, considering how soft-spoken she was. It drew attention and made her blush, so she didn't laugh often. She smelled like wool and rosemary. One of her front teeth was chipped from an accident when she was small, and she was self-conscious about it. She'd sometimes cover her smile or duck her head. You hated that.

"Her hands were callused from her work, but gentle— especially when you were unwell. And when you needed to talk, she would stop whatever she was doing and face you. She always gave you her complete attention, so you knew how important you were."

My throat went tight and hot, and it was suddenly difficult to breathe.

I could see her again, sitting at her loom by the

window. Could hear the hum of the spinning wheel, the sound of her laugh.

My voice came out raw, hoarse.

"How do you…" Of course. Demos had made me talk to him in that dungeon. As soon as I was strong enough, he'd insisted I keep talking, even when I'd wanted nothing more than to let my grief and hopelessness swallow me whole.

I just hadn't expected him to have memorized everything I'd told him.

My mother's image was firmly back in my mind. The way she smiled. Her scent. I swallowed around the lump in my throat, unable to speak. Reaching out, I squeezed Demos's arm.

He went still. I yanked my hand back. We didn't touch—unless I was at risk of dying or he was training me. Any other time, it was as if there was a barrier between us.

I wasn't sure which one of us had raised that barrier.

"Thank you," I croaked.

His eyes darkened. "There's nothing worse for me than knowing you're hurt. When you're sick or injured or sad, I want to fix it. It's a kind of helplessness I've never felt before."

And he loathed it. I could see that truth, written across his face. Demos loathed that feeling, because he'd been helpless for two years in that cell beneath Regner's castle. He'd been helpless while his friends, his family were slaughtered with the dawn, and he was left there— alone. And he'd been helpless when Prisca was risking her life to get all of them out.

I'd watched him in that dungeon, day by day, as he'd fought not to break. As he somehow continued to be a source of support for Pris and bullied me into staying awake when all I'd wanted was to retreat into the void.

Demos was a natural protector. At some point, he'd decided I was one of those people he had to protect. Likely, it was when he met Prisca and saw her determination to keep me alive. Once he learned she was his sister—and I was her best friend—that was enough for him. I'd chafed at his controlling, overprotective ways each day in that cell, but he'd kept me together when I'd wanted to break.

"Demos," I said gently, and his eyes widened slightly. It wasn't often I spoke to him in a lowered tone, my voice serious. He leaned in, and I took a deep breath. "Thank you for everything you've done for me. You… you kept me alive in that cell—in all the ways that count. And then you did it again over the past few days. But you don't need to do it anymore. You're no longer responsible for me."

His eyes *were* different from Prisca's. Only someone who'd studied his eyes enough would notice, and I wrestled with that even as I watched him. While Prisca's eyes were closer to gold, Demos's held green undertones. Now, they turned cold.

He opened his mouth, leaning even closer, and I knew whatever he was going to say would cut like the sharp edge of a blade. He'd always been good at that—knowing exactly where to strike to get the result he wanted.

His expression turned blank as he pulled himself back from that edge.

"Message received," he said.

I opened my mouth, frustration roaring through me. I wasn't trying to hurt him. I was trying to let him know I wasn't just another person he had to look out for. I was trying to set him free from the expectation that he had to keep me safe.

That I was another *task* he had to complete.

But he was already stalking away.

LORIAN

The days passed in grim silence, all of us alone with our thoughts. Asinia was still pale, and the healer had ordered her to take plenty of breaks. Still, she'd mostly refused to stop—except when we'd come across Regner's men. Then, she would stay in the shade with the horses and our supplies, and together, Demos and I would find the highest-ranking of Regner's guards and corner them when they least expected it.

Demos's power was particularly helpful. Where I would have used brute force, his strategy gave us the best possible route each time, ensuring we only killed those we *wanted* to kill.

And we always, always let them hear just why they'd been chosen—within earshot of those who would spread the message: The last regiment had betrayed them. They'd told us to come here.

At first, it was simple. The generals never expected to be targeted. It was an easy matter to kill the few guards with them at any time and take them into the forest for a discussion.

Eventually, the generals refused to even take a piss without several guards surrounding them—all armed with fae iron. We worked around it, but it took longer, and the monster inside me roared at the wasted time.

When we couldn't find any more regiments, we turned to the guards in charge of keeping the peace in villages across Eprotha. They ensured compliance during Gifting and Taking ceremonies, and the only time they held a crossbow or sword was when they were terrorizing villagers. They knew nothing of the hybrid heir.

"We need iron guards," Demos spat after a particularly gruesome few hours with a guard who'd taken a respectable amount of time to break. "These men know nothing."

I'd sent a message to Telean, updating her on the situation. She had her own contacts and was mining every one of them for information. As soon as we found Prisca, Telean would travel to us, but for now, we needed someone in Gromalia who could keep an eye on their king. And she was still working to find leverage to turn the Gromalian king.

Eventually, we came to a village so tiny, it had no name. It boasted a single inn, and Demos arranged for rooms while Asinia pulled on a cloak and strolled down to the market. There, she heard rumors of a group of black-armored guards traveling south.

"Could be a trap," Demos said while we slumped in his room, picking at a light meal. "By now, Regner knows we're hunting for Prisca."

I just nodded. It felt as if I was losing the ability to communicate. My body shuddered with fresh rage each time I thought of Prisca in Regner's dungeon, until all I could do was call to her in my mind.

Stay alive, wildcat. Please. Just fucking stay alive for me.

Someone knocked, and I stalked to the door, throwing it open.

Rythos, Galon, and Marth crowded into the room. Some of the tension melted from my neck and shoulders. They must have traveled quickly to meet us this far north. For the first time in days, a tiny spark of hope slid into the dark cavern of my mind. More of us searching meant we had a greater chance of finding Prisca quickly.

Asinia hugged each of them, while Demos nodded a greeting.

Galon's eyes met mine. "What happened?"

I had to tell them. And I had to do it quickly. But the words burned up my throat, until I could barely force them out of my mouth.

"Cavis was one of the king's spiders."

Rythos went eerily still. "I don't believe it."

"It's true," Demos said tiredly. "He was fighting against whatever orders he'd been given, but the moment we got to the hourglass, those orders must have overridden his will. He took Prisca."

"We'll fix him," Rythos announced. Someone who didn't know him might assume he didn't understand the gravity of the situation. But he'd immediately channeled his unwavering determination and optimism. His response was so like Prisca's, I had to turn away.

"Let's get some sleep," Galon said. "We'll leave at first light."

And so we continued to travel, choosing our direction based on the slightest rumor, the tiniest spark of hope.

Sleep had become something foreign. Instead, I spent my nights writing letters to Prisca. Letters I would probably burn.

Wildcat

I don't know if you'll ever see this letter. I don't know if I'll ever give it to you. But I spend my days talking to you in my head. By now, I know you well enough to know how you would answer most of my questions. Your quick humor, sarcasm, and the way you occasionally take my breath away with your honesty...

Gods, I miss you.

Rythos told me that writing to you might help. I

snarled at him, and he just gave me that steady, patient stare—you know the one. Galon nodded, and finally, with nothing else to do, I stalked away to the river to talk to you.

Some of our biggest moments have been by water, wildcat. The day you almost died, when Galon was the one to save you—that day still haunts me now. Sometimes, I wake from nightmares that you succumbed to the river and I never knew you. My life would have remained dark and cold if that had happened.

I would have deserved it.

In my best dreams—the dreams I don't want to wake from—I manage to get to you in those caves. I pull you from Cavis's arms, and we find a way to help him. A way to undo the evil Regner spawned in him.

But in my nightmares, all I see is your face. You were terrified—I could see it in your eyes. But your expression was strangely calm. Subdued. I'm not sure if you knew there was no way out of the situation, or if you were still planning your escape.

You're the best thing that's ever happened to me. Did you know that? Some part of me is sure you must have known. But I've never been good at letting anyone in. When I think of you, alone and afraid, never knowing just how much I love you…it's all I can do to stay sane.

Just…stay alive for me. Stay alive, and I swear I'll find you.

-Lorian

And so, each day, we slaughtered our way across the kingdom. Each night, I wrote long letters to Prisca, until the early hours of the morning.

Each moment stretched as long as a lifetime, until I began to question my own sanity. And still, we continued to search. We knew Regner's secret dungeon wouldn't be in a city. So we traveled north through tiny villages and large towns, not bothering to hide our path. Regner had painted my people as monsters, so we became the monsters who raged through his kingdom.

Until one morning, Galon received a message from someone I'd almost forgotten existed. Prisca's friend Madinia.

"I know where she is."

My people often referred to those with Madinia's magic as dragons. They were believed to have a closer connection to the gods.

Perhaps that was why Prisca's dragon had somehow achieved what none of us had managed.

Written in Tibris and Prisca's code were the directions to Regner's secret dungeon.

PRISCA

They came for Cavis later that day.

Three guards held me down while I howled, screaming threats which quickly turned to desperate pleas.

"Where are you taking him?"

"Worry for yourself, Hybrid Heir," a heavyset blond guard sneered, the long scar down his cheek tightening with the expression.

The red-haired guard laughed and locked my cell behind him, shoving the keys into his pocket.

I knew Cavis wasn't here anymore. Knew his body was just what was left. Everything that had made him *him* had gone. But for the first time, I felt truly alone.

Eadric didn't return. I'd heard the guards whispering, and apparently, he'd fled—likely unwilling to be here after killing Cavis. Regner wasn't going to be pleased with him. That knowledge was the only satisfaction I could find.

If Eadric was working for my cousin, had he arranged for Cavis to die to ensure Regner couldn't use him for information? Perhaps he'd always meant to kill Cavis and had simply looked for his chance. Or was Eadric playing both Regner and Zathrian?

Someone began to sing a bawdy tavern tune in a surprisingly pleasant voice. One of the guards snarled a threat, and the voice got louder.

I wasn't the only prisoner here. Just how many of us were there? I craned my neck, attempting to see around my bars, but all I could see were the legs of the guards as they kept watch.

Several hours later, the guards began walking faster

as they strolled up and down the corridor. Their posture was different, shoulders back, serious expressions on their faces.

They spoke in hushed voices. The kinds of voices that told me Regner would be here soon. For the king to come to me, it meant he was losing trust in the security of his own castle. His own city.

Usually, I would have celebrated at that news—and the fact that his paranoia and distrust were growing. But if I'd been transported to the city, I would have had a much greater chance of escape.

No one was going to rescue me but me.

And I'd promised Cavis.

Whenever I was alone, with no guards peering in at me, I scraped the chicken bone. Gently. Carefully. Never risking taking too much from one side. Finally, I'd sharpened the end of the bone into a point. I slowly sat up, my head swimming as I pulled my knees close to me, the chain between my manacles clinking. That chain was short enough that this would be difficult.

The bone I'd been sharpening would work as a makeshift tension wrench. Angling my wrist, I ignored the way the cuff scraped against my raw skin. The bone fit into the keyhole, and I slowly used it to apply pressure on the internal cylinder. Sweat poured down my face, my palms grew damp, and I had to pause, forcing myself to take long, deep breaths. It was painstaking work—the pins needing to be held in place without breaking the bone or jamming the lock.

If I lived through this, I would have to thank Demos for his insistence on making me pick locks for days at a time when we were at the hybrid camp.

Taking the second bone, I inserted it into the lock, wincing as it scraped against the metal. The bone hit the first pin, and I sucked in a breath as it clicked, falling into place.

It took an eternity. Twice, I had to pause as the guards passed by my cell. Each time, I buried my head in my knees and hunched my shoulders—a broken prisoner.

Finally, the tension bone turned slightly.

The click of the lock mechanism turning was the sweetest sound I'd ever heard.

The cuff opened. Savage pride surged through my veins, and the light, uplifting sensation made my head spin. But I didn't have time to celebrate. The other lock was waiting.

My hand shook, and I rubbed at the lacerated skin of my wrist. One more. Inserting the tension bone into the remaining lock, I held it steady, slowly pushing the other bone next to it. I pressed it against the pin, squeezing gently.

The bone snapped.

The sound that came out of me was half moan, half roar. I choked it off, placing my head on my knees. But a pair of boots was slapping against the stone.

I leaned my head against my legs, holding the chain in my lap as my shoulders shook. The guard waited, and I sucked in a long breath, letting out another false sob.

He snorted. "King Sabium will be here tomorrow, Hybrid Heir. Your tears won't save you." Slowly, his footsteps faded.

I lifted my head. I could sense my power—flickering at the periphery of my awareness. It lingered tantalizingly close, yet remained elusive. If I didn't remove the second manacle, my power would remain out of reach.

Crawling to the scraps of the one and only meal they'd given me, I picked through the remaining chicken bones.

The bone I chose wasn't as flexible as the first. There was a very real chance it would also snap. But I was out of options.

Achingly slowly, I used the tension bone to press against the internal cylinder. Sliding the new bone into the lock, I held my breath until the world dimmed around the edges.

Stop. Breathe.

There would be no rushing this. I either picked this lock, or I died.

I kept my movements small, manipulating the pins gently. One by one, I felt for the pins, the world reduced to the cold iron around my wrist and the fragile hope still fluttering in my chest.

It felt like hours later when I turned the tension bone. *Click.*

The manacle fell open.

Feral delight kindled in my gut, spreading hungry flames throughout my body. The rush was heady, and my head spun, my spine tingling with *possibility*.

I yanked my wrist from the cuff, carefully placing the manacles on the floor next to me, hidden by my body. Rolling my shoulders, I waited for my power to slam into me. To come roaring back.

Nothing.

Panic clawed at me, until I leaned over, battling nausea. I was down to hours before Regner would arrive. My power was closer than before, but still out of reach. And without that power, I was his prey.

I took a deep breath, leaned my head against the wall, and closed my eyes.

Then I begged whichever gods were listening for help.

8

PRISCA

As usual, the gods weren't listening to my pleas. I didn't receive a sudden influx of power.

But slowly, as the guards' shift changed once, and then again, a few drops of my power began to return. It was sluggish, buried deep within me. But I could use it.

At this point, I *had* to use it. There was no time left to wait.

I shuffled over to the bars of my cage.

The first guard didn't spare me a glance as he stalked past. He wasn't who I needed. The blond guard came a few minutes later, rushing past as if he were late for something incredibly important.

He was the guard in charge of the keys today.

I pulled the thread of my power toward me and launched to my feet, reaching through the bars to his pocket.

Empty.

Taking hold of his shirt, I pulled until his frozen body fell against the bars. Panting, I grasped my power with everything I had, refusing to let go until…

There.

I scooped the keys from his other side, swiping them off his belt. The lock was on the outside of my cell, and I twisted my arm around, pressing the key inside and twisting. At this point, I half expected the iron key to snap.

But it didn't.

The cage opened with a satisfying click, and the guard fell inside my cell. Pressing a foot to his back, I shoved him in farther, slipped his dagger from his sheath, and slammed the cell door shut. Now I was the one in the corridor.

My grasp on my power slipped.

Time restarted.

Our eyes met. His screams cut through the air.

I angled my head. These men had tormented me for days. The guard fell silent at whatever he saw on my face.

But the red-haired guard was sprinting down the corridor toward me, his sword in his hand.

"You're dead, bitch."

I ignored that. He swung his sword, and I jolted back, my head swimming dizzily.

"Don't kill her, you idiot!" another guard roared from down the end of the hall. Lifting his hand, he aimed a torrent of water at me. I ducked, slipping on the water as it hit the wall behind me, flooding the corridor.

More guards joined the first. I had to get out of here.

Quickly.

I fumbled for my power. It came to me easier this time, but my nose dripped blood—a clear sign I didn't have access to as much as I needed. My heartbeat hammered against my ribs, my breath coming in shallow pants.

Stepping toward Red Hair, I plucked the sword from his hand. Then I pushed his frozen body against the wall and let time resume.

Shock flared over his face. He bared his teeth. I bared mine back.

"Where are we?" I demanded.

"I'm going to rape you," he said. "And then I'm going to kill you."

I slammed my knife into his throat and ripped it free as he gurgled, slumping to the floor. Blood sprayed, wetting my face.

Swinging his sword with my other hand, I squinted at the others. "Who's next?"

"Witch," one of them hissed.

"Where are we?"

"Get back in your cell, and we'll allow you to live long enough for His Majesty to arrive," one of the guards said. I knew him. He was the short one with curly dark hair who'd slid the tray of food into my cage.

My power was almost depleted. If I didn't get out of here soon, I wasn't going to make it. My mind helpfully provided me with a series of visions of my dead body crumpled on the stone floor of this dungeon.

I stalked down the corridor toward the guards, past several empty cells to my left. Until the sound of a chuckle wound toward me. I flicked a glance to the left, recognizing the voice.

This was the man who'd been singing.

I pulled my power with everything I had. It took me far too long to disarm the remaining four guards, but I threw their weapons into the cell with the male prisoner, who eyed me.

"Let me out," he said. "And I'll fight by your side."

He was larger than most of the guards, with eyes so dark they were almost black, his beard overgrown, clothes filthy.

His lips curved, even as his dark eyes glittered with suppressed wrath. Dangerous.

Freeing him was an easy decision. *This* man hadn't locked me up.

Throwing him the keys, I positioned my knife at the curly-haired guard's throat. Time resumed, and I could taste copper as blood dripped down my face, into my mouth. The guards gaped at me.

Jerking my head at the dead guard behind us, I gave them a sweet smile. "I suggest you tell me what I want to know."

The man from the cage swung open his cell and buried his sword beneath the ribs of the first guard who barreled toward him. The guard groaned, falling to his knees. "Answer her," the man said.

"We're near the remains of Crawyth. But you won't

get far. The king is already almost here."

The man cursed. Our eyes met. "I owe you a life debt for my freedom," he said.

"Anyone would have done the same." If Regner had him imprisoned here—for torture—I was willing to bet he was no ordinary prisoner. No, he was likely a political enemy.

"No, they wouldn't." His expression was grim, as if he knew that reality firsthand. "My name is Calysian. And I insist on helping you in some way."

We didn't have time to argue about this, so I merely nodded.

"Is there anyone else here?"

"No. I was alone until they dragged your unconscious body across the floor."

I felt my lips twist at the thought, and he let out a rusty laugh.

Together, we directed the remaining guards into the cell and locked the door. It warmed my heart to know that when Regner arrived, he would find his prisoners gone and his guards either locked up or dead.

The sun was blinding as I stepped outside, my eyes used to the dim light of the prison. Fresh air teased my nostrils.

We were out. My last sight wouldn't be stone walls and iron bars.

Calysian stood close enough that I felt when he went still. My knees weakened, and I turned.

Bodies littered the ground surrounding the building.

Torn apart, they lay in piles. Here, a leg, bloody and mauled. There, an arm, the male hand still clutching a sword. A few footspans away, what remained of a head.

The hair on the back of my neck stood up. Something else had rampaged through the area.

I glanced at the man. "Your people?"

He shook his head. "Yours?"

"No. They would still be here."

We pondered the bodies for a long moment. Whoever had brutally murdered these people, I hoped they didn't plan to come back.

"I hear horses."

I couldn't hear anything. He met my eyes. "Trust me. We need to hide."

"If it's Regner, we can surprise him." We could win this war within a few moments.

"He'll be traveling with at least thirty guards. He would have sent half of those guards ahead, for just this possibility. You're covered in blood, Hybrid Heir. How much of that power do you have left?"

So he knew who he was. I narrowed my eyes. "And you?"

"My power is slowly returning, but I've been in that cage for months." He grabbed my shoulder. "You would die."

"Let her go." A voice rang out, low and dangerous.

I whirled. "Are you seeing what I'm seeing?"

"Oh yes," Calysian purred. "I see her too."

Madinia sat on a horse, leading another bay mare

behind her. Her hand was raised, several bright-orange sparks floating threateningly through the air, and her red hair was now so dark, it was almost black. She wore leather leggings, a tunic, and a dark scowl.

I wasn't hallucinating. I craned my neck, searching for a sign of anyone else behind her. But she was here alone. "How…? What?"

She tossed her long, darkened hair over one shoulder. "I'm here to help you escape." She wrinkled her nose at the bodies strewn across the ground. "If you didn't do that, then we need to be on our way before they return."

Fascination flickered over Calysian's face. "Well, well, well," he murmured.

Madinia just gave him a withering look and glanced back at me, her gaze lingering on the bloodstains. "Are you well enough to sit on a horse?"

"Yes."

"Then let's go."

"What about your life debt?" Calysian asked.

I shrugged one shoulder. "Madinia has just saved my life. Give your debt to her."

Madinia ignored us and made a motion with her hand that clearly told me to move faster.

"You'd leave me here?" Calysian asked, still staring at Madinia.

She opened her mouth, and he sent her a wicked grin. "Forget it. I have some…unfinished business to take care of. But I'll see you again. In the meantime, good luck to you both."

I nodded. "Good luck, Calysian."

He turned and stalked into the forest. The distant sound of hooves cut through the sudden silence. "Someone's coming," Madinia said, as if I'd suddenly gone deaf.

I glanced at the carnage surrounding the dungeon. If Madinia had gotten to the guards first, they would have been little more than charred bone.

"It's Regner and his guards. We can't take them now," I said. "They'd slaughter us."

Frustration gleamed in her eyes, but she nodded. "Then let's go."

PRISCA

"Well, this is familiar," I mumbled. "Us on horses, fleeing for our lives. Me barely conscious, you bullying me relentlessly."

Madinia just snorted. "I sent a message to Galon with your location. I assumed if you'd been taken, Lorian was likely dead or dying."

My breath stuttered at the thought. "He's not." I refused to even consider it.

She just let out a "hmm" sound, and we plodded

through the forest, allowing our horses to recover from their gallop.

We'd had a head start on Regner's men, but I had no doubt they would be spreading out after us. Our best hope was to reach the closest town or village and get a message to Lorian and the others.

"What happened?" she asked.

"Cavis…" My throat closed up.

I could feel Madinia studying the side of my face as I kept my gaze on the forest in front of me.

"I'm sorry. He was always kind to me. He was kind to everyone."

My breath hitched. Yes, Cavis was kind to everyone.

Perhaps that was all we could hope for. That when we died, we would be known for our kindness.

Would those platitudes mean anything to Piperia as she grew up without her father?

The ache in my chest grew agonizing. "Something else," I managed to get out, meeting her eyes.

Madinia nodded. "It was the queen who helped me find you." She changed the subject.

My muscles tightened, and my horse flicked her ears in response.

"Why would you trust her?"

"Because before she sent that message, she informed us of a hybrid camp in the Gromalian capital. One that was about to be under attack. I managed to get a message to Vicer. Kaliera wasn't lying, Prisca. Her information saved hundreds of lives."

"How is she tracking you?"

Madinia narrowed her eyes. "I don't know. No one else knew where I was, and I've been careful."

"I don't like it."

"Neither do I. She wants you free for her own reasons—that bitch doesn't have a heart. But she still helped. If I hadn't found a way to decode her message, you'd be wandering around the forest, hiding from Regner's men."

She had a point.

"Poison's Homeland," she said. "She knew I'd figure out what that meant."

"Poison's Homeland?"

"Her horse. His name is Poisoned Apple. He was purchased from a breeder near the dungeon. Once I knew the general area to search, all the guards coming and going made it easy to see where you were being kept."

"Maybe too easy. You weren't worried about it being a trap?"

She gave me a derisive once-over. "Of course I was. But decisions had to be made."

"Thank you for coming for me."

She sniffed. But her shoulders straightened, and I hid a smile. Prickly Madinia.

"What do you think she wants?" I asked. My horse snorted, and I gave her an encouraging stroke.

Madinia sighed. "There is only one thing she has ever wanted. Her son."

"You think she'd work with us if we freed him?"

She shrugged one shoulder. "I spent years watching her. I know how her mind works. She's calculating and clever. If she doesn't know the truth about the man she married, she at least knows something isn't right. And she's helped us twice now."

"You *truly* think this is all for Jamic?"

She pushed her hair off her face. "Somewhere along the way, she became his mother—against her will. He is the one thing she cares about. We find him, and we'll control her."

I felt my brows shoot up. Not long ago, Madinia had been concerned we would use Jamic—just like everyone else had. But obviously, when it came to her relationship with the queen, it was personal.

"Think about it, Prisca," she said when I didn't reply. "She's in that castle, close to Regner all day, every day. The only way he has managed to keep her in line is by dangling Jamic in front of her. Once Regner kills him and takes his place, he has no use for her, and she knows that too."

She was right. Either way, we needed to find Jamic before Regner reinforced the barrier. And if Kaliera was willing to help us make that happen, we should listen.

Still, I couldn't let myself fully trust her.

Not after I'd seen what she had done to Wila.

We fell into silence after that. All I could see was Cavis's face. The grief for his family. And the acceptance that this was how he would die. I hadn't been enough to save him.

Depression would suck the life out of me if I let it. It would steal the strength from my muscles and the courage from my bones. I wasn't ignorant enough to think I could merely choose not to feel what I'd been through. But I would lock it in the box that held the loss of my parents—all of them—the loss of Wila, Thol, Cavis. The loss of the person I might have one day become if I hadn't been clawed by grief and rage.

At some point, that box would open.

If I weren't careful, it would become too full—the lid no longer able to close. And all the pain I refused to feel would flood me.

But for now, I slammed that lid shut, buried it beneath a pile of rubble, and nurtured the flame of my fury.

Madinia turned in her saddle, facing me. "There's a village ahead. But I don't think we should stay there. It will be the first place Regner's guards check. You hide with the horses, and I'll buy supplies." Madinia raked her gaze over me and wrinkled her nose. "Supplies such as soap."

My mouth twitched. Something that might have been relief flickered in her blue eyes. Those eyes widened as a shout cut through the forest.

"Go," I said, nudging my horse with my heels. The mare was tiring, but she gave me a canter, dutifully following Madinia's horse as she picked up speed.

We needed to hide. But if the guards had hounds with them, they'd find us anyway.

I'd die out here before I allowed them to put me back

in those manacles. My power was like a tiny spark within me, but I'd use it until I burned myself out if that was what it took.

The shouts turned to screams.

Horrifying, blood-curdling screams.

Madinia chanced a look over her shoulder, her mouth open, before facing forward once more.

The screams continued. Had the guards found someone else? I slowed my horse. I couldn't allow anyone else to die. If those guards thought they could slaughter their way across this kingdom as they searched for us...

"Prisca," Madinia hissed.

Silence.

No screaming. No hooves. No shouts.

My skin prickled, and the tiny hairs on my arms stood up.

A ball of fire appeared in Madinia's hand. Her horse tossed its head, but she expertly reined her in.

Something rustled in the undergrowth to my left. Madinia bared her teeth.

Vynthar stepped onto the path, the sunlight catching his horns. His fur was covered in blood, his teeth stained with red.

"Stop!" I screamed, reaching for the wisp of power I had left. But it was too late. Madinia let her fire loose, aiming straight at the Drakoryx.

Panic swallowed me whole. I swung my leg over my horse, a shriek ripped from my chest—

The Drakoryx opened its mouth and swallowed her

fireball.

Madinia let out a sound that was somewhere between a snarl and a hiss. Another fireball appeared.

"Don't you dare," I snapped.

She gaped at me. "Monster."

"Well, yes. But he's *our* monster."

I slid off my horse and dropped to my knees, holding out my arms for the Drakoryx.

"Did you eat all the bad men?"

He stepped into my arms, butting my chin with his head like a big cat. *"I did."*

"Thank you."

Madinia stepped up next to me. "Next time," she gritted out, "you may want to let me know when you've befriended magic-eating monsters."

I ignored her, scratching Vynthar beneath his chin. "Were you the one who took care of the guards around the dungeon?"

"Yes. But one of them escaped. And he would have alerted more of them. I had to chase him."

A long tongue slid over his muzzle, letting me know Vynthar had enjoyed the chase—and the spoils of that chase.

Regner would send more men when the ones Vynthar had killed didn't check in with their superiors. But hopefully those men would be a lot more wary once they saw the bodies Vynthar had left behind.

With a final scratch beneath Vynthar's chin, I mounted my horse. Vynthar slunk through the forest surrounding us, only appearing in glimpses. I could finally breathe easier with him on guard against threats.

The sun was high in the sky by the time we finally made it to the village. Since I was covered in blood and grime and would only draw attention, I waited with Vynthar in the forest while Madinia slipped into the market to purchase supplies.

While she was gone, I told Vynthar about Cavis. Tears dripped down my cheeks, and he let out a low growl.

"Where is the fae prince?"

"I don't know. Eadric said he'd set a trap for him, Demos, and Asinia in those caves."

Vynthar seemed to think about that, his black eyes focused on something in the distance. Or perhaps he was just daydreaming. It was difficult to tell.

I turned away, facing the small homes at the edge of the village. "Why...why didn't you come into the caves with us?" I'd attempted to understand it at first, but now, after everything that had happened, I couldn't.

If Vynthar had been there, perhaps Thol wouldn't have died. Maybe we could have saved Cavis. At the very least, he could have helped Lorian, Asinia, and Demos once we were taken.

"Trap."

"I know it was a trap." That was my point.

Vynthar stepped into my line of sight, almost poking me in the eye with one of his horns. *"Trap for Drakoryx. Wards."*

Ah. The wards would have trapped him in those

caves. I shuddered.

"I'm glad you're here now. Do you know where Lorian and the others are?"

"No. I'm connected to you."

My shoulders slumped. Still, whatever connection he had to me had likely saved our lives, and I stroked him beneath his chin.

As soon as Madinia and I found somewhere safe to rest, I needed to send some messages. By now, Tibris should be on his way back from the hybrid camp. I wanted an update from Vicer about the hybrids he'd attempted to convince to move down to the camp in the fae lands. And of course, we needed to send a message to the queen. We had to know without a doubt that we could trust her.

And then?

Then we would strike where Regner was weakest.

"You're going to free them, I know it. Promise me, Prisca. Promise me you'll free them. And one day, you'll come back and burn this fucking place to the ground."

9

LORIAN

Regner's dungeon was well hidden, deep in the southern forests of Eprotha. We'd been traveling north, certain he would have picked a spot farther from the fae lands. Instead, the dungeon was in a forest close to Crawyth—just hours from the caves.

If I thought about how much time we'd wasted, I might slip off the edge of sanity. Yet no matter how I retraced our steps, I couldn't see any hint we should have moved south instead.

Now, we were hidden in the forest as the sun went down, all of us watching the entrance of Regner's hidden prison closely for any sign of movement.

It went against all my instincts not to stride directly into the dungeon and search for my mate. But Galon and Demos had been right. This would make the perfect trap.

Body parts had been strewn across the ground outside of the dungeon, as if some beast had torn those bodies into pieces. Asinia had retched, stumbling into the forest to lose her stomach, and even Demos had swallowed at the sight. But his eyes had met mine, and we'd shared the same thought.

If this was the state of the bodies *outside* the dungeon...

Prisca—

I didn't even allow myself to finish that thought. "We've waited long enough. I'm going inside."

Galon clamped his hand on my shoulder. "We need someone to guard the entrance."

"Asinia and I will do it," Demos said, his jaw clenched. "Just find my sister."

Asinia returned, wiping her mouth. She glanced up, and I followed her gaze to the pigeon as it circled down to us.

Holding out my hand, I allowed it to land, carefully removing the message from its leg.

Fuck.

"What is it?" Demos asked.

I lifted my head. "It's Tibris. The Gromalian rebels used his pigeon to send a message back to us. They've taken him hostage."

Prisca's face flashed before my mind. The grim resolve in her expression as she'd made the decision to send him, along with the sorrow at the thought of putting him in danger.

Asinia's lip trembled. "But we sent him as an act of faith. Because he's a healer. He's no threat to them."

"Tibris knew there was a chance this could happen." Demos ran a hand over his face. "The rebels are likely suspicious for good reason. Right now, they may be holding him, but as far as we know, they haven't hurt him."

The rebels would have to be idiots to have harmed Tibris. But I'd been alive for long enough to be painstakingly aware of just how many idiots were in this world. Still, I kept that thought to myself.

Asinia got to her feet, eyes stark with hopelessness.

Demos and I were silent as she walked several steps away, slumping to the ground and leaning against a tree.

"I'll watch her," Demos said. "Go find Prisca."

His eyes were hard, and I nodded. We should have been under attack the moment we got close to this place. Instead, it was silent.

Prisca wasn't here.

And that thought, the disappointment that clawed at me, the sheer hopelessness and terror for her...

Thunder sounded, followed immediately by lightning that seemed to split the sky in two. My power had slipped through my control, announcing our presence as I strode toward the iron doors. Galon directed his power at the doors, his water blowing them off their hinges. Someone moved inside, and I launched myself into the entrance of the dungeon, ignoring the scream of the guard.

In front of us, a corridor stretched, a stone wall on one side, a row of cages on the other. I snarled, drawing Prisca's scent into my lungs. Rythos disappeared to investigate, and I slowly turned to the guard hiding behind several chairs in the corner of the room.

My hand circled his throat, and I held him in place against the concrete wall. His own hand dropped to the sword at his side. With the twist of my wrist, I broke his arm, reveling in his scream.

Rythos returned, his expression solemn. "Empty," he said.

I slammed the guard against the wall. His dark eyes darted frantically, his terror palpable.

"Where are they?"

Silence.

My lightning escaped, striking the wall next to his head. The sharp tang of urine hit my nostrils, sweat glistening on his sallow, pockmarked skin.

"Speak."

He cringed. "The fae is dead."

The words ripped into the air. Time stopped.

Cavis.

A weight pressed on my chest. For a long moment, all I could do was stare at the human.

Rythos let out a choked sound. We'd all retained a shred of hope.

The beast inside me howled for vengeance. *I will make them pay, brother.*

The guard swallowed. He reeked of fear. It rolled off him in waves, penetrating the dungeon. I could feel the others stepping closer.

"The woman?" I demanded.

"She w-was weak. Sick. She spent all day sleeping. We thought she would die."

Fae fire exploded from me. I managed to channel it into the wall behind us, gritting my teeth and pulling my power back down where it belonged.

When the last spark disappeared, everyone looked at me. My hand tightened around the guard's throat, and I stared back at them.

"How long has that been happening?" Galon asked.

"It only happened one other time. At Eryndan's castle."

Rythos angled his head. "Because Prisca is your mate. And you haven't truly claimed her."

The guard choked.

Ignoring him, Rythos shook his head. "I'd wondered."

Turning my attention back to the guard, I shook him. "Speak."

He shuddered, his eyes so wide, they were mostly white. "She somehow managed to get the manacles off and escaped her cell. Tiran attacked. She disarmed him and held him at swordpoint. I'm not sure how she was even standing," he said, reluctant admiration coating his words. "She asked Tiran where we were. He told her he was going to rape her and kill her. She stabbed him in the throat."

Sounded like Prisca in a rage. It didn't happen often, but her temper occasionally rivaled mine. Pride warred with the fury churning through me.

"What happened next?"

"She kept stopping time. She'd disarmed all of us. She also…freed the other prisoner."

I tightened my hold. "Who is the prisoner?"

"I-I don't know. I swear. When I asked a few weeks ago, Gorris said he'd been here for a while."

Was this man still with Prisca? Why did she free him? I almost shook my head at the thought. She'd freed him because she couldn't help herself.

"What. Happened. Next?"

"We told her what she wanted to know," the guard said, as if the answer was obvious. I supposed it was.

Behind me, Rythos let out a low, admiring whistle.

"Where did she go?"

"I don't know. I swear."

"Marth," I said, keeping my eyes on the guard.

"You want me to look?"

"Yes."

The guard shuddered, likely unaware of what that meant, but fearing it all the same. His eyes wheeled, his feet shifting as I held him in place.

Marth stepped up next to me, and I surveyed him. His eyes were already turning cloudy as he focused on the guard.

"He watched through the cage as Prisca was tortured," Marth said. "She refused to break, and that's when they killed Cavis."

I looked at Marth. His eyes were wet. He'd just witnessed Cavis's death. And I'd made him see that.

"I'm sorry, brother."

He just shook his head. "This guard has the power to hide from all senses, but only every few days. He slipped into the forest and spied. Madinia arrived and left with Prisca on horseback. The man she freed traveled in the opposite direction."

Despite the situation, I almost laughed. Madinia had not only found Prisca's location first, but she'd helped her escape before we'd even arrived. If Madinia ever chose to *truly* care about someone, she would be a force to be reckoned with.

I killed the guard with a glance, my power making his body dance as he died.

"Then we go. Now."

THE QUEEN

I had thought things couldn't get worse. But such thoughts were not just useless, they were a temptation for the gods. Things could *always* get worse.

I'd imagined that Madinia would save the hybrid heir, and we would enjoy a brief respite while she gathered her allies. Instead, just days after I'd sent Prisca's location to Madinia, Pelysian was standing in my rooms once more, his eyes haunted…

My palms began to sweat.

Pelysian was always, always calm. Composed. Usually, I found it infuriating. But seeing fear on his face was worse.

"Sabium has begun planning his trip to the barrier."

Nausea swept through me, until I stumbled to the closest chair, burying my head in my hands. "When?"

"Soon. By the next full moon."

Eight days. I lifted my head. "Your mother said my sacrifice would buy Jamic time!"

"And it has. The problem is the king. According to my source, he no longer wishes to keep the barrier up. After all, it is now far too late for the fae and hybrids to find the help they need. Even if they could get to the eastern continents and convince another kingdom to help us, the political machinations of that would take months. Not to mention the time it would take for any allies to ready their own armies for war."

A tiny spark of hope appeared deep in my chest. "Then...then Sabium doesn't need Jamic. Perhaps he could be convinced to let him go."

Pelysian's eyes gleamed with sympathy. "He *does* need him, Your Majesty. He will sacrifice him at the barrier. Only, instead of using that power to reinforce the barrier, he will take all the power from both your son and the barrier into himself. That power will make him unstoppable. A god."

I didn't care about the influx of power Sabium would receive. I certainly didn't care what happened to this continent or the people living on it. Because if Sabium received that power, I would already have nothing left to live for.

Jamic would be dead.

My arms ached for him, and for a moment, I could almost feel the last time I'd hugged him. I'd noticed how tall he was in that moment—much taller than I. Had he grown taller still? He'd reached nineteen winters while imprisoned by the man he'd thought was his father.

"Your Majesty?"

I raised my gaze once more, and I must have looked as hopeless as I felt, because Pelysian crouched in front of me.

"We will get this information to the woman you have the connection with."

"Madinia," I mumbled. My face had turned numb.

"Yes."

Pelysian melted away, and I wandered through my rooms, my mind replaying our conversation again and again.

I made my way to the library, spending the day huddled in front of a fire. The numbness had spread to my entire body.

Eventually, I got up to pace. But my attention was caught by movement outside.

Sabium's carriage was entering the castle gates, surrounded by guards. Pressing myself against the window, I watched as he stepped out of that carriage, his expression twisted with rage.

The tumultuous chaos in my mind quieted, until only

stillness and silence remained. Unclenching my fists, I stretched out my stiffened fingers. If Sabium had managed to kill the hybrid heir, he would have been beaming. He would have also been dragging her corpse behind his horse.

Madinia had trusted me. She'd gotten to Prisca in time.

But I was in an extraordinarily dangerous position. Sabium had a tendency to lash out when his plans were impeded. It was one of the only times his mask of civility would fall.

By now, Sabium would have heard about the hybrid camp in Gromalia. According to my spies, the Gromalian king was furious, implying that Sabium had set some kind of trap in retaliation for hosting the hybrid heir. Eryndan had demonstrated a surprising amount of spine, his message to Sabium terse, verging on threatening.

Sabium had blamed Eryndan's people, accusing them of leaking the information. But he would be looking to his own people as well. If Tymedes chose to risk implicating me…

Or if Sabium learned that the woman who rescued the hybrid heir had once been one of my ladies…

My memory supplied me with an image of his graveyard, and the back of my neck grew clammy.

I remained in the library, twitching at every footstep on the stone corridor outside. Half of me expected several guards to march in and drag me to the dungeon.

But Sabium was far too controlled for that. When he

had me killed, I would be taken from my own rooms and dragged to that graveyard. Or perhaps, he would simply poison me at dinner, his eyes alight with suppressed mirth. My death would be a quiet, private agony. And directly after, Sabium would no doubt publicly mourn the "love of his life."

More footsteps. Despite my logical analysis of the situation, some part of me still expected the door to slam open at any moment.

Instead, a quiet knock sounded.

I cleared my throat. "Enter."

The servant bowed. "The king requests your presence for dinner, Your Majesty."

He backed out of the room at my nod. Steeling myself, I returned to my chambers, splashed water on my face, and pinched my cheeks until some of the color returned. Finally, I made my way down to the man I wanted dead more than I'd ever wanted anything in my life.

Sabium raked his gaze down my body as I entered the room. Seated at the table, he kept his spine erect, shoulders squared. Yet his jaw was set, his fingers curled slightly inward, nails pressing into his palm. Though his expression was carefully neutral, tension lingered at the corners of his eyes as they met mine.

"Not even bothering to dress for dinner?"

"I wasn't expecting you to be back tonight."

One of the servants stepped forward and pulled out my chair. I sat down, waving him away.

The oak table was laid with ornate silver and fine

bone china, Sabium had chosen the more intimate dining room in his chambers tonight—likely in an effort to ensure I was off-balance.

He raised one eyebrow. "I hadn't realized you paid such close attention to my comings and goings."

"People talk. Everyone in this castle knows you captured the hybrid heir. I assume she's dead?" I asked, voice casual as I gestured for a servant to fill my wine.

The muscle that twitched in Sabium's cheek told me my question had struck true.

"No. Somehow, she managed to free herself and disappear. My men arrived to find the guards dead or locked in a cage, the heir gone."

My heart pounded so hard I could feel it in my throat.

"I don't understand." Was he telling me this because he suspected me somehow? And why hadn't he mentioned Madinia?

"She picked the locks on her manacles. The guards were so useless, they allowed my greatest enemy free. Their idiocy may have cost this kingdom *everything*."

Shock sucked the breath from my lungs. Sabium's gaze clung to my face, and our eyes held for several excruciating moments. Finally, he leaned back in his chair. He'd suspected me somehow, but I'd been exceedingly aware of his body language for decades now. He'd decided my reaction was believable.

It wasn't surprising that the hybrid heir had escaped. That crafty bitch had humiliated Sabium time and time again.

No, I had only one question. A question that made my shoulders slump.

Where was Madinia?

Had she chosen not to trust me?

If she refused to trust me, all of my planning was useless.

Eight days.

Panic clawed at my chest, and I fisted my hands beneath the table, my nails digging into my palms. I couldn't free Jamic without help.

Eight days.

I would never have the daughter I would have adored. I'd sacrificed that life for the ability to find Madinia, and the stupid little whore had ignored my message.

"Your fury surprises me," Sabium remarked.

I cleared my throat, raising my gaze to his. "The hybrid heir made a fool out of me. She infiltrated my closest circle. To learn that she escaped is…disappointing."

That seemed to please him, and he lifted his cup once more, drinking deeply. This was the most we had spoken since he had begun "courting me" all those years ago. It was…unsettling.

I moved some of the food around on my plate.

"Something on your mind?" he prodded.

I gestured at the table between us. "Why…"

"A private dinner?" Sabium shrugged one shoulder. "It can be…tiring to wear the mask at all times. But I don't have to wear that mask with *you*, do I, Kaliera?"

No, he didn't need to wear a mask with me. I was

one of the few people who knew exactly who and what he was.

"I heard about the carriage situation."

I lifted my head, attempting a casual tone. "Tymedes overstepped."

He smiled. "I hadn't realized how much you loathed him. That, more than anything else, will keep him alive during the coming months."

My skin prickled with suppressed hatred. How this man loved to taunt me.

Sabium took a sip of wine, ignoring the plate in front of him. "I expect you think I'm a monster."

I gave him a dry smile. "You *are* a monster."

Amusement darted over his face. He turned his head, gaze distant as he stared out the window.

"My son could have lived, you know. If humans were given stronger power. If the gods hadn't given most of that power to the fae and hybrids."

I kept my expression carefully neutral, suppressing my urge to sneer. I needed to be very, very careful of Sabium in this mood.

"Crotopos was a good man," Sabium said.

I drank my own wine, using the movement to hide my grimace. Many people in this kingdom could have lived if not for Sabium and his obsession with his dead son.

Sabium raised his eyebrow, as if reading my mind. His gaze met mine. "Crotopos would have been a firm, unyielding ruler. His son…"

The death of Sabium's son had unlocked something dark inside the king. But when Crotopos's wife and son died during childbirth, all that darkness had come spilling out.

Because if Sabium hadn't declared war on the fae, there would have been healers in the castle who could have saved his daughter-in-law and grandson. Sabium couldn't live with the guilt. Couldn't accept that his actions had led to their deaths. So he fanned the flames of his hatred instead.

Rather than mourn his family, Sabium stole a newborn son from a poverty-stricken village woman and told the kingdom his grandson had survived. He had his men slaughter the villager's entire family—including her three other children—so his actions could never be discovered.

Sabium could have raised that boy as his grandchild if family had been what he truly wanted. Instead, he'd come up with his despicable plan.

And all these years later, he still lied to himself. He still insisted that if his family hadn't died, he would have been a better man.

Sabium would never have been a better man. Whichever evil had been planted in his mind—either when the gods created him, or when his father raised him—had simply been waiting to be set free.

My silence hadn't pleased him. He met my gaze, and his mouth twisted. "I suppose there are worse things than being a monster," he said. "Such as being leashed by one."

Fury twisted in my stomach.

Sabium's lips curved into the mimicry of a smile. Pushing his chair back, he got to his feet and stalked from the room.

Eight days.

MADÎNIA

Prisca exuded rage.

She sat, appearing almost relaxed in her chair in our room at the inn I'd chosen—that monster taking up far too much space as he sprawled at her feet. But I could see something in her eyes that hadn't been there before. Something cruel and vicious and burning with suppressed vengeance.

She'd gotten out of bed, eaten, slipped food to the monster—who followed her around as if guarding her from *me*—even washed the blood out of his fur. She'd changed into the fresh clothes I'd bought at the market, used my pigeon to send a message to her aunt, wrote more messages for Tibris and the others, brushed her hair... And the entire time, it was as if she was somewhere else entirely, her gaze burning with wrath.

She didn't sleep. When she lay down, she jolted awake, and the dark circles beneath her eyes—already startling when I found her—seemed to grow worse by the hour.

I supposed it wasn't surprising. Prisca had taken a number of blows that would have been crippling on their own, and all of them had come in a short period of time.

But her timing was definitely inconvenient.

We took turns on sentry duty each night. I'd been careful to appear as if I were traveling alone, Prisca using her power to sneak up to the room I'd secured. But it was only a matter of time before Regner's guards began going door-to-door in every village within a few days' travel of his dungeon.

My worst fear was that we would stumble across a town or village just as they were readying for a Taking or Gifting ceremony. While both of us carried blue marks on our temples, the king's assessor and the priestess would be the most likely to recognize one or both of us. If they traveled with a null or managed to take us by surprise with fae iron...

My hair had been darkened, but Prisca's long blond curls and amber eyes were recognizable. We needed to take care of that. Soon.

I considered my strategy as we ate. I'd ordered food to be delivered to the room, well aware that we couldn't draw attention to ourselves. And so, I sat on my bed, plate in my lap as I eyed the creature. Prisca had attempted to convince him to stay in the forest, and he'd argued.

Argued. Because the beast could talk. In our minds.

Last night, he'd slunk out the window, climbed up

the side of the building, and strolled along the roof, where he'd kept watch.

A knock sounded on the door. Prisca went still. The Drakoryx slowly rolled to his feet.

I held up one finger, and Prisca buried her hand in the fur along the back of his neck. My power came to me easily, warming my hands. Prisca nodded. She could pause time if necessary.

Crossing the room to the door, I cracked it open.

The messenger stood at attention. I glowered at him. He just sighed, handing me the note and holding out his hand for the coin I dropped into his palm.

I closed the door, locked it, and opened the message.

"Kaliera," I said.

Prisca curled her lip, her eyes flashing. But she leaned forward, gesturing for me to continue. She had always been at her best when there were plans to be made, action to be taken.

"I don't like it either. Somehow, her messengers always seem to know where I am. Clearly, she thinks we're still her fucking puppets, even if we're no longer at her beck and call. But this is important. Regner is going to kill Jamic before the next full moon. He's bringing down the barrier."

She frowned. "Why would he bring it down? That's exactly what we want."

"He knows we're a true threat to him now. And he's going to end this war before it even begins. According to the queen, he'll draw all that power into his own body, until he's the most powerful creature on this continent. Completely unstoppable. All of us using our power together wouldn't put a dent in the magic he has been hoarding for all these centuries."

Prisca placed her plate on the ground, and the Drakoryx got to work finishing her stew. "That amount of power in a human would make him insane."

"We could argue that he already is insane."

Prisca's eyes were sharp now. "He'll need to get Jamic to the barrier."

"According to Kaliera's spies, Regner is taking no chances, and he's planning to move him closer to the castle. But one of the patriarchs knows where he will be kept. The same man responsible for creating the dungeons that have held Jamic since he disappeared."

"Rothnic Boria." Prisca curled her lip at the name, but I could practically see her pondering our options. "Taking Jamic when he's in the city is our best chance. When is it happening?"

"Within a few days. Regner will then take Jamic and a handful of his most loyal guards with him to the barrier."

"Which part of the barrier?"

I shrugged. "The queen doesn't know. The barrier stretches along most of this continent."

"That means we need to rescue Jamic before they leave. Otherwise, Regner could hide his tracks and we'd have no idea where to search." She stood, leaning down to pet Vynthar as he craned his neck. She was still pale, but her mouth was tight.

"Which means we need to get to Rothnic," I said. "After what I did to his son, he's likely being very careful." My mind threw me back to Davis Boria's hot breath on my face, the sharp pinch of his fingers, his huge hands squeezing my arms.

It had taken weeks for his fingerprints to fade from my skin.

Occasionally when I bathed, I found myself scrubbing until my skin was red and raw. At least until I could convince myself he was still dead.

It was Prisca's turn to study me. I gave her a mock snarl, and she shook her head at me.

"Think about anything else you know about him," she said. "Even the smallest things can be helpful."

I placed my plate on the table next to me. My knowledge of the castle and the people in it was one of the only things that made me uniquely helpful to Prisca's little group.

"He's friendly with Patriarch Greve. They both gamble in some of the illegal dens on the outskirts of the slums. The king knows about it but turns a blind eye."

She nodded, leaning against the wall. "You're sure you haven't heard anything from Tibris?"

I shook my head. She frowned. Then she seemed to shake it off.

"How far are we from Lesdryn?"

"A few days if we buy fresh horses here and travel from dawn to dusk."

Prisca's eyes burned until she looked more fae than

hybrid.

"What are you thinking?" I asked.

"I'm thinking we're going to gather our people. Then we'll go to the city. We're going to find Rothnic, locate Jamic, sneak into the castle…"

"And then?"

"And then we're going to burn that fucking place to the ground."

10

MADÎNIA

The next day, we traveled east along one of the smaller trade routes. Both of us were cloaked, but we still moved our horses off the trail whenever we heard someone approaching.

Prisca had asked me to send a message to Vicer, requesting that he briefly return to the city to help with our plans.

Vynthar prowled alongside us, putting the horses on edge. Each time we came across other travelers, he would melt into the forest, his steps silent. The monster was the perfect hunter, and losing sight of him made the hair on the back of my neck stand up.

By the time we found an inn that still had rooms available and Prisca used her power to stroll into the inn and up the stairs, both of us were mostly silent.

Of course, she'd been silent all day. I'd given her time since that was what *I* would have wanted, but perhaps she needed more…support.

She sat on the threadbare armchair next to the bed, Vynthar curled next to her. He'd appeared at the window, and I'd almost jumped out of my skin as he'd shown me his teeth through the glass in an obvious demand to let him in.

I closed the window, cleared my throat, and sat on the edge of the bed. "Are you…all right?"

Prisca gave me a look that was caught between exhausted and amused. "Are you truly interested?"

"Yes." Surprisingly, I wasn't lying. She watched me, and I shrugged. "All of us are relying on you."

The amusement disappeared, until only the exhaustion was left. Exhaustion and something hopeless. It was an expression I'd never seen her wear before, and it made my stomach churn uneasily.

Prisca let her gaze drop to the monster curled at her feet. She was silent for a long moment. Finally, she shrugged. "I can twist time whenever I like, and everyone will just…stop. But sometimes, more than anything, I wish I could be the one to pause. To be frozen for just a few seconds while the world goes on without me."

A dull panic spread through my chest. While our relationship had progressed from when we were both serving the queen as her ladies, we weren't friends. And I didn't have the words she needed. Didn't know *what* I could say to remove the increasingly wounded look in her eyes.

She needed Asinia. Lorian. Tibris. Demos. Someone

who understood feelings.

"You're tired. You're mourning. You're worried about the others. It's…natural to struggle."

Her expression cleared, and she nodded, dropping her gaze to her hands.

A pit opened in my stomach. Useless. I was *useless*.

The door slammed open. I loosed a fireball, which was immediately doused. The torrent of cold water swept through the air toward me, barreling into my face.

Prisca let out a sound I'd never heard from her before. I whirled, ready to fight, to *kill*.

But she wasn't looking at me. And she wasn't afraid. No, her expression had twisted into a kind of tortured relief, and her eyes…her eyes…

They glimmered with hope and sadness and fury. With liberation and passion—and with a love so pure, I had to look away.

Vynthar yawned. Clearly, he wasn't worried.

Lorian crossed the room in a movement almost too fast to see. He snatched Prisca up with a kind of possessive fury—a dragon regaining its stolen hoard.

He was running his hands down her arms, her back, as if checking for injuries. When he was satisfied she wasn't hurt, he tipped her chin back, staring into her eyes as if he could search her mind for damage. Prisca just shook her head, buried her face in his neck, and held him so tightly, her knuckles turned white.

PRISCA

I held on to Lorian for a long time. He clamped me to him, his huge body trembling. When he raised his head, it was to scan my face slowly, as if he couldn't quite believe it was me.

"I'm fine," I told him.

He shook his head, but his mouth found mine, his hand sliding to the back of my head.

I breathed him in, soaking up the feel of him. He was really here.

Someone cleared their throat and my cheeks heated. I pushed against his chest, and he let out a rumble of displeasure but lifted his head, dropping me back down to my feet.

Lorian refused to let go of my hand as I hugged the others. Demos squeezed me until I yelped, while Asinia swore if I ever put her through anything like that again, she would make me pay.

Rythos and Galon and Marth...

I stared at them, my heart pounding until I could feel it in my throat. "Cavis..."

Lorian pulled me close. "We know, wildcat."

Rythos met my eyes. I'd expected blame. Maybe a hint of judgment. Instead, all I saw was understanding. "We heard about how you escaped. Cavis would be so proud of you, Prisca."

A hollow ache settled beneath my ribs. For a long moment, I couldn't say a word.

But I'd promised Cavis.

"He…he wanted you to know…" My voice cracked, and I forced it to steady. "Cavis wanted you to know that being your brother was the honor of his life."

Lorian squeezed me tight, burying his head in my hair for a long moment. Devastation flickered through Marth's eyes, but he nodded, stalking to the other side of the room to gaze out the window.

Rythos's eyes glistened. "Thank you, Pris."

I turned my attention to my own brother. "You must have already been close before I sent my message. How did you find me?" I asked.

They filled me in. Asinia had been hurt—badly enough to need a healer. And it had cost them time. With no other leads, they'd worked their way through any enemy camps they could find—enemy camps Regner had obviously put into place to ready for his march forward.

But the time to consider his tactics would come later. Now, I was too busy laughing as Demos ruefully admitted that even after all of their hunting and killing, Madinia had been the one to let them know my location with her note.

I glanced at Madinia, who was squeezing water from her hair while sending Galon a killing look.

Lorian was still holding my hand, his gaze on my face. He was watching me as if afraid I would disappear without warning, even as he held up his free hand.

"Everyone out."

Surprisingly, no one argued, although Madinia rolled her eyes at me. Rythos ruffled my hair, and Asinia let out a chuckle but wandered out of the room with everyone else—including Vynthar, who showed Lorian his teeth.

"I won't let anything happen to you ever again," Lorian murmured in my ear as Demos shut the door behind them.

I turned in his arms. For the first time in days, I felt safe. I nuzzled his chest, drawing in the wild scent of him. "Are you planning to be completely unreasonable now that I'm back?"

He gave a low, unamused grunt. Clearly, that was indeed what he was planning.

"Never again, Prisca. I'll kill anyone who tries."

I stifled a sigh, but Lorian seemed to be waiting for me to agree, so I nodded. Losing me for so long, and learning about Cavis…it had cracked something open in him.

"What are you thinking?"

He slid his hand down my throat and then stilled, stroking my skin with his thumb.

"I'm resisting the urge to drag you away from Regner, from your cousin, and from this entire war."

My heart thumped against my ribs. Some part of me wished we could do that. Just disappear. But I could never live with myself.

"I wouldn't go."

He nuzzled my hair, and I could feel him breathing

me in. "I can be very...persuasive."

A tiny hint of humor slid through Lorian's low voice. He was stepping back from the brink of the cliff he'd been poised on, and I let out a breath, nestling closer.

I raised my hand to his face, gently running a finger along his strong, stubborn jaw, drifting up to the sharp angle of his cheekbone. Touching him again, feeling his arms around me....it felt like a dream after Regner's dungeon.

"I'm sorry," he said, his voice tight.

"For what?"

He gave me an incredulous look. "For not getting to you in time. For every second you suffered in that place. I should have been faster."

My chest clenched. I tilted my head, peering up at him. "Did I undermine your rescue plan with my own audacious, highly impressive escape?"

His eyebrows furrowed. I smirked at him. "As much as I would have enjoyed waiting for you to stroll into that prison and slaughter everyone in sight, I had things to do."

Ah. There. My smirk turned into a grin. His mouth had twitched.

His hand slipped to my chin, his head lowering until it felt as if he were staring into my soul.

"You had things to do." His words were flat.

"Well, yes. I couldn't sit around for days and wait to be rescued. Besides, if I'd done that, you would have arrived and roared at me for not working harder to escape."

Amusement flickered in his eyes. "Is that right?"

"Well…yes." I sighed, dropping my nonchalant tone. "Asinia was hurt, Lorian. Do you think I would've wanted you to leave her?"

His jaw hardened in a way that told me he'd considered it. "No."

And he'd lost time. But Asinia was healthy now.

"Cavis…" My throat tightened, and I forced the words out. "They killed him early. You wouldn't have made it in time, even if you'd left Asinia. Even if you'd known exactly where I was. It was too late, Lorian." The admission killed a part of me.

"I could have spared you some pain."

I shook my head. "Once Cavis died, I didn't see Eadric again. Cavis was supposed to stay alive, and I think Eadric fled because he knew Regner was on the way."

He stiffened. "Who is Eadric?"

"Do you remember the man at the inn? The day you were flirting with that fae woman?"

"I wasn't—" He narrowed his eyes at me. "Not amusing." A slight frown appeared between his brows. "The man who approached you was the same one who just tortured you? I should have killed him at the inn. My instincts told me he was a threat." Several sparks rose from his skin, crackling above us.

Time for a change of subject. "I heard your voice in my head, you know," I told him.

He released my chin, his hand sliding to the back of my neck. His expression was still shuttered, his eyes hard. "Is that so?"

"Yes. I heard you saying that I couldn't give up. That I had to survive. I had to escape. When I was in that cell…It was the lowest point of my life, Lorian. And even though you weren't there, you kept me alive. You ensured I kept fighting."

His breath shuddered out, and then his mouth was on mine and he was spinning me, urging me back toward the bed. I opened for him eagerly, twining my tongue with his, until he pulled his mouth away to press kisses down my neck.

"Need you," he rumbled, and I nodded, lifting my arms so he could pull my tunic over my head. He froze.

I glanced down. His gaze had caught on a line of yellowed bruises along the right side of my rib cage. I wasn't even sure when that had happened, but my ribs had only just stopped hurting over the past few days.

Lorian angled his head in that strange fae way of his. More sparks began to lift from his skin, the scent of lightning filling the air.

"If you set this inn on fire, I will be very upset," I murmured.

His eyes had turned lifeless. The last time I'd seen him look like that was when we were beneath the king's bedrooms. The day he'd learned the amulet he'd risked everything to find wasn't there.

"Lorian," I said, keeping my voice quiet, even. "I'm not hurt. But if you make me wait much longer without your hands on me, I won't be happy."

A hint of warmth returned to those frigid eyes.

He was with me. We were together. I just had to convince my mind that I wasn't still in that cell. That I was free.

Lorian seemed to feel the same, because he pressed a heartbreakingly gentle kiss to my mouth.

"I missed you so much, I sometimes thought I'd die from the agony of it."

My eyes stung. "I knew you were coming for me, Lorian. I freed myself, but I knew you were on the way."

He leaned down and nuzzled my nose with his. "Seeing you hurt, imagining your pain, it makes me insane, Prisca."

"I know. But I don't want to think about it anymore. Make me forget."

He finished stripping off our clothes. His hands were hot—likely from suppressing his power—and I shivered as he ran them up my legs, massaging the tension from my calves, stroking my sensitive inner thighs, sweeping up my hips. My breasts ached for him, and I arched my back until he cupped them, his mouth finding my nipples.

I was more than ready for him—swollen and desperate—but he swept his hands along every inch of me, pressing his lips to my skin, nibbling and kissing, leaving reddened marks behind.

Lorian's expression was dangerous, eyes fierce as they met mine. Heat pooled between my legs, and he kissed my neck, his teeth grazing my most sensitive spots, until my head spun and I clawed at his shoulders, desperate to feel him inside me.

I'd thought we would never have this again.

Sliding one hand down my body, he growled as he eased my thighs farther apart, finding me slick. "Mine," he crooned in my ear, and I forced my heavy eyelids open.

"Yours," I agreed, and he rewarded me, slipping one finger inside, quickly followed by another. His thumb found my clit, and I opened my thighs even wider, silently urging him on.

"Need to taste you," he said, sliding down my body and immediately fastening his lips over me, stroking his tongue in time with his clever fingers.

I buried my hands in his hair and held on, curving my legs around his shoulders as if I could hold him in place. He chuckled, and I gasped at the vibration.

I needed more. Needed to feel him inside me, filling me up. Needed to prove to myself that this wasn't a dream. That I was no longer in that cell, wishing for him with my every breath.

His tongue lashed my clit, the pleasure washing over me as I let out a moan so filthy, he laughed once more, spurring me on.

"Inside me," I ordered, although it was more of a plea.

He lifted his head. "Need to get you ready for me, wildcat."

I *was* ready. I opened my mouth to tell him exactly that, but he'd already lowered his head once more, and the combination of his tongue, the slow, steady thrust of his fingers, and the feel of him, the *scent* of him…

I erupted, clamping down around his fingers. He thrust deeper, continuing to flick his tongue, ignoring as I let out a choked plea—suddenly too sensitive.

Lorian curled his tongue around my clit and then sucked.

I fell apart again, my body turning limp as he let out a pleased laugh. I opened my eyes to find him watching me as I trembled with aftershocks. Removing his fingers, he licked them clean.

"There is no better taste than you," he said.

I didn't even have the energy to blush. Lorian merely grinned at me, clearly pleased with himself. As he should be.

With a yank on my legs, he pulled me farther down the bed toward him, then flipped me over, guiding me up onto my knees. This was no longer just our reunion. It was a claiming.

Even after two incredible orgasms, I sucked in a breath as he pressed against my entrance, slowly pushing inside me. He was so large in this position. His hands found my hips, tilting me to the exact angle he wanted me, and I buried my hands in the sheets, holding tight as he eased his full length into me.

When I was stretched around him, he didn't hesitate, his thick cock pulling back and immediately driving back in again. I sucked in a breath, and he slipped his hand down to my clit, stroking once.

I tightened, letting out a low groan.

"There you go," he said. His hand stayed teasingly

close, but he continued to thrust into me slowly, driving deep, the constant pressure driving me higher. When I let out a low, desperate groan, he paused. And I understood.

Lorian was claiming me on his terms. And I would come when he allowed it.

All I could do was stay there, ass in the air, body trembling, entirely exposed, and at his mercy. And just that thought almost tipped me over the edge.

"Not yet," he warned, and I was so close, I let out a desperate mewling sound that would have made my cheeks heat if I weren't out of my mind with lust.

He cursed, picking up the pace, and my thighs trembled. I was just on the edge of pain in this position, and yet I loved the feeling of being entirely owned by him. Of knowing it was I who made him grunt with need as his hands tightened on me.

"Please," I gasped out.

He let out a low, wicked chuckle. "I could keep you on the brink like this for hours. Maybe one day, I will. I'll fuck you until your voice is hoarse from begging, and when I finally let you come, you'll soak the bed."

I moaned at his filthy words, and he slipped his hand down once more, barely brushing my clit. I was so close, but it wasn't enough. Just as he'd known it wouldn't be.

"Or perhaps I'll make you come and come and come, until you don't think it's possible to come anymore. We'll see just how many times you can find your pleasure with me, hmm?"

"Lorian…please…"

He growled, and I almost smiled. He might have the upper hand, but when I begged using his name, he lost all control.

He thrust deeper, hitting that spot inside me that made my vision turn fuzzy. One flick of his thumb across my clit and I shattered, pleasure consuming me as he continued his long, steady strokes.

I went limp, slumping to the bed, but Lorian flipped me over, slid back inside me, and cupped my face.

"Like this," he said. "One more time, just like this."

"I can't."

He smiled, sliding one hand down to my nipple and tweaking it as he ground into me.

We came together, and Lorian shuddered against me, pressing his lips to mine. I wound my arms around his neck, holding him tightly, unwilling to let him go. We lay like that for long moments, until Lorian rolled away, pulling me with him until my head rested on his chest.

But he was quiet. It was a strange quiet, as if he was deep in thought. I craned my neck, studying his face.

He was surveying the ceiling, mouth tight, a frown on his face.

"What is it?"

He glanced at me, and his arm tightened around me.

"Nothing," he said.

My heart tripped, and I laid my head on his chest, my throat tightening.

Lorian had just lied to me.

11

PRISCA

The sky darkened. The others had probably gone downstairs to eat, but Lorian ordered dinner to be sent up to our room.

Our room.

Lorian stroked my back, and I listened to the sound of his heart beneath my head. But we'd spent what little time we could spare. Lifting my head off his chest, I forced myself to roll away, reaching for my tunic. Lorian studied me. "You need to talk about it."

I shook my head. "I can't. Not yet." I couldn't linger on the way I'd lain on that stone floor as if it were the bottom of the world. As if I were lying in a pit I could never climb out of.

I couldn't tell him I'd left a part of myself there in that pit. And that I might never get it back.

Lorian was still studying me with those eyes that saw far too much. "When you're ready to talk, I'm here," he said. "I will always be here."

My throat ached. "Did you find

Cavis?"

The muscles around his eyes tightened. "Regner took his body with him."

A thousand images assaulted my mind at once. All of them various ways that Regner could be disrespecting Cavis's body. I closed my eyes, and Lorian caught my wrists.

"There are…spells Regner can use to try to recover his memories. His knowledge."

My head spun, my stomach churned, and Lorian placed a cool hand on the back of my neck as I fought not to vomit.

I couldn't fall apart. That wouldn't help anyone. I forced my eyes open. "We can't let that happen."

"We won't."

"I'm sorry." There was nothing else I could say.

"Nothing about this is your fault."

"Lorian…Cavis knew I wouldn't be able to hold on. He knew I couldn't watch him be tortured. Eventually… eventually, I was going to break. *I* was the weak one. And he knew it. He died for it."

His expression hardened, even as grief darkened his eyes. "He would never have let them take him alive, Prisca. Never. Don't take that decision from him."

I drew in a deep, shaky breath. Lorian was a solid support next to me. But I wanted to be *his* support. I reached for his hand.

"I know you're hurting too," I said. "You don't have to pretend with me, Lorian."

"I…" He paused. Swallowed. "He should be here, Prisca. He should be right here. With us." His voice was hoarse, and I nodded, just letting him talk. "The hurt will come later. When I have to—" His voice broke now. "When I have to tell Sybella he's not coming home. That she's all alone now. And I didn't do what I was supposed to. I didn't bring him back alive."

I thought of the way Cavis had doted on his daughter. How they all had. Lorian's last words to the man he'd considered family. He'd promised him he'd be there for his daughter.

He wouldn't let anyone else tell Sybella. That wasn't how Lorian was made. No, he'd do it himself. He'd see it as the least he could do for Cavis. But I had messages to pass on to Sybella too. And one day, when Piperia was old enough, I would tell her about her father. I would tell her that he *was* a hero, and that he'd left a hole in our lives that would never be filled.

"He was the best of us," Lorian said. "The kindest. There was no one better. No one who cared more. But… now, he's gone. And somehow, we all have to live with that. I've lost people before. Over and over again. So have Galon, Rythos, and Marth. But I don't know if we'll recover from this. I don't see how we can."

Leaning down, he buried his head in my neck, breathing me in. I stroked his head, giving him the time he needed.

He wasn't ready to talk about it either. All I could do was be there when he was. And right now, it was obvious he wanted a change of subject. I understood what it was not to be able to think about it. Not to be able to feel the pain.

"I have a new power," he muttered.

"You…what?"

"Do you remember the fae fire I used that time in Eryndan's castle?"

I shivered. "Yes."

"It appears that wasn't a unique experience."

"Are you…"

"I've only been able to use it during times your life has been directly threatened. I need to learn how to wield it without you being in peril. If I lose control, the world burns."

I flinched. "We'll find some damask powder," I said. "Just in case we ever need it."

He lifted his head, and I ran my thumb over his jaw, meeting his gaze.

"I took the disk from you," he said.

"You did."

"I won't apologize."

"I didn't think you would."

He sighed. I just watched him. Finally, he wound one of my curls around his finger. "It was Parintha, the woman who was my nanny when I was a boy. She hadn't eaten with the rest of the castle that night when my uncle came for our magic. She was old and tired, and she fell asleep. If she hadn't fallen asleep, she might've raised some alarm. Or perhaps she might've noticed the strange silence in the castle and hidden me away. She couldn't forgive herself."

"And she took her own life."

He nodded.

"It was selfish of her. You'd lost your parents, and you needed her."

He hesitated, his gaze still on my hair. But he nodded again.

"I will never leave you willingly," I vowed.

His wild gaze jumped to mine, and he scanned my face. After a long moment, the tightness around his eyes eased.

"I wish I *could* apologize for taking the disk from you. For taking that choice away. But I'm not sorry."

"I'm not either. I wanted to live, Lorian." I took a deep breath. "We need to talk to the others. Make plans," I said.

He nodded. A muscle twitched in his jaw, but he swung his legs off the bed, pulling on his pants. "I'll tell them."

He hesitated, watching me. Getting to my feet, I walked over to him, slid my hand around his neck, and guided his lips to mine. "I'll stay right here," I promised him.

His eyes darkened. He didn't like it. But he nodded, stalking out of the room.

I remade the bed, splashed water on my face, and paced. When Lorian returned, he gestured for me to follow him.

Madinia and Asinia were sharing the room next

to mine now. The others had likely doubled up as well. Someone had dragged in extra chairs, but Lorian slid down onto the floor, his back against the wall, and I sat with him, leaning back against his chest. His arm remained wrapped around me from behind, his chin resting on my head as his huge body encased mine.

Asinia was standing by the window, scowling down at the street. Something was bothering her, and we were overdue for a long conversation.

She could have died.

I could have gotten out of that cell and learned that Asinia had succumbed to her head injury and was no longer here. My skin suddenly felt too tight, my lungs burning. My heart pounded against my ribs, so hard it felt as if they might break.

I couldn't fall apart here. I had to lead. We had to make plans.

Lorian tightened his arms around me, and I took a deep breath. Then another. Rythos took a seat next to us, while Marth chose a low chair in the corner, his expression dark.

Madinia was the last to arrive. She sat on the edge of the bed, and Galon closed the door.

Lorian created a silence ward, and Demos got to his feet. He pulled the hourglass from beneath his shirt and slid the chain over his neck, holding it out for me. It seemed to suck in all the light in the room, reflecting it back at me.

The room went silent, as if everyone were suddenly

holding their breath. So much suffering and death had occurred so that I could get my hands on this.

I slowly reached out to take the hourglass. My hand shook.

The moment my fingers brushed it, I gasped.

I'd expected it to be warm. But it burned with cold fire, calling to me. The power thrumming from it teased the edges of my senses. With trembling hands, I lifted the fine chain over my head. The hourglass came to rest beneath my collarbone, that cold fire spreading beneath my tunic, curling out into each of my limbs.

My heart stuttered, then aligned itself to the rhythm of the glittering, incandescent sand. Power sang through my veins, wild and intoxicating. Each grain of sand seemed attuned to the seconds of my life. Scenes from my past flashed before my eyes in vivid bursts—Tibris, my father, Mama.

Then flashes of what could only be my future. Fire. Ice. A feeling of suffocation. A desperate love. A kingdom torn apart. A kingdom healed. Choices. The future was fluid.

I could hear voices. Whispers flying through my mind from across time—past, present, and future. Slowly, the visions faded, the whispers ceased, and I released my hold on the hourglass.

At some point, I'd clutched at it. Now, it radiated a comforting warmth against my chest.

Everyone was staring at me. Asinia had turned white, Galon had gotten to his feet, Rythos's hand was on his sword, while even Madinia looked perturbed.

"What's wrong?" I asked.

"You were…flickering," Demos said, his voice tight. "Your whole body was here and then not here."

Craning my neck, I met Lorian's gaze. His eyes were solemn. "I was holding you, but you kept disappearing, slipping through my fingers."

I rolled my shoulders, my stomach churning uneasily. Still…I was *supposed* to wield the hourglass. It felt as if some part of me had finally clicked back into place.

Clearing my throat, I attempted a casual tone. "Well, I'm fine now. The hourglass feels…right."

Demos grinned at me. After a moment, I grinned back. Despite everything we'd been through so far, we'd achieved something incredible. We'd taken back the artifact that belonged to Lyrinore—the hybrid kingdom. It was finally in our people's hands. In *my* hands.

It felt like it was just yesterday when I'd been planning to hand this hourglass back to our people. I'd hoped one day someone else would be gifted time magic. And that they'd be able to wield it. I hadn't believed I could be queen. Hadn't dared imagine I could become someone worthy of ruling.

Now, I knew better. All of us were only as strong and as capable as our belief in ourselves. I might not have chosen to rule, but I would choose it every day. For my people.

"Now that I have the hourglass, why couldn't I just… get close enough to Regner to stop time and kill him?" I hadn't dared attempt such a thing in the castle. Not with my power barely lasting a few seconds. I would have been instantly killed by his guards the moment I dropped the threads of time.

But I was stronger now.

Galon's mouth trembled. "Delusions of grandeur, Prisca?"

I scowled at him. "It's a legitimate question."

"Regner is always warded. That was his original magic, long before he stole any of the amulets. Many of our people have attempted to kill him over the centuries. If it were that easy, Lorian would have slaughtered him the moment he saw him in that castle. But Regner's ward has only grown stronger as he collected more and more power. It's a good plan, but we would need to find a way to break his ward first. Then you could kill him."

Behind me, Lorian tensed. Galon gave in to his grin as his gaze flicked to Lorian. "Or one of us could kill him, while you stayed far away from any danger."

When I glanced at Lorian, he was giving Galon an approving look. I squinted at him. "When I asked why you didn't kill Regner at the city gates, you told me it was because it wasn't his time to die."

Lorian nodded.

"But he was warded. You couldn't have killed him anyway."

"You didn't trust me. If I'd told you that, you'd probably have attempted to escape me and gone after him yourself."

I opened my mouth to argue, then snapped it closed. I was so, so angry at Lorian when I made that deal with him. If I'd thought there was a way to shift my helplessness and rage into action...

"I might know of someone," Demos said, pulling me back to the present. "He used to use his power to eat away at the guards' wards. I'll ask around. See if he's still alive."

"You don't know if he's still alive?" Marth scratched at his cheek. His beard was growing out, and he looked more rugged than usual. Almost...disheveled.

Demos shrugged. "I haven't seen him since before the rest of us hybrids were arrested and taken to Regner's dungeon. He was one of the few who managed to escape the guards that night." For the barest moment, his eyes filled with so much anguish, a lump formed in my throat.

"Speaking of escaping, how exactly did you three get out of the caves?" Madinia asked.

The lump in my throat grew even bigger. She didn't even like Demos, but she'd changed the subject to distract him.

"Skill," Lorian rumbled.

"Preparation." Demos's expression was hard.

"Luck," Asinia said wryly.

I exchanged a knowing look with her, and Lorian pinched me lightly beneath my ribs.

They spent a few minutes slinging insults and telling bad jokes until the remaining tension had dissipated. Finally, Lorian held up a hand.

Everyone silenced. He glanced at Madinia. "Prisca said the human queen helped you. Explain."

Madinia's eyes flared at the order, but she told the others about the messages.

"We can't trust her," Marth said from his spot in the far corner of the room.

So far, I agreed with Marth. But just because we didn't trust her, didn't mean we couldn't use her.

"She wants something," Galon agreed. "But so do we. She gave us Prisca's location for a reason." His eyes met mine, his expression serious. "You said she wants us to free her son."

"Yes. And we want to do that anyway. Once that happens, she will come after us. So, we'll need to be prepared."

Madinia nodded. "She wants to put him on the throne, but she can't do that until Regner is dead. So she's playing a long game. That means, until we separate Regner's head from his body, she will cooperate with us. But the entire time, she will be moving us into position for when she's ready to strike."

"So we need to be moving her into position too," Demos said.

I took a deep breath. "In the meantime, we need to begin moving children and their mothers away from the fae camp, along with the weak and sick. If the wards fail…"

"Conreth won't allow them to go deeper into the fae lands," Lorian said.

I didn't *want* them to move deeper into the fae lands. But my lip still curled at the mention of Conreth's callousness.

Demos smiled. "We're not taking them deeper into fae lands, are we, Pris? We're taking them home."

"Yes. But not yet. We need to make plans for their journey. I'll need to make sure the elders will allow it." And the thought of asking them for anything felt like swallowing acid.

Demos nodded. "I'll communicate with Vicer, along with our own generals. They'll need to be well-guarded as they move."

Asinia grinned at me. Even Madinia looked pleased, her eyes brighter than I'd ever seen them.

But Lorian had shifted slightly behind me.

"There's something else, Prisca."

I didn't like his tone. Wiggling out of his arms, I turned to face him. "What happened?"

His expression was solemn. "Yesterday, we received a message from Eryndan."

I rubbed at the bridge of my nose. "I'm assuming he wants to know why we haven't taken care of the Gromalian rebels yet."

"Yes."

Asinia snorted. "He's still attempting to play both sides. If Madinia hadn't managed to get a message to Vicer, Eryndan would have killed everyone living in the hybrid camp, simply because Regner told him to."

Lorian was silent. Something was wrong. "What is

it?"

A muscle ticked in his cheek. "I want you to know that I will fix this."

What was he—

Horror swept through me. "Tibris. The rebels."

"Yes. When I hadn't heard from him, I sent Aquilus. The rebel leader responded with a message. He has sworn that no harm has come to your brother, but he knows about Eryndan's orders, and he says he's keeping Tibris as insurance. Now that Tibris is living at the camp, the leader believes you'll be especially motivated to make sure it's protected."

My vision speckled, my mouth suddenly bone-dry. I'd sent Tibris alone. I'd thought he could negotiate with them in good faith. Instead, he was probably in some dark cell, wondering where we were and why we hadn't come for him yet.

"When were you going to tell me?"

Lorian's jaw clenched. "I sent a fae delegation to attempt to negotiate. I was hoping they would be successful." He held up another piece of parchment. "Unfortunately, the rebels refused to engage with them. And if they were to attack, your brother could be killed."

Fury raged through me. "You were hoping to fix this with your fae delegation and get Tibris back before I even knew what had happened, weren't you?"

Lorian gave me a steady look, and I ground my teeth. I was *not* overreacting. Did he think I was fragile now? That I needed to be coddled?

Demos got to his feet. "The rebels will negotiate with me."

My heart pounded in my chest. Time had suddenly sped up, out of my control. I forced myself to focus on his words. "Are you sure?"

"Yes. By now, the rebels will know I'm alive. They also know I'm the *Hybrid Prince*—" he rolled his eyes at the title "—and that I can negotiate on your behalf. By the time I get to the camp, their spies will have learned of your attack on Regner. If we're lucky, it will make them wary. They may even be grateful that it was I who arrived and not the hybrid heir herself." He gave me a faint smile.

"You're not going alone," I said. I ran my gaze over the others, considering our options. Lorian wouldn't leave my side, and truthfully, I couldn't bear to be separated from him right now either. Marth could have been helpful, but he was barely functioning, his eyes wounded as he sat silently in the corner and sharpened his knives. Galon—

"I'm going with him," Asinia said.

I sucked in a breath even as I nodded. At least Asinia and Demos would guard each other's backs.

Demos glanced at her, but unsurprisingly, he didn't argue. My brother preferred Asinia where he could see her, even if he still refused to admit such a thing to himself.

Pinching the bridge of my nose, I refused to think about the risks. Instead, I considered the tactical implications. We could have used Demos's power for Jamic's rescue. Asinia was also becoming incredible with her crossbow.

Vynthar prowled over to me. *"I will go with them."*

"Really?"

"I do not say things I do not mean."

Some of the weight lifted from my shoulders. "Thank you."

"You are welcome."

LORIAN

While Prisca cooed to the monster—who preened for her like a house cat—I nodded at Galon, who rolled out his map, laying it on the floor in the middle of the room.

Everyone leaned closer.

"While traveling, we heard rumors of Regner's ships moving south along the eastern coast," Galon said.

Madinia nodded. "I heard the same."

"And then there are his regiments," I said. "We visited a number of them while searching for Prisca."

Her eyes met mine, her expression softening slightly.

Demos moved until he was sitting in front of the map. "Regner's positioning his foot soldiers southeast along your border, while he readies his fleet to attack from the coast."

I studied the continent. "They'll either attempt to take Quorith or bypass it completely as they navigate the southern coastline. From there, they'll attack the fae lands from both the south and the northeast. If Eryndan cooperates with Regner, and so far, I can't see why he wouldn't, then the Gromalians will also attack from the east."

"They're not attempting to get to the hybrid kingdom," Galon mused.

A tiny bit of luck. We wouldn't have had a chance if the humans had been able to attack on both fronts.

"No," I said. "Thanks to the sea serpents, they can't get their ships across the Sleeping Sea. And they know the hybrids on this continent are currently forced to rely on the fae for protection. Regner's aware of the hybrid camp. It's why he wants to break the ward."

"You think he can break it?" Marth spoke up from his spot in the corner of the room.

I met his eyes. "If Regner brings down the barrier and takes that power, there's no question he could break our ward. It may be ancient, but since the theft of the amulet from the fae responsible for shoring up that ward, it has barely been reinforced. Even without the barrier, if he feeds enough of his stolen power into those on the front, they could likely take it down." And the slaughter would be unimaginable.

Prisca paled. Turning her attention back to the map, she pointed at the border between Gromalia and the fae lands. "Eryndan can't position himself along this section of the border yet—since the Gromalian rebels still hold it."

Asinia let out a bitter laugh. "Eryndan was never

going to ally with us. He wanted us to lay waste to that camp so he could station his own people there, ready to march on the fae lands."

Prisca nodded, but she raised her head, addressing both Asinia and Demos. "We need the rebels on our side—and not just for our own tactical reasons. If they don't ally with us, they're dead."

It was risky, but the rebels had no one else to turn to. I watched Prisca as she squared her shoulders. They'd taken her brother, and she was still trying to save their lives.

Regner had taken her, and I'd slaughtered hundreds.

I wasn't fit to be in the same room as Prisca. But I was keeping her anyway.

Demos nodded, glancing at Asinia, who stuck out her chin. "We'll take care of it, Pris."

I considered our options. If Prisca succeeded with Rekja, convincing him to turn on his father...

Regner would be forced to position his own people near the rebel camp—hoping to go *through* the rebels—or he'd risk our people cutting through the same land and attacking him from behind.

As the night grew darker, our plans solidified. All of us would leave tomorrow. But most importantly, I would be with Prisca, where I could see her and hear her and know where she was at all times—firmly clamped to my side.

Prisca would practice using the hourglass as we traveled, sneaking most of us back into the city. We would find Rothnic, learn Jamic's location, break him free, and take away Regner's greatest weapon—all in one night. Meanwhile, Demos and Asinia would rescue Tibris and convince the rebels to ally with us.

It was a huge, audacious, risky plan.

In the back of my mind, I knew we also needed to search for the other two amulets. Desperately. But Jamic had to take priority. We couldn't risk Regner gaining access to that much power.

I glanced around the room as the others talked quietly. Cavis's missing presence was a wound that would never heal.

It would always be this way. Never again would we be the same. I'd been too slow in that cave. I should have noticed. Should have known something was terribly wrong. But I hadn't. And now Cavis was dead.

Prisca glanced my way, and her gaze held mine, the concern evident even as she gave me a considering look.

I'd broken her trust by not telling her immediately about Tibris. It didn't matter that I'd been attempting to fix the situation before it could hurt her. Now, she was wondering what else I was keeping from her.

And from the way she'd just firmed her mouth, those amber eyes burning into mine, we were about to have that exact conversation.

It was time to tell her the truth. About everything.

12

PRISCA

"We should all get some rest," Lorian announced, not taking his eyes from mine. "If anyone thinks of anything else, we'll discuss it in the morning before we leave."

Catching my wrist, he tugged me toward the door. A moment later, we were back in my room.

Lorian released my wrist, and I backed up several steps, narrowing my eyes at him. He watched me back, and even now, when I was furious, it was all I could do not to step closer, slide my hand up to the back of his neck, and guide his mouth down to mine.

I took another large step farther away from him, and his eyes gleamed.

"I shouldn't have kept the news about Tibris from you," he said. "I'm sorry."

My heart skipped. Lorian wasn't someone who apologized often. Because it wasn't often that he thought he was in the wrong. He stalked through life with the sheer self-assurance that all his moves were the right ones. Except, perhaps, when it came to me.

"It's difficult for me, Lorian, because not only did you lie, but I can tell you're still hiding something now."

His eyes sharpened, but he waited me out.

Lorian loved me. I felt the truth of that deep in my bones. I'd considered what he could possibly be keeping from me that he'd feel the need to hide. He was, after all, someone who was used to roaming this continent, making choices based on his own moral code.

Well, that—and his brother's orders.

I took a deep breath, watching Lorian closely. "Tell me the truth. Am I your mate?"

Surprise flashed across his face before he could hide it. My mouth went dry.

"That looks like a yes."

His gaze was locked with mine. His eyes blazed like two emeralds, filled with stubborn tenacity. I hadn't seen that exact expression since the moment I'd asked him to let me go—right after he'd healed Demos. And he'd refused.

"This isn't how I wanted to tell you. But you deserve the truth. Yes. Yes, you're my mate."

I let out a strangled sound that made his nostrils flare. He took a single step closer, and I backed up. If he touched me, I'd do something stupid like jump into his arms. He froze.

Flashes of memories were flicking through my mind.

Lorian, snarling at Eryndan, fae fire encircling me. Lorian, leaving his brother and following me when I went after the hourglass. Lorian's face in my dreams before we'd even met.

I swallowed around the lump in my throat. "Is this… is this why I dreamed of you?" I asked, and my voice somehow came out steady.

It wasn't unheard of for the fates to meddle in dreams. I'd imagined it was simply because Lorian had played such a huge part in my life. Meeting him had set off the chain of events that had allowed me to rescue Asinia, save the hybrids in the castle, and accept that I really was the hybrid queen.

But from the predatory focus in Lorian's eyes, the fact that I'd dreamed of him was more important than I'd thought.

He met my gaze unflinchingly. "It's a sign. That we could be mates. While fae men often have the *Knowing* before their mates, the women occasionally recognize their mates when they meet them…"

"Because they've dreamed of them."

He nodded. A hint of what might have been panic slid through his eyes, almost too fast for me to catch.

But I had caught it. Lorian was desperately terrified of losing me over this. My stomach tumbled, but I forced myself to stay focused.

I remembered mumbling that I'd dreamed of him one night when we were traveling. "And did you know?"

Silence.

"Lorian. Did you know?"

"I believe some part of me knew. The fact that you saw through my glamour in the castle… It was a sign. A sign I ignored. Because I didn't *want* to know, Prisca."

I let out a hollow laugh. Well, that made more sense. Why would he tell me about something he had rejected?

He caught my hand, ignoring me as I attempted to yank it away. "Not because I didn't want *you*. Gods, no. I'd never dreamed I would have a mate. After everything I've done, I imagined such a gift was reserved for those whose hands weren't covered in blood. I ignored any signs of our mating—even though all I wanted was you."

"Why?"

"Because I knew I wasn't worthy of being a mate. I could never be worthy of *you*. By the time the knowledge had truly hit me, I was in love with you. And I knew I would never recover if you stayed with me simply because of our mating. I needed you to choose *me*, Prisca. Because I would choose you ten thousand times over, every day for the rest of my life."

My heart thudded until it felt as if it might fly out of my chest. A strange lightness had filled me, urging me to pull him onto the bed and forget everything else.

I was a mess of competing feelings. Fury, because he'd kept something from me *again*. An all-encompassing love, because, despite myself, I couldn't imagine living without him. Understanding, because I'd met Conreth, I'd learned about Lorian's past, and I knew why he didn't feel worthy of happiness.

But I couldn't stay with someone who kept hiding the truth from me. Something in me had changed in that cell. I felt both stronger and more brittle.

"How many more lies, Lorian?"

"There are none," he swore. His eyes hardened. "Let me be clear, wildcat. You can take all the time you need to forgive me, but you're mine. I'll wait for you to realize that too. No matter how long it takes."

Stubborn fae. My head was spinning.

"Give me a few minutes."

Lorian's hands fisted, as if it was taking everything in him not to reach for me. But he nodded.

Turning away, I gazed unseeingly out the window. I couldn't explain all of my feelings—even to myself. Because even though I was furious Lorian had kept the information from me, something like elation had made my heart trip and my lungs expand.

I wouldn't have to worry that he'd meet his mate one day and look at me with regret.

I could keep him.

I'd spent so much time picturing what would happen when we won this war—and we *would*. I would take the hybrid throne and stabilize my kingdom. But Lorian would stay at his brother's side. Where his true loyalties lay.

It was why I'd been wary of getting too close, even if I hadn't admitted it to myself. I'd decided our story would end in misery. Seeing the potential life we could have had…it would only make the heartbreak worse.

But then, when I was in that cell, desperate to see his face just one last time, I'd...*loathed* every moment I'd wasted. Each second I hadn't spent in his arms had seemed almost offensive.

War made things clear. The threat of losing the people I loved had thrown my priorities into sharp focus.

I was furious with Lorian and would likely be furious for some time. Some part of me would always wonder if he was mine because he'd loved me first or because fate had determined he would love me.

But he *was* mine. And I would always choose him.

"Look after Lorian. Hold him tight and savor every moment. He's been waiting a long time for you."

Cavis's words burned through my mind, turning my doubts to ash. He'd known. Somehow, Cavis had known. For a moment, I couldn't even breathe as the grief swamped me.

Dropping my hand to the hourglass, I lifted it, studying the incandescent sand.

Time. It all came down to time.

I'd been convinced we would one day be separated. Because he would have to go back to Conreth and I would take my throne.

I'd been certain that love was being willing to give someone up if that was what was best for them. But I was wrong.

Love was being willing to fight.

It was being willing to stand up and say, *It's you and me, we're in this together, and gods help anyone who attempts to tear us apart.*

It wasn't up to me to manage Lorian's relationship with his brother. If he tried to do that to me, I would be livid. No, all I could do was love him, support him, and make it clear that no matter what he lost, even if he shattered into a million pieces, I'd be right there to put him back together. Just like he'd done for me.

Something frozen in my chest began to melt.

I turned, and my heart stopped as I surveyed every inch of him, from his dark hair to his knife-sharp cheekbones, that strong jaw, his large hands, which could kill one moment and be so incredibly tender the next. He took up so much space in the room—in *every* room— his shoulders back, feet spread wide, arms crossed, as if daring me *not* to accept him.

"I'm finished thinking," I said.

His face remained blank. But his green eyes had taken on a feral gleam.

"When I was captured…all I could think was that you'd told me you loved me and I hadn't said it back. But I feel it, Lorian. Gods, I feel it. And I never want you to wonder if I love you the way you love me. We have a lot of work to do, and you need to promise me you won't keep anything like this from me again. I can't stand you lying to me. You know how I feel about lies."

A ravenous hunger had entered his eyes, as if it was taking everything in him not to touch me now. But he was waiting. And he was listening.

"I know, wildcat. And I'm sorry."

He might regret his actions, but he would do the same thing again. Because he couldn't bear the thought of my thinking he only wanted me because of our mating.

"I get why you did it. I'm annoyed, but I understand why you waited."

"You love me." He smiled, and it was so beautiful, my breath hitched.

I nodded. "I love you. Even when you're pushing me to the brink of madness with your domineering attitude."

His grin widened. "And you're mine."

My throat tightened. "I'm yours. Just as you're mine."

His eyes darkened with triumph, and he pulled me to him, backing me toward the wall. "Swear it."

"I swear it."

He caught my chin, staring down at me. "Now hear this—I love you. I'm yours forever. I will never leave you. If you want to take back your kingdom, I'll be by your side. You want to hide in mine? I'll be there too. If you want to bring down the barrier and get on a ship to some far-flung continent with new lives and no titles—as just Prisca and Lorian—I'll make it happen. Just tell me what you want."

A heady rush surged through me, and I cupped Lorian's face. He really meant it. He would do anything, go anywhere, as long as we were together. I'd done nothing to deserve a love like his, but it was mine now. And I'd never give it up.

"You," I said. "I just want you."

He shuddered against me. And then his hand was tangled in my hair and he was kissing me like he was drowning and I was his air. I angled my head and opened for him, and his tongue stroked mine, his other hand cupping my face, holding me as if he was afraid I'd disappear.

He let out a ragged sigh against my mouth, and I inhaled him, drawing in his desperation, his need. He slid his hands beneath my tunic, gently caressing the skin across my lower back, before pushing my tunic over my head and expertly removing the flexible band covering my breasts. I shivered as the cool air hit my skin, my nipples peaking as he stroked and played.

We kissed for long moments, until tenderness turned to something darker. Lorian stepped back, pulling his shirt over his head and revealing smooth, tanned skin and the hard slab of muscle that was his chest. I let my gaze drift down, and his pants fell to the floor. My mouth watered.

"Now," I said. "I need you now."

For once, Lorian wasn't in the mood to tease. Lifting me into his arms, he took several steps, holding me easily with one hand while he used the other to pull my leggings down. I let out a choked laugh as he tripped on his boot, cursed, and cupped my head, preventing me from hitting it on the wall.

He swallowed my laugh with his mouth, and I let out a breathless moan as he slipped a hand down, stroking the wet heat of me.

"Already so slick, wildcat."

My cheeks heated—as they always did when he used that tone. And as always, he let out a dark chuckle, enjoying my blush.

"How are you still so innocent and yet willing to be so filthy with me, Prisca?"

My cheeks were blazing now, and I lifted my hands to cover them. Lorian caught them in one of his own, using his body to hold me in place against the wall as he positioned himself against me, immediately thrusting deep.

It was fast and hard and intense. My body shuddered against his as he plowed into me, his steady rhythm designed to make me insane.

I came with a shriek, and he slammed his other hand over my mouth, his eyes wild with lust as I clamped down around him. With a string of curses, he slapped his other hand against the wall, barely holding both of us up as he emptied himself inside me.

For a long moment, neither of us moved, both catching our breath.

He lifted his head, and his gaze was a little bleary. Cupping my butt, he carried me back toward the bed.

Lorian stumbled, tightening his arms around me as he tripped on the same boot. He cursed, glowering at me as I burst into a peal of laughter.

"I'm sorry," I choked out. "But I've never seen you be anything less than graceful. I'll forever store that away in my memory."

Leaning down, he gently scraped his teeth over my

chin. Despite the incredible climax I'd just enjoyed, I shivered.

"You make me clumsy," he purred, kissing his way along my chin and cheek, until his lips found my earlobe.

As much as my body was ready for more, I had things to do.

"I need to talk to Asinia before she leaves tomorrow," I said. "I'd like to speak to Galon and the others too."

Lorian's eyes glittered. "You want to leave my bed looking like that?"

I had a pretty good idea of what he was talking about. Rumpled sex hair, swollen lips, several red marks decorating my throat and breasts. But I raised one eyebrow. "That's exactly what I want."

Within a few minutes, I'd braided my hair, pulled on my clothes, and was watching, entranced, as Lorian stalked toward his saddlebag for a clean shirt.

"Keep looking at me like that, and we won't be leaving this room," he warned.

I took several large steps back and attempted to drag my gaze away from him. But my eyes caught on a stack of parchment he'd shoved aside while searching for his shirt. Each piece was covered with scrawled words.

"What is that?"

He hesitated, and then his head canted, something that almost resembled...embarrassment sweeping across his face.

But he squared his shoulders. "While you were gone, I wrote to you. Some days, it was the only way I stayed sane."

I could picture him, slaughtering his way across Eprotha during the day, writing to me at night. He would have continued that way for years if that's what it would have taken. The realization of that was almost impossible for me to truly understand. But I knew I would do the same for him.

"Will you show me?"

He frowned. "I wasn't...myself during that time, wildcat."

Curiosity was flickering through me now, and I waited him out. He sighed.

"You can read one of them."

I greedily snatched it from his hand.

Wildcat,

I don't know if you'll ever see this letter. I don't know if I'll ever give it to you. But I spend my days talking to you in my head. By now, I know you well enough to know how you would answer most of my questions. Your quick humor, sarcasm, and the way you occasionally take my breath away with your honesty...

Gods, I miss you.

My eyes burned as I continued reading. He told me how much he loved me. How much he missed me. That I was the best thing that had ever happened to him. He swore he would find me.

And he had.

Drawing in a shaky breath, I lifted my head. Lorian's eyes flared at whatever he saw on my face.

"I want the rest."

He slowly shook his head. "Not all of them are filled with pretty words, Prisca."

"I want all of your words. Always."

He heaved a sigh, but he couldn't argue with that. He wanted the same from me.

His eyes glittered with calculation. "I'll give you one a week."

My mouth dropped open. "You—"

His lips firmed. I knew that expression. I wasn't changing his mind. At least, not right now. Carefully folding the letter, I placed it in my own satchel. "I'll convince you to hand them over," I muttered.

Lorian laughed. "I bet you could."

But I knew why he wasn't. We were going to war. So Lorian was keeping them for when I'd need them the most. Those letters would be a beacon in my darkest hours. Just as he was.

He stepped up behind me, nuzzling my neck as I reached for the door.

"You smell like me. I like it."

I liked it too. But I gave him a warning look that made his eyes heat.

I swung open the door. Asinia stood there, her fist raised to knock. She smirked at my rumpled clothes, but her face quickly cleared.

"It's Madinia," she said. "She's planning something."

LORIAN

I found Galon, Rythos, and Marth sitting on the roof of the inn. All of them were silent as they watched the village below them.

Rythos glanced up. His eyes met mine, and he gave me a faint smile. "You look…better."

"I told Prisca. That she's my mate."

Galon's expression was carefully neutral. Marth just nodded, his gaze sliding away from mine.

I felt my hands fist. These were my brothers, but that didn't matter to the most feral part of me. That part whispered that they were a threat.

If I could arrange it so that no other males were ever around my wildcat again, I would make it happen without a second thought.

Galon was still studying my face. "I see the mating is hitting you hard."

I showed him my teeth. He shared a look with Rythos, and I suppressed the urge to throw them all off this roof.

They'd heal.

Galon stretched out his legs. "Let us know when you've managed to find your self-control," he said. "We'll wait."

His sardonic tone was enough to dull the edge of my

rage. I took a deep breath, forcing the beast inside me to go back to sleep.

This was Galon. Rythos. Marth. Prisca considered them brothers. They wouldn't touch her.

Because if they did, I would kill them. Slowly.

No.

I clenched my jaw and forced myself to chain the worst part of me. It wasn't unlike clamping down on my power, and after a long moment, I could meet Galon's eyes once more.

"I'm sorry."

"It's to be expected."

For a long moment, the world spun dizzily around me. I was suddenly exhausted. Rythos nodded at the empty spot next to him, and I sat.

"Your brother sent a message." He handed it to me, returning his gaze to the lights of the village below us.

I scanned the parchment.

L,

I was saddened to hear about what happened to Cavis. I understand your reasoning behind your search for the human Regner pretends is his son—and preventing him from using the power of the barrier. However, I must insist you return your attention to finding the second amulet as soon as possible.

And, brother, I'll take this opportunity to remind you: I gave you three weeks.

Meldoric has been traveling throughout the territories in an attempt to make them cooperate. Of the five wardens, only Thorn has appeared willing to at least listen to the threat. Verdion, in particular, seems to believe he can remain entirely neutral.

I still retain the power to summon all territory rulers to Aranthon for the summit. And if the fae are to join forces to meet the threat Regner represents, I need the Bloodthirsty Prince at my side.

Your brother,
-C

No mention of Prisca. Or the fact that she could have died too. In his mind, Prisca was the reason I wasn't falling into line. So he would treat her as if she were irrelevant.

I'd be lying if I said it didn't sting. But I was becoming used to Conreth's stance. He wouldn't be content until I returned to the fae lands and resumed following each of his orders—regardless of what that meant for the woman I loved and the people she was willing to sacrifice everything for.

And yet, our people needed me too. I'd fought this hard for them, for this long.

"Did he even mention Cavis?" Marth's voice was bitter.

"Yes."

Marth just snorted. I couldn't blame him. Things had deteriorated so badly with Conreth. It was difficult to reconcile my brother with the man who'd once gently teased me about the woman who'd distracted me from my brooding. Of course, that was before Prisca had become a threat to him.

"It still doesn't feel real," Rythos said. "That Cavis is gone."

"Because he shouldn't be," Marth growled. "If Conreth had been worthy of that fucking crown, he would have united our people and killed Regner decades ago."

Galon was quiet. I was so used to him being the voice of reason, and yet now, he had nothing to say. None of us could reason this away.

"We're going to make Regner pay," I said. "It won't bring Cavis back. Nothing will. But no one else will suffer his fate. No other sons or daughters will grow up without a parent."

"It's not enough," Rythos said.

"I know." I had to stifle the grief that wanted to swallow me whole. If I could turn it to fury, and turn fury to action, perhaps one day I could look Piperia in the eye.

PRISCA

Since the bed in my room was rumpled, I'd followed Asinia into hers. Madinia was nowhere to be found.

"She probably went to get something to eat," I said.

"Let's just wait for her."

"Good idea." She slumped onto her bed, gesturing expectantly. "Why don't you tell me what happened between when we arrived and now? You can skip the sex if you'd like. Or not. One of us should be enjoying ourselves."

I choked out a laugh. And then I told her about the mating. When I was done, my eyes were hot and my throat burned.

"I accepted the mating. I love him. But some part of me is still afraid he doesn't really feel this way—and it's all just *fate*."

"I'm sorry he didn't tell you. But…I can also see why he didn't. You've been so busy worrying about all of us—and by all of us, I mean all of the hybrids. And whatever you have with Lorian, even though it's difficult, it makes you happy, Pris. *He* makes you happy. I've been watching you since the castle, and some days, he has been the only person to make you smile. He knows you inside out, and he knew learning you were his mate might make you doubt if any of it was real. He didn't want that for you."

I sighed. "I'm scared, Asinia. Because if I lost Lorian…I think it would break me."

She got up and wrapped her arms around me. I sank into her.

"You're braver than this, Pris. But I saw what happened to him when you were missing. There was nothing left of him except death."

I sighed, squeezed tight, and pulled away. "Why do you always sound so reasonable?"

"It's much easier to give advice about other people's lives than it is to navigate your own."

"Is...is there anything you want to talk about? Perhaps with Demos?"

Asinia shrugged. "Demos is Demos."

Uh-huh. I hesitated. Part of me wanted to try to help. I didn't want either of them to get hurt. But the worst thing I could do was get involved, even if I wanted to lock them in a room together until they'd figured it out.

"You'll be careful when you travel to Tibris."

She nodded, but a slight frown had appeared between her brows.

"What is it?"

Asinia sighed. "It's fine, Pris. I'm just tired of being a liability."

All of my muscles went tight. "Who called you a liability? Demos?" He often bullied Asinia into training, but if he'd said such a thing, we would have words.

"No," she said instantly. "But once again, I was the reason we had to spend a night at that fae woman's house. Because I got hurt in the caves. What if that night had been the difference between you living and dying?"

My heart ached. "It wasn't. Is that why you're going with Demos? You have nothing to prove, Sin. Just promise me you'll look after yourself. And Demos."

"You know I will."

The door swung open. Madinia's gaze met mine.

"Good. You're here. While you and Lorian were *reuniting,* and everyone else was shoveling badly cooked stew into their mouths, I made a few plans of my own."

My lips twitched, and I waved my hand. "By all means, fill us in."

She closed the door behind her. "Wars aren't only won with armies and magic and iron. In Regner's court, I saw firsthand just how much damage could be done with a few carefully worded rumors."

I nodded. I was also sure Madinia had done much of that damage herself.

"When I was younger, my father told me one thing that has stayed in my mind for all these years. *'Swords may clash in battle, but words shape the destiny of kingdoms.'"*

"Regner knows that," Asinia muttered. "It's what he has always counted on."

Madinia angled her head. "Yes. But we know it too. Regner's winning this war. Not just by sheer scale of soldiers and ships, but by propaganda."

My jaw ached as I clenched my teeth. But she was right.

"He has the power," Madinia continued. "Because he has those fucking priestesses and assessors who continually lie. Not to mention the guards who visit the towns and villages with messages from the castle."

I frowned. "You want to compete with him? Send messages of our own?"

Next to me, Asinia angled her head. "Many villagers

can barely read. And those who can read will be unlikely to believe us."

Madinia sighed, clearly frustrated. It wasn't often that she was this…passionate about something. "I can see why you'd be hesitant to devote time and attention to this kind of approach," she conceded. "But I know it's worth a try."

I tried to imagine what her plan would look like.

"Wait," I murmured. "We don't need to target everyone in each village. We just need to convince a few." Madinia understood nobles and royalty. But Asinia and I understood *people*.

Asinia smiled at me, "Healers. People who have seen things they can't explain. People who've kept secrets because they truly care about their friends and neighbors. People who are trusted. People like Tibris."

My spine tingled. I could almost *see* how it would work. "We need some way to… Where's Finley right now?"

"He went with Vicer," Asinia said. "Which means he's likely in the city. But it would take him months to replicate the amount of parchment we would need."

I chewed on my lower lip. "You're right. He once replicated my dagger, but it took a lot out of him."

"Your dagger is made of iron," Madinia said. "It naturally repels magic. It's likely he can replicate other things much more easily."

Asinia's eyes glinted, and then the hope in them dimmed. "The villagers will think *we're* the ones lying.

Most of them won't believe us."

She was right. Still… "Some of them will. Even if it's just a few at first. Some of them will begin to question. And they'll look a little harder at what they've been taught to believe."

"I'll travel ahead," Madinia said.

I didn't like it. Madinia shook her head at whatever she saw on my face. "I've rested enough. We won't have much time in the city, and if what we're planning is going to work, we'll need every minute. I'm leaving now."

I met her eyes. Madinia had good instincts. If those instincts were urging her to go now, we needed to listen. And this could work. I knew it could. "Go," I said. "Travel fast but stay safe."

13
THE QUEEN

Of all the worst times in my life, counting down each second until Sabium would kill my son was the most horrifying.

That countdown had begun the moment he'd handed the squalling infant to me, of course. But now, with barely any warning, I was down to mere days. Hours.

Pelysian had pled with me for patience. He'd urged me to wait. We'd sent another message to Madinia, and the hybrid heir knew what would happen if that barrier came down.

Yet, Sabium was watching this castle—and all the people in it—so closely, it had taken hours before my messenger could finally slip out undetected.

Hours of agony as I felt time slip through my fingers.

I was done with waiting. If the hybrid heir didn't save my son, I would find a way to do it myself. I didn't know how—would likely die in the attempt—but I couldn't delay any longer.

And so, I paced my library, waiting for some form of acknowledgment from Madinia. What good was she if she wouldn't respond—wouldn't tell me the hybrid heir would free Jamic?

Movement caught my eye, and I strode to the window. In the courtyard below, Sabium's guards were filing out of the castle, Tymedes overseeing them. He glanced up at the library, and I ensured the heavy curtain was covering my body. Still, his smirk told me he knew I was watching.

Only one guard carried the object they were removing. As tall and wide as a person, it was covered in several blankets, which hid its exact form from prying eyes. Curiosity pricked at the back of my neck, and I leaned closer.

Sabium stepped out of the castle, watching as a carriage pulled to a stop next to the guards. Longer than most, the carriage had been modified, allowing the guards to open doors at the back for added storage. More blankets had been piled strategically inside.

Whatever this was, it was clearly important.

Squinting down into the courtyard, peering around the curtain, I barely breathed.

While only one guard had been necessary to carry the object, he nodded to the others, who jumped into action, each taking a side and loading it into the carriage.

Slowly, carefully, they moved, as if the object was something infinitely precious. My stomach twisted. Anything Sabium was paying this much attention to—

One corner of the blanket slipped. Tymedes snarled at

the guard, who immediately covered it, his face flushing.

But I'd seen.

The barest glimpse of a scrolled black edge that glimmered in the sunlight. A strange glass that seemed to absorb the world, instead of reflecting it back.

Sabium stepped forward, and I realized he was holding a book. A book bound in red leather with gold lettering. My breath caught in my throat.

One of his footmen opened another door to the carriage. Sabium began to step inside. I'd expected him to slide out of sight. Instead, he turned his head, meeting my eyes. He knew I was here, and he didn't care. Some of what Tymedes had said was the truth after all. Sabium had so efficiently declawed me that he found it *amusing* to allow me to see what he was doing.

I backed away from the window, my head spinning.

Centuries ago, Sabium had used that mirror to spy on the hybrids and fae. While I didn't believe it was the *reason* for his covetousness, resentment, and spite, it was certainly the tool that had allowed him to see how much more powerful they were compared to us.

If he was taking the mirror out of the castle, along with the book…

I had no doubt Sabium had been using that mirror for much, much deadlier tasks than spying.

MADÎNIA

A symphony of laughter and clinking glasses swelled around me. The air inside the tavern was heady with the scent of the stew currently bubbling over the hearth. Patrons sat on every available seat—and a few tables too. Barmaids navigated through them with practiced ease, arms laden with plates and mugs.

After arriving in Lesdryn, I'd stabled my horse and made my way directly to this tavern, finding a table in a darkened corner. Across from me, Vicer was grimmer than I'd ever seen him. A new scar wound along his forearm, and his eyes looked older, his expression resolved. When all of us had left the hybrid camp in the fae lands, he'd traveled to the foothills of the Normathe Mountains. His plan had been to convince Kaelin Stillcrest—the leader of that hybrid camp—to begin moving south. Clearly, that plan wasn't going well.

Thankfully, his problems had nothing to do with me.

"What exactly are you looking for?"

I took a sip of my watered-down wine, stifling a grimace. And then I explained exactly what I was thinking.

His eyes lit up with interest. "It might be useless. We've considered similar tactics in the past."

I'd expected that response. "Humans hadn't seen thousands of their own people killed in the past. Thanks to Regner's hybrid hunt, many of them are still living through that unique terror."

Some people only cared when either they, or someone they loved, were affected. My father had been that kind of man. He'd been happy to watch hybrids burn, knowing there was nothing *corrupt* about us. But the moment he'd learned I was one of them, he'd agreed to help us.

I was both disgusted by his weakness and reluctantly appreciative that at least he hadn't turned me in.

"I'll see what I can come up with. I'll meet you at the safe house."

I nodded, and Vicer got to his feet, stalking away. My eyes drifted closed.

I'd managed to travel much faster alone than the others would in a group. If Prisca learned I'd allowed my horse to plod along the most deserted trails while I'd dozed, she would have snarled at me. Still, I'd saved myself at least a day of travel by only stopping for brief naps when I was so tired I thought I might topple from my horse.

But this was worth it. I knew it was. Surviving Regner's court had taught me to scheme and lie and use my words as weapons. It was only looking back now that I could see exactly how Regner had used his own lies to control not just the court, but the population. I may have grown up in a castle, may have slept in lavish surroundings, but I'd lived with the same anguish Prisca had. Terror that clawed at me, waking me in the middle of the night until all I could do was curl up and shake, icy sweat sliding down my back.

Because I was *corrupt*. I'd somehow angered the gods. And one day, when I was discovered, I would burn.

Now I knew my mother must have been a hybrid.

That day when my father learned the truth, he'd seemed sickened. In the following days, he'd been distant, and I hadn't had a chance to ask him anything about my mother before Regner's guard killed him in front of me. He might have been the last family I'd had left, and I would never know.

The fact was, if we were going to win this war, we had to fight Regner everywhere. And that included the hearts and minds of his people.

I opened my eyes and jolted. A large man had slid directly into Vicer's chair. He'd moved so quietly, I hadn't seen or heard him. Hadn't sensed him.

My hands heated, and he grinned at me. I recognized that grin. This was the man who'd escaped Regner's dungeon with Prisca. *Calysian*. That was what she'd called him.

No longer was he wearing bloodstained, torn clothes. Instead, his shirt, dark pants, and cloak seemed to have been designed so as not to attract any attention. Plain, almost boring, but he'd chosen good quality fabrics in a cut that flattered. His beard was gone, although a hint of scruff remained. And when our eyes met, a hint of wicked humor glittered back at me.

He was a handsome bastard, that was for sure. Handsome and far too large. What exactly was he doing here?

"Tired?" he asked.

"What do you want?"

"I did a little research about you, Madinia Farrow," he said.

"Did you?" I purred. "Then you know I could turn your insides to kindling."

Calysian laughed. "Relax, beautiful woman. I'm here to help you."

I gave him a bored stare. "And why would you do that?"

"I owe your friend a life debt. Since she didn't seem inclined to let me pay it before we went our separate ways, and she told me to give it to you, it's yours."

"I don't need a life debt." And I didn't trust anyone who wanted to go out of their way to help us.

"Too bad," he said. "Where I come from, a man's honor rests on his word. Who do you need killed? Or perhaps you have someone who wants to kill you? Name the time and the place, and I'll be there to protect you."

His expression was serious, his words solemn. But I knew better than to trust strange men.

"I can protect myself."

"Something else, then."

Reluctant fascination cooled my hands. "What is it you think you could help me with?"

"You'd be surprised what I can help you with," he said. I rolled my eyes, and he laughed at me, folding his arms. "I know this city. I know the people in it, and I'm relatively confident I know what you're planning."

Every muscle in my body tensed.

He waved a hand. His fingers were strangely long and elegant. "I want you to succeed," he told me. "So I can go home."

"Home?"

One side of his mouth curved. "I'm from…elsewhere. When Regner's little barrier went up, it trapped me on this continent."

Of course. Of course there would have been people here who became stuck, unable to get home. Curiosity slid through me despite myself. If I'd known this man, I might've asked him to tell me of his homeland. And any other places he'd seen.

"Why were you in Regner's dungeon?"

Calysian shook his head, giving me a faint smile. "Irrelevant. Just tell me what you want."

If there was a chance he truly *could* help…I'd be an idiot to lose that chance.

"What kinds of people did you say you know?"

"All kinds of people."

"Get me a meeting with Caddaril the Cleaver," I said.

One dark eyebrow shot up. "You continue to surprise me."

I shrugged. "Can you do it?"

"Yes. You're sure this is what you want to use your life debt for?" Doubt coated his voice, and I understood. A life debt was called such a thing for a reason. Because it was usually used to save lives. But at this moment in time, gaining access to the Cleaver *could* potentially save hundreds of those lives.

We needed a distraction.

"I'm sure."

He nodded. "In that case, I'll find you when I've arranged the meeting."

I opened my mouth to tell him it wouldn't be that easy to find me, but from the calm confidence on his face, he wasn't exactly concerned about locating me. His huge body uncoiled, and he got to his feet. "Be careful."

I made sure my expression was coolly blank, not deigning to reply. He angled his head, curiosity glinting in his eyes.

"Prickly," he said. "I like that."

"Come closer," I said. "And you'll see just how prickly."

His laugh was strangely compelling. He did it often, as if he were sucking the joy from every moment of his life.

"I'll see you soon, Madinia Farrow," he crooned, his voice low, ensuring no one would overhear my name.

I waved my hand, a clear demand for him to leave.

He strolled away.

The heat was becoming stifling in the crowded tavern. Slipping between swaying drunkards, I made my way to the door, the din muting as it swung shut behind me. My boots echoed on the cracked cobblestones, the fresh air clearing the fog from my mind as I wound through the slums and back to our safe house.

Most of the humans and hidden hybrids in this city

wouldn't believe us if we told them Regner had lied to them all this time. If we revealed he'd lied to their parents, their grandparents, their great-grandparents.

Their beliefs were like roots entrenched in ancient soil—clinging fiercely, digging deep. Those roots reached into their minds, smothering any whispers of truth, any longing to understand. Prying those roots free would be almost impossible. Some people would refuse to listen. But others...others might. And for every person we convinced...

It was worth it. I had to believe it was worth it.

I didn't know why I was so determined to do this. Perhaps it was because my father had known the truth— and let me live with the terror. Perhaps it was because I'd never get to meet my hybrid mother—and this was something *I* could do for our people.

Perhaps it was just because I enjoyed thinking about the look on Regner's face when he learned of it.

Either way, I would make it happen.

I was just a few feet away from the front door when I felt a gaze on the back of my neck. Whirling, I put my back to the wall, lifting my hand.

The queen's messenger stuttered. "I-I'm sorry."

The same messenger who continued to find me each time. I ground my teeth. "How did you find me?"

"I-I only go where Her Majesty tells me to go." His gaze dropped to my hand. "P-please."

Sighing, I dampened my fire and took his message. "Ahem."

With a roll of my eyes, I handed him a coin. He gave me a solemn nod and scampered away.

"Who was that?" Vicer asked when I'd climbed the stairs to the hidden safe house within the brothel.

"The queen's messenger. She continues to find me."

Vicer let out a vicious curse which I chose to ignore. Unrolling her message, I scanned it. "It's a reminder the full moon is approaching, and Regner will be taking Jamic to the barrier." The man had an obsession with the moon. Although, I wouldn't be surprised if it was tied to his power somehow. That, or the mythical book I kept hearing about.

Vicer scowled. "We have five days. I'll send a message to Prisca and the others."

Less than an hour later, Calysian knocked on the door of our safe house. By the time I made it downstairs, he was surrounded by hybrids, his expression holding its usual sardonic amusement.

The hair on the back of my neck stood up. Either the man was an idiot, which was still to be determined, or he was so dangerous, he didn't see any of the hybrids in this place—and the power we wielded—as a threat.

Vicer let out a snarl. "Who is this?"

"Madinia and I are old friends." Calysian gave him a cold smile, his gaze flicking between us consideringly.

I elbowed Vicer aside. "He owes me a favor."

"A favor?"

"I'll tell you later."

If Vicer had access to my fire, he likely would have

set both of us alight. Something had changed in him recently. He was quiet, continually brooding. I hadn't seen him smile once.

Vicer met my eyes, clearly attempting to stay calm. "You're not meeting the Cleaver alone," he said. "Prisca would never allow it."

Fury sparked through me. "Prisca's not here. I make my own choices, Vicer. Don't forget that."

He narrowed his eyes. "If you go missing and fuck up our plans, no one is coming to rescue you."

"Haven't you heard?" Calysian smirked. "Madinia Farrow doesn't need rescuing."

I ground my teeth. The mockery in his words had been unmistakable.

Vicer met Calysian's eyes. "Don't come back here," he warned him.

Calysian merely shrugged one shoulder, clearly unconcerned, strolled away.

I followed him. "How did you find me?"

His eyes turned cool for the first time. "Surprisingly easily. Your people will be tempted to return to this place when you've executed your plan. You'll likely have injuries to tend to and will be exhausted. Don't let them."

My heart tripped, and I kept my gaze on his as I nodded.

Calysian led me through the slums, his expression relaxed, even as his eyes scanned the streets relentlessly.

By the time we arrived at what appeared to be an abandoned building, my hands were hot, smoke curling from them. Calysian raised one eyebrow. "Scared?"

I ignored him. He just nodded. "That's good. Only an idiot wouldn't be scared. You're smarter than you've demonstrated so far."

"What is that supposed to mean?"

"You shouldn't have come here alone. I could have killed you nine times already."

My hands fired at that. "Try," I dared him.

His eyes glittered. "You'd like that, wouldn't you? To be able to kill something? Or for someone to finally kill you and put you out of your misery?"

My spine tingled with fury. "You don't know me."

"I've seen everything I need to know."

It didn't sound like a compliment. Ignoring the way his words twisted in my gut, I turned away, surveying the building. It was cracked and ragged, like a piece of parchment that had been folded and unfolded so many times it had worn through in places. The air was filled with the scent of dust and decay.

"You believe you're invulnerable," Calysian murmured, and I had to clamp down on the urge to jolt. He'd leaned close, his breath warm against my ear. "So, go on. Wander into that building alone."

I shrugged, stalking toward the dilapidated excuse for a door. My heart may have been thundering in my chest, but I would never allow this bastard to see it.

It was a test—only I wasn't sure if he wanted to see if I was a coward or to prove I was reckless. Either way, I was going into that building. Hesitating would simply make this take longer or confirm to whoever was watching me from inside that I was afraid.

Only an idiot allowed predators to see their terror.

Calysian let out a choked laugh behind me. "Gods, woman. Do you have no fear?"

I glanced over my shoulder. "Yes. I fear that you'll continue to draw this interaction out even longer. Leave."

His expression turned flat. "The debt has not been satisfied."

"It has."

"Weren't you listening? *I* decide. One day, I will find you, Madinia Farrow. When you're ready to be the woman I think you are."

Cold fury slid through my veins. "If I see you again, you'll regret it."

He chuckled. "Likely, I will. But I'll still find you." Turning, he strolled away.

I'd already put his presence out of my mind. My power burned through me, ready to char and destroy at any moment. My hand found the cracked doorknob, and I risked one last glance behind me.

He was gone.

I stalked into the building—which, from the debris strewn across the floor, had been occupied earlier today— and watched as a man turned. Short and balding, with a face crisscrossed with scars, he still managed to stand with an air of menace. His gaze swept over my skin, appreciation gleaming in his eyes. I immediately longed for a bath.

Strolling closer, I angled my body so my back was to the wall. The last thing I needed was for someone to sneak up on me.

"The Cleaver," I said.

He looked me up and down once more, and this time, his gaze was detached. "I know you. You were one of the queen's bitches."

"And now, I'm a free bitch," I said coolly, and the corner of his mouth quirked.

"What is it you want?"

"Let's talk about what you want. Revenge for your son. I know you were responsible for the riots. But Regner managed to suppress them."

He sneered, several of his scars turning white as his skin stretched. "My son wasn't corrupt."

"You know the corrupt don't exist."

He turned away to gaze down at the city. "Well, he wasn't a *hybrid*. He was a human. And Regner burned him anyway. Then he tried to invite me to his castle," he spat. "As if we could *talk* about it."

That was my opening. "You want revenge?"

"I do. But why would I imagine one of the queen's bitches could help? I know," he said before I could speak. "You're a free bitch now." His laugh was low and mocking.

I suppressed the urge to set his shoes on fire and watch him dance. While it would be amusing, it was unlikely to secure his cooperation. So, I took a moment to wrestle with my temper. He turned back, watching me.

Amusement was written across his face.

"We're going to kill Regner one day," I told him simply. "You don't have to do anything to make that happen. It's inevitable. But something tells me you'd like to look your son in the eye when you see him at the end of this life. And you'd like to tell him you helped avenge him."

The amusement drained from his face. It wasn't real amusement anyway. "What do you want?"

It was my turn to smile. "I want chaos."

14

PRISCA

"*Tell them, Prisca.*"

Blood, so much blood.

Cavis's blood.

I launched myself at Soltor, but my movements were slow. I was pinned in place. Trapped.

Eadric's knife, so close to my eye. I choked on a sob.

"Prisca."

Cavis's eyes, steady and accepting. And then blank, as if he was already gone, and the deepest memory of who he'd been was what kept him moving.

I was free. Somehow, I was free. And I leaped at Soltor, hope spreading its wings in my chest.

Everything went silent. And that sound Cavis made...it echoed, over and over and over. A rough, choked gurgle.

I screamed and screamed.

"Wildcat."

I couldn't breathe, I couldn't. I—

"Prisca, wake up. Now!"

I came awake swinging. My hands lashed out, as if still chained together, smashing into Lorian's face.

He didn't make a sound, just leaned back, giving me some space. His mouth was bleeding. Bleeding because—

"I'm...I'm going to—"

My head spun as he pulled me into his arms. And then we were in the tiny bathing room, and I knelt in front of the toilet, heaving and shuddering.

When I was done, I lifted my head.

"I'm sorry."

"Don't." He handed me a cup of water, pressing a damp cloth to my forehead, before using it to wipe the sweat from my chest, the back of my neck.

It was my fourth nightmare of the night. Each time, I'd jolted awake to find myself in Lorian's arms, and he'd held tightly, stroking me gently as I'd trembled.

"Can I take you back to the bed, wildcat?"

"I can walk." Just as soon as my knees solidified again.

He merely lifted me once more, depositing me on the bed and placing several pillows behind my back. My hand shook, spilling the water, and he held it to my lips before placing the glass on the bedside table.

I reached for his hand. He looked as if he was the one who'd been tortured. "I'm fine," I murmured.

He pressed a gentle kiss to my cheek. "You're so tired, Prisca. Will you sleep again?"

I shook my head.

"Then rest. With me."

It was still dark outside, so I curled into him, and he stroked my back until I finally managed to stop trembling and was still.

When I gave up on resting, I shifted away, swinging my legs over my side of the bed. Lorian wasn't brooding. He wasn't seething. But he was...something.

"Say it," I said.

"I haven't seen you cry."

"I know. I can't." Demos's words had kept me from falling apart in that cell. *"First rule of being a prisoner. You cry, and you're done."* Unfortunately, I seemed to have clamped down so tightly on my grief, I now *couldn't* cry. Because I was relatively sure that if I allowed even the tiniest trickle of that grief free...the ensuing flood would drown me.

Lorian frowned. "I'll allow you to refuse to think about it for a little while. But eventually, we're going to talk about this. And you're going to mourn."

I shot to my feet so fast, my vision blurred. "You'll *allow?*" My voice was very soft.

I was doing the best I could. I'd shoved everything that had happened to me down deep where I didn't have to look at it, and I was able to go most of the day without permitting my thoughts to fester. I had more than enough distractions to help me suppress the memories of the look in Cavis's eyes. The—

No.

I brought myself back to the present by sheer force of will.

Lorian was watching me closely, as if he could see into my mind. And I recognized that cool expression on his face. It was the same expression he'd worn every time he'd pushed me to be smarter, stronger, faster. Every time he'd forced me to become a better version of myself.

But this wasn't the *same*. I was holding almost enough pressure on a wound so deep, just the thought of it overwhelmed me. And if I removed that pressure, I'd bleed out.

Lorian's brow lowered, and he slowly got to his feet. "You don't have to talk about it today. Or tomorrow. Or three months from now. You don't even have to talk about it with *me*. But you won't spend the rest of your life ignoring what has happened to you, Prisca. Because one day—likely a day you won't get to pick—you'll be forced to face it. All that pain you're hiding away will be as fresh as the day you decided to turn it to rage. And right when you need to be strong the most, that pain will cripple you."

I wanted to scream at him. But that would only prove him right about the rage part. So I waited until I was sure I could speak without my voice trembling with fury, and I met his eyes.

"I don't need this from you right now."

"Did you think my love for you would dull my claws?" He gave me a grim smile. "Now I know exactly what I have to lose. And I refuse to lose you."

The fury drained. Replaced immediately by the numbness that continued to creep into my limbs, and I welcomed it.

Lorian seared me with a look I so rarely saw from him. Disappointment. "Death will come for all of us, Prisca. Do you think this is what Cavis would want? For you to let his death poison you? You think it's better to lock it all down? To attempt to feel nothing?"

"I just need...time."

"Then you'll have it. But don't take too long."

He was letting it go. For now. My breath shuddered out of me, and his expression softened just enough that I crossed the room and leaned my head against his chest.

But we didn't have the luxury of time. So we readied ourselves for the day and made our way outside, waiting for the stable hands to bring out our horses.

Lorian was acting strangely. We needed to leave, but he seemed to be dragging his feet. And as I watched, he waved a stable hand away and insisted on checking my mare's hooves. Again.

He must have felt my eyes on him, because he glanced up, the slightest frown etched between his brows. Rythos muttered something about time-wasters beneath his breath.

Slamming my hands onto my hips, I gave Lorian a beady stare. "What is it?"

He glanced behind me, and his face smoothed into relief.

Someone sucked in a breath, and I turned. Telean had stepped into the stables.

My breath caught in my throat, and I felt my chest

contract. My aunt just smiled at me. I let out a choked sound and darted straight for her, launching myself into her arms. We squeezed each other tightly, and when we finally let each other go, her eyes were wet.

"Never again," she said. "Never, Nelayra."

"Never again."

It was a promise I might not be able to keep. Both of us knew that. But I said the words anyway.

One glance at Lorian told me he'd made this happen. And that he'd wanted to surprise me. He was watching us with a faint smile on his face, and my heart tumbled in my chest.

Telean dried her eyes with the heel of her hand, reaching for Demos.

He pulled our aunt into his arms, towering above her smaller frame. Leaning up, she patted him on the cheek. "You're a good boy."

He grinned. "Let me guess, you were supposed to arrive last night?"

"Yes." She nodded at me. "Your prince ordered a carriage for me, but we lost a wheel at midnight last night. I took one of the horses."

I reached for Lorian's hand and squeezed. "Thank you."

He pressed a kiss to my knuckles. "Since your aunt has made it, we can depart."

Rythos shook his head at him. "You didn't think to tell us?"

"She was supposed to be here last night."

Lorian nodded at the stable hand, who jumped into motion, and we led our horses out to the small courtyard.

Vynthar had already said his goodbyes before dawn, slinking out of the inn and into the forest so he wouldn't cause any alarm this morning.

I hugged Demos and Asinia. They were still barely looking at each other, but they would work together when it counted. And if I was hoping for them to work something else out…well, that was none of my business.

"We're going to bring Tibris back, Pris," Asinia promised.

I nodded, suddenly unable to speak. Demos slung his arm around my shoulders and led me to my horse. "Remember what we talked about."

I nodded again. He'd given me strict instructions about our plans for the city. "I will."

We mounted, and I watched Demos and Asinia travel in the opposite direction.

The soft rustle of feathers sounded overhead. A plump gray pigeon circled, then fluttered down, landing on my outstretched hand. Its tiny claws flexed against my skin, and I unrolled the parchment.

It was written in our code, and I recognized the handwriting. Vicer.

Barrier to come down with full moon—five days and counting. Regner currently out of the city. Whereabouts unknown.

-V

My breaths stilled. "How far are we from the city?"

Lorian shifted his horse closer to mine. "Two and a half days if we travel from dawn to dusk."

"We need to move faster. Regner is taking Jamic out of the city before the next full moon. We've got five days." And we would need at least two of those days to put our plans into motion.

"In that case, we'll need to travel through the night." Lorian glanced at the others. "Rests will be few, and sleep will be short."

Everyone nodded. I nudged my mare, pulling my cloak over my head as we headed through the tiny village and back toward the main trail.

Five days. Regner knew if he could swallow down all of the power from both Jamic and the barrier, his chances of wiping all of us out were much, much higher. And if we were all dead, there would be little stopping him from conquering this continent and killing anyone who opposed him. He'd already made it clear exactly how much he enjoyed slaughtering my people, and with nothing standing in his way...

Bile burned up my throat, and I lost myself in a fantasy in which Regner had never been born. What would all of our lives have been like without his evil infecting them at every turn?

Perhaps it all would have been different if his son had lived. But I didn't think so. Regner had already ordered the fae from his kingdom by the time his son died.

I could make myself crazy, attempting to analyze him. Attempting to understand the impossible. I couldn't apply logic where there was none.

Telean angled her horse next to mine, and my chest lightened as she gave me a faint smile.

I attempted a smile back. It felt strange, and I let it fall. "Where are we with the Gromalian prince?"

"We followed every rumor about what really happened to his mother, and the most likely outcome is that Eryndan killed her. We've encouraged these rumors to spread, but we don't have any proof until we can manage to locate Rekja's aunt. She disappeared around the same time. If she was smart, she ran and she's been in hiding all this time. But it's possible that Eryndan had her killed."

I leaned my head back, attempting to drain some of the tension in my neck. "We're running out of time."

"How do you want to respond?" Telean asked.

What I wanted to do and what I needed to do were two separate things.

"Can we guarantee Rekja's lover's protection?"

"What do you mean?"

I attempted to ignore the little voice in my head that urged me not to go down this road.

"Prisca?"

I met Telean's eyes. "If the king was to learn that his son was fraternizing with a guard…"

Riding ahead of us, Rythos turned in his saddle, and our eyes met. "Are you sure about this?"

There was no such thing as a private conversation

around the fae. A few footspans away, Lorian sat as if he'd been born on his horse, his expression distant, but I knew he was paying attention to every word.

"We'll only do it if we can keep the guard safe. We let it leak, and then we rescue the guard directly after. We *have* to keep her safe." Despite my unconcerned tone, Rekja's face flashed in my mind, complete with the way his expression had hardened, his eyes turning to ice. "Can we do that?"

Lorian shifted on his horse. "I have a spy in Eryndan's court. He hasn't yet reached the inner circle, so his information hasn't given us anything we haven't found elsewhere. We can use him to get her out."

My mouth went dry. These were the decisions I struggled with the most. The ones I wouldn't feel any true repercussions from. The ones that could ruin or even end other people's lives. Here I was, casually discussing a woman I'd never met. At the very least, her career would be over after this.

"Pris?" Rythos asked.

I just shook my head, returning my attention to the conversation.

"Eryndan could kill Rekja when he learns of the guard," Galon mused, scratching at his beard.

"He won't," I said. "Rekja is his only son. His heir. He would make him suffer, but he wouldn't kill him." I met Lorian's eyes. "Do it."

Telean's eyes sparked. "I'll let it leak. At the very least, this will prove a distraction for Eryndan."

We fell silent after that, all of us quiet as we traveled east toward Lesdryn.

Our horses' hooves clopped a steady rhythm on the leaf-strewn trail—the only sound as we plowed onward. When the sun began to sink toward the horizon, sunbeams slanted through the trees, bathing our trail in a golden light.

We stopped for a brief break to water the horses and stretch our legs, and I refilled my waterskin in a nearby stream.

A shrill cry pierced the stillness, and I jolted, spilling the water. Above us, a hawk was circling high overhead, gliding on outstretched wings. With a few lazy sweeps, it spiraled lower. I'd expected it to settle onto Lorian's shoulder. But it wasn't Aquilus.

Instead, it fluttered down to settle onto my shoulder. I tensed, but it held steady, its talons flexing. My heart pounded at the damage those talons could do. I could feel the strength in them as it regarded me with inscrutable onyx eyes.

With delicate precision, the hawk extended its leg, offering a small piece of parchment. Placing my waterskin on the closest rock, I unfurled the tiny scroll, scanning its contents.

Nelayra,

Remember our little deal? The hour has come for you to settle your debt. Don't keep me waiting.

—Daharak

"The pirate queen is calling in her favor," I announced.

And of course, the timing couldn't have been worse. From the put-upon look on Lorian's face, he was in agreement.

Galon lifted his head. He was crouched next to the stream, splashing water on his face. "What exactly did you promise to do for her?"

"Something of equal value to what she did for me. She helped us avoid the Gromalian fleet and sneak through Thobirea without either Eryndan or Regner learning where we were."

Marth was leaning against a tree close to the horses. He glanced at me. "You're planning something."

"This is our chance to convince Daharak to ally with us. I'm not going to waste it."

I would go to Daharak. But she was going to have to wait a few days. First, we needed to get to Jamic. Panic began to press on me, tightening my chest.

Voices sounded from the trail behind us, and Rythos angled his head. "We need to go."

My thighs burned as we walked back to our horses.

Lorian held out his hand, helping me to mount. I didn't need his assistance, but I'd be lying if I said I didn't enjoy the way his large hands guided me into the saddle. The way he stroked my thigh with a gleam in his eye before turning away to hold out his hand for my aunt.

As usual, she waved away any assistance. The

moment she was in her saddle, Lorian was gesturing us forward.

"Let's go."

ASINIA

Demos and I had said thirty-six words to each other since we'd left Prisca and the others behind. I'd counted.

All thirty-six had been travel-related. I wasn't sure if I should be impressed by how well we could communicate with just body language and quick glances—or irritated that we didn't *need* to speak.

The constant silence was giving me far too much time to think. And those thoughts inevitably returned to my mother and the last time I'd seen her face—immediately before she was murdered.

From the time I was old enough to hold a needle and shears, my tasks were mending and adjustments. I would sit at my spot near the door, patching trousers, hemming dresses, and listening to my mother consult with the wealthier women in our village. The women who lived behind the gates. The kinds of women who threw parties.

I had seen eleven winters when I realized there was something different about the way I worked. I could spend my time watching my mother design and cut and weave—taking my eyes completely off my work—and my hand would still dance over the fabric. Each stitch would land precisely where it needed to be. I was small and quiet, working in a corner of the room. So no one else noticed. But I knew something was terribly wrong.

One night, after my mother had gone to bed, I sat in my chair by the door, finishing my mending. An odd kind of dread had taken up residence in my chest. A breathlessness that drove my next move. Closing my eyes, I randomly stabbed my needle through the backside of the fabric and back down again. Repeating the stitch a few more times, I finally stilled my hands, opening my eyes.

My stitches were perfect. As if something else had guided my hands. Something invisible.

My mouth turned watery with fear. My tongue itched, while my skin was suddenly too tight.

And I knew.

I was one of the *corrupt* the priestess cursed so often. A deadly weed that had somehow grown in the garden of goodness. A weed that must be plucked out to save the other flowers in that garden.

I told no one. I didn't understand exactly what my power was, but since it only seemed to work when I was sewing, it wasn't the type that would be likely to get me discovered.

No, as long as I kept my head down and was unfailingly polite to our customers, my tiny, precise stitches and remarkable speed were considered natural-born talent and skill.

Now, when I looked back, I could see other things had come to me easily. Complicated dances for various celebrations were simple for me. And while I may have been terrible at playing King's Web, none of our friends would play me when Natan had found an old dart board and hung it from a tree in the forest. I'd hit the bull's-eye every single time, until Natan banned me from playing.

I'd unconsciously been stifling my power in public ever since, especially when Prisca and I had trained with Tibris and his friends. But the next time I'd picked up a crossbow, I'd felt a strange sense of...comfort.

What would my mother think of that?

If the queen had worn my creations, my mother would have been so proud of me. Now, I was hoping we would be able to kill that same queen before she became even more of a threat to us. Shame curled in my stomach as I imagined my mother's reaction to *that*.

I wasn't like Pris. I couldn't shove my grief down deep and refuse to think of it. I understood why she did it. I didn't know how she would function if she allowed herself to feel that grief. And we all needed her to function.

I would give anything to hear the sound of my mother's voice. All I wanted was just one moment.

Your heart doesn't stop beating when you lose someone you love. The world doesn't end. It just feels like it does.

Vynthar stepped onto the trail, spooking my horse. I sighed, and he turned his head, his elongated eyes narrowing further. My mouth twitched, and I glanced at Demos.

Our eyes met. His expression softened, but he immediately looked away. On the trail ahead of us, the

Drakoryx was carrying something in its mouth. Some kind of animal. He stepped back off the path, disappearing into the forest.

Happy hunting.

Demos was frowning into the forest now, clearly deep in thought.

His voice ran through my mind—as it so often did. *"Close your eyes. I won't let anyone hurt you."*

He'd been trapped in the cell next to me, his body fighting to heal from the iron that had been slowly poisoning his body. If one of the guards had come for me, there was literally nothing he could have done.

And yet, something about the glint in his eyes, the determined set of his mouth, and the almost arrogant way he held his head…

I'd believed him.

Demos had been keeping his vow ever since. And now he thought I'd thrown it back in his face. Thought I'd deemed it unnecessary. Thought I'd rejected his natural need to protect.

I was tired of it.

"I hadn't thought you were the type to choose silence," I told him.

He wasn't. Demos was the kind of man who fought relentlessly for what he wanted. I would have preferred his vicious temper over this.

His shoulders stiffened, the only sign of his irritation. "I don't know what you want from me, Asinia. When you figure it out, let me know."

15

PRISCA

Two days later, we were all exhausted, irritated, and hot.

There was an empty space where Cavis should have been riding next to Marth. And it was quiet without Asinia and Demos sniping at each other. Too quiet.

Insects buzzed in the underbrush, our horses kicked up clouds of dust, and I drank greedily from my waterskin, the summer heat suffocating, even in Eprotha.

When we marched against Regner, would our soldiers be exhausted from the heat? Would they be drained from flicking away bugs, enervated from dehydration, and irritated at the unrelenting sun?

Or would Regner wait until winter, knowing his soldiers were used to the cold, while the fae and hybrids tolerated the heat better?

Worse yet, would there be no need for a war, because he would take down the barrier and kill us all?

If I didn't learn to manage the

grim thoughts that constantly plagued me, I would be useless for the next part of our plan. I pictured my mind as a lake, each thought a ripple that disturbed the clear surface of the water. It helped for a while.

Gray flickered across the sky to my right. A pigeon fluttered downward toward Lorian, a tiny scroll bound to its slender leg. Lorian held out his hand, and the pigeon dropped into it, cocking its head as he slipped the message free.

"My spy has reported in. He took Rekja's guard by force. Just hours later, news of her relationship with the prince was delivered to Eryndan."

My mouth tasted like ash. I didn't even know this woman, and I'd had her kidnapped with just a few words. She had a life, and I'd yanked her from that life without warning. Worse, I'd ensured that until Eryndan was dead, she would never be able to return to that life.

"Keep her safe," I managed to get out. Lorian pinned me with an intent look, but I dragged my gaze away.

We stopped to rest near the river before the main route to the city walls. Everyone was quiet, well aware that this would be my first time using the hourglass. Stretching my legs, I wandered over to Rythos, who was staring into the water.

He looked at me, and his eyes were so grief-stricken, all I could do was wrap my arms around him.

"It doesn't seem real that he's gone," he said, his own arms encircling me and squeezing. I stroked his back, helplessness eating at me.

Lighthearted, playful Marth had become someone who could explode into rage at any moment. Galon was grim, barely speaking, his eyes hard. Rythos kept disappearing, preferring to be alone, while Lorian was burning with suppressed wrath.

There was nothing to say to make anyone feel better. None of us *wanted* to feel better. The sheer suggestion seemed like a betrayal to Cavis's memory in itself.

Rythos sighed, his body relaxing slightly. Then he drew away. "Let's go make Cavis proud."

My eyes stung, but I nodded, turning to find my aunt waiting a few feet away. A hint of concern slid through her eyes, quickly replaced by determination.

"Are you ready?" Telean asked me.

I nodded. But beneath my false confidence, the first glimmer of fear tightened my chest. The hourglass channeled my own power. That meant it would bypass the natural warning of my body and take what it needed. I could die and not even know it was happening.

"Control," Telean told me as we walked back toward the horses. "Usually, the rulers in your line are introduced to the hourglass when they are still young. Your mother would have first practiced with it as a child, under your grandmother's watch. She would have continued to use it over the years, so that she would be prepared for it when your grandmother eventually passed. You haven't had that luxury."

No, I hadn't. My stomach fluttered, but Telean had prepared me enough to know that these kinds of artifacts must be used by someone confident. Someone who had the sheer strength of will to demand their cooperation.

Telean placed her hand on my shoulder. "The hourglass will rip your power from you if you're not careful. It will take it all at once, and you'll have nothing left. It's up to you to prevent that from happening."

I nodded. I could do this. The hourglass was my birthright. It *would* work for me. I refused to believe otherwise.

The others were getting ready to mount. Lorian met my eyes, and I saw his complete and utter belief in me. Something settled in my chest.

"Give us a moment," he told Telean. Taking my hand, he pulled me several footspans away from the others.

I gazed up at him. I'd never get used to the way I was drawn to Lorian. When he was close, it was as if I lost sense of everything around me. The air seemed charged with his presence, and my senses were attuned to him. Sound faded into the background, and when those green eyes locked on to mine, my breath caught in my throat.

Surely, at some point, this need for him would fade. This obsession would turn into something closer to contentment.

"Just what are you thinking, Prisca?"

My cheeks heated, and his gaze sharpened. "I see." He gave me a wicked grin. "Perhaps I didn't satisfy you this morning."

My mind flashed me back to the feel of him behind me as he'd thrust inside me before dawn. I'd been so...

vocal, he'd needed to cover my mouth with his hand.

"You satisfied me…fine."

Those eyes lit with challenge. As I'd planned.

"Fine?" he purred. "I'll remember that for next time." He took my hand. "Do you remember the last time we were in this area?"

Despite the situation, my mouth curved. Lorian's gaze dropped to my lips.

"Tibris had just found us," I said.

"Because he's smart and stubborn, just like you."

I took his hand. "You kissed me once we were through the city gates, and I knew I could never let you kiss me again."

A feral gleam entered his eyes. "I had no idea my kisses were that powerful, even then."

"In another life. That was what you said." I gave him a mock scowl. "And then you insisted on this one instead."

His huge palm cupped my cheek, tilting my face up. "In every life, wildcat. No matter what happens, you hold on to that. It's you and me in *every* life."

He lowered his head, and I sank into his kiss, turning boneless. When he lifted his head once more, his eyes were serious. "Are you ready for this?"

My conversation with Telean had focused me, but Lorian had steadied me out.

"I'm ready."

Lorian led me back to the others. Not one of them looked concerned. I wasn't sure if they were purposefully controlling their expressions or if they truly had that much confidence in me. Either way, seeing the calm assurance on Rythos's, Galon's, and Marth's faces helped.

Telean nodded at me. "Control," she warned again.

"I know. Is everyone ready?"

We mounted, making our way back to the main road leading to the city. I maneuvered my horse in front of the others. The bend in the road appeared, and I focused on it, reminding myself of the position of the city gates, which would be visible as soon as we rounded it.

My left hand clutched the reins, while my right held the hourglass. I closed my eyes, feeling the deep well of its power, hot and wild as it waited for me.

I nudged my mare into a gallop and *pulled*.

Time stopped.

But the power swamped me. For a single terrifying moment, it was as if the hourglass was alive and my own will didn't matter at all. Yes, Telean had warned me, but I still hadn't understood just what the hourglass could do. I was so used to yanking at the threads of my power, I was unprepared for so many to come free at once. Power roared through me, until my head spun with it.

Control.

But how could I control something that seemed to have no end?

I attempted to push the threads back down, but they weren't going anywhere. Someone hauled me onto their horse, and Lorian's masculine scent surrounded me. I could see nothing except a blur in the periphery of my vision as we slowed.

Our horses were walking. I could feel that much. It meant we'd made it through the city gates and past the guards. But I couldn't release my grip on either the hourglass or my power.

"Prisca." Lorian's voice was tight. "You can let go now."

"I'm trying."

"Release the hourglass. You don't need it anymore." Telean sounded concerned, her tone high and thready.

I was attempting to do exactly that, but my fingers were curled tightly, frozen in place.

Lorian's hand clamped around my wrist. "Just open your hand, wildcat."

Open my hand. That was all I had to do. I could do that.

One finger first, and that was all it took. Once the first finger lifted, I managed to loosen the rest, and the hourglass thumped against my chest. I swayed, and Lorian pulled me tighter into his chest.

My eyes found Telean's. Her gaze was steady, reassuring.

"You did it," she said, approval coating her words.

"It almost took me over. I was…"

"Almost means nothing," Lorian rumbled, nuzzling my cheek.

Telean watched me. "This is why you must always hold the hourglass when you use it. It's a physical reminder that you are linked to it. When you let go, your power will unlink too. This is how children train."

I was too tired to feel embarrassed by that implication. "I will."

"I wish Demos had seen that," Telean said. "He would have been so proud."

I nodded, but a lump had formed in my throat. Tibris would have been just as proud.

Gods, I hoped he was unhurt. I hoped he knew we'd make sure he was freed. The anxiety gnawing at me wouldn't disappear until I could see him unharmed with my own eyes.

Lorian lifted the hood of my cloak, hiding my hair. While Regner was unlikely to expect us to return to his capital, we'd take no chances, and the others were cloaked and tense as well.

I turned in Lorian's arms as someone murmured my name. Vicer had appeared next to us. He'd put on muscle—and it looked good on him. But new frown lines were etched between his brows, and his eyes were guarded.

"Vicer."

He nodded at us. "Follow me to the safe house."

As I'd expected, the safe house was in the slums. But just as Vicer's original headquarters had been carefully hidden in plain sight, so was this one.

It was a brothel.

We dismounted, leaving our horses with several of Vicer's people, and he led us through the front entrance. It was surprisingly quiet, perhaps because it was the middle of the day. I peered into the dim front room, but Vicer was already turning, unlocking another door—just footspans from the first. I swallowed at the sight of the small supply closet.

"You just need to walk straight through the wall," Vicer said.

Lorian went first, gently pulling me with him. And my heart jumped into my throat when he walked *through* the back wall. I held up one hand, and it melted into the wall. Moments later, we were walking up another set of stairs.

"How?" I got out.

He winked over his shoulder at me. "Magic."

I gave him a long look, and he pressed a kiss to my forehead as we reached the top of the stairs. Booted footsteps sounded behind us as Vicer led us down a hall and into a suite.

I surveyed it as Rythos, Galon, and Marth spread out, making themselves at home. Telean sat on one of the stuffed chairs with a long sigh as she rubbed her feet. The suite was large, with five separate bedrooms connecting to a main living area. It was comfortable enough, but I was already fantasizing about curling up on a bed.

First, though, we needed to talk.

"Any luck with the hybrid camp?" I asked Vicer.

"Kaelin Stillcrest wouldn't cooperate. I did everything I could. Both she and her *generals* refuse to move south." Grief battled with helpless fury in his eyes. Since the moment his lover died, Vicer had been fighting for the hybrids. He was one of the most stubbornly determined people I knew. Leaving that camp before he'd finished convincing Stillcrest to abandon her suicidal ideology had likely killed a piece of him.

"They're going to die," Marth said.

I winced.

Vicer snarled, whirling on him. Marth stepped closer, and Lorian slowly moved between them. He didn't say a word, but both men seemed to regain control of their rage. Vicer turned back to me, ignoring Marth.

Clearly, Vicer was on edge. And I couldn't blame him. But I was going to have to consider the problem of Kaelin Stillcrest another time.

"We traveled through the night. We'll need some rest," I said.

Vicer nodded, gesturing to Ameri as she stepped inside the room. She looked tired, but she smiled at me—a very different attitude from when we'd first met. "Nice to see you, Prisca."

"You too."

"Let me show you your rooms," she said.

Telean nodded. "I could use a nap."

Rythos and the others followed her out of the room, but Vicer gestured for Lorian and me to sit at the small table.

"Where's Madinia?" I asked.

"Working with Finley. She has been with him all day, creating these."

Vicer held out a strange, ink-stained device about the

size of a book. He gave a faint smile at my confusion and handed me a piece of parchment. The message had been stamped onto the parchment.

The Eprothan King is lying to you.

Brothers and sisters, hybrids and humans: None of us are corrupt.

I glanced up. Vicer's smile widened. "Madinia wrote it. We're using our contacts to get them into as many hands as possible."

My pulse thudded as I continued reading. She'd explained almost everything. And she hadn't used her haughty, queen's lady tone. At some point since leaving the castle, Madinia had learned how to talk to people—villagers, townsfolk, and city residents alike. Or perhaps she'd always known how and just hadn't bothered to use that skill until now.

Either way, she presented the truth in compelling, matter-of-fact prose. She pointed to the facts—the gods were not taking our power, but the king was. The corrupt weren't corrupt at all. We were hybrids, and we wanted nothing more than to live our lives. The king had instilled such terror and loyalty that this would seem impossible. That was no mistake on Sabium's part.

It will be difficult for some people to live with the fact that they have betrayed their neighbors. Their family members. Their friends. That those people were not rejected by the gods, but were hunted by a tyrannical, power-hungry king.

Denial might seem the easier path, brushing aside these truths as mere fabrication. Yet a moment of reckoning is upon each of us.

Will you rise, defending future generations and guarding the innocent? Or will you allow Sabium's lies to destroy the little goodness left on this continent?

Choose wisely.

My heart beat with something I hadn't felt in a while. Hope.

Most people wouldn't believe. They would see it as rebel propaganda.

My first day in this city—directly after I'd left Lorian and the others and located Vicer's safe house with Tibris—I'd met Margie in the kitchen of that safe house.

She was the one who'd told me how the artifacts worked, what Regner had done, and how his lies had flourished. When I'd asked her how he'd gotten away with it for so long, her expression had turned bleak.

"How do you control a population? You keep the people poor and uneducated. Tell them the same lie for centuries, and tie that lie to religion. Those people will believe you even when the truth is dancing naked in front of them. Because to believe otherwise would mean their entire world has always been a lie. And that realization is too difficult for most people to take."

It wasn't just a case of countering Regner's lies. We would have to make these people question their religious beliefs. Regner's tactics were both clever and insidious.

But it was something.

I handed the parchment back to Vicer. He was studying my face, and he nodded. "We keep our expectations low. If this reaches just one person who believes it—and doesn't turn on their neighbor, or refuses to fight in Regner's army…"

I blew out a breath. "It's worth it. At the very least, it's a distraction for Regner."

"We have a distribution plan in place," he said. "They'll go out to every town and village within the next few days. And they'll keep spreading the word, even after you've left the city."

"Thank you."

Someone thumped on the door. Lorian got to his feet and opened it, revealing Marth. Likely, the poor man had been just about to lie down and get some rest.

"What is it?" Lorian asked.

Marth narrowed his eyes at him. "Someone's here for Prisca."

For me? No one else knew I was here.

Lorian angled his head. Likely, he was thinking the same. "What do they want?" he demanded.

Good-natured, flirtatious Marth let out a sound that made me freeze. Half growl, half snarl, all warning.

Lorian went still. "Are we going to have a problem?"

"I'm not your messenger."

Oh, Marth. Gone was the easy humor, the sly grin that was so often a fixture on his face. It had been replaced by pure rage.

"I'll go down," I said.

Squeezing between the two fae, I ignored the tension in the air as they stared at each other. I almost kept walking. But Marth was practically radiating frustrated misery. Leaning up on my tiptoes, I pushed his blond hair away from his face and pressed a kiss to his cheek.

Surprised eyes met mine. I smiled at Marth, making a mental note to talk to him. Soon. Behind me, Lorian hissed out a breath.

"Never mind that," a voice said behind Marth. "I let myself up."

Vicer stalked past me. "How the fuck—"

A short man with hunched shoulders strolled into the room, and I sighed.

"Tymriel." My voice was cool.

I hadn't exactly enjoyed my first meeting with him. As one of the five elders who had ruled the hybrid kingdom since Regner attacked, he'd interrogated me, told me my mother would be ashamed of the coward I'd become, and finally—along with the other elders—had refused to give me basic information, such as if the hybrid kingdom still had a functioning army.

Tymriel smiled at me, the lines in his face deepening with the movement.

I didn't smile back.

Lorian shifted, stepping closer to me. Tymriel's smile disappeared.

My visit to the hybrid kingdom had ended with the elders telling me I wasn't yet the queen I should be. It was only after talking to Lorian that I'd realized the truth.

Their refusal to help me hadn't really been about me at all. My cousin had gotten to them first.

So just what exactly were the hybrid elders hoping to achieve now—after they'd refused to help me mere weeks ago?

My hourglass warmed against my chest, and the realization slammed into me.

The elders knew I'd found my birthright.

And they wanted to take it from me.

PRISCA

"This man managed to find the location of this safe house. We're now compromised." If my voice had been cool, Vicer's was pure ice.

"I have not told anyone of your location, and I have not been followed. I would never risk your plans," Tymriel said into the awkward silence. "Is there somewhere we can speak privately?"

"As long as you understand that Lorian will be part of that conversation," I said.

Tymriel frowned at Lorian. "I don't believe your presence is necessary."

"Anything you want to say to me can be said in front of him," I said.

Tymriel sighed but didn't argue.

Vicer was a silent, seething presence. He led us down the hall to what seemed to be a small meeting room before stalking out after one last furious glanced Tymriel's direction. He was likely about to begin poring over every detail of his security. And while he'd wait until I'd spoken to Tymriel, there was no way Vicer would allow him to leave without learning exactly how he'd found us.

Tymriel's frown deepened, but his gaze dropped to the hourglass around my neck. "You truly did it."

I inclined my head. "Yes, I did."

"While I'm pleased you managed to find the hourglass, the other elders may order you to give it to your cousin."

Lorian's expression turned lethal. "They won't *order* Prisca to do anything."

Tymriel glanced at me. As if he was expecting me to be oh-so reasonable and simply hand it over.

I met his gaze. "Zathrian has a man working beneath Regner. A man called Eadric. Eadric killed our friend. A man who had a wife and child. A good man. Eadric also tortured me. For days."

Tymriel opened his mouth. I shook my head. "Listen carefully because I will only say this once. If anyone attempts to take the hourglass from me to give it to Zathrian, I will not hesitate. I will not show mercy. I will kill them without blinking."

Next to me, Lorian practically glowed with pride. Of course, he wasn't a good judge of my own morality.

My mate still considered murder to be the best solution to most problems.

Tymriel gave me a look as if I'd greatly disappointed him. "Is that the kind of ruler you will be? A tyrant?"

"No. But I care about Lyrinore. All of us have suffered and lost loved ones for it, and there will likely be more to come. And yet you would prefer that Zathrian rule. A liar and a murderer, whose parents dropped the wards that day, killing thousands of hybrids."

I'd once been determined not to blame Zathrian for that. But now that I knew just how evil he was, I was willing to bet he had much more in common with his parents than I'd ever imagined.

Tymriel sighed. "You had my vote. I would prefer the crown sit on your head."

My pulse increased. If that was the truth, perhaps he could be convinced to actually help us.

"Since when?"

"Do you remember what I said to you that day we met?"

You have seen more horror than anyone of so few winters should have to. But you are still hiding. Become the queen we know you can be, and we will do whatever we can to help you.

Fury burned deep in my gut. "So now I'm suddenly worthy of your help?"

"The other elders agreed I would watch you from afar, studying your choices. I learned of your attempts to ally with the Gromalian king and the way you manipulated his son. I heard of the torture you survived, and rather than allow it to break you, you have used it to grow stronger. I know your plans to take Jamic, and if you can truly succeed, you will deal Regner the greatest blow he could imagine."

He knew a lot of things. And none of us had been aware that he was watching me.

Lorian let out a vicious snarl. "And just when did you hear of Prisca's torture?"

Tymriel's gaze stayed steady on my own. "After you had already escaped that situation," he said.

I wanted to believe him. But the words he'd said when we'd first met were looping through my head.

"Just as your blade had to endure the intense heat and the force of the hammer to become a strong, reliable weapon, so must you. Except you must choose to be forged in fire so you will become the queen we need."

Was this man ruthless enough to allow me to be tortured—to allow Cavis to *die*—all to ensure I was a strong enough *weapon*? So he could declare me worthy enough to lead?

I wasn't sure I wanted an answer to that question. From the sparks simmering on Lorian's skin—and the ominous, metallic scent in the air—my mate most definitely did. I reached for his hand.

I could practically hear him grumbling as his hand swallowed mine, but he brought it to his lips, dropping a kiss to my knuckles. Still, he fixed Tymriel with a stare that promised retribution.

"Once again, the so-called *elders* have proven less than useless," a hoarse voice said from behind us. My aunt stepped into the room, mouth twisted in a sneer as she watched Tymriel. Likely, Vicer had woken her from her nap. A good choice. My aunt clearly had her own thoughts about the elders.

Tymriel attempted a smile, but his eyes were blank. "Telean. It has been a long time."

"Yes. A long time, indeed, since I was forced to flee with Nelayra's parents. Directly after her grandmother was brutally killed."

His jaw clenched. "I remember what happened."

"Do you?" she asked. "And what about the rest of the *elders*? Do they remember? What exactly have you achieved for all these years, while our people have been fighting and dying on this continent?"

Tymriel's nostrils flared. "We've kept the wards up, protecting those who were able to stay. We've ensured the sea serpents guarded our sea. We've slowly built up our military—small though it may be—with the hopes that one day we would be able to save our people."

"That was your tactic?" Lorian asked incredulously. "Hope?"

It was small of me, but I had to hide a smirk. They had said everything I was thinking, and from Tymriel's dark scowl, the hits had landed. Unfortunately, we needed Tymriel on our side so we could convince him to help us begin moving some of our people back to their kingdom.

I cleared my throat. "Which council members voted

against me?"

"Gavros, Sylphina, and Rivenlor."

I had Ysara on my side, then. "Was my cousin tested by the Drakoryx?"

Tymriel's gaze focused on a spot right above my head. He was attempting to hide things from me even now.

"No," he admitted.

"Why not?"

"There are only a few of the creatures left. Unlike when you arrived, they were nowhere to be found when he approached us."

Frustration clawed at me, and Telean let out a bitter laugh. "He dosed himself with hinianseed. And you didn't test for it, because you were desperate."

"Hinianseed?" I asked.

"An herb," Telean said, keeping her eyes on Tymriel. "One that repels the Drakoryx. Because your cousin knew if he were to encounter one of them, he would be found wanting."

"At the time, we didn't know Nelayra had survived," Tymriel rasped. He turned to me. "Zathrian had already traveled to us before we knew of your existence. Once we learned of you, he returned, insisting he was the better choice. You're young. You didn't want the crown. Didn't feel worthy of it. Your cousin…he was very persuasive. He has been preparing for this since before you were born, and it is easy for him to paint you as young, inexperienced, and weak."

I nodded, bitterness flooding my mouth. "It changes

nothing," I said when I could speak again. "I'm not giving up the hourglass. If the other elders want it, you can tell them to come take it from me."

Amusement danced across his face, and he shook his head at me. "You are very much like your grandmother."

The memory of her tripped through my mind. Ysara had shown me the hybrid queen's final moments before she died. My grandmother had been fighting to the end, and her power had been both incredible and horrifying as she'd aged those who came for her before she was finally overrun. She was the one responsible for the blighting of the Cursed City.

"I'll take that as a compliment," I said.

The quirk of Tymriel's mouth told me he might not have meant it as such.

"Do we have an army?" I asked.

"We do." Tymriel's face had turned a gray color, and I braced myself for his next words. "Zathrian has taken control of them."

I closed my eyes. Next to me, Lorian let out a soft snarl. For the first time, I was glad Demos wasn't here. The thought of fighting our own people... This news would devastate him.

"How many?" Telean asked.

"Twenty thousand."

Twenty thousand hybrids that my cousin would no doubt turn on us at the worst possible time. Likely, at the end of this war, when we were attempting to recover.

"I...may have someone who can help with that. I

will have to convince him to override the other elders."

I was so tired of the elders. I'd tried to be patient, but all they had done was hinder our ability to fight this war. Why hadn't they found any other allies?

"What is to the west of the hybrid kingdom? Was there *no one* to help our people through all these years of suffering?"

Tymriel shook his head, his expression mournful. "All that lies to our west is a continent of ice. Our people could never get close to it. And they tried again and again after your grandmother was killed. Huge, hidden icebergs capsized many of our ships—no matter how much magic we used. And the water was too cold, even for the sea serpents. There are many rumors about the creatures that make that continent their home, and…it is likely in all of our best interests that those creatures stay where they are."

I wrestled my mind back to our plans. "Regner is moving his regiments south. He's going to attempt to take down the fae ward. And at some point, he will attack the hybrid camp. He won't be content until all of us are dead, Tymriel."

His brow dropped in a dark scowl. "What is it you're asking?"

I wasn't *asking*, but I kept my voice even. "We need to start evacuating. It's going to be a long, dangerous journey. But we need to begin moving the young, old, weak, and sick back to our kingdom."

Tymriel's eyes lit up, and he suddenly appeared years younger. "This is what I have always dreamed of but could never achieve. It will be dangerous. We will need powerful, experienced hybrids to guard them." His mouth twisted. "There's a reason this hasn't been done before. If Regner learns of those plans, his soldiers will be waiting."

"Which is why you need to convince the elders to send anyone capable of wielding a sword. We need them stationed along the Asric Pass. This won't be like last time, when our people fled in the snow, unprepared and terrified. We'll get them out within weeks, when the temperatures have dropped enough to become tolerable for walking long distances. And we have guides, healers, soldiers—all to keep them safe. As soon as they get through the pass, they can use the tunnel and get to Lyrinore. Once they're in the hybrid kingdom, they'll be safe."

"Who will lead them home?"

"I will," Telean said.

I turned to face her. She stuck out her chin. "I am old and tired. Who better to set the pace for the weakest among us?"

"You're not weak."

She smiled at me, leaning up on her tiptoes to pat my cheek. "I'm not. Which is why I'm a good choice."

"We'll need to make arrangements," I said. "It will take time."

Telean nodded. "Agreed. I'll wait as long as you need. And then I'll take our people home."

17

ASINIA

From the moment we'd left the others in Eprotha, a stifling politeness and awkward silence had descended between Demos and me. We'd always ignored our simmering tension, yet now, without the terror of Prisca's fate between us, our interactions were filled with strained courtesies and stiff formality.

Even Vynthar seemed to have gotten tired of it, disappearing into the forest yesterday and failing to return when we'd made camp last night.

Thankfully, just a few hours ago, we'd finally managed to locate the rebels. There was no question that we were close. The smell of damp soil intermingled with the distant scent of searing meat from their fires.

They were well positioned, the fae lands sprawling to the west, while a wide river made a surprise attack almost impossible from the south. Enemies could only approach from the north or east, and the dense forest surrounding the camp also acted as a natural defense, while making it difficult to spot from a distance.

We'd left our horses and supplies, slipping through the forest on foot so we could survey the camp before we made our move.

Rustling sounded somewhere deeper in the woods, and I flipped my crossbow from its position hanging over my shoulder into my hands. Demos's sword had appeared in his hand so fast I hadn't seen him draw it.

"Behind me," he ordered.

I didn't argue. He waited until I was in position, and together, we crept forward. His power allowed him to move nearly soundlessly through the forest, and I stepped where he stepped.

"Up," Demos instructed, gesturing to a tree. I climbed it slowly, carefully, well aware that the crack of a branch might draw attention. I'd expected Demos to choose his own tree, but he waited until I was carefully balanced before hauling himself up until he was crouched next to me—one foot on my branch, the other on the branch next to us.

My skin prickled as he leaned closer, until both of us were hidden among the leaves. Something tugged in my stomach. My tree had suddenly become crowded with Demos and his scent.

Scowling, I peered through the forest and into the rebel camp.

Tents—likely made from scavenged materials, but astonishingly well crafted—had been arranged in groups, all surrounding a central hub. Men and women in mismatched leathers and homespun tunics went purposefully about their tasks—training in their arena, cooking on the fires, hauling water from the river. The steady clang of hammer on steel rang out from a makeshift forge, while horses were led in and out of the large wooden building that served as their stables.

I knew now why the Gromalian king hadn't been able to snuff out the rebels. They were a well-organized, self-sufficient army. Next to me, Demos leaned even closer. His gaze was intent as he watched a man sitting in a chair by the largest fire, signing the pieces of parchment brought to him, consulting with those who were clearly the highest ranking, and giving orders to groups of rebels as they returned to camp.

This was their leader.

Finally, when the sun began lowering in the sky, Demos seemed to have all the information he needed. He gestured, and we both climbed down from the tree, boots hitting the ground with low thumps.

"Wait here," he said. "I'll come back for you once I've talked to their leader."

"I don't think so." Tibris was the closest thing I had to a brother. Besides, Demos was the kind of man whose very presence was a palpable threat. Infiltrating their camp would likely prompt an immediate attempt on his life. They would be more hesitant to kill a woman at first sight, which meant it was safer if I went with him.

Demos slowly turned his head, menace pouring

off him in waves. I rolled my eyes. This was the exact problem.

"They're not going to like that we made it past their sentries," he said.

So he knew there was also a chance they might attack before asking any questions. I gestured to the crossbow slung over my shoulder. I was now deadly with it—thanks to his relentless training.

"We're wasting time," I pointed out.

He glanced at the skies, clearly reaching for patience. "I wouldn't have brought you if I'd known—"

"If you'd known I would want to do everything *I* could to save Tibris, too? I didn't need your permission to come here, Demos."

He scanned my face, as if searching for a hint of weakness. I kept my expression carefully neutral and waited.

"If things go bad, you run."

I would never run, but if I didn't agree, he'd never relent. I nodded.

"Your word."

"We're wasting time."

"I'll have your word, Sin, or you're waiting here."

He hadn't called me by the nickname in days now. I hated how the word made my heart thump harder, even when we were mid-argument.

"I'll run."

I'd run, then I'd circle back, and save the stubborn ass.

He narrowed his eyes at me, but footsteps sounded. A group of rebels was marching this way. Either we strolled into the clearing on our own, or we'd be discovered anyway.

Demos shook his head, rolled his shoulders, and stalked toward the clearing.

Shouts sounded, and I sighed, following him. Instantly, we were surrounded.

Bodies pushed close, cutting off any escape routes we might have attempted. The rebels' expressions ranged from fury to shock, while their weapons ranged from short daggers to broadswords.

Demos ignored the weapons leveled our way and pinned the leader with a hard stare. His amber eyes were wild, his hands fisted. Anyone who didn't know him might have thought he was scared. But I knew he was holding himself back from tearing through these rebels before they knew what had happened, his instincts vehemently opposed to allowing both of us to become surrounded.

"You have something of ours," Demos said.

Surprise flashed into the leader's eyes, followed by dull fury. He had an interesting face. Not exactly handsome, but...compelling. All sharp angles, with a high forehead. The kind of face you remembered.

The rebels came closer, tightening their circle surrounding us. I wasn't claustrophobic like Pris, but sweat dripped down my back just the same.

The leader swaggered toward us, his gaze stilling on Demos's face.

"I assume you're the hybrid prince. How fortunate that you've chosen to grace us with your presence."

Demos angled his head. A man holding a large knife took a step closer to me, and I leveled my own crossbow at him. Another man approached from my left, getting close enough that I jolted.

Demos was suddenly there. He wrapped his left arm over the man's knife hand and twisted. The knife dropped, the man fell to his knees, and a loud crack echoed across the clearing. The man screamed, and Demos stepped back, the knife in his hand. He returned his gaze to the leader, expression placid.

"Where is Tibris?"

Something I couldn't place flickered across the leader's face. "You came all this way, placing both of you in danger, for one man? A human?"

Demos's face might have been carved from stone. "I came all this way for my brother."

I was watching closely enough that this time, I caught the flicker of relief at Demos's words.

What exactly was happening here?

The rebel leader narrowed his eyes at Demos. "You have no brothers."

Demos bared his teeth in an expression that would never be mistaken for a smile. "The brother of my sister is my brother. I've claimed him as such."

My chest squeezed. Demos didn't say things he didn't mean. And I knew him well enough by now to know that he would die for those he'd claimed as family.

When Prisca learned that Demos—who had resented Tibris from the moment he learned who Prisca was—had claimed him as his brother...

"Is he alive?" Demos demanded.

The leader nodded. "Yes."

My shoulders slumped, the relief almost dizzying. "Is he hurt?" I asked.

He flicked his gaze to me. "No."

Demos tensed. Obviously, he'd also caught the hesitation before the word.

"*Was* he hurt?" I hissed.

"We found their horses, Herne," someone called. "Just the two of them."

Herne nodded. "Why are you here?" he asked. His refusal to answer that question made it very clear. Tibris had been hurt. And from the way Demos's eyes had darkened, he was well aware of that fact too.

"I told you. My sister wanted to communicate with you. And for some insane reason, you decided to provoke the hybrid heir by taking her brother. You should be thanking the gods that I'm here instead of her. Of the two of us, I'm the calm, reasonable one."

I fought to keep my expression neutral. Demos was most definitely not "calm or reasonable" when someone he cared about was in danger.

"We don't need to communicate with the hybrid heir or anyone else."

Demos raked him with a contemptuous glance. "War is coming, and you've managed to position your little camp in the most dangerous place possible."

Herne's eyes flared at *little camp*. Demos was incredibly strategic. He was attempting to enrage the rebels for a reason, although I couldn't understand exactly what that reason was.

"Explain," Herne ground out.

Demos smiled. "Gladly." His smile dropped, and his eyes turned icy. "Your position along the fae border is going to be critical for Regner's attack. It's why the Gromalian king is humiliated by his failure to kill all of you. Regner has been moving his regiments south, while Eryndan is likely attempting to negotiate how much of the fae lands he'll be able to take for himself if they're successful in their plans."

"They'll never take the fae lands."

"No." Demos shook his head. "There are creatures there that would kill an entire regiment without blinking. But they could kill my people in our own camp. They could kill thousands of fae and rape their land of magic and resources. Ultimately, if you want to die, that's your choice. But you won't take Tibris with you. Where. Is. He?"

Someone gasped. One of the men who'd first approached us dropped his weapon and stepped back. Herne's face drained of color.

There was only one reason for a reaction like that.

Vynthar stalked out of the forest, his curved horns gleaming in the sunlight.

"What is that?"

"He's a Drakoryx," Demos said. "The hybrid queen considers him a friend."

Vynthar showed his teeth. It was either a threat or his version of a smile. Either way, everyone flinched.

"I suggest you show us where Tibris is," Demos said. The amusement in his voice was so faint, I had a feeling I was the only one who heard it. Well, me and the Drakoryx who'd glanced over his shoulder at Demos.

"I'll take them," a voice rang out.

A woman stepped into the center of the camp. She moved with a kind of feline grace, almost as if she were—

Fae. She wore her human glamour, but I'd spent enough time with Lorian and the others to recognize the way she moved. My eyes narrowed, but Demos slid me a warning look.

I wrestled with the urge to slap him. Of course I wouldn't say anything.

Herne nodded, and at the gesture, the people surrounding us stepped back, sheathing their weapons.

"Fine," he said. "You will see him, and then you will leave."

Both of us ignored that. Herne truly seemed to think we would leave this place without Tibris.

The woman led us down one of the paths, toward the far end of their camp. I hadn't been able to see this far from our tree, so I paid careful attention to the tents, which increased in size as we moved closer to the river.

"What is your name?" I asked.

"Quirala."

"And what are you doing here?" Demos growled.

"I follow my king's orders," she said, her voice so low it was almost a whisper. It was clear she didn't mean Herne. No, Conreth had placed her here. Just how many other spies did the fae king have in places we weren't aware of?

"Do the others know what you are?" I asked.

Quirala gave one sharp nod. "There are other fae here too. Those who lost faith in our people, yet craved a community."

It was clear from her tone that she wasn't one of them. She was solely here to spy for Conreth.

Demos obviously wanted to question her further, but she'd stopped at one of the tents. She gestured for us to step inside, and Demos caught my wrist, neatly stepping in front of me.

As I'd expected, no one was lying in wait to attack us. Instead, Tibris shot to his feet. With a laugh, he threw his arms around me and squeezed. I squeezed back, pressing a kiss to his cheek. "From Pris."

He grinned at me. Demos stepped forward and hugged him as well, slapping him on the back. "Good to see you're alive."

"Good to be alive."

I surveyed him. No scars or visible sickness. He'd jumped up quickly, walking without limping. Some of the tension left my shoulders.

"What happened?" I asked.

Tibris sighed, sat on his cot, and gestured for us to sit

with him. I planted myself on the end of the bed, while Demos shook his head and prowled the tent like a caged animal.

"I did everything wrong when I got here. But…they did a few things wrong too. When I arrived, I thought the best option would be to walk right up to the sentries and announce my presence."

It made sense. Tibris was a healer, and coming in unarmed *was* the best option.

"And?" Demos asked.

Tibris winced. "One of the sentries got a little too excited. He shot me."

Fury bubbled in my stomach, and I let out a low hiss.

A hard glint entered Demos's eye. Tibris waved a hand. "Thankfully, he wasn't a very good shot. His bolt went through my arm. But it was enough to throw me off-balance, and when I fell, I hit my head on a rock." He winced again, this time clearly embarrassed. "When I woke up, the most beautiful man I'd ever seen was leaning over me, scowling as if I'd been created to make his life more difficult."

I hid a smile. I knew that look. I'd seen Lorian giving Prisca that exact look more than a few times.

"And the name of this beautiful man?" I asked.

"Herne."

I sighed. Of course it was.

Demos echoed my sigh. "The rebel leader. Did they have a healer?"

Tibris glanced down. "That's the problem. The last time the Gromalians struck, Eryndan had ordered his men to wait until the rebels were dragging away their dead and healing their injured before the rest of his regiment attacked. Herne had two healers with my kind of power. Both of them were killed."

My stomach clenched at the thought. These were the kinds of men we were dealing with. Those who would purposefully aim for innocents and healers.

"If they had no healers with magic, who helped you when you arrived?" I asked.

Tibris shrugged. "They cleaned my wounds, used healer's paste, and my wounds healed naturally."

Fury burned in my belly. The rebels' sentry had wounded Tibris, and they hadn't even had a healer to help him. What if it hadn't been his arm that had been hit?

Tibris was still talking, and I forced myself to focus.

"After I'd rested for a couple of days, Herne came back. I told him who I was. And that I was a healer. He made it clear he had no interest in allying with the hybrids or fae."

"I'm assuming you tried to leave?" I asked.

Tibris nodded, although something in his expression told me he hadn't tried too hard. I narrowed my eyes at him, and he sighed. "They didn't have any healers," he said again.

On the other side of the tent, Demos pinched the bridge of his nose. "So you decided to prove to them exactly how useful you could be?"

Tibris glowered back. "They knew who I was. It was evident I was a hostage—at least until they sent a message to Prisca."

And he hadn't been able to help himself. Healers were compelled to heal, and Tibris's heart was bigger than most.

"A fae delegation showed up a while ago," Tibris said. "Herne refused to allow them entry. I assume that was Lorian's doing?"

"He was trying to get you back before Prisca learned you'd been taken."

Tibris's expression softened slightly.

Demos folded his arms. "We're staying a few days. We need to wait to hear if Prisca and the others free Jamic—and where we need to travel next. That gives us some time to convince Herne to drag his head out of his ass. I want to get a good look at how this camp runs. Since you're so close to him, you can convince him not to make this an issue."

PRISCA

A cool breeze ruffled my hair, the air tinged with the distant scent of salt from the sea. A blanket of stars had emerged above our heads, while below us, the sounds of the slums cut through the night. Someone was cursing, low and vicious. Several children ran past, little more than barefoot blurs in the dim light. Dogs barked, carriages rolled down the cobbled streets, and laughter spilled out when someone opened the brothel door.

Next to me, Galon and Rythos passed a flask between them, murmuring quietly. Lorian had flung his arm around my shoulders, while Telean had climbed up with us, insisting that she wanted to watch the gatehouses as well.

It was difficult for her—being left behind so often. She wanted to fight, and yet she knew her body wasn't strong or fast enough.

We'd sent a message to Vicer while we were still traveling here, asking that he familiarize himself with the shifts. Still, all of us had wanted to watch the guards come on and off shift, to ensure we'd know exactly what to expect.

"How exactly will we take down the barrier?" I asked, turning my gaze to the gatehouses in the distance.

No one spoke. Finally, Galon met my gaze. "Regner used the dark book to create it. I don't know if we would need that book to *uncreate* it, or if the barrier could be broken with brute force. Perhaps if we gathered enough people with enough power, we could finally take it down."

It was a huge risk. But I couldn't see any other option. "No one has ever tried that before?" I asked.

Galon shook his head. "So many hybrids still don't even know what they are. And those who do are often distrustful of the fae. And our people?" He glanced at Lorian.

Lorian's expression turned grim. "Conreth couldn't even convince the fae to cooperate long enough to attempt to bring it down as soon as he learned of it—before Regner had reinforced it multiple times."

"There's one thing we're not taking into account," Galon said. "It's possible the barrier will recognize Jamic's power. Not only will he be brimming with stolen human power, but his magical signature will be the same as the other boys who were sacrificed before him. We can't rely on this, however. We need to gather the most powerful hybrids we have. As for the fae," he sighed. "We need more people. Regner will do everything he can to prevent us from bringing down that barrier."

"We're going to need to negotiate with Conreth," Rythos said.

Lorian nodded, stretching out his long legs as he took my hand. "My brother will be difficult to deal with after the way I left. But once he learns of Regner's plan to take down the barrier and steal the power, he will listen. Besides, we need to be able to protect Jamic while we determine if he can actually help us bring the barrier down."

I took a deep breath. "Perhaps you should go to the fae lands, and I'll travel directly to Daharak—"

"Not happening." Lorian's expression was blank, except for the stubborn look in his eye that told me he was unrelenting in this. He'd made a decree, and he expected that everyone would fall in line. Including me.

I reached for patience. I didn't have much available.

"I don't want to separate either," I said, my voice even. "But if we successfully rescue Jamic, it's likely that

Regner will lash out. We need to be moving forward with our own plans."

"I said no."

I pulled my hand from his. I loved this stubborn fae bastard with everything in me, but gods, sometimes I wanted to slam my fist into his gut. If some miracle occurred and we went on to grow old together after this war, this would be what our lives would be like. A never-ending battle for dominance.

His brows lowered into a dark scowl. "Think, wildcat. Do you really believe this is the best action, or are you just mad because I told you no?"

"You don't *tell* me anything, Lorian."

Rythos chuckled. Everyone else had various expressions of amusement on their faces. Except my aunt, who leaned past Rythos to shake her head at me. "You could have had a nice hybrid man," she told me. "You took him on, and now you'll have to live with the consequences."

My life was ludicrous. Despite my fury, a laugh bubbled up from deep inside me. My aunt was right. If I was going to fall in love at the most inconvenient time in my life, I could have found someone even-tempered and rational. Instead, I'd somehow found the opposite.

I fixed Lorian with a hard stare.

He raised his eyebrow.

"Imagine we weren't mates," I said. "Would you still make the same suggestion?"

"Imagine you weren't grieving for Cavis and

drowning in guilt for his death. Would you still be attempting to protect everyone at the risk of your own life?"

Lorian's question sucked all the air from my lungs, and I flinched. There was no amusement on anyone's face now. He took my hand once more, pressing his mouth to my knuckles. "The pirate queen isn't going to ask you to do something easy. You'll need our help. Besides, I can't negotiate with Conreth on behalf of the hybrids. That's up to you."

I could see his point.

That didn't mean I was happy about it.

Lorian gave me a faint smile, clearly amused. As much as he enjoyed it when I outmaneuvered him, he also loved when he did the same to me.

I wasn't going to win this argument. At least not right now. So I moved my attention to other concerns. "Stillcrest is a problem. I respect the fact that she's managed to keep her people safe, but the chances of them staying that way are decreasing by the day."

Galon sighed. "She's unlikely to change her mind anytime soon. I have a few fae in the area. I trained them myself. I can ask them to help guard the camp."

Some of the tightness in my chest eased. "Thank you."

"Don't thank me yet. We need to talk about what will happen if we can't get the boy out of the city."

For a moment, I didn't understand. Was he referring to the amount of power Regner would suddenly have at his fingertips?

Our eyes met, and I sucked in a breath.

"You're suggesting killing him if we can't rescue him."

Rythos cleared his throat. "We have to think about the worst that can happen, Pris. If we can't get Jamic out, and Regner uses him…we're all dead. If Regner can't use Jamic to take his power—and drain the barrier of that power—then we're no worse off."

"You think he's a reasonable loss." My stomach hollowed out. Just the thought made me want to vomit.

Lorian's expression was carefully blank. But I knew him. This was the man who had brutally murdered my attacker at the inn that night so long ago. That decision had come easily to him—the man had hurt me, so he was dead, and I should appreciate it.

Unlike that occasion, Lorian wouldn't enjoy killing Jamic. But if there was one thing my mate was good at, it was making logical, often cold-blooded, decisions.

He was—and always would be—exceptionally ruthless. Part of me loved that about him. He made me more strategic with my own decisions, helping me remove the emotion from them.

But I couldn't remove emotion from this one.

"We do everything we can to keep him alive. Please."

Lorian nodded. "Of course we will. He's much more useful breathing."

That wasn't what I'd meant. But the conversation was irrelevant anyway. Jamic wasn't going to die—not just because he'd spent so much of his life locked away and hadn't even truly gotten a chance to live. No, he wasn't going to die because I refused to let Regner kill him.

Someone let out an irritated huff, and I glanced over my shoulder. Madinia stuck her head out of the attic window. "We need to get ready to go. Now."

17

PRISCA

Rothnic's favored gambling den wasn't far from our new safe house. Vicer had quickly realized that if we wanted to get close to him, we needed to blend in to his surroundings.

Rothnic would instantly recognize Lorian and Marth. Galon and Rythos were too large and threatening to be able to spend too much time around the illicit gambling haven. They would draw far too much attention.

That left Madinia and me.

My blond curls had been loosened, covering most of my face. The heavy rouge, red mouth paint, and dark kohl changed my appearance significantly—as did the low-cut gown I was wearing.

When I stepped into the main room, Lorian took one look at me and growled, his gaze hot as it drifted over me. I knew that expression. He was wondering if there was some way for this plan to go ahead without me.

Rythos laid a hand on his arm. "Necessary," he told him.

I met Lorian's eyes and gave him a bawdy wink. "Well hello, handsome."

A flicker of amusement entered his eyes. "I'll be staying close while you're walking through the streets baring that much skin." His gaze landed on my collarbone before trailing lower, and I shivered at the heat in his eyes.

"If you're nice to me, perhaps I'll keep the dress on later," I breathed.

He took a single step closer and leaned down, his nose brushing my throat. "I'll be very, very nice to you, wildcat."

My knees turned weak, and he smiled against my neck.

Rythos made a gagging sound. Without looking, Lorian lashed out with his fist. Even I could hear the dull thump as it made contact, and Rythos cursed.

"It's time," Vicer announced, leaning his head in the door. I wiggled out of Lorian's arms, and Vicer nodded to me. "You know what to do?"

"Yes." Tonight, I would finally learn what Vicer's power was. Without him and Marth, we would have needed to torture Rothnic. As someone who'd recently been tortured myself, I'd felt my stomach churn at the thought. But when I'd broached the subject, Vicer had shaken his head. "Marth can get what we need," he'd said. "And I can make sure he doesn't know what we've done. But I'll need several minutes alone with him, and the guards on the door of the gambling den would notice me loitering."

I moved into the main room, where Madinia was dressed similarly to me. While I felt—and likely looked—awkward and uncomfortable, her dress fit her like a glove. Her hair was still dark, although it had faded enough that it was rust-colored in places. The dark kohl encircling her shockingly blue eyes made them almost appear to glow. Even her cheekbones seemed somehow higher. Sharper. She radiated a cool, amused confidence.

"I could really learn to hate you," I muttered.

She just raised an eyebrow. "Stop slumping over like that."

I sighed, pulling my shoulders back, and she nodded approvingly. Vicer, Madinia, Lorian, and I all filed downstairs. Marth had already left with Galon earlier, Telean was writing letters to her contacts in Gromalia, while Rythos was at the tavern, keeping an eye on Rothnic.

Vicer walked out of the brothel first, hands in his pockets, stride unhurried, his dark ponytail stark against the crimson velvet of his jacket.

He looked like a rich, bored noble—likely with a wife at home. I stood next to Madinia, and we watched out the small window until he'd disappeared down the street. He would walk slowly so we could follow him.

Lorian leaned over and nuzzled my cheek. "Be careful."

"I will."

He nodded at Madinia. "Good luck."

She shot him a cool smile. "I don't need luck."

Linking her arm through mine, she steered me out of the brothel exit, and we strolled away, as if getting some fresh air between clients.

A woman passed us, her dress a dark emerald green, her cheeks brightened with just a little more rouge than my own. Her lush mouth curved as our gazes met, eyes glittering. I'd seen her whispering with Vicer earlier. She knew what we were up to, and from the smirk on her face, she approved. I nodded back at her.

Lorian had prowled into the night, but I could feel his eyes on me. He was close, and he'd stay that way.

Eventually, we caught up to Vicer, staying at least ten footspans behind him. He was standing, hands clasped behind him, peering into a store window. When he wandered away, we slowly followed. Madinia leaned close to whisper in my ear.

"You look like you're about to vomit."

I threw my head back and attempted a laugh. She just sighed.

Vicer tapped three fingers on his thigh and then hurried away. Just a few footspans later, we were standing across the street from the gambling den.

Even without Vicer's signal, the location would have been obvious by the large, burly men who stood against the wall outside, clearly guarding the door. The one on the left was shorter than the one on the right, but both looked as if they could punch through the stone wall, sprint to the city gates and back, and then casually hold a conversation without even breaking a sweat.

Several other women of the night had taken up residence on the street, leaning against doorways or positioning themselves near conveniently located alleys. Madinia and I found a free spot—moving after a woman hissed at us that our first choice was *her fucking territory*.

Dirt lined the cobblestones beneath our feet as we placed our backs against the brick wall of the building behind us. I scanned the street, lingering on the broken windows gaping at us from the building next to the gambling den.

The street smelled dank, heavy with the aroma of burned wood and the pungent odors of stale sweat, cigar smoke, and cheap perfume.

All we could do now was wait, listening to the clicking of heels on the cobblestone, the jingle of coins in pockets as groups of men and the occasional couple strolled into the gambling den.

Vicer had asked one of his rebels to study Rothnic's routine. Apparently, it was likely he'd stumble out of the gambling den within the next hour or two. The longer we stayed in the city, the more dangerous it was for us, so we'd gotten here early, unwilling to risk missing Rothnic and wasting a night.

With nothing else to distract me, my thoughts returned to Tibris. To Demos and Asinia. Tibris was kind, warmhearted, and prone to putting others before himself. But he was also iron-willed, unwavering in his determination. I had to remember that. Had to remember that he was more than he'd pretended to be while we were growing up in that village. He'd been a rebel. He'd managed to find me when I was with Lorian and the others. He'd healed Asinia and Demos, and hundreds of other prisoners, and worked to free them—right beneath Regner's nose.

Madinia nudged me.

A thin, well-dressed man was walking toward us, and I snapped my mouth closed, pasting an inviting smile on my face. He looked at Madinia, and his eyes widened in awe. "You're beautiful." He glanced at me. "So are you. How much for both of you together?"

I could feel Lorian's eyes on me, a warm comfort. Madinia tilted her head, giving him a disparaging look. "It's not enough for you for one of us to pretend to be satisfied by your fumbling incompetence? You need both of us to feign pleasure to feed your ego?"

His mouth dropped open. So did mine. Somewhere above us, Lorian chuckled, the sound so low, I doubted the man could hear it.

"You fucking whore," the man snarled, leaning close to Madinia.

She just gave him a bored look. "Leave," she ordered imperiously.

His eyes widened. Shock flickered across his face, followed by confusion. But he stumbled away, practically running down the street.

I surveyed our surroundings, but thankfully, no one was paying any attention. Madinia's temper had gotten progressively worse lately.

She turned her attention back to me, as if we hadn't been interrupted. "You're worried about Tibris."

"Yes."

"You should be."

I shouldn't have been surprised by Madinia's bluntness. Yet I constantly was.

This time, Lorian's low growl was clear and full of threat. Even Madinia cast a wary look upward.

But she met my eyes anyway. "You'd be an idiot if you weren't worried. But you have to focus on what you can control. You've done everything you can in this moment to help him. Demos knows how much he means to you." Her mouth twisted. Demos and Madinia still didn't get along. "And Asinia..." Her voice trailed off, and she glanced away.

"What is it?"

"She would do anything for you," Madinia said. "Just like you would for her."

"Yes." I couldn't read her expression, and I leaned close. "What is it?"

"Nothing."

"Madinia—"

She lowered her voice, until I was sure even Lorian would have struggled to hear her. "You should appreciate what you have, that's all. A friend you can trust that much is a gift."

She'd said it as if she'd never experienced such friendship. I cleared my throat. "What about Lisveth or any of the others?"

She sent me a poisonous look. "You were there. You know what they were like."

"Yes, I was there, and I remember *you* were the one who was constantly lashing out."

Her mouth tightened. "When I had seen fifteen winters, Alcandre started a rumor that I was sleeping with the king. When I had seen sixteen winters, Pelopia convinced me we could be friends, and when I fell asleep after talking to her that night, she cut off all my hair. When I had seen eighteen winters, Caraceli and Katina put some kind of charmed herb into my drink, ensuring I lost consciousness at one of Regner's balls. Thankfully, my father was the one to find me and not Davis. Those were just a few of the incidents over the years."

I ground my teeth. Caraceli was the one who'd poisoned me in the castle. If not for Lorian, I would have died.

"I'm sorry."

Madinia's face somehow turned colder. "I don't need your apologies. Just stop feeling sorry for yourself. Instead of dwelling on how the people you love are in danger, try turning your attention to how lucky you are to love and be loved by that many people."

She was right. After watching Cavis be murdered, I was crippled by fear. I still woke screaming several times a night, fresh from nightmares where Lorian was the one being tortured. And then Asinia. And then Tibris. My mind provided constant fuel for the nightmares, and during the day, my thoughts spun uselessly, attempting to control the uncontrollable.

I opened my mouth, but Madinia let out a low hiss. "Here he comes."

Rothnic walked with the careful stride of the impaired. He didn't stumble, but his movements were slow, steps meticulously precise.

I'd left the hourglass with Galon, unwilling to risk wearing it through the city. Using my power without it felt...awkward and slow in comparison. But I pulled at the threads of my magic, drawing up my power and focusing on everyone except Madinia and Lorian.

"That's him, Lorian," I said in a hushed whisper. "Tell Vicer."

"Leaving now. Be careful, wildcat."

I could hear in his voice just how little he wanted to leave me.

"I have the dragon," I said, and Madinia let out an amused snort.

"Let's get this done," she said.

We'd positioned ourselves perfectly. Rothnic would have to walk directly past us. Hopefully Galon was ready with our distraction.

My heart raced. Rothnic was ten footspans away. Eight. Six.

My pulse quickened. His cold gray eyes appeared almost black in the dim light, and his features seemed to have sharpened.

Four. Where was our distraction?

Madinia stepped toward Rothnic. He lifted one hand

to wave her off and then froze.

"You."

She grinned. "Me."

"You killed my son."

"Believe me, the bastard had it coming."

A carriage drove past, several drunk passengers singing a bawdy tune. Finally.

Rothnic charged. I leaped forward, tripped him, and guided him into the wall. His face hit with a thunk, and I positioned my knife at his throat. The sound of the men in the carriage echoed down the street.

"Walk," I said.

He was shaking with rage. I let him feel the cool metal of my blade, right up against his throat. "Don't make me tell you again."

I watched him consider his options. Madinia stepped closer, using his body as a shield to hide the fire burning in her palm. "It would be so easy," she crooned.

It *would* be easy. And Madinia knew Rothnic would hunt her for the rest of his life for what she'd done to his son. I gave her a warning look, and she shrugged at me.

Rothnic allowed us to steer him down the alley, stiffening as he noticed Vicer and Marth waiting at the end. Marth was leaning against the wall, arms folded, while Vicer watched us approach with his hands on his hips. "What took you so long?"

Madinia muttered something under her breath, but I was too busy waiting to see Vicer's power. I'd wondered what it was since the moment I'd seen him again after so many years. He'd once told me his power was useful to the king, but he hadn't been able to talk about it.

I'd understood. Even with a power as useful as his was rumored to be, it hadn't been enough to save his lover. She'd been a hybrid with the misfortune of having been captured right before Gods Day. Vicer hadn't been released until after she'd been burned at dawn.

Lorian's gaze was on me once more. I could feel it. I glanced up but couldn't see him.

Marth stepped closer to Rothnic, who slashed out with a knife of his own, aiming it at my gut. I sidestepped, mouth going dry, and Marth caught his hand, easily plucking the knife. A low, dangerous snarl ripped through the night. Rothnic froze.

"I'm fine," I murmured to my overprotective mate.

Marth leaned close to Rothnic, his eyes turning distant. "Jamic was moved because Regner wants him to travel in his carriage to make his defenses more secure. He currently has him in one of the gatehouses along the city wall. Three—no four—to the left from the entrance we used when we arrived."

Rothnic whimpered. Marth just angled his head. "Four guards on the door, three at various points on the stairs, and four up the top of the gatehouse with Jamic. The boy is wrapped in fae iron. We'll need a key for the chains. One of the guards will be holding the key." He stepped back and glanced at Vicer.

"Look at me," Vicer whispered, fixing his gaze on Rothnic. His voice seemed to echo in my ears, and all the fine hairs on my arms stood at attention.

Rothnic looked, and his face turned slack, blank, empty.

Vicer leaned close. So close, their noses were almost touching. And Rothnic's eyes began to flicker back and forth. As if he were dreaming with his eyes open.

Vicer's own eyes darkened, the pupils expanding until only a tiny sliver of gray was visible.

They stood like that for a long time. Long enough that I leaned against the alley wall. Madinia stood so still, she might have been a statue, her eyes burning as she watched Vicer with a considering look.

Finally, Vicer lifted his head. "It was nice to see you tonight," he said. "But you still owe me a rematch."

"I still owe you a rematch," Rothnic repeated. Then he grinned, young and boyish. "Next time, drinks are on me."

"Remember, you had a great time gambling tonight. Nothing out of the ordinary happened. When you walked out of the tavern, you went straight back to the castle."

Rothnic nodded. "Nothing out of the ordinary happened."

He turned and wandered out of the alley, paying no attention to Madinia or me. For a long moment, my mind struggled to understand what we'd just seen.

"He was strong," Vicer said.

"Explain." My voice was hoarse.

He sighed, rubbing his temple in a way that made it clear using his power had hurt him. "I have the power to take and replace memories. It was what made me so useful to the king. I was still learning how to use my power when he killed Rosin, but I knew at some point I would be forced to move in to the castle. And to work directly for him."

The thought of Regner wielding that kind of power made me shiver.

"You could have told me," I said.

Vicer just sighed. "No one truly wants to know what I can do." He nodded at Madinia, who was staring at him as if he were a particularly poisonous creature she needed to kill. "She's wondering if I've ever used my power on her. I could have. I could have used it on all of you, and you would never know."

Both of Madinia's hands lit up, flames at the ready. But I shook my head. "Except that you wouldn't do that. It's not the kind of man you are. If you don't want us to tell anyone what you can do, we won't. But don't be ashamed. You've just saved Jamic's life. And in turn, that will save thousands and thousands of lives. Lives that Regner would snuff out without a second thought."

His eyes met mine. His pupils had returned to normal, and I saw gratitude there now. "Thank you, Pris."

Marth glanced around the filthy alley and sighed. "Let's get out of here."

By the time we got back to the safe house, my eyes kept sliding closed, and my head was pounding. We had one day to ensure Madinia's plans were finalized, Vicer could get his group of hybrids out, Lorian could get to

Jamic, and Madinia and I could get into the castle.

Marth and Rythos left to watch the gatehouse where Jamic was being kept. The choice of location was a clever move by Regner. Not only were the gatehouses incredibly secure, but no one would notice if one of them had a few more guards than usual. They each had just one entrance point and could only be accessed by the guards stationed along the city walls. Not to mention, Jamic was guarded by Regner's most loyal men. By hiding him somewhere other than the castle, he'd ensured none of our spies would be able to find his location. Without Kaliera, we would have been unlikely to have located him in time.

Still, there was still so much that could go wrong.

Lorian's arm came around my stomach, and he closed the bedroom door, holding me in place as he pressed a kiss to my neck.

"It will work," he said.

That was what I was telling myself.

"I have a surprise for you," Lorian murmured.

I attempted to turn in his arms, and he held me still. "What kind of surprise?"

"Come with me." Leaning around my body, he opened the door once more. Taking my hand, he led me through the common room and to the hall near the stairs. He turned, frowning at the wall near a suggestive painting of a barely dressed woman reclining on a sofa.

Raising one hand, he measured a few handspans from the bottom right corner of the painting and pressed against the wall.

The wall swung open. Lorian gave me a smug smile and patted my butt, gesturing for me to enter.

"What is this?"

"A little something I organized. You'll like it."

I had no doubt I would. Taking his hand, I stepped into the dim room. A touch of claustrophobia stole my breath, and Lorian squeezed my hand.

"Almost through." He pressed against something to our right, and another door swung open.

Soft, muted colors painted the walls, which were covered by ornate tapestries. Many of those tapestries were stitched with scenes of couples in intimate positions. Golden sconces were affixed to the walls at regular intervals, casting a soft glow over the plush chaise longue next to the curtained window and the lush velvet cushions scattered on the floor.

In one corner, a fireplace crackled, a set of silver goblets and a carafe of wine waiting on a table nearby.

But it was the tub that held my attention. Carved from what looked like a single piece of opulent white marble, it rested on an elevated platform, the dainty wooden table next to it holding an assortment of bath oils.

Next to me, Lorian shook with laughter, and I realized my mouth was hanging open. And that he'd already stripped off his shirt and was working on his pants.

"What is this place?"

"According to Vicer, it's reserved solely for the wealthiest patrons who refuse to be seen by anyone who could report them visiting such an establishment."

I winced at the thought of Lorian having that conversation with Vicer—and arranging access to such a place. Lorian poked me in the ribs. "Prude. Vicer was only too happy to owe me a favor. Besides, I enjoyed reminding him you're mine."

I gave him a look. There was not, and never had been, anything between Vicer and me. Lorian shrugged. "The water is losing heat."

Steam rose from the tub in gentle curls. I shook my head at his attempt at distraction, but I couldn't help drifting toward the tub. "This is incredible. Thank you."

He was already untying the back of my dress. "I know exactly how I want my payment."

I laughed, and his mouth found mine, stealing the sound as my dress fell to my ankles. He slid his hands up my rib cage, thumbs teasing my nipples, and I let out a shaky breath, my knees weakening.

Lorian pulled away just long enough to step into the tub, pulling me in with him. The warm water slipped over my skin, the heat enveloping my body. I let out an appreciative groan, leaning back against Lorian's chest. I could feel him, hard and thick, behind me, but he pulled me close, plucking one of the glass bottles at random and pouring it straight into his hand.

The scent of jasmine and something I couldn't place wound toward me. Something sensual and heady. Lorian's huge hands found my shoulders, and he began working the tension from my muscles. I groaned as he found a particularly large knot near my neck, and he gently worked on it until I was limp against him.

"Your turn," I said, reaching for the oil. I wanted to soothe him too. Wanted to make him feel as good as I did in this moment.

"This *is* my turn," he murmured into my ear, his slippery hands cupping my breasts.

He tortured me, those hands drifting over my skin, fingers coming close to my nipples but never touching. I groaned, arching for him, and he nibbled my earlobe.

"Why must you always make me crazy?"

He let out a low laugh. "Because hearing you beg for me, seeing you so needy, so *desperate*…there's nothing else like it."

It took some maneuvering, but I slid my hand beneath my back, grasping his cock.

He sucked in a breath, and his thumbs finally grazed my nipples. I attempted to turn, but he slid one arm around my middle, easily holding me in place.

"Not yet," he said. "Let me play with you for a while."

I let out a choked laugh at that, and he pressed a kiss to the side of my neck before slipping his hand slowly down my body, the muscles of his arm bulging in the dim light. He teasingly moved that hand down, between my legs.

I rolled my hips, and he slid his other hand into my hair, angling my head for his kiss. Fog rolled over my mind as heat spread through my body, warmer than the water surrounding us. His tongue moved against mine, his fingers drifting gently over my clit, and I shivered. He'd somehow always known exactly how I longed to be touched.

I gasped against his mouth, and he let out a low growl, his legs pressing against my own and spreading my thighs wider. There was something almost...lewd about this position. And I liked it.

His expert fingers drove me higher and higher, until I threw my head back, arching my hips. My climax rippled through my body, until all I could do was shudder and moan in his arms.

I went limp, and Lorian let out a low chuckle. "Beautiful." He easily lifted me one with arm, positioning his cock at my entrance with the other.

The water lapped at the top of the tub as he pressed into me, guiding my hips down. I groaned, suddenly so full in this position it was almost painful. Lorian went still, returning his fingers to my clit. He gently stroked my swollen nub until I clenched around him, needing *more*.

He began to move, angling his hips up. My belly began to tighten, my nipples becoming even harder.

"Are you going to come for me again, wildcat?"

I nodded, jerking my hips, falling into the rhythm of him thrusting into me.

The pleasure hit with no warning, rolling through my body, and I clamped around Lorian as he cursed, drawing out my pleasure. He slowly rocked his hips, scraping his teeth against my neck as I melted against him.

I needed to see him. Needed to ensure I was giving

him just as much pleasure as he was giving me. Lifting my hips, I turned, my gaze meeting his.

Gods, the way this man looked at me.

Slowly, I slid back down his cock, both of us groaning as I pushed my knees wide, angling him deep. I was swollen, overly sensitive, but the feel of him stroking against my inner walls, caressing that spot deep inside me…

I lifted my hips, sinking back down. His expression tightened, his eyes blazing as they met mine. He moved his hands to my butt, moving me faster, harder.

My head fell back, a strangled moan leaving my throat. He slid his hand into my hair once more, holding me still for him as he claimed my mouth, still ruthlessly plowing into me.

My vision went white as my climax slammed into me with a strength I wasn't expecting. Lorian let out a groan, holding me tight as he continued to thrust, flooding me with warmth.

We clutched each other for a long time. When I finally opened my eyes, the water was cooling around us, and Lorian was leaning back in the tub, his eyes closed.

Some of the tension had drained from his face. He looked suddenly younger. Until he must've felt my gaze on him and opened his eyes. Lightning sparked within them, and I tensed.

"Shh. It's fine, Prisca."

"Is this why you haven't been using your power as much? You've been storing it?"

He nodded. "We'll need it for tomorrow."

"What was it like? Growing up with so much power?"

"Conreth once told me I was born with all this power because the gods had decreed I would protect our kingdom. Our people." A slight frown had appeared between his brows, and I lifted my hand, running my thumb over the lines until they vanished.

"Did you believe that?"

A pause. "It seemed like as good of a reason as any. I never understood it—why I would have been given so much more power than my brother, who would rule. Our parents were gone, so I couldn't ask my father."

"And now?"

He tucked a piece of hair behind my ear. "Now, I believe it was all leading up to this. I had to be powerful for this war, so I could protect you. My mate."

My heart strained, and I pressed a kiss to his knuckles.

"Why have you followed his orders for so long, Lorian?"

"He's my king."

I stayed silent and he sighed. Vulnerability gleamed in his eyes for just an instant. "And he's my brother."

Conreth didn't deserve Lorian. He never had. Lorian had more loyalty in his little finger than Conreth could even conceive of.

I nestled closer to him, and he stroked my back.

"It's the fae, too, isn't it?" I murmured.

I felt him nod. "My people…they've suffered. Not like your people. But losing our power, fighting against

Regner's constant attacks, it has worn them down. They're now just as likely to turn on one another as they are to fight our enemies. And Conreth…" His voice tightened, and he was silent for a long moment. "He could have achieved so much more. Over the last few decades, at every opportunity to make our people stronger, he focused instead on cementing his power. My father would be so disappointed in him, Prisca. And yet my mother would be brokenhearted at the fact that we can barely look at each other."

My throat ached. How had Conreth turned out this way? Why?

"He sees you as a threat," I said.

"Yes. I would never turn on him. I never wanted power. I just wanted a brother. Seeing the way you love yours, the way you'd do anything for them without question, it hurts."

"I'm sorry."

"No, wildcat." He dropped a kiss to my head. "Don't misunderstand me. I adore seeing it, and I'm so fucking happy you have family like that. Family who would protect you, no matter what. But I look at how you and Demos would die for each other already—I'll never forget how he took that arrow for Tibris, simply to spare you pain. And yet Conreth…"

I nodded. Conreth would wrestle any happiness from his brother without a second thought if it was more convenient for him. And yet…Lorian was naturally respected by his people. He was also ruthless, arrogant, unyielding, and stubborn. Not to mention, he was more powerful than Conreth. So why had he put up with Conreth for so long?

"What are you thinking?" he asked.

I told him and he sighed. "Galon and the others. Conreth allows us to stay together simply because I follow his orders. Bad things happen when we separate."

He was silent for a long moment, and I knew he was thinking of Cavis. His arms tightened around me. "Once, twenty years ago, I refused to follow one of Conreth's orders. In retaliation, he decided each of us was needed in different places across the fae lands and Gromalia."

"He split you up."

"Yes. Marth…with most of his power gone, he was vulnerable. He nearly died. Conreth made his point."

I was shaking with fury, retribution burning in my gut. Lorian attempted to soothe me, gently stroking my back, and I forced myself to take a deep breath. I couldn't make Conreth be the brother Lorian deserved. It was unlikely that would ever happen.

Lorian's hands slid low on my back. "Leave it, Prisca. Be with me."

I heard what he wasn't saying. We had such little time together like this. We needed to make the most of each and every moment. Turning to run my lips along his neck, I smiled as he tensed. "Why don't you distract me then, hmm?"

18

PRISCA

By the time we were ready to go through with our plan the next night, my heart seemed to have lodged itself in my throat. Even after reluctantly agreeing that this was the best strategy, Lorian held me close, nuzzling my hair. "I don't like this."

"I don't either. But I'll have the dragon."

Next to me, Madinia heaved a put-upon sigh. Lorian's chest shook with his chuckle.

He clasped my chin in his hand, tilting my head until he was staring down into my eyes. "Be careful," he said.

"You too."

"Time to go," Rythos announced. "Everyone else is ready."

Lorian's gaze met his, and Rythos nodded. "I'll bring her back to you."

I glanced at Galon, who rolled his eyes at me. "And I'll bring him back to you. You'd think you two had never been parted before." But he gave me a faint smile of understanding. He had, after all, been present while Lorian had killed his way across this continent looking for me.

Lorian's mouth found mine, and I breathed in the scent of him one last time before forcing myself to step out of his arms.

He turned, following Galon and Marth, while I fell into step with Rythos and Madinia. We needed to be in position. It was time to rescue Jamic.

Winding through alleys reeking of rot and piss, we made our way deeper into the slums. Someone let out a hacking cough, while a child wailed incessantly. The cool night air did nothing to remove the sweat on the back of my neck.

Gradually, the dwellings shifted from sagging wood and crumbling brick to tidy inns and stores. We kept walking silently, cloaks pulled over our heads as our surroundings transitioned to sprawling homes with sculpted gardens in the neighborhood surrounding the castle. I barely breathed as we turned toward the castle itself. It loomed over the city, the dark stone walls swallowing the light from the many lanterns and light orbs surrounding it. Next to me, Madinia maintained a cold, distant expression. I couldn't imagine spending most of my life here and then fleeing the way she'd had to.

The guards were stationed in their usual spots at the castle gatehouse.

My heart thundered in my chest. I reached for my power, even knowing I needed to save it for later. But

Rythos caught my hand and squeezed. His eyes were calm, reassuring. The next part of the plan depended entirely on him.

"Oi, you!"

Rythos smiled at the guard stalking toward us. And then he seemed to come alive. His skin glowed, his eyes turned lively and warm, and he grinned at the guard.

The guard grinned back. "About time you got here," he said. "The others won't believe you've stopped in."

My breath caught in my throat. It was working.

The guard glared at me and Madinia. "Who are they?"

"They're my friends," Rythos smiled easily.

"I thought *I* was your friend." The guard's lower lip stuck out. Behind me, Madinia made a choked sound.

"You are. I wanted to introduce you to my other friends too. It's so nice to have lots of friends, don't you think?"

"I suppose. But I'm your *best* friend." The guard slitted his eyes threateningly at me.

I clamped down on the inappropriate laugh that wanted to escape. Rythos just nodded at the guard. "That's right. Can you open the gate for us?"

The guard waved his hand. "You'll have to keep quiet. We've had a little trouble recently," he confided. "The king has us all on lockdown, and Marinith won't like that I'm letting you in. Paranoid old bastard."

This was both astonishing and incredibly unsettling. The guard actually believed Rythos was his close friend.

And he was complaining about his superiors to him as if he'd done so many times before.

I understood now, why Rythos had been so hurt soon after I'd first met him, when Lorian had succumbed to what I now knew was jealousy—implying that Rythos had used that power on me. Lorian had known he hadn't, of course—had lashed out in a way that was extremely rare for him.

If Rythos had used his power on me, I would have told him anything he needed to know. He would have instantly been my best friend, my only friend, and if he'd told me to trust Lorian and the others, I would have done it without question.

I shivered.

In the distance, something exploded, the sound ripping through the night even this far from the city gates.

My eyes met Madinia's. That was our signal. The Cleaver had struck. Now, chaos would reign on the streets of Lesdryn.

"Stay safe," Rythos told us. He melted away. If everything went according to plan, his new best friends would find Cavis's body so we could take him home—all while Rythos kept the other guards and servants contained.

Meanwhile, we'd be creating our own chaos right here in the castle. But first, we had to meet with Kaliera.

Lorian hadn't been happy about this part of our plan. But she was helping us—for her own reasons, yes, but she was still helping us. One quick conversation could save us days of messages back and forth. Besides, I wanted to look into her eyes and judge just how much she could be trusted.

Reaching for my power, I paused time. The hourglass tugged at my magic, urging me to use more and more. Wrestling with it, I clamped down, refusing to allow it to drain me completely. Just the thought of being powerless in this castle made my hands tremble.

We sprinted through the servants' entrance and up the stairs, making our way to the queen's chambers. Strolling past the lone guard on the door, we let ourselves in, Madinia closing the door behind us.

I dropped the threads of my power. Watching the queen whirl, her back to the window as fear flickered in her eyes...I'd be lying if I didn't admit I enjoyed her moment of helplessness.

Still, her face immediately settled into its usual bored arrogance. She cast a dismissive gaze over Madinia, tutting at her faded hair, before turning a considering look on the hourglass around my neck.

"Why aren't you busy freeing my son?"

"We are. But how do we know we can trust you, Kaliera?"

Her eyes flared at my use of her first name. But I would no longer bow and scrape to this woman. Those gray eyes shuttered, her mouth twisting, and she seemed to steel herself.

"Because Sabium will kill him otherwise."

"You expect me to believe that someone like you cares about someone other than herself?"

Her mouth thinned. "I also care about my own life. It is far too late for you to get help from any other continent. If Sabium takes that power, he will be a *god*. Unstoppable."

I knew that much. "After we free Jamic, then what happens?"

"You find a way to kill Sabium, and this continent will finally see peace."

Peace. And where would Kaliera end up after the war? I was betting she was already mentally redecorating the throne room of this castle.

I glanced at Madinia, but she wasn't looking at me. No, she was studying the queen carefully.

The moment I killed Regner, Kaliera would come for me. I wasn't stupid enough to believe she would allow me to become a threat to her power by claiming the hybrid throne. But just how close was she to her son? When we freed him, would he turn on us when we least expected it?

I crossed my arms. "What exactly are you proposing?"

"A formal alliance."

"And what would this alliance look like?"

"We both want the same thing—Jamic free and Sabium dead."

It was strange that she still called him Sabium, even knowing his name was truly Regner. It was as if she was unable to reconcile the fact that he'd lived for much, much longer than she could have imagined.

"And what will you be doing while we're risking our lives?"

"You don't think slipping you information is risking my own life? I am the one who told Madinia where Sabium was keeping you. And yet you haven't thanked me for it, Hybrid Heir."

Her voice had turned frigid, as if I were still one of her underlings. Not long ago, such a tone would have made me feel achingly small. Now, I just raised one eyebrow, staring back at her.

"You needed Prisca alive to save Jamic," Madinia said, her tone bored. "Don't pretend you helped us for any other reason."

Kaliera sent her an irritated look, then turned back to me, her face tight. "You'd be a special kind of idiot to turn down information directly from this castle. From Sabium's table. His throne room."

Unfortunately, she was right. I might not trust her, but she wanted Regner dead just as much as I did. And she knew she couldn't accomplish that herself.

"If he finds out you helped us, he'll kill you."

She gave me a humorless smile. "No, he'll make me wish I were dead. For months. Believe me, I know exactly how high the stakes are. I'm trusting you not to betray me either."

I kept her secrets. She kept mine. And at the end, when Regner was finally dead, we would turn on each other.

Just the thought made my muscles ache with exhaustion. But I took a single step closer to her. "If you betray us, we'll make what Regner would do to you look merciful."

Surprise flickered through her eyes. She stared at me for a long moment, and I let her see just how serious I was. I let her see just how much I'd changed, and how little tolerance and patience I had left.

She sighed. "You need to—"

One of Kaliera's mirrors was flickering. My knife seemed to jump into my hand, while Madinia created a fireball the size of my head. We stepped farther apart, giving each other room to move.

An old woman walked through the mirror. The first thing I noticed about her was her eyes. They were dark and yet somehow familiar. The second thing I noticed was her power. The dark magic leaked from her, until the tiny hairs on the back of my neck stood up. A glance at Madinia told me she was just as wary, one of her palms still lit with orange flames as she watched the woman.

"Are you mad?" Kaliera asked in a strangled whisper. "You can't come here."

The old woman cast her an unconcerned look that made Madinia snort a laugh. Kaliera looked at Madinia for a long moment before narrowing her eyes at the old woman.

"Miss the chance to meet the hybrid heir? I think not." The woman stepped close to me, and I tensed. Next to me, Madinia moved closer as well. The woman paid no attention to the threat she presented.

"Who are you?" I asked.

"Never mind that. I have dreamed of you, Hybrid

Heir. In fact, I've had visions of your future for years now."

A seer. I couldn't seem to escape them.

"My name is Prisca."

She waved that away. "You will travel to my daughter," she said to me. And I stared at her. Her daughter?

"Daharak," she said.

I opened my mouth. What was the pirate queen's mother doing in this castle with Kaliera?

She held up her hand before I could speak. "Your plan is a good one, and if my daughter can be reasoned with, she will give you what you so desperately need. But listen closely because if she does not get what she is looking for, she will never work with you again. Even if she cannot blame you for the mistake, her pride and rage will overtake her sense. It may only be temporary, but it will be long enough that you will lose this war, and everyone in this kingdom will suffer."

My skin itched, as if it had shrunk around me. "Tell me what I need to know."

"When bound by blockade's tightening fist, heed the drifting shadow, else all be lost. To prevail, dance the sails toward the sun."

"That's it?" Why was it seers so often spoke in strange riddles?

She nodded, and her expression turned mournful now. It was difficult to know if she truly felt the emotion or if she had placed it on like a mask.

"In my dreams, I have seen what will come to pass."

I swallowed. From her tone, what was coming to pass wasn't exactly going to be joyful. "And?"

"You believe you have lost enough. That the gods wouldn't be cruel enough to take more from you." She shook her head. "You should never believe such things. The gods delight in cruelty."

My mouth turned dry. So dry, it took me a moment to speak. "Who?"

"When the land itself repels war and unnatural clouds obscure the sun…

When the waves are coerced…and reflection deceives…

The Bloodthirsty Prince will die."

LORIAN

Crouched in shadow, we watched the gatehouse. Torches flared along the parapets above, the orange glow flickering in the slight breeze. Shouts and clashing steel echoed from the street as our distraction raged within the city.

All of my instincts rebelled at separating from Prisca. Yet I knew this was the best plan. The human queen would likely be closemouthed in my presence, while my power ensured I was necessary to free Jamic. Still...

"She will be fine," Galon muttered. "If you lose focus, we'll be the ones who fail to walk away from this."

He had a point. With Prisca's time magic, Madinia's fire, and Rythos's own inexplicable power, we'd prepared for every eventuality. Yet I knew my wildcat. If there was an extra chance to strike at Regner, or a way to free an imprisoned hybrid on her way out of the castle...

The first gatehouse exploded. Marth grinned at me, his eyes wide. "You have to admit, Madinia was smart to involve the Cleaver."

She was. Now the criminals the Cleaver had summoned would be attacking from all angles, ensuring the guards were confused and distracted.

The iron guards Regner had in place were his best. They would tighten security in Jamic's gatehouse. But we'd prepared for that too.

Another gatehouse exploded. The guards surrounding Jamic would be wondering if they were next. Some of them would be convinced that this attack had nothing to do with Jamic, and if they didn't flee the gatehouse, they were dead.

Others would insist that they needed to stay, trusting their instincts.

I smiled, picturing the chaos.

The air reeked of smoke and fear-sweat. The gatehouse we needed stood silent, its heavy wooden door likely still barred.

A flicker of movement appeared in the upper level. Galon tensed, and I nodded. I'd seen it too. Four iron guards peered out into the chaotic city.

Now.

"Are you ready?" I asked.

Galon nodded. While his mastery of water was his strongest power, his wards were also some of the best I'd seen. They would ensure we weren't taken by surprise.

"Now," I said.

The three of us moved toward the gatehouse. Immediately, arrows filled the air, the bolts gleaming in the dim light of the torches. Fae iron.

Galon grunted as they hit his ward.

Focusing on the wooden door, I pulled my power to me, basking in the feel of it crackling beneath my skin. It exploded in a lethal arc, shattering the door before us with a resounding crack. Wooden shards flew inward, instantly killing anyone stupid enough to be in the way.

The boy was upstairs on the second level. And by now, he would be surrounded by all four of the guards who'd disappeared from their spots by the window.

Just as we'd planned.

Marth twirled his sword in his hand, his expression colder than I'd ever seen it.

Acrid smoke billowed from the obliterated entrance, and we strode inside. I stepped over the charred remains of a guard caught in the blast zone, turning to meet the sword that slashed toward my face.

Spinning out of the way, I sliced at his side. My

sword carved through muscle and bone, and he screamed, collapsing to his knees. Another swipe of my sword, and he fell, eyes empty.

Galon and Marth had already killed the other three guards. I flicked my gaze to the stairs and back to them. Galon nodded.

No sound came from the second level. But I could feel them up there, waiting. I raised my eyebrow at Galon. He nodded again. He could continue warding us just long enough to get upstairs. It wouldn't protect us from hand-to-hand anyway. Wards were best suited for projectiles and power-based attacks.

Marth positioned himself near the remains of the door, ready to guard it against anyone who approached.

Silently, Galon and I climbed the stairs. They had the advantage—we'd be exposed as soon as we crested the top steps. But if Galon said his ward would hold, then it would hold.

The iron guards struck fast from the shadows. Arrows hit Galon's ward and dropped. I counted six. And there would be more, still guarding the boy. "Ward," Galon warned.

"Drop it," I said.

His ward disappeared. I whirled, smashing bone, slicing limbs, conserving my power for later. Next to me, Galon fought with methodical precision, his every movement perfectly calibrated to do maximum damage with minimum effort.

I ran my gaze around the upper level. Shadows clung

to the circular chamber's stone walls, dispelled only by the flickering of mounted torches. The room was sparse—a wooden table and chairs, a couple of narrow cots, a few weapon racks lining the perimeter.

In the rear of the room, a heavy oak door was reinforced with iron bands. The entrance to the cells.

A door that was currently swinging open.

PRISCA

"The Bloodthirsty Prince will die."

My lungs seized, my stomach hollowed out, and a fine trembling began in my limbs.

"You're lying." The word was strangled. Next to me, Madinia took a step closer.

"His death will ignite a rage in you that has never been seen before and will never be seen again." The seer glanced at Madinia. "You must find a way to help her channel that rage and not become lost to it. Or she will doom all of us."

Madinia's mouth thinned. Her face was pale. The old woman scowled at her before turning back to me. "Even now, you refuse to believe me. You must direct that stubbornness into a will to survive. To make sure your people survive."

"Why would you tell her this?" Madinia hissed. "Are you trying to torture her? To make her second-guess her every decision?"

"I am trying to prepare her. She can control many things, but she cannot control the fates."

"Fuck the fates," Madinia snapped.

I seemed to have become incapable of speech. My mind had gone cloudy, as if I couldn't even fully form thoughts. All I could see was Lorian's face.

And then Ysara's voice tripped through my head. *"Enjoy your time with your fae prince. But know this— you cannot keep him."*

Had she been warning me, even then?

"You must go," the woman said. "You have lingered here for too long."

With a final glance at the queen, I turned away, stumbling toward the door. Madinia led me along the servants' hall, both of us ignoring the choked gasps from anyone who recognized us.

"If you want to keep your life, stay away from the throne room," Madinia announced to any servants we came across. She lit up her hand and kept her fire burning threateningly as we made our way down the stairs. It was eerie, with most of the servants and guards busy with Rythos. Many of the others were with Regner, while still more were outside gawking at the carnage beyond the castle gates.

The queen had prepared ahead of time, ensuring that Auria was out of the castle on some useless overnight errand. As a null, she was one of the few threats to this part of the plan.

I would never forget how she had removed my ability to access my power.

"Prisca," Madinia prodded me, her voice grim.

"Don't tell Lorian." Was that my voice? It sounded so far away.

She grabbed my hand, forcing me to stop, and her eyes narrowed at whatever she saw on my face. "If you think you're carrying this alone, you're wrong."

I blinked, forcing myself to focus on our conversation. But all I could hear was the seer's words.

"When the land itself repels war, and unnatural clouds obscure the sun... When the waves are coerced... and reflection deceives... The Bloodthirsty Prince will die."

What if...what if he wasn't known as the Bloodthirsty Prince anymore? Could I trick the fates that way?

Some of the weight slipped off my shoulders. I would fix this somehow. Prophecies didn't always come true. I refused to believe that we were all just the gods' playthings, destined to act out whatever fate they had written for us. I wouldn't let Lorian die. It wasn't going to happen, so the old woman's words were irrelevant.

"We need to go," I said. My voice didn't sound like me. Madinia shook her head, but she knew I was right.

I forced myself to focus on the next part of our plan. There were enough people with water magic in this castle that our fire would be contained quickly. This was a symbol. A statement. A way to prove to those suffering in this city that they weren't alone. That we were still fighting for them.

The throne room stretched out like a cavern. I'd never seen it empty like this before—without even the usual guards on each door. In front of both thrones, a wooden altar had been built, surprisingly sparse for the otherwise ostentatious space. Frowning, I took a few steps forward. What was it?

My breath caught. Bile crawled up my throat. Manacles hung from each corner of the wood. Blood had soaked into the pale grain.

Madinia let out a string of curses.

How many hybrids had Regner tortured here, in front of his court? How much blood had he spilled? How many families were missing their loved ones?

She glanced at me, and I nodded, unable to speak.

Madinia waved her hand. The bloodstained wood ignited with a crackle, orange tongues of flame leaping to the plush silk cushions sitting on each throne. The cushions smoldered, the material turning black as they shriveled until they were little more than ash.

I took a few steps backward, listening carefully for the sound of anyone approaching from beyond the throne room. I needed to conserve my power, but I refused to be disturbed until we were finished here.

The heavy floor-to-ceiling curtains were next, and I basked in the acrid tang of smoldering opulence as Madinia's fire roared through them. She glanced at the wooden chairs lining the walls—where Regner's court had no doubt sat and watched while he engaged in many of his torture sessions. The chairs turned to little more than kindling, but Madinia was already refocusing on the thrones.

The gold was blackened, but that wasn't enough for Madinia. She lifted one hand and poured her power into the thrones, slowly walking toward them. The gold began to warp.

Impossible. Lorian could melt gold with his fae fire, but this…

Madinia smiled, and her whole face changed, lit up with a joy I'd never seen from her before. Molten droplets wept from the disfigured thrones, sizzling as they splashed onto the marbled floor below.

My breath hitched. *It's not the entire castle, Wila. But I hope you're watching. Wherever you are.*

The heavy jewels were freed from their golden prison, several of them falling to the ground. Blood began to drip from Madinia's nose.

"That's enough," I told her.

She ignored me.

"Madinia." I grabbed her arm. "I need you to save your power. There's something else I want you to burn."

She ignored me. The flames were greedily scaling the walls of the throne room now, the smoke heavy and thick. I froze them with a thought, and Madinia whirled, lips pulled back in a snarl.

"Please," I said. "This is important."

She glanced back at the thrones. They weren't entirely melted. But they were buckled, drooping, ruined.

The symbolism was clear.

Finally, she nodded. The knot in my stomach loosened, and I bolted toward the doors, allowing time to resume. Madinia staggered through the doorway behind me as I urged her to the right, bursting from the castle and into the courtyard.

Rythos's gaze jumped to mine. A huge group of guards was gathered around him, sitting on the cobblestones and watching him attentively. Obviously, he'd already found Cavis and ensured his body would be transported out of the castle. My throat tightened.

"We need a few minutes," I said.

"Pris," Rythos warned.

"I know."

I would use my power again if I had to.

I couldn't explain the compulsion. But I had to do this. Beside me, Madinia panted. "You're going for the sanctuary."

"I want it destroyed."

She smiled. "Done."

Her upper lip was smeared with blood. She noticed my gaze and shook her head. "I'm fine."

The sanctuary walls were made of white stone, which wouldn't burn. But the chairs would. The light-blue cloth draped over the walls would. The wooden ceiling, etched with gold, would. As would the wooden floors. My heart pounded as the flames curled through the building, and we made our way outside, all while Madinia ensured even the smallest sliver of wood was burned to ash.

When it was done, the stone had begun to fall in places, the sanctuary crumbling where it stood. But blood ran freely from Madinia's nose. I'd never seen her even close to a burnout like this before. "We need to get back to Rythos."

"Prisca."

"What?"

"You need to tell Lorian. About the seer."

I shook my head. I didn't need to tell Lorian anything, because he wasn't going to die. The seer had clearly been tainted by the same madness that had gripped Vuena.

"Find the prince," she'd told me. *"Find him and meet your fate."* At the time, I'd assumed her mind was breaking.

Now that there was nothing left to burn…

It hurt. Oh gods, it hurt. Even just the thought of losing him was enough to make me…

I leaned over and vomited. Madinia's hands were surprisingly gentle as she pulled my curls out of the way. When I was done, she grabbed my waterskin from where I'd tucked it into my belt. Handing it to me, she sighed. "Either you tell him, or I will."

Pulling away from her, I attempted a glare. She rolled her eyes at me, and then her expression returned to grim determination. "You're not losing sleep and wrestling with grief and scheming and plotting and looking for a way out. At least not alone. You're telling him. And you're telling the others too. Or *I'm* telling them."

"Fuck you, Madinia."

Was that a hint of relief in her blue eyes? "Fuck you too, Prisca."

The thought of Lorian's death had hit me like a fist to the face. But I was recovering from the shock now.

The gods thought they could take Lorian from me? From all of us?

Let them fucking try.

19

LORIAN

The door swung open, and the guard peered out at us. Deep frown lines were etched in his face, his eyes hard. He raised his hands, making it clear he was unarmed. "Take what you want and leave."

I watched him closely. Even cowards occasionally overcame their baser instincts during their final moments. "We want the boy."

"Regner will come after you with everything he has."

Galon snorted. "Your concern for our safety is touching."

"I will not stop you from taking him," the guard said.

I didn't bother asking why he was cooperating. His gaze was currently clinging to the dead men at our feet.

"In that case, show us the boy."

"Will you spare my life?"

"How about we kill you and then take the boy?" Galon asked mildly.

The guard's mouth twisted. "Your distraction may have allowed you entrance here, but the moment your attack began, iron guards were dispatched from all directions. You have minutes at most."

"We're aware. And you're wasting our time."

The guard opened the door wider, and I held my lightning in my fist. His gaze dropped to it. "You truly are the Bloodthirsty Prince."

Ignoring him, I scanned the room with all my senses. No one was here. Other than the boy, of course.

Jamic's cage was directly across from the doorway, created from so much fae iron, it set my teeth on edge, even from several footspans away. He was taller than I'd expected, thin, unshaven, with a sparse beard that reminded me just how young he was. His clothes were clean, and so were his hair and skin. Someone was making sure he was looked after.

I looked at the guard. His hand shook as he pulled the key from his pocket. But he unlocked the cage. Behind me, Galon let out a rough curse. Both of us stepped closer to the cage.

Chains were wrapped around every inch of Jamic. He might be human, but stolen fae and hybrid power were being poured into him. All that fae iron must have felt as if he were being smothered. As if he were suffocating, little by little, for every second of every day.

He opened his eyes. They were completely black, no white to be seen. My instincts prickled. We had no choice but to free him, and yet this could go very, very badly.

"Do you know your name?"

He turned his head at the sound of my voice.

"Jamic," he hissed.

"Good enough for me," Galon muttered.

I held up a hand. "If we free you, will you attack us, Jamic?"

"Nooooo." His lips curved, and I shook my head, waiting him out. If he wanted us to trust him, he'd have to tone down his eerie little display.

His face cleared, and he sat quietly, as if we didn't hold his life in our hands.

I nodded at the guard. "You don't know what you're doing," the guard said.

"Put the key in the lock," Galon growled.

The guard's hand was shaking so much, it seemed to take him an eternity to unlock the first manacle. Gone was the man who'd bargained for his life. Now, I wouldn't be surprised if he lost his bladder.

There were nine locks in total, and the guard began panting as he got to the last lock. "Pull the chains away," Galon ordered. We could touch them, but fae iron often felt like acid against our skin.

The guard shook his head but complied. The boy smiled and stretched languidly, as if waking from a long sleep. One glance at the guard, and the man began choking.

Galon's ward jumped into place. The guard was slowly turning purple, the air stolen from his lungs. He gasped and clawed at his throat, eyes bulging as the boy watched closely. Finally, the guard slumped to the ground.

Jamic's eyes met mine. "Forgive me," he said with a long blink. "That guard was particularly cruel."

I could understand that. Still, I nodded to Galon, who kept the ward in place.

Jamic slowly unwound, shuffling forward, out of the cage. His knees straightened, as if he would take his first step of freedom.

His eyes rolled back in his head, and he collapsed.

Galon caught him, and I went still, staring at the object that had slipped from the neckline of Jamic's shirt.

"Is that…"

Galon nodded. "One of our amulets. Regner has been using it to channel power into him."

Despite myself, I laughed. "Oh, if only I could be there when he learns about this. We can't remove it now. The power withdrawal could kill him. We'll wait until we have a healer close by."

Galon leaned down, heaved the boy over his shoulder, and glanced at me. "Truthfully, I prefer him like this."

I met his eyes. "If he wakes up, you drop him."

He didn't look pleased at the order, but he nodded. The boy was jumpy, clearly traumatized, and over-powered. If he woke up while Galon was hauling him around, there was a chance he would steal his air before asking questions.

I wouldn't lose another brother.

PRISCA

While the guard towers burned and chaos reigned, our people fled. They took only what they could carry, but unlike the prisoners we'd rescued, these hybrids were healthy and prepared. With as little notice as he'd had, Vicer had still used Lesdryn's hidden tunnels to save close to two hundred lives.

Even with the hourglass around my neck, I was almost out of power. Yet no blood dripped from my nose, and the headache I usually suffered was thankfully missing. Still, I could sense the threads becoming weaker and weaker as I lifted them.

I pulled that power toward me, freezing time so the hybrids could sprint past the burning guard towers and the guards themselves, who were slashing at anyone who moved.

Vicer had insisted on sending the hybrids northwest to Kaelin Stillcrest's hybrid camp.

We'd argued bitterly about it, but I'd been forced to concede when he'd pointed out that our priority had to be getting Jamic down to the fae lands where we could protect him. We couldn't risk drawing attention to ourselves by attempting to lead one hundred and eighty hybrids south—through a forest currently crawling with Regner's soldiers.

But I could see Vicer's underlying tactics. He was

hoping that when these hybrids arrived, desperate and terrified and speaking of the horrors they'd seen in Lesdryn, Kaelin Stillcrest would be forced to at least consider moving her people to safety.

As soon as those who couldn't fight began traveling toward the hybrid kingdom, the hybrids we'd freed today would leave Stillcrest's camp—either to also travel through the gap to Lyrinore or to move down to the fae lands to join our army.

Both Vicer and I were hoping at least some of Stillcrest's people would travel with them. But at the very least, Vicer had assured me she would protect the hybrids who would arrive at her camp in the next few days. He'd also ensured they were taking as much food and other supplies with them as possible to contribute to the camp.

I swayed on my feet, my head spinning, and Vicer grabbed my elbow, steadying me. "Your power is almost drained."

Another group of hybrids made it to the tower we'd taken, and I steeled myself as a little girl screamed her displeasure in her mother's arms. "I can probably freeze time once more."

Vicer nodded. "Wait. We'll give as many as we can a chance to get to the meeting point."

I stayed quiet as we waited for more hybrids to arrive, a few at a time. Their expressions grew more and more desperate, well aware that they'd almost missed their chance for escape. Despite all our planning, some of them would get caught up in the protests and looting and wouldn't make it. No matter what we did, there were always losses. Always.

Finley and Lina slipped in behind the hybrids. I nodded to both of them. "Thank you," I told Finley. "For helping Madinia."

"Anytime." He smiled shyly. "I wish I'd thought of it."

I studied Lina. When I looked at her, I couldn't help but visualize the day she'd been found to be *corrupt* so long ago in our village. We'd all watched as her grandparents were ruthlessly beheaded in front of her.

While her eyes were still shadowed, she'd put on muscle, and she moved as if she'd been training. Even without that training, she was a smart choice for these kinds of...activities. Luck may not be an active power, but having Lina around was likely helping all of Vicer's carefully crafted schemes go as planned. Madinia slipped in behind me, eyes dark with fatigue. "I've put out the worst of the fires in the city."

"Thank you."

Where were Lorian and the others? I'd been forcing myself to focus on the hybrids, determined not to give in to the fear crawling through my veins. But the terror was slowly clamping around my throat, my hands shaking.

"The Bloodthirsty Prince will die."

Was that why Madinia was standing so close to me? Was she wondering if tonight would be the night, and the queen's seer had told us just in time for me to lose him?

It was possible that this was all an elaborate trick,

created by the queen to ensure I would be second-guessing my every move. To make me weak.

I couldn't—I couldn't take this. I couldn't—I…

"Pris." Vicer's voice was low. "It has to be now."

My vision swam, but I harnessed my thoughts, taking the hourglass in my hand, clamping down on my power and channeling all my fear and rage. I yanked the threads toward me. "Run," I ordered.

The hybrids scattered.

I managed to hold on until they were almost out of sight, but the power drained before I could stop it. Several of the guards fired at the fleeing hybrids, and I choked out a scream.

The bolts burst into flame, dropping to the ground. "They've used all their fae iron," Madinia said. "Those were wood and regular iron." Her face was bloodless, and it was clear she was now at the dregs of her own power.

"We need to go," Vicer snapped. "What the fuck is taking them so long?"

Had I told Lorian I loved him before we separated? I didn't know.

He could be dead even now. Or he could be dying, while I waited here, my breath frozen in my lungs.

No. I would know if he were dead. I would feel it.

"What's wrong, Pris?" Vicer demanded.

"Quiet," Madinia ordered him.

His brows shot up, and he glanced back at me. Whatever he saw on my face made him snap his mouth closed.

My knees quaked, the ringing in my ears turning into a roar.

Behind us, something exploded. I had to focus. Had to—

Lorian was striding toward me.

I choked. Was I seeing things? But no, Galon and Marth were behind him, an unconscious man over Galon's shoulder. And Lorian...

Lorian looked tired and irritated and so fucking alive. The world slid back into place, and I leaped into his arms, pressing my mouth to his.

LORIAN

I woke, wrapped around Prisca. She lay so still in my arms, her long lashes dusting her pale cheek.

Some days, it took everything I had to clamp down on the urge to take her someplace quiet, away from this war. To watch her eat and laugh and raise a family. I stroked my hand over her flat stomach, and I imagined it rounded with our baby.

Gods, she would make an incredible mother. And if she didn't want that, I would have her to myself for the next several centuries. Either way, she was mine.

She sighed, shifting her ass against me, and I

harnessed my self-control. She needed sleep.

We'd made it to this camp in the early hours of the morning. Since I had every intention of making Prisca scream before we left, I'd ensured our tent was farther away from the others, closer to the river.

Unsurprisingly, Vicer had taken Prisca aside as soon as we'd left the city, determined to return to Kaelin Stillcrest and her hybrid camp. I'd be impressed by his determination if it weren't so fucking misplaced.

Prisca was just as hopeful that Stillcrest would see reason. Madinia, on the other hand, had been out of patience.

She'd given Vicer a look of such fury, it was almost impressive. "You don't think we could use someone with your power?" She'd hissed. "Think of all the things you could do if we got you close to Regner's generals."

"I'll go wherever Prisca asks," he'd muttered. "I just need a few more weeks." His gaze had met Prisca's. "I can't give up on her yet."

"Just use your power on Stillcrest," Madinia had ordered.

Vicer tensed. Slowly, he'd turned his head, pinning her with a look so dark, a tiny flame had appeared in one of her hands, despite her drained power.

Part of Prisca had agreed with her. I knew her well enough to know that much.

But there were two kinds of people in this world. Those who justified the confiscation of one person's free will in exchange for hundreds or thousands of lives, and those who felt it was such a slippery slope, such an action should only be taken under the worst circumstances.

I was someone who could easily justify such a thing without a second thought. So were Madinia, Galon, and Demos.

Rythos was not. Neither was Marth, although that might be changing. Tibris was in the second category as well, and so was Asinia.

Prisca naturally felt the same as Rythos and the others. But the decisions she'd had to make in this war were wearing on her. And she knew exactly what would happen if Regner discovered the hidden camp.

Vicer's eyes had flared as he'd watched Prisca deliberate. And I'd seen the moment he'd realized just how much she'd changed. She hadn't yet been formally crowned, but it weighed on her just the same, along with the lives of each of her people.

"Two weeks," Vicer had said hoarsely. "Two weeks, and I'll convince everyone I can to leave. The hybrids we've just freed will help. If I…if I can't make them leave after that, I'll make my way back down to you. And I'll use my power however you want." Bitterness dripped from his voice.

Prisca had nodded. "Two weeks. Convince as many hybrids as you can. We'll have safe places for them to stop and rest on their way to either the hybrid kingdom or the fae lands. Galon has offered a group of highly trained fae to help guard the camp." Her amber eyes turned colder than I'd ever seen them. "Attempt to make Stillcrest see reason and allow them access. And tell her I'm personally holding her responsible for the lives of every hybrid in her camp. If they die because of her stubbornness, she better hope she dies too."

Rythos sucked in an audible breath. Vicer's eyes had turned flat. But he nodded. Madinia smiled at her, clearly pleased. Galon flicked me a glance, but I had already been watching Prisca once more. Something had happened. And whatever it was, I would get it out of her.

Prisca shifted some more.

I growled. "I know you're awake."

She chuckled, her eyes still closed.

"Was there something you wanted, wildcat?"

Her eyes slid open, so gold, I caught my breath. "You," she said.

Gods, this woman.

I nuzzled her hair, breathing in the sweet scent of her as I pushed up the shirt she'd worn to sleep—*my shirt*—and slid my hand slowly up her body.

She sucked in an unsteady breath, arching her back, urging me on. I took my time, enjoying the way she melted for me.

"Lorian…"

Her nipples were already hard, and I played, teasing them, enjoying her gasps and moans. When I pinched one of them, she ground back into me. I smiled against her neck.

I hauled her even closer, trapping her right where I wanted her. Sliding my hand down, I groaned at the wet heat of her.

"You're dripping, wildcat."

She let out a choked moan, her cheeks burning red. I laughed, stroking her clit until her hands found my arm, nails digging into my skin as she urged me on.

I thrust two fingers inside her, and she let out a whimper that made me groan. My cock ached, desperate for her.

"Inside me," she demanded.

As much as I would've liked to tease her some more, the way she was writhing against me was eating at my self-control. We hadn't had nearly enough time alone recently. If it were up to me, I would spend days inside her.

Removing my hand, I spread her thighs farther apart. Sliding my cock against her sensitive folds, I hissed out a breath as she pushed her ass back invitingly.

I thrust all the way in. She let out a shaky moan, tensing at my size, angling her hips away.

"No," I told her, holding her still for me.

"You're so big."

"And you're so wet."

Prisca whimpered, and I pulled back, teasing her clit until she was on the edge once more. She let out one of those strangled sounds, and I drove into her, angling her right where I wanted her.

"Oh gods."

I nibbled on her earlobe. "It's Lorian, wildcat."

I wrapped my hand around her throat, and she

tightened around my cock. She liked it when I stole her air. Perhaps because she knew I'd cut off my own hand before I hurt her. And maybe because she liked just that hint of fear. That feeling of being out of control.

We would have the rest of our lives to explore *those* fantasies.

I thrust harder, again and again. She'd devolved into those low, steady moans that told me she was close. "You were made for me, weren't you, Prisca?"

She nodded, desperate. "I need to… Please, Lorian."

It had always been difficult to say no to her. Even when I was pretending I loathed her. Rolling to my back, I freed my other arm, holding her in place as I thrust up into her. Tightening my hand around her throat, I slid my other hand to her clit, stroking once, twice.

She shuddered, clenching around me so tightly, she almost took me with her. But we weren't done.

When she was boneless, gasping, I caressed her clit again.

Her internal muscles squeezed me, even as she shook her head. "Too much."

"No, it's not. Look down, wildcat. Look how sexy you are, filled with me."

She angled her head, and I drove up into her, lifting my hips as I bounced her on my cock.

"See the way you stretch around me? The way I fit you so perfectly? You were made for me."

She was trembling again now, driving her hips down against me. I thrust deeper, rolling my hips and hitting that spot inside her. The one that made her wild.

Once. Twice.

Her body melted, and she let out a low groan. There was no better sight than Prisca finding her pleasure, and I ground my teeth as I came, filling her up, my entire body aflame.

I clutched her tight for long minutes, just enjoying the feel of her in my arms. There was never enough time.

"When this is all over, I want days with you," I murmured. "With no interruptions."

"Deal." Turning her head, she attempted a smile. But something that looked a lot like panic flickered across her face.

"What is it?"

Her expression cleared, and she attempted to wiggle off my body. I leaned down and nipped the shell of her ear. "Lie to me," I said, "and you're in big trouble."

"I'm not ready to discuss it."

"Something is hurting you. Do you think I'm going to quietly tolerate it?"

Sliding her onto the blankets beneath us, I caught her chin. "What is it, Prisca?"

The gold in her eyes dimmed. Something in my chest wrenched, and I cast my mind back.

She'd been beyond relieved when I'd made it to the meeting place last night. When she'd jumped into my arms, I'd enjoyed the display of affection. But something had happened while we were separated.

"Stop trying to figure out what it is," she muttered.

"There's an easy fix for that. Tell me yourself."

"You're so…"

"Handsome? Sexy? Unwilling to stand idly by when I can help fix the problem?"

Her eyes slitted. "Overbearing. Imperious. High-handed."

"Enough, Prisca. You said we were in this together. Was that a lie? Because it's too fucking late to change your mind. I'll never let you go."

"Arrogant. Presumptuous. Tyrannical," she continued.

I leaned over and bit her gently on her neck, sucking the skin between my teeth until she let out a breathless moan.

"You can tell me," I murmured against her throat, "or I'll find out myself."

She heaved a sigh. "I will tell you. I just need to think. Just…just wait until we reach Aranthon," she said quietly. "And then I'll talk about it. Please."

I considered it. I was a patient man. At least, I'd thought I was. And yet with Prisca, I wanted nothing more than to peer inside her mind and immediately understand what it was that had made her so furious last night. And so solemn this morning.

"Lorian," she said, and I sighed.

"As soon as we get to Aranthon, you'll tell me."

She nodded. I waited, my hand tightening on her chin.

She yanked her head. "You can let me go now."

"I will. Just as soon as I have your word."

"I promise," she snarled. "Would you like a blood vow?"

"That attitude isn't making me want to let this go."

Prisca bared her teeth. I slipped my hand down her body, slowly, teasingly, reminding her just who that body belonged to.

"That's not fair," she muttered as I found her slick and swollen.

Footsteps sounded outside our tent, and my ears twitched. "Telean received a message from Gromalia," Madinia called. "It's important."

I sighed, nuzzling one of Prisca's wild curls to the side so I could press a kiss to her cheek.

"We're awake," Prisca called back. "We'll be right there."

She pushed her hair off her face. "I need to get to Daharak, Lorian. I can't stay for long in the fae lands."

She'd asked me to send a message to the pirate queen last night. I'd advised Rostamir that Prisca would come but needed to handle something else first. We hadn't heard back from her yet.

"You mean *we* can't stay for long." I leaned over and nuzzled her neck, reveling in the scent of her—and the way I'd imprinted her scent with my own. "Don't think I didn't notice your nightmares last night. Or the fact that you still haven't let yourself grieve." She hadn't cried once. It would have been impressive, the way she'd clamped down on her emotions, if the sorrow and rage weren't slowly poisoning her.

Prisca stiffened, and I pressed gentle kisses to her throat until she relaxed once more.

"Speaking of grief, you need to talk to Marth," she said.

"I know. I've tried. He's not ready to talk yet."

She tutted. "Men."

I poked her in the ribs, and she let out a tiny yelp.

"I'm just saying," she said. "Maybe he doesn't need space."

"He does. For right now. If he doesn't talk to one of the others, I'll irritate him until he hits me. Then we'll get to the bottom of this."

She stared at me. "That's your solution?"

I shrugged. I wouldn't fail Marth the way I'd failed Cavis. I was paying close attention to his mental state. But I knew Marth well enough to know he would explode eventually. And I'd be there to pick up the pieces.

We were both quiet as we dressed. It was times like these that I wished I could read Prisca's mind. Fae were possessive, but I'd never imagined that I would crave her every thought, emotion, breath.

After everything we had been through so far, this should be when we were happiest. Prisca loved me. She'd accepted that she was my mate. *Mine*. And yet this war would rip us apart if it could.

Telean was waiting with the others outside, sitting near the remnants of our fire. Marth and Galon were talking quietly near the tent they'd dedicated for Jamic—a ward in place around it—while Rythos said something that managed to make Madinia crack a smile.

We would need to leave soon. My spies had discovered the current locations of Regner's regiments and mapped out our best route to the fae lands. But thanks to those regiments, the best route was through Gromalia. Prisca needed to recover as much of her power as possible, so we could get across the border and through the nearby towns.

Prisca took my hand. "Cavis's body?"

"Rythos arranged for it to be transported to Aranthon by boat." My chest clenched. He should be here with us, excited to see his wife. His baby. There was no conversation I was dreading as much as the one I would soon have with Sybella.

Telean met my eyes briefly before turning her attention to Prisca and holding up a piece of parchment.

"I learned the truth about what happened to the Gromalian queen. Our suspicions were correct, as were the rumors we began spreading. Eryndan had her killed."

Prisca's shoulders tensed, and I could feel her refocusing, steeling herself for whatever was to come next. "Tell us."

"Eryndan's wife was named Brynne. When Rekja had seen three winters, she traveled to see her sister, who still lived with their parents. Her carriage was attacked by human bandits, and a group of fae saved their lives. One of them was a fae ambassador from Quorith. His name was Althor."

I glanced at Rythos. He shook his head at me. He didn't know the ambassador.

"They fell in love," Telean continued. "Over the next few months, Brynne began making plans to leave Eryndan. She was also looking for ways to take Rekja with her. But she knew if she were to take Eryndan's heir to the fae lands, Eryndan would likely declare war on the fae. She told her sister Losorli what was happening, and Losorli warned her to be very, very careful. Eryndan was controlling. He would have his men spy on her, would make her account for every moment of her day."

"He learned of the affair, didn't he?" Madinia asked.

Telean nodded. "I asked one of my friends to convince Losorli to tell us the truth, promising her we wouldn't let Eryndan know she'd talked." Telean held up the message she'd clearly just received. "One day, when Brynne was visiting Losorli, she suddenly became sick and confused. One of the guards had offered her a valeo to eat while they were traveling. It was poisoned. The guards rushed her back to the castle, where she died—apparently of natural causes. But Losorli knew. The next time the guards came, she was warned to stay away from Rekja. To pretend she had never had a sister. But she had noticed the remains of the valeo while the guards had been loading her sister back into the carriage, and she'd tucked it into her gown. She'd taken it to her neighbor, who used her power to test for poison."

Prisca's face was flushing, her hands fisting as she wrestled with her fury. She'd loathed Eryndan since the moment I'd met him. I couldn't say I was surprised to learn what he'd done, but I ran my hand down her back until she let out the breath she'd been holding.

We couldn't help Brynne. She was long dead. But her son wasn't.

"How do we convince Rekja of the truth?" Prisca asked.

"We set up a meeting between him and his aunt."

"He won't believe her," Madinia said.

I considered what I knew about him. The day Prisca and I had traveled to Gromalia to meet with them, Eryndan had given Rekja a long, disappointed look. *"You are your mother's son,"* he'd told him.

And Rekja had almost flinched.

"Perhaps he will," Prisca said, likely remembering the same moment. "Either way, we need find a way to make the meeting happen."

"You honestly think he'll break from his father over this?" Madinia asked.

Prisca shrugged one shoulder. "He's...*better* than Eryndan. He can be reasoned with. At the very least, it'll sow discord between them."

Telean nodded approvingly.

Prisca got to her feet, pacing the clearing. "What will happen to the power Regner used for the barrier if we manage to take it down?"

Galon gave a languid shrug. "It is difficult to know."

Telean stretched out her legs. "There's a chance it could return to the humans it was stolen from. And if that happens, we have an opportunity."

Excitement flashed in Prisca's eyes. "Because they believe their power was sacrificed to the gods. If some of it were returned, that would be difficult for Regner to explain."

"And if the power doesn't return to those it belongs to?" Madinia asked. "If it goes to whoever is closest?"

Prisca chewed on her lower lip. "That would make it easy for Regner to continue his propaganda against us."

"It won't," a voice said, and Prisca jolted.

Jamic stepped out of his tent. I glanced at Galon, who shrugged. Clearly, he wasn't worried about the over-powered boy we'd freed.

"I can feel them," Jamic said. "All of the tiny sparks. Each spark is a soul, and the power wants to return to those souls."

Prisca's eyes met mine. And her smile was brilliant.

20

PRISCA

Six days after leaving Lesdryn, we arrived on the outskirts of Aranthon. None of us had been happy about the time it had taken to travel all the way to the southern fae lands. But Marth had sent Lorian's hawk to a friend, who'd agreed he would loan us his boat to sail northeast to Daharak when we were ready to leave.

And still, we'd traveled fast, pushing our horses as hard as we could and only resting for a few hours each night. Impatience clawed at me, but I knew the summit was necessary. Lorian had explained a little about what to expect. While Conreth was still the ultimate ruler of the fae lands, they were divided into territories. And the leaders of those territories were known as wardens. They had the right to choose if they would get involved in a war that would risk their own people.

I glanced at Lorian, Rythos, Galon, and Marth. All of them had discarded their human glamour. My eyes met Lorian's, and he gave me a wicked grin. He knew I was captivated by the sight of him in his fae form.

We approached Aranthon from the north, and my breath caught in my throat at my first sight of the city. While Quorith had dazzled with its color and vibrancy, Aranthon glimmered as elegantly as a polished pearl.

The guards wore silver, and the moment they noticed Lorian, the huge gates swung open, and they looked at him with awe in their eyes. Awe and a little fear.

The city sloped down toward the water, and I pulled my horse to a stop. A salty breeze teased my hair, and I tasted the tang of the ocean, mingled with the heady scent of jasmine and some kind of herb. The cobblestones were spotless here, practically new. I peered down at them.

"It's a ward. Prevents Conreth's precious city from becoming *dirty*." Lorian smirked.

Madinia snorted, studying the cobblestones. She'd argued with me before we left our first camp after taking Jamic, determined to return to traveling alone. She'd heard rumors that a drunk in Gromalia knew where the third amulet was. It was incredibly unlikely that was the case, but she was determined to find it. I'd convinced her to come to the fae lands first. Not only was she excellent at reading body language, but she would be able to analyze current alliances and sniff out secrets far better than I could.

Finally, she'd agreed to come, but she wouldn't stay more than a few days. I'd watched her closely enough to know she was running from something. And that despite her longing for family, she wanted to be alone.

Telean was brimming with energy. Ever since our conversation with Tymriel, she'd seemed younger, almost. We'd talked about my parents every day. About my mother's wicked sense of humor and my father's sly remarks. About how they'd been considering adding to their family before my mother was killed. If Crawyth hadn't been destroyed, Demos and I might've had a younger brother or sister.

Telean glanced wide-eyed as we traveled through the city, clearly intrigued despite herself.

And Jamic?

That amulet still hung around his neck, until it could be removed under the supervision of a healer.

Galon had allowed him to ride his own horse, but he was keeping a close eye on him. Jamic pretended not to notice, but I knew better. He noticed *everything*. He'd stared hungrily at the clouds, the trees, the horses, the small villages we'd passed…and I couldn't blame him.

Lorian had made it clear he didn't want me anywhere near Jamic. When he'd told me about the fae guard Jamic had killed, I'd understood. Still, I couldn't help but offer a smile to Jamic whenever he glanced my way.

He'd been locked away for two years. Lorian had told me all about where he'd been kept—suffocated by fae iron and yet forced to hold Regner's stolen magic. It was surprising he hadn't gone insane. And I knew Galon was watching Jamic for any signs of him teetering over that edge.

A couple of days ago, Jamic had quietly asked me why we were bothering to be nice to him. He'd assumed we would attempt to slit his throat to bring down the barrier. The way Regner would have.

I'd stared at him, speechless. Finally, I'd assured him that we were hoping he would voluntarily join with us to bring the barrier down. But we would never hurt him.

He hadn't seemed fully convinced. Given the way he'd grown up, I didn't blame him.

My horse pricked her ears. Somewhere, someone started singing. Someone else joined her, and I basked in the simple joy of a normal day.

Aranthon was so…open. Our horses clopped down the warded cobblestones, and I could feel Lorian watching me as I surveyed the city. The buildings lining the street were so vastly different from anything I'd seen in my village—or anywhere in either Gromalia or Eprotha— that I found myself staring.

The fae here didn't seem to value privacy at the expense of enjoying the sun or the salt-soaked breeze. Large, stately homes relied on pillars, rather than full walls. My gaze clung to the fae who strolled in groups along breezeways connecting the buildings above and the cobbled walkways winding between them below. The breeze shifted toward us, carrying the sounds of laughter.

Emerald vines curled around the slender columns supporting arched rooftops, but I caught glimpses of sprawling atrium gardens within central open spaces of the buildings.

Along the walkways, artisans plied their trades in jewel-hued stalls bedecked with silk awnings. Fountains burbled at intervals along the street, but within the buildings, I occasionally spotted larger waterfalls and streams trickling through beds of lilies and moss.

"Do you like it?" Lorian asked.

He was still watching me, as if memorizing my reaction. "It's incredible. You grew up here?"

"Until I was nine winters."

The thought of just how young he'd been when he'd been *removed* from this city soured my thoughts. He just shook his head at me. "I'm glad you like it."

I studied him. Since we'd arrived, some of the tension had left his face. His eyes were warm, and he looked more relaxed than I'd seen him since before we'd traveled to find my hourglass.

"You love this city," I said.

He gave me a faint smile, turning his head as Galon called to him. Did Lorian even realize he loved Aranthon? Or had he convinced himself he didn't want to be here in an effort to make it easier on himself when Conreth ensured he spent most of his life elsewhere?

I'd spent the long days on horseback considering the seer's prophecy and studying the clouds. What did it mean if they were *unnatural?* Was it a shape? A color?

Reflection deceives seemed to have something to do with mirrors. Lorian would likely think I was crazy if I had them removed from our rooms.

That was the problem with prophecies. They could make you mad.

Lorian had been surprisingly patient. Likely, it was because he knew I'd promised to tell him—although I wondered how much of it was him indulging me after he'd kept our mating from me.

That mating seemed to become stronger every day. The strange awareness I'd always had around him had become deeper, until I could immediately tell if he'd entered a room. Gone were the days when I struggled to know what he was thinking behind his indifferent mask. Now, I felt like I knew him on a soul-deep level.

Guards bowed to him at the castle gates, immediately opening them for us as we made our way into the courtyard.

We were traveling light, and the moment we dismounted, our belongings disappeared. I jolted, and Lorian pressed his hand against my lower back. "Our bags have been placed in our rooms."

Conreth strolled out of the castle, dressed in an icy blue that matched his eyes. He was wearing his crown, and it glittered in the sunlight. Did he find it heavy? Or perhaps he wore it often enough that his neck muscles had compensated for its weight.

His gaze immediately caught on the amulet around Jamic's neck and lingered there for a long moment.

"Ah, a personalized greeting from my brother," Lorian said. "What an honor."

Conreth rolled his eyes, and for a moment, I caught a glimpse of the brothers they could have been. Perhaps the brothers they still occasionally were. Gently teasing, competitive without attempting to break each other.

If they'd ever had that kind of relationship, I wanted them to find it again. But from the way Conreth's mouth thinned when he glanced at me and the way Lorian's eyes burned in response, it was unlikely to happen.

A woman followed Conreth out of the castle, her steps unhurried, graceful. Long, golden-blond waves cascaded over her shoulders, contrasting beautifully with her gossamer gown—a soft violet. Delicate gold chains dripped from her throat and wrists, studded with crystals and pearls. Her eyes were a shockingly bright blue, which gleamed with curiosity as they met mine.

"Emara," Lorian said, and his eyes softened slightly. He liked her. The next time Lorian displayed unreasonable jealousy, perhaps I'd bring up this moment. I ran a hand over my mouth, hiding my smirk.

"Lorian. It has been too long." She took his hands, smiling up at him. Then she turned to me. "And you must be Nelayra."

I nodded. "But you can call me Prisca."

"Prisca." Her smile widened. "It's nice to finally meet you." She hugged Rythos, Galon, and Marth, then introduced herself to Madinia, Telean, and even Jamic, who studied her as if she were some unknown species he'd never seen before.

Lorian was having a wordless conversation with his brother. From the way Conreth's jaw hardened, it wasn't a pleasant one.

Emara smiled again, still radiating that calm contentment. "I'll show you to your rooms so you can freshen up."

Madinia frowned, and I understood why. Kaliera would never have considered doing such a thing herself.

Within a few minutes, I was standing in a tastefully decorated room that begged to be explored. And yet, all I could do was fantasize about falling into the wide, plush bed.

Lorian turned to me and smiled humorlessly. "We're in Aranthon now, wildcat," he said silkily. "So why don't you tell me what you've been keeping from me since we left Eprotha?"

THE QUEEN

Sabium did not rage.

His cheeks did not flush.

His hands did not fist.

Instead, his face was blank, his posture relaxed. But his eyes…

His eyes gleamed with a dark malevolence.

We sat at a circular table in his war room—a damp, underground room with stone walls and wooden chairs—Sabium's advisers talking over one another as they competed for his attention. The patriarchs were shaken by the seemingly random attack. Most of them would never know my son had been taken. Any guards who had known Jamic's location and survived the attack had been slaughtered for their alleged crimes against the kingdom. Just another way for Sabium to ensure word of the true reason for the attack would never spread.

But my son was free.

Beneath the table, my hands shook, and for the first time since I was a young girl, my eyes ached with suppressed tears. Joyful tears. Jamic wouldn't bleed to death like a stuck pig, his body dumped into the sea when Sabium was finished with him.

I sat still, expression attentive, pretending to listen to the suggestions made by those who couldn't comprehend the reason for the attack. Of course the hybrid heir hadn't been able to resist freeing more of her people. Hundreds of residents of the city had gone missing overnight—likely hybrids in hiding.

This had given Sabium the perfect smokescreen for the true reason behind the attack. As far as the court knew, the infiltration of the city had merely been a raid to free those hybrids. An incursion that, while embarrassing, was not at all a threat to his plans.

Finally, Sabium waved his hand. The room went silent. "I must think on this," he said. The advisers filed out. I stood, and Sabium shook his head. "Not you."

My hands turned numb. Distantly, I wondered how much longer I could keep doing this. Sabium was becoming suspicious. I knew he was. Tymedes watched me constantly, and I knew he was bribing several of my servants.

Sabium hadn't just lost Jamic. No, Pelysian's spies had learned of an error much worse. My son had been wearing one of the fae amulets. It would have slowly tortured him, the flood of all that power likely excruciating. But Sabium had risked it, greedy as always for extra power when he killed Jamic and took the barrier down.

The loss of Jamic was a blow. But the loss of the amulet, after so many years of scheming and killing?

Blood drummed in my ears at the thought of his retaliation.

"I suppose you're pleased," Sabium said mildly. His gaze met mine. For a long moment, I lost the ability to breathe.

But I hadn't worked this hard just to fall apart now.

"Pleased?" I said scornfully. "The hybrids will likely torture Jamic. They will see him as a valuable prisoner— despite the fact that he knows nothing of your plans. His pain and suffering will increase morale for them." I shook my head, turning my gaze to the ground, as if I couldn't even contemplate his fate. "At least you would grant him a quick death. The hybrids will make Jamic pay for *your* failings."

My heart slammed into my ribs, until I thought they might break. Sabium's expression had turned cold.

"Interesting arguments," he hissed, and I raised my gaze. "If I find out you had anything to do with this, I will have your lips sewn shut, so no one can hear your screams. Then I will have your fingers removed, one by one. And that will just be the beginning."

I clamped my mouth shut, a chill rippling over my skin.

Slowly, his gaze on my face, Sabium got to his feet. "If I cannot use the boy, I will ensure they cannot use him either." His smile was cold, humorless, and empty. My stomach turned to lead, and his smile widened.

He turned, his mind clearly already on his plans as he walked out of the room.

I shuddered, sweat dripping down my spine. Now that I was alone, my entire body trembled, my breaths little more than shallow pants.

Sabium was enraged, yes. But he was handling this setback far too calmly. It didn't make sense.

Pushing that thought away, I focused on my own fate. Jamic was free. If everything went according to plan, the next time he returned to this castle, my son would be the Eprothan king, and both of us would finally be safe. Sabium would be watching me even more closely after this.

But I could feel the seconds of my life ticking down one by one. With Jamic gone, Sabium had nothing left to keep me in line—except fear for my own life. Soon, I would receive a dagger in the back. Perhaps poison at dinner. A pillow over my face by a trusted guard. Or Sabium might prefer to watch my death himself.

Pelysian would help me get out. He'd made it clear

he was available years ago, before accepting I would never leave Jamic.

But before I left, I needed to deal Sabium one final blow.

ASINIA

What should have been a few days in the rebel camp had turned into over a week. Today, I'd received a message from Prisca, letting us know they'd managed to free Jamic.

It felt as if my entire body was suddenly lighter. As if I was floating above the ground instead of walking on it. We really had a chance now.

I'd sent word back, letting her know we were all fine. I'd been waiting, hoping to be able to tell her we had an agreement with Herne in place. But that wasn't the case.

Each day, Demos attempted to reason with him. And Herne refused to listen.

Soon after we'd arrived, Tibris had shown us around the rebel camp. I'd expected the people here to be suspicious of outsiders, unhappy we were here. But simply being close to Tibris meant most people had seemed to accept us by default. Although they tended to freeze whenever Vynthar stalked into camp.

Tibris had always been likable, but he'd settled in

here in a way I hadn't expected. He was content.

And we were going to rip him from that.

Oh, he would want to be where he could do the most good—especially if Prisca were in danger. But I knew him well enough to know he would have stayed here if he could.

And not just for the camp itself. I'd caught the way he looked at Herne. And the way Herne looked back when Tibris wasn't paying attention.

Demos and I had slid neatly into camp life. For Demos, that meant training with some of the younger rebels, ensuring they could handle a knife and a sword.

I gave a daily class, teaching technique with my crossbow. I'd come a long way from the woman who'd refused to train with Demos in the hybrid camp.

Today, I found myself watching Demos stretch after training. Along with what seemed like half of the female population of the camp—who seemed to sense whenever he was about to strip off his shirt.

When he glanced over at me and winked, I glowered back at him, turning to stalk away.

He caught up with me. Still shirtless.

"You're done with training?" he asked.

"Yes. I thought I might go help with the traps." Anything to avoid looking at the way his muscles tightened each time he moved.

"I'll go with you."

Perfect.

We walked in silence for a while, checking the traps,

resetting the ones that had been knocked over. As much as I attempted to keep my eyes from wandering to his body whenever he leaned down to check a trap, I found myself ripping my gaze away each time he gave me that knowing look of his.

Smug bastard. Still, we fell into a companionable silence. I didn't have to tell him I was worried Herne wasn't going to relent. He didn't have to tell me he was planning to increase the pressure until Herne's back was against a wall.

On our way back to camp, I looked up to find Demos studying my face. His expression was serious.

"What is it that you want, Sin?"

"What do you mean?"

"After all this. If we finally achieve peace and we get to go home. What then?"

I shrugged. It was difficult to imagine such a thing, knowing how much we still had to achieve to win this war. "I want to open my own store in the hybrid kingdom. I want to be a great seamstress who brings joy to people through my clothes. I want to help people find the clothes they'll wear to weddings, balls, ceremonies—to all the *best* days of their lives.

"I want to know that when I use my power, it won't be to shoot a bolt directly through an enemy's throat. Instead, it will be to *create* something. Something that brings a little beauty into this world." I blinked. I hadn't expected all that to come out. It was as if a weight had been lifted from my chest.

"I'm going to make sure you get that life. It will happen. I promise you." His voice was so assured. And if there was one thing I knew about Demos, it was that he kept his promises. He stopped walking and turned to face me fully. "But you're not being honest with me. What is it you really want?"

I felt my eyes widen and glanced down in an effort to hide my reaction.

Demos wouldn't approve of what I wanted. If he learned my true goal, he would do everything he could to keep me out of this war.

It wasn't his fault. The day he'd met me—and for weeks after that—he'd seen me at my weakest. Now, when he looked at me, he would always see someone who needed to be protected.

One day, I *did* want to be a great seamstress. But first, I would make an impact. Pris wouldn't have entered this war if I hadn't been taken. I had been the catalyst. And I refused to live the rest of my life knowing I was merely one of the reasons this war had begun. The day Prisca had shown me the headstone she'd had made for my mother, I'd silently vowed that I'd also be one of the reasons this war ended. Maybe one day I'd share that with Demos. When I was sure he saw me as more than just a victim.

"That *is* what I want."

Demos angled his head, and I folded my arms. "I shared with you. What do you want, Demos?"

He was quiet for a long moment. "For two years, all I wanted was either to die alone with some shred of dignity or to escape. Now, all I want is to win this war and bring our people home. I don't—I haven't let myself think about what comes after."

I wanted to reach out and touch him. I wanted to hold his hand—so much that I physically hurt with the need to feel his skin. But that was stupid. Demos had only ever seen me as yet another person to keep alive. I was a promise he'd made to his sister.

And most days, I was fine with that.

Today…today, it ached.

Perhaps a change of subject. "Do you think we'll be able to convince Herne to work with us?"

The corner of his mouth quirked. "I think if anyone convinces that man to do anything, it will be Tibris. He's our best hope."

"We need him to make a decision. Soon." Regner wanted this border secured. And Eryndan wanted to save face.

"I know. I have a plan for that."

We were silent for the rest of the walk back. A few hours later, not long after I'd washed away the sweat of the day, I wandered toward the main fire. My gaze caught on Demos. He was standing near the camp entrance between Tibris and Herne. Uh-oh.

"He's not going anywhere," Herne growled as I walked over to them. "We need him."

Demos swiped his hand over his mouth in the way he did when he was hiding a smile. But his eyes remained serious. "You've made it clear that your people have no interest in our help. Your ability to heal your people is your own business. Tibris is needed on the front lines. Where he will be most useful."

Herne's face turned white with fury. "You're not taking him to the front."

Tibris was watching Demos and me closely. I knew him well enough to know he wasn't happy with either of us, but anyone else would likely assume it was the situation that irritated him. Still, I was willing to bet he would play along. Besides, he couldn't refute that he *was* needed on the front. With us.

Herne turned on him. "You wouldn't leave our people. You know we need you."

The truth beneath Herne's words? *I* need you. My chest clenched.

Tibris turned his steady gaze our way. I barely hid a wince. Demos just lifted one eyebrow.

"I know you need me," Tibris said, turning back to Herne. His voice softened. "But you have enough non-magic healers here to help with delivering babies, bandaging training wounds, and treating stomachaches. I've been training them myself."

Herne's eyes flared. "You're not leaving. If you try, I'll have you brought back." He turned and stalked away.

Demos smiled.

"You made me manipulate him." Tibris's voice was cool.

The smile dropped from Demos's face, and he sighed. "I know. I'm sorry."

Surprise flashed in Tibris's eyes. I couldn't blame him. Demos wasn't exactly known for his frequent apologies.

Tibris sighed. "I don't—"

A sentry sprinted past. Demos grabbed his shoulder, pulling him to a stop, and the sentry lashed out with his knife. Demos plucked it from his hand, and the sentry flushed purple.

"What is it?" Demos asked.

"We're under attack." Shaking Demos off, he sprinted toward Herne's tent.

All the air disappeared from my lungs. A prickly sensation engulfed all of my nerve endings. Under attack. Here.

Tibris's eyes hardened. "Are you responsible for this?"

I shook my head, heart pounding. "No. I swear."

"This isn't one of Prisca's schemes?"

Demos shook his head, expression grim. "Show me where they keep their weapons."

Tibris led us toward the armory, his steps quick.

"You did this!" Herne hissed, intercepting us.

"I can see why you'd think that," Demos acknowledged calmly. "But we didn't. Whatever is happening, it didn't come from us."

To Herne's credit, he didn't waste time arguing. Turning, he began snarling orders to his generals. When he glanced back at Tibris, his expression softened almost imperceptibly. "You need to go now. Take a horse and leave."

"We're staying to help," I said. "Which direction were they spotted coming from?"

Relief darted across Herne's face, gone in an instant. "The east."

"How far away?"

"They'll be here by nightfall. Perhaps faster."

"Are you certain none of them are coming from the north?" Demos asked.

Herne's mouth twisted. "Yes."

"What colors are they wearing?"

Herne hesitated. When he finally spoke, his voice was haunted.

"There were no colors. Our attackers are not men. They are some kind of twisted creature my sentries have never seen before."

All of us went silent at that.

"I'll join you on the front lines," Demos said. "Asinia will join the archers in the trees. Tibris—"

"The healer's tent." Herne glanced at Tibris. "It's where you're the most useful. You know that."

Tibris nodded. "I'll be there." He swept his gaze over all of us. "Be careful."

21

ꟼRISCA

Lorian was waiting for me to speak. I should have known he'd insist on having this conversation the moment we arrived in Aranthon.

"I want you to stay in the fae lands while I go to Daharak."

Lorian tilted his head in that infuriating way he did when he was endlessly amused.

"And why would I do that?"

"Because it's what I want."

He laughed at me. "Try again, Prisca."

I hadn't thought it would work. Still, I had to clamp down on the urge to stick out my lower lip. Heaving a sigh, I sat on the edge of the plush bed. "When I was with Madinia in Regner's castle…when I made my alliance with Kaliera…a woman stepped down out of her mirror."

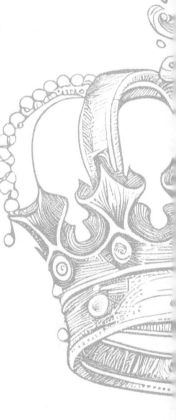

All humor had left Lorian's face, and something feral glittered in his eyes. "Who?"

"Daharak's mother. A seer. You've heard of her," I said, spotting the recognition on his face.

He nodded, and I straightened my spine. It felt as if a knife were being dragged down the back of my throat. "She knew things. About me. She said she'd had glimpses of my future for years."

Lorian's gaze was steady on mine. For once, I couldn't tell what he was thinking. "And what did she say?"

"She gave me two prophecies. The first was about Daharak and fulfilling the blood vow."

He didn't say a word, just watched me, waiting.

"The second was about you. About your d-death." My voice cracked, and Lorian's eyes softened.

"Tell me."

I recited both prophecies, and he sighed. "Is this what you've been so worried about? I told you, Prisca, I'll never leave you."

I glanced away. He didn't believe me. And why would he? He was lethally powerful, a force that had carved his way across this continent and protected his people for decades.

"All I'm saying is, based on her prophecy and the mention of water...perhaps it's best if you stay here. Temporarily." I dragged my gaze to Lorian's. His lips curved, and I glowered at him.

"Prisca..."

"Please," I begged, and my voice broke.

His gaze turned gentle, and he cupped my cheek. "I'll give you anything you want," he said. "Anything but that."

I had to hurt him. I had to lash out. Or worse, I had to betray him in such a way that he would be eager to leave. The thought made me want to vomit. But there were no lines I wouldn't cross to save his life. None.

"I know the way your mind works." His voice was achingly soft, but his eyes had turned predatory. "Listen carefully, Prisca. No matter what you do, I will *never* leave your side."

"Please."

"If I'm going to die, it will be while I'm protecting you."

"That's what I'm afraid of."

He slowly shook his head. "I can think of no better death."

I pushed out of his arms and turned away, unable to even look at him.

He wrapped his arms around me from behind, nuzzling my hair. "I don't want you to obsess over this."

My laugh was bitter. It turned into a sob, and I wiped at the tears streaming down my cheeks. "I can't lose you, Lorian. It would break me."

"You won't. Our story doesn't end that way. I know it doesn't."

I wanted to believe that. Most of the time, I'd been able to believe that. But I had this terror lodged in my chest, and no matter what I did, I couldn't shake it.

"Promise me."

"I promise." His body pressed close to mine, and

he kissed me so gently my breath hitched. "My fierce wildcat," he murmured against my mouth. "You've been holding this in, attempting to bargain with the fates for days, haven't you?"

I lifted my gaze, meeting forest green. "They can't have you."

"And they won't."

He lowered his head again, and I let my eyes drift closed.

His lips brushed against the sensitive area beneath my ear, and I let out a small gasp, opening my eyes.

"No." He nuzzled me. "Keep your eyes closed. Just feel me."

I complied, and he pushed my tunic aside, sliding his hand to cup my breast. I was aching for him, my thighs shaking, and he thumbed my nipple, his mouth finding mine as I moved restlessly. I needed to be closer. Needed him inside me, making me forget.

Lorian pulled away, and I let out a mewing sound that made him chuckle. "Soon, wildcat."

My tunic was over my head in an instant, and he let out a low growl. "It somehow always manages to shock me," he said, "just how fucking beautiful you are."

My cheeks heated, and Lorian cursed. Suddenly, I was on the bed looking up at him, my heart pounding. In one of his too-fast-to-see movements, he'd placed me carefully on the covers and was slowly rolling my leggings down my legs.

He lowered his mouth, kissing his way along my

thighs gently, teasingly. He nuzzled my lower belly. "I want you to feel how much I love you. I'll always be with you, Prisca. It's you and me."

Me and him. Forever. My breath shuddered from my lungs, and a tiny chunk of the terror in my chest began to melt.

Removing my undergarments, he ran his lips over my stomach, my breasts, my neck. I arched for him, wanting his lips on mine, but he was already kissing his way down my arm, making me shiver as he found sensitive places I hadn't known existed.

I was lost in sensation. In the way his hair tickled my skin. The way his lips caressed and soothed. The way he continually made me feel *cherished*.

He nudged my thighs apart, and I opened for him, watching as he positioned himself between my legs. His eyes met mine. "I've been craving this all day." His gaze stayed on my face as he slid his hand down, eyes heating as he found me slick for him. He stroked my clit, and my eyes drifted shut. "No, look at me," he demanded. "Let me see what I do to you. How good I can make you feel."

Lifting my hands, I traced his shoulders, brushing over his warm skin. He gave me a stern look. "Don't distract me."

I laughed, and he lowered his head, pressing his lips to me and blowing gently on my clit. I lifted my hips, and he smiled against me. "Insatiable woman."

"*You* make me this way."

"And no one else ever will." He stroked with his

tongue, teasing me the way he so enjoyed.

"More," I groaned, and he gave me more. His tongue slid through my folds, circled my clit, flicked and played and found the places that made me tense and moan. The spots that made my thighs shake. I was rocking my hips, grinding against his face, and his gaze remained locked on mine, his hands holding me in place. The message was clear. I would take whatever he chose to give me. Even while worshipping my body, Lorian made it clear that he was in charge.

My climax hit me like a hurricane, a force that locked my body, pleasure rolling through my limbs as it went on and on. Lorian groaned against me, continuing to stroke until I buried my hands in his hair and tugged.

He growled, clearly put out, but I tugged harder. "Inside me," I begged. I needed to feel him moving within me. Needed to know he was alive and he'd stay alive and everything would be fine as long as we were together.

He kissed his way back up my body, pausing to tease my nipples until I was writhing, hips lifting as I slid my hand down to his cock.

He caught my hand, pressing a kiss to my palm. "I don't think so."

One day, I was going to make *him* beg for me. Lorian smirked at me. "Don't pout, wildcat. I'll give you what you need."

Achingly slowly, he thrust into me, his eyes darkening as he watched me. It felt like he was coming home. Like I was born to be his.

His mouth found mine, his palm caressing my throat, stroking along my pulse point. Our kiss was slow and gentle and deep. He moved, taking his time, and I *could* feel how much he loved me. And I could feel that he was born to be mine too.

He told me with the way he watched me so closely, adoration mixed with pure possession in his eyes. He told me with the way he brushed my hair back from my face, cupping my cheek as he balanced on his other arm and moved deeper. He told me with the way he paid such careful attention to the change in my breathing as his cock found the spot inside me that made warmth stir in my belly.

He pressed deeper, harder, hitting that same spot again and again. Our movements grew more desperate, his teeth dragging across the skin of my neck as I gasped out his name.

His eyes had turned so dark they were almost black. He stared down at me like he would burn the world for me.

What he didn't seem to understand was that I would do the same for him.

"Mine," I gasped out, right as he angled his hips, his pelvic bone stroking my clit.

"Yes, wildcat. Yours. Now, come for me."

He linked our hands, pressing mine back to the bed as he thrust so deep my breath hitched as I lay poised on the edge.

Another thrust and I shuddered, groaning through

a climax that swept through me like wildfire. Lorian pounded into me, drawing it out, until my muscles went lax and he pressed his mouth to mine, trembling as he fell with me.

ASINIA

My mouth was so dry, I would have paid almost any price for a gulp of water. My hands trembled, and I fought to steady my breathing, leaning into the bark of the tree limb I was sitting on.

The creatures had arrived before dusk. According to Herne's scouts, some of them had flown toward the camp, and his sentries had picked off a few of them from the trees. Still more of the rebels had been slaughtered as the creatures made their way on the ground.

Herne's rebels had slid almost soundlessly toward the edge of the forest, close to where Demos and I had approached from the road. I was surrounded by archers—all of us poised on branches above the rebels on the ground, ready to defend them.

The tree I'd chosen was close enough for me to keep an eye on Demos, while still ensuring I was well hidden, nestled among its branches. My quiver was slung across my back, filled with arrows. I had already nocked one of them, ready to draw and release in an instant.

Someone let out a choked gasp to my left. A woman I recognized from training was poised in the branches, her crossbow in her hands. I hadn't had a chance to talk to her, but she attempted a smile, her face ashen.

I smiled back.

The sun was setting, shafts of fading light filtering through the gnarled canopy above my head. But a sense of foreboding clutched at me, ice sliding up my spine.

Pressing myself against the trunk, I watched Demos. He was positioned around ten footspans away, sword in his hand, his back to me.

"You stay in that tree, or I'll haul you back to camp myself," he'd growled moments ago.

I hadn't dignified that with an answer. There was no time anyway.

The temperature plummeted. I steeled myself.

Boom! Boom! Boom!

I jumped, clutching at the branch above my head. Herne had warned us about the traps surrounding their camp. Demos and I had been lucky not to stumble across any of them.

A feral screech cut through the silence. I was panting now, and I wasn't the only one. Next to Demos, a boy white-knuckled his sword, his entire body trembling. He must have only been eleven or twelve winters. What was Herne thinking, allowing him at the front?

Demos glanced at him, a muscle feathering in his jaw. And then he went still.

The forest surrounding us was silent—as if even the

animals knew what was coming.

I caught a single glimpse of feathered wings extending from a warped spine. Red eyes glowed malevolently beneath a heavy brow ridge as the creature shot toward the ground…and the rebels positioned to meet it.

I fired, my bolt sinking deep into the creature's throat. It fell, but not before letting loose a shriek of retribution.

A shriek echoed by the creatures attacking from both the forest floor and the sky.

My teeth began to chatter.

I drew and fired. Again and again, in rhythmic succession. In the trees surrounding me, the other archers did the same, until the sky was filled with arrows. The creatures ducked and dodged, shockingly fast. But we were managing to keep them at bay. For now.

Vynthar was suddenly there, his movements just as fast as the attacking beasts. I'd wondered where he was, worrying for hours about whether one of them had found him and killed him earlier. I should've known he'd arrive on his own time.

"Don't shoot the monster without the wings!" I screamed.

Vynthar let out a roar as one of the creatures dove at him. In a vicious movement, he launched himself at it, burying his teeth in its neck. The creature flapped its wings, attempting to fly away, but Vynthar's huge jaws clamped down harder. He shook his head, those long teeth driving deep. The creature went limp. Dead. Vynthar merely released him and aimed for another.

I risked a single glance as I nocked my next arrow. On the ground, Demos and the other rebels sliced and stabbed, fighting with a vicious fury. Something in my chest released.

Somewhere, in the distance, Herne roared orders.

I let loose another arrow, straight into the spot where the creature's heart might have been. It didn't even falter. My stomach knotted.

"The wings!" I screamed, hoping the others could hear me. "Aim for the head or the wings."

More creatures fell from the sky. But they were getting smarter. A blur of black shot toward me, and I loosed my arrow, only for it to dodge it entirely. It aimed for the tree next to me and the woman who'd smiled at me.

I spun, almost losing my seat on the branch. But I was too late. The creature had her in its claws, and he flapped strangely beautiful wings, taking her higher and higher. She screamed, legs kicking.

I aimed. Missed. No, no, no!

The archers surrounding me fired again and again. But the creature had flown too high.

It let the woman go. Her scream echoed over the sound of the battle, abruptly ending as she hit the ground with a thud I imagined I could hear.

My eyes burned, but I fought myself to focus, filing away the details. That action implied some level of malevolence. A dark intelligence. We'd hurt and killed its people, so it had publicly displayed what it could do to us.

My pulse pounded at my temples.

The creature shrieked, and this time, there was no mistaking the triumph. Its red eyes glowed, it tucked its wings tight, diving at Demos. My heart jumped into my throat. Demos was cutting a path through the creatures. He'd killed so many that they lay in piles around him.

And the creature had clearly noticed.

My hands trembled, but I took a long breath, focusing only on the feel of the crossbow in my hands. On the way my arrow would strike true.

I drew, fired, aiming right for the huge, winged monster. My bolt slammed straight into its wing. But it didn't matter. It was still diving. Straight toward Demos.

Acid boiled in my gut. I nocked, aimed, fired again.

A breeze tickled the side of my face. I ducked, barely avoiding claws. One of the monstrous creatures careened toward my tree, razor-sharp claws extended from its gnarled feet as it dove for me.

It barely missed.

But now, it was too close. I fumbled my knife from its sheath, pressing myself against the rough bark and slinging my crossbow over my shoulder. The creature's hot, fetid breath washed over me, and it dodged around my tree branch, snapping at my leg.

My eyes met blood-red orbs. There was a bloodthirsty intelligence peering out from its monstrous face. It wanted me dead.

I yanked my leg away, and its teeth closed with an audible "snap." Slashing out with my knife, I sliced along its scaled arm.

It shrieked, slamming its clawed arm into my wrist. My hand instantly went numb, fingers opening, and my knife dropped to the ground. Blood pounded in my ears.

One of its brethren shrieked back. The creature snapped again, its movements fluid, predatory. My tree was dense enough that it was finding it difficult to snatch me up as I scrambled away, moving between branches. It flapped huge, feathered wings, until it was above me once more.

It tucked those wings tight, slicing through leaves and twigs as it plunged, claws extended.

Hunching my left shoulder, I swung my quiver toward me, fumbling for an arrow…

The beast barreled toward me. My vision dimmed at the edges, until it was all I could see.

Wait.

Wait.

Now.

I drove the arrow toward it with all my strength. The iron sank into its red eye with a wet pop.

The creature's scream was something out of a nightmare. Taloned feet scrabbled on the tree branch as its wings tangled in smaller branches and leaves. It slashed out, and all I could do was cover my head with my arms, huddling against the tree. Claws raked at my arm, and I screamed as pain erupted, driving up toward my shoulder. I peered beneath my arm. Long, bone-white teeth snapped, inches from my throat. I clung to the branch above my head. I was going to die. I was—

One wing tangled briefly in the branches surrounding us, and the creature snarled, shaking it free. It leaned back.

Now.

Pulling my leg back, I slammed it into its face. It shrieked, a high, bone-chilling sound. I kicked again and again, desperate sobs escaping my throat.

The creature fell, steadied itself, flew higher. I braced for its return.

But it wove through the air, its eye ruined, likely impacting its balance. Retreating. It was retreating. I shuddered, unwilling to move, until finally, it was a tiny speck in the sky.

Everything hurt. My hands were scraped and bleeding from clinging to the tree. Blood dripped from my arm. But I wasn't dangling high above the forest, about to be dropped.

Demos.

I peered through what remained of the leaves and branches on this side of my tree after the creature had stripped so many of them bare. Demos was fighting the winged beast that had aimed at him. A dry sob escaped my chest. He was still alive. Still moving faster than should have been possible.

The creature dove again and again with alarming speed, massive wings smashing branches as it hurtled toward him. Each time, Demos rolled away, just as the monster's talons rent the soil where he'd stood.

Snarling, the creature snapped at Demos. He dodged

its razor teeth, slashing out with his sword. A bloody gash opened near its neck, but that just seemed to enrage it further.

Demos matched the monster in ferocity, cunning, speed. A claw swipe here, a sword slash there—for a long moment, all I could do was hold my breath and watch, helplessness warring with fascination.

He'd been born for this, I realized. The gods had created Demos for just this reason—to wage war. To kill. To *protect*.

But he was still just a man. Swinging my bow over my shoulder, I aimed.

In a burst of fury, the creature pounced, wings spread wide. Demos sidestepped, muscles bunching as he swung his sword in a wide arc.

His blade cleaved through membrane and feather and bone. With an unearthly howl, the creature crashed to the ground, one feathered wing gone. It thrashed in agony, kicking up plumes of dirt.

I lowered my bow. Demos's expression was cold as he approached the beast. His sword reflected the last of the light as he swung it straight through the creature's neck.

Several of the creatures began to flee. It appeared the one Demos had felled was one of its leaders.

But one of the creatures turned, teeth flashing in a snarl. And it aimed for the boy.

The boy who'd just tripped on a tree root and dropped his sword

I was already scrambling down my tree, jumping the last few footspans.

Demos sprinted, aiming for him.

The boy fell onto his ass, shuffling backward. Demos wasn't going to make it.

The creature slashed out.

I nocked an arrow. Fired.

Demos lunged.

My arrow struck true, straight through the creature's open mouth. But it was still moving.

So was Demos.

His sword flashed. But he was too far away. I saw the moment he chose. The life of the boy over his own. Time seemed to slow.

"Demos!" My scream was swallowed by the din of the fight around us.

Demos was off-balance. But he leaped, propelling himself in front of the boy. The creature's talons shredded through his shoulder and one side of his back. But Demos stubbornly held his ground.

Another scream was ripped from my lungs. I fired again, but the creature was already slashing out once more, burying its claws in Demos's side. My next arrow lodged in the creature's eye, and it fell back.

But Demos slumped to the ground as well.

22

ASINIA

The beasts still circled high above our heads. But they were no longer attacking, merely dodging the arrows our archers continued to send their way.

I sprinted toward Demos, falling to my knees.

"I'm sorry," the boy choked out. "I'm so sorry."

"Pick up your sword," I said. Gods, there was so much blood. "And get back to camp."

He scrambled to his feet and ripped off his shirt, handing it to me. His face was wet as he stared at Demos. "He saved my life."

"So don't waste it. Go."

I pressed the boy's shirt against Demos's side. I wasn't a healer. I needed Tibris. I didn't know what to *do*.

Demos's eyes met mine. They were clear. Fearless. And tender. "Run," he ordered, but his voice was barely a whisper. "They might circle back."

I would never leave him. And I was keeping one eye on the sky. "Just as soon as you can run with me."

"Sin."

"How bad is it?"

"Bad," his eyes told me. But he didn't say a word.

I took a deep breath, removing the pressure I was putting on his side. Pushing up his shirt, I found the deepest wound. His blood was still spilling out onto the ground around us. Dropping my crossbow, I pulled off my tunic, leaving me in just the flexible band around my breasts.

"The closest I get to undressing you, and I can't even make the most of it." His words came out weak, but still soaked in humor.

"Survive this, and I'll let you undress me," I said recklessly.

He laughed, but it was a mere puff of air.

I scanned the sky. The creatures had disappeared. But who knew if they'd fled for good or if they were planning to return?

Around us, the wounded moaned. Demos wasn't the only body lying flat on the ground with someone next to him. Nearby, a woman burst into tears, sobbing a name over and over. Herne would dispatch the human healers without power, but he wouldn't risk letting Tibris near the front. And we needed his magic.

I tied my tunic to the boy's shirt, wedging it beneath Demos's torso. He grunted but helped me by rolling slightly, allowing me to encircle his torso with it. I tied it in a knot to put a little pressure on the wound. But it wouldn't last for long. Especially when I moved him.

"Sin."

"Either help, or shut your mouth. I need to think."

He shut his mouth.

The way he was bleeding... If I moved him, I could kill him. But I had to get him to Tibris.

Prisca wasn't losing her brother here.

And I wasn't losing my...whatever he was.

Demos didn't get to make me think about him night and day and then die in front of me.

He was too heavy to drag. I couldn't carry him in my arms, but...

"I need you to help me get you up."

If I could get him closer to camp, I could scream for Tibris.

"Sin."

"Just try, Demos. Please."

Our eyes met, and the faint smile he gave me almost tore my heart in two. "Whatever you want."

He thought it would make him bleed out faster. And if I didn't move quickly enough, it would. And yet he cupped my face, his thumb brushing over my bottom lip.

Tears blurred my eyes. I needed Prisca. In that moment, I would have given anything for her power. Anything for her to be here to stop time long enough for Tibris to get here.

"You said your power makes you heal faster," I choked out.

"It can't achieve miracles, Sin."

"We'll see about that."

He made it to his knees. At some point, he was going to pass out. But if I could maneuver him into the right position, I could carry him. Not for long, but I could do it.

When he was on his feet, he buried his face in my neck and sniffed. "You smell like home."

Swallowing around the lump in my throat, I helped him sling an arm around my neck. With most of his weight slumped against me, I was as unsteady as a drunk. But I'd paid close attention to the route we'd taken here. He was on his feet. We were getting to Tibris. I would entertain no other option.

Demos's head lolled against me, his blood warm against my bare stomach. The metallic scent of his blood put me on edge, until I wanted to scream.

He didn't speak. I don't think he had it in him. All his energy was consumed by helping me steer him. By putting one foot in front of the other. Tiny steps, but steps all the same.

Halfway there, he let out a breath. "I'm sorry."

He went limp. But I'd prepared for this. Leaning against the closest tree, I let it take his weight. Then I crouched, pressing my leg between his legs to steady him. Grabbing his right hand with my left, I draped his arm over my shoulder. He was so much taller than me, but I squatted anyway, attempting to distribute his weight as evenly as I could over my shoulders.

I stumbled, cursed. Recovered. Hooking my arm around his knee, I straightened. Immediately, my legs wobbled beneath his immense weight. But I gritted my teeth. Ignoring the spasm in my back, I took one step, then another. My shoulders screamed in protest, my breath already coming in labored gasps. Demos let out a groan.

"I know. I'm sorry."

He was alive. If he was making those pained noises, he was still alive. My breath exploded from my lungs in a sob, and he let out another sound, tensing slightly.

He was worried about me. I had to keep my sounds to myself or he would stay conscious, when passing out again would be the best thing for him.

The forest seemed to close in on me as I staggered on. Gnarled roots threatened to trip me with every step. The sun had slipped behind the trees, and if I weren't careful, I'd fall, break an ankle, and Demos would die.

My body was slick with sweat. One of my arms was still bleeding from my fight with the creature in the tree.

I stumbled again and almost went down. My hand caught on something warm and furry.

Vynthar prowled beside me. I let out a shaky breath. He could help.

Place him on my back.

"I can't. I'll drop him."

Then use me for balance.

I choked out a sob. "Thank you." I reached for him, my hand sliding into his fur and holding tight. He pressed his body next to mine, helping me stay balanced as he guided me over the uneven forest floor with his superior sight.

When the glow of campfires finally pierced the night, I let the sob caught in my lungs free.

"Help!" I screamed. "Help!"

Several people stumbled toward me. "More survivors?" a man asked, his own tunic damp with blood. "Gods, how are you carrying him?"

"Tibris," I demanded. "This is his brother. Get Tibris now."

Someone called for him, while the men helped gently pull Demos from my shoulders. His face was so pale, my heart stopped. But he cracked his eyes open, his gaze scanning me as if for injuries.

His eyes rolled back in his head as one of the men pulled off the tunic I'd tied around him. And then Tibris was there, his expression grim. Tears rolled down my cheeks.

"Move," Tibris ordered the men.

"Don't let him die," I begged. "Tibris—"

"I know. I know, Sin."

He'd likely been healing for hours. But he held his hands over Demos's body. And then he closed his eyes.

MADÎNIA

Jamic was a strange man.

It was unsurprising, given how he'd spent the last however many years. But still, the way he stood on his balcony, staring down at the wild fae gardens below us...

It was as if he was memorizing everything. So he could store it away. Did he think he was destined to be locked up once more?

I'd knocked on his door a few minutes ago, after bathing and dressing. It was warm in the fae lands, and my dress was made out of some gauzy material that danced in the breeze.

Jamic had opened the door and gestured silently for me to enter. He didn't speak often. Today, we would finally remove the amulet from around his neck, and it would be returned to the fae. With Prisca and the others mourning Cavis and strategizing for the summit, I'd arranged to be here with Jamic for this.

He had no one else.

"You didn't need to come," he said, as if reading my mind. With the amount of power I could feel simmering within him, I wouldn't have been surprised if he could.

"I wanted to."

Someone approached, and I turned. A short, pale fae woman stood behind me—unremarkable except for her eyes, which were a strange mix of blues, greens, and browns. Next to her, a tall, solemn-faced man shifted on his feet.

"I am Nortris, and this is Metral," she said. "We are healers."

Jamic nodded. He appeared unconcerned, but I'd caught the way his jaw tightened. "Come in," he told all of us.

When we were all seated in the plush chairs near

Jamic's fire, Nortris gave Jamic an encouraging smile. "We have no way to know what the effect will be once we remove the amulet. Never before has a human worn such an artifact—and His Majesty said you have worn it for years. So this is just the first attempt. Metral will remove the amulet while I balance the power within you, reducing the drain to a steady trickle."

Because she didn't know what would happen if the power was removed suddenly.

My stomach began to twist. We needed Jamic alive or there was little chance we could take down the barrier. But from what Lorian had said, there was no way the fae would cooperate if Jamic attempted to take it down with that amulet still around his neck.

And…I didn't want to watch him die. I understood firsthand his desperation to live every moment he could. He deserved more time.

I studied the amulet. It was identical to the one I'd seen that day at the city gates, when Prisca and I had galloped through the streets, only to learn that Lorian and the others were fae.

The middle of the stone was dark, as if draining all the light from the room. Yet it lightened at the edges, until it was almost the same color as both the silver setting and the chain around Jamic's neck.

"What happens if you can't remove it?" I asked.

Nortris exchanged a glance with Metral. "We change our approach. We'll bring in someone with more power, and we'll try again. And again. Eventually, it will work."

She smiled at Jamic, and he gave her a placid nod back.

Did he ever show his true emotions? I shook off that thought. Likely, Regner had stifled such urges while Jamic was still learning to walk.

"I'm ready," he said.

Metral got to his feet and moved until he was standing behind Jamic, his hand poised over the chain of the amulet. Nortris stood in front of him, her gaze on Jamic's face.

My skin prickled. Nortris paid me no attention. But Metral glanced at me. There was something on his face...

Metral slammed his hand onto Jamic's head. And a thick spider web appeared on Metral's left check.

I was already up and moving, but Metral shoved his power into Jamic. Jamic let out a low, agonized sound as his skin began to turn gray.

Metral was killing him.

Jamic's eyes rolled up into his head, and he began to seize. Nortris screamed, hands fluttering as she attempted to push Metral away from Jamic.

Metral smashed his free hand into her face, and she fell.

I could taste ash on the tip of my tongue. Dread crept up my spine until my entire body shook with suppressed adrenaline.

"Let him go," I said quietly.

Metral bared his teeth. The web had encompassed the entire side of his face. "I can't. Kill me."

I knew what that web meant. And I couldn't let him

kill Jamic. Still, I hesitated.

Metral did something to make Jamic scream.

My flames came to me easily. Hungrily.

I aimed my fire at Metral's heart, and he slumped to his knees. Within moments, he was dead. Just footspans away, Nortris sobbed and sobbed.

The door burst open. Fae guards streamed inside, their armor gleaming silver. One of them aimed his power at me, but Nortris had raised a ward. The guard gaped at her, betrayal clear on his face.

She just pointed at Metral, her hand trembling.

My stomach turned. I'd burned a man alive. It wasn't the first time, and it wouldn't be the last. But I'd looked into his eyes. He hadn't wanted to die. But he hadn't been able to control himself. So he'd made the honorable choice.

Just as Cavis had.

Metral's body was blackened, extremities curled in. But I'd been careful not to burn his face so they could see Regner's mark. The proof that their healer was one of the human king's spiders.

Jamic was slumped in his chair, barely breathing. I glanced at Nortris, and she placed her hands on either side of his face.

Taking a step closer, I watched her carefully, my pulse still racing. She sent me an anxious glance but didn't protest.

"He'll be okay," she said softly. "I know Metral's power, and I know how to nullify it."

The guards were removing Metral's body. "We will order protection for the boy," the one who'd attempted to kill me said. "His Majesty will be notified immediately."

Within minutes, the room was empty. If I ignored the scent of charred flesh, the gray tinge to Jamic's skin, and the way Nortris's hands shook as she healed him, I could almost pretend nothing had happened.

This had been an assassination attempt. Regner had obviously decided he would rather kill Jamic than allow us to use him.

If I hadn't been here, he would have succeeded.

Jamic opened his eyes. They were blurred with suppressed pain and fear.

"Take it off," he demanded.

"You almost died," Nortris said.

"Off." His hands fumbled for the amulet, his eyes stark with desperation. "Now."

"Do what he says."

Nortris glanced at me. "You will have to help."

In the end, Nortris and I worked together. She shoved her power into Jamic, while I slowly, and with great care, lifted the chain.

Every few moments, she would tell me to stop, and I would freeze as she did something I couldn't see. Jamic sat quietly, but I could feel his anticipation.

"Now."

I lifted it over his head.

"Stop."

I froze. The chain was no longer around his neck, but

the amulet was still pressed against his chest. This would be the biggest test.

"Now."

My lungs burned as I held my breath, slowly pulling the amulet up.

We both looked at Jamic.

His smile was beautiful.

He was free.

The amulet felt warm in my hands, and I eagerly handed it over to Nortris. She met my eyes. "Thank you for what you did for Metral. I don't know if I could have done it."

I almost flinched. She was looking at me as if I had done something heroic. "I killed him."

"You freed him. His family will be grateful." She leaned close to Jamic, checking his eyes, his pulse, his coloring. When she'd examined his reflexes and had him walk around the room, she ordered him to rest.

And then we were alone.

"You saved my life," Jamic said. "Thank you."

"We need you. For the barrier."

I'd expected my words to remove the gratitude from his eyes. Perhaps he'd stop looking at me as if I were his savior. Instead, he just laughed at me.

"Does it hurt?" I asked.

He shook his head. "I can feel the absence of it, but...I can suddenly hear myself think. Humans aren't meant to wear fae artifacts." He glanced at the balcony. "Would you like to sit outside?"

His eyes shone as I nodded, following him out. He wore that same wide-eyed expression as he gazed out at the world.

"Will you help us?" I asked.

He shrugged one shoulder, leaning over the balcony handrail to peer down at the garden below. "I didn't know I had a choice."

"You do. Of course, if you don't help us, there's a good chance Regner will find you and kill you. This little incident proves that. But the choice is still yours."

His mouth twitched as he glanced at me. He had such old eyes.

"Yes, I'll help you. I want him dead more than anyone."

We stood in a comfortable silence for a while, until he sighed.

"Everyone is worried about the barrier. But you should really be focusing on the grimoire."

"The grimoire?"

He grimaced. "You all keep referring to it as a 'book.' As if it would fit neatly in a library."

"It's not?"

"Calling the grimoire a book is like calling the barrier a fence."

"How do you know this?"

He gave me an impatient look. "I was there when Regner learned the grimoire could do more than he'd ever imagined. And I was there when he learned that there are others—and that he'll never be able to find them, thanks to the barrier he constructed. This war isn't the only reason he now wants that barrier down." He turned his gaze back to the city in the distance, where fae buildings glowed as white as exposed bone. "What exactly do you know about the grimoire?"

I studied his face. Now that he wasn't wearing that amulet, Jamic was almost…loquacious. Although, I *had* also saved his life. Perhaps he'd decided he could trust me.

"Conreth told Prisca the book—grimoire—was created by a dark god. It's the reason Regner was able to create the barrier. He found instructions teaching him how to do it."

He nodded. "There is much I don't know. And what I do know, I overheard in snippets. But there is a priestess Regner favors who was often…kind to me." His cheeks warmed, and he hunched his shoulders. "If we can find a way to speak with her, we will learn everything Regner knows."

"Tell me what you *do* know."

"The dark god knew his siblings were going to strip him of his power. His memories. They were tired of the favoritism his father showed him, and they didn't approve of his plans for this world. Before they could attack him, he learned of their plan. He poured much of his knowledge, power, and *self* into three grimoires, casting them out into this world. He knew they would be used, and when they were, that knowledge would call to him."

If Regner ever found the other two grimoires, we

were doomed. I couldn't let him become that powerful. He didn't get to win. After everything he'd taken from all of us... The life I could've had...

Would I have known my mother if Regner hadn't relentlessly hunted our people for so long? Would I have grown up somewhere safe? Would I have been surrounded by love?

"Madinia?"

I forced myself to focus. "What has Regner used the grimoire for?"

"I don't know. But...I think he did something to change how the oceartus stones worked. To make it possible for him to drain and keep our power."

I went still. If Regner had used the book to change the oceartus stones from their true purpose...

To take their power...

We could undo it.

We could give that power back.

Just as long as we killed Regner and took the grimoire.

"Galon said Regner's wards are impenetrable."

Jamic nodded. "When Tronin gave the fae their amulets and Bretis gave the hybrids their hourglass, Faric gave us humans a mirror. Regner used the grimoire to tie his wards to the mirror, and just as the mirror casts back a reflection, Regner's wards cast back any magic aimed his way."

I could see where he was going with this. "If we destroyed the mirror, you think his personal wards would be destroyed too."

"The priestess said she believes the fae and hybrids would have to cooperate to destroy the mirror."

His cheeks had flushed again. Clearly, he held the priestess's words in high regard. But was it because she knew what she was talking about, or because he wished to remove her blue robes?

I smirked. Either way, I would talk to Prisca about this.

"I need something from you," Jamic said.

"Hmm?" I blinked, pulling my mind from everything I'd just learned.

"I'll help you. With everything you need. But in return, you must do something for me."

"Me, personally?"

"Yes."

I eyed him. "What is it?"

"I can't tell you yet."

"When does this need to happen?"

"I can't tell you that either."

I turned, fully facing him. "And you think I'll blindly agree?"

"I would never hurt you. You just saved my life."

I studied his face. "You won't help us without my agreement?"

His jaw clenched. "I will help only as much as I am forced. Prisca seems like a good person. She would feel badly if she had to force me to cooperate."

And I'd thought he was innocent. Guileless.

Inexperienced. He may have been locked up, may be desperate for freedom, but he had still seen nineteen winters. And he was still Kaliera's son. I wouldn't forget that again.

I sighed. "I won't do anything to betray the others. Or anything that puts our plans at risk."

His back stiffened, a flash of indignation flickering through his eyes. "I would never make you do that."

"Fine."

PRISCA

Lorian was gone when I woke up, groggy from my nap. Peeling myself off the bed, I suppressed the urge to climb beneath the covers, and I bathed instead, choosing one of the dresses Emara had insisted were for guests. A pretty pale blue, the gown was tight along my torso, falling to the ground in gentle folds.

I would have liked to check my reflection, but I'd ordered the mirrors to be removed from our rooms.

And reflection deceives...

A knock sounded on the door. Crossing the room, I opened it, expecting to find Madinia, perhaps Rythos or Galon. Instead, Emara smiled at me.

"I just wanted to check on you." She scanned me. "That dress looks lovely on you."

"Thank you." I opened the door, and she strolled in.

"I hope your rooms are adequate."

"They're perfect." We'd been making camp in the forest for the past week. A seedy inn would have been an improvement over the hard ground. But it truly seemed to matter to Emara that we were comfortable.

I got the sense that she was…lonely.

"I spoke to your aunt. She said to tell you she'll rest for the remainder of the day. And Lorian is speaking with Sybella."

Pain shot through me, sharp and unrelenting.

All I could do was nod.

"There is…something else. As you'd discussed with Conreth, two healers were dispatched to remove the amulet from Jamic."

My heart stuttered. "The power drain killed him."

"No. But one of the healers tried to."

"What—" Shame and shock warred on her face, and I understood. "He was one of Regner's spiders."

"Yes. Your friend Madinia killed him. The amulet has been removed, and Jamic is fine. We have increased security—with Conreth's most trusted guards. And Madinia is staying with Jamic."

Even here, Regner had people lying in wait. If I let myself dwell on it, I would scream. Still, I made a mental note to talk to Jamic.

Emara's expression creased, and she turned toward the balcony, then seemed to change her mind, pacing the room.

"Is something wrong?" I asked.

"No," she said quickly. "Nothing is wrong, I just…" She stopped moving, and her gaze found my face. Her eyes were guarded, but she licked her lips, glancing away. "Lorian has been incredibly loyal to Conreth for all these years. I know it hasn't always been easy, and there were times when he didn't agree with those orders, but he always followed them. Now…" she sighed. "It seems Lorian no longer wishes to be a part of this family."

Her unspoken question hung in the air. So many potential answers jumped into my throat that I almost choked on them. After a long moment, I rolled my shoulders, attempting to force myself to relax. "Do you think Lorian feels as if you are a family?"

"He has always been welcome here."

I kept my face expressionless and watched her silently. She frowned. "I think I understand what you are implying. But my question remains unanswered. I know Lorian is enamored with you—anyone can see that. But he has had other women before. He has never risked his relationship with Conreth for any of them."

I winced. I wasn't sure if she was *trying* to annoy me with the "other women" comment or twisting the knife with the "risked his relationship" part.

A blush rose to her cheeks, but she kept her eyes on me. And I understood. Behind her warm, welcoming exterior, she was still the fae queen.

"Lorian is my mate," I said. And it was my turn to watch her.

The blush disappeared, taking any other color remaining in her cheeks with it. I shifted uncomfortably on my feet. Was she...in love with Lorian?

"When...when did you learn this?"

Irritation began to chew at the manners I was working so hard to display. I didn't even know this woman, and she felt entitled to private details about my relationship. If Lorian had once had some kind of intimate relationship with her and hadn't told me...

Emara was still waiting for my reply.

"With all due respect—"

She waved a hand through the air. "Forgive me, I can see the conclusion you would naturally come to. But no, I'm not and have never been in love with your...mate." Her nose wrinkled slightly, even as humor flickered in her eyes.

Something in my chest relaxed. "I only learned this information recently. Lorian didn't want me to feel... trapped."

Her expression softened. "You must have been upset when you discovered he'd lied to you."

"Yes," I admitted. "I understand why he did it. But..."

"You're still carrying that lie of omission with you."

I didn't like her tone. As if I had no right to that feeling. She caught my frown and lifted her hand, playing with one of the pearls hanging from her necklace.

"I may have only just met you, but I like what I've seen so far. I know you were raised human, and I can imagine our ways must seem foreign to you. Would you allow me to offer you some perspective?"

I didn't know what to say to that. But I nodded.

Her expression turned solemn.

"I'm in love with Conreth. And he is in love with me. Together, we have enjoyed a wonderful life and a relationship filled with mutual respect. One day, gods willing, we might have a child. Despite everything we have, I would give anything for Conreth to be my mate. *Anything*."

Her eyes flooded, and I opened my mouth, unsure what to say. Emara simply shook her head. "I have to live with the fact that his true mate is out there somewhere. The other half of his soul. And no matter how much I love him, our relationship can never be what he would have with her."

I couldn't imagine such a thing. Could I have kept Lorian, knowing there was someone else out there for him—someone his people believed had been crafted by the gods to be the other half of his soul?

As much as I would like to believe I could, the jealousy and insecurity would eat me alive.

"I'm sorry."

Emara wiped at her eyes. "I used to think that knowledge might destroy me. Now, I can admire Conreth for doing what he saw as best for his kingdom, even as I wonder if my own mate might be out there somewhere, waiting for me. I apologize for involving myself in your relationship, especially as we have only recently met.

But…Lorian gave me some advice of his own a long time ago, and that advice helped me greatly during one of the darkest points of my life. So I'm going to give you some advice too. When the fae love, they love deeply and unreservedly. And with their mates…that love has no limits. I know Lorian, and his love for you will be a wild, possessive love. He will cherish you above all, but he may forget that you have other responsibilities. And he will give up *everything* for you."

My eyes blurred, and I turned away. "Do you think I want to get between him and his brother?"

"No," she said softly. "I don't believe you do. Conreth has made some mistakes—"

"Mistakes?" The word whipped from me, and I forced myself to temper my tone. This was still the fae queen I was speaking to. "Conreth's only job was to love his brother. And instead, he turned him into a weapon and watched him lose his soul one piece at a time."

Emara flinched. But from the way her gaze briefly lowered, some small part of her agreed. "I apologize for interrupting your day. I think…I think the relationship between Conreth and Lorian will likely get worse before it gets better. Both of them are stubborn men, and nothing you or I do will change that. But I hope one day we can be friends."

I attempted a smile. Emara seemed sheltered, despite her title, her responsibilities. But she also seemed to have a good heart. "I hope so too."

She smiled back, walking out of the room. She didn't

rush, yet her steps were purposeful, graceful.

When her footsteps faded down the hall, I wiped my face and went to find Galon and the others.

I found Marth sitting on his balcony, a bottle of wine in his hand. He drank straight from the bottle, turning his attention away from it just long enough to nod at me.

"Galon is training. He made noises about finding you for a session."

I looked down at my pretty dress ruefully. Marth sniggered.

"Where is he training?"

"Below the castle. There's a small arena down there for when Conreth and his guards wish to train alone."

His expression had hardened once more, and I sat next to him. "Do you want to talk about it?"

He shook his head.

We sat in silence for a long time. Occasionally, he sent me a glower, as if silently asking why I was still in his space. I just smiled at him, waiting him out.

Finally, he sighed.

"I saw them."

"Who?"

"Sybella and Piperia."

I flinched, and Marth nodded, his gaze still on the wild garden below us. "That's where Lorian is right now. I had to look Sybella in the face, knowing I am one of the reasons Cavis isn't coming home."

I couldn't imagine how painful it had been. Marth and Cavis had been friends for decades. He'd treated

Sybella as a younger sister, gently teasing her and spoiling Piperia.

"You're not to blame, Marth."

"Spare me your meaningless platitudes."

"Tell me, then," I said, attempting to keep my voice calm, level. "Tell me how it's *your* fault."

He slowly turned his head. And for the first time since I'd met him, he looked truly dangerous. "You want to hear all about how I failed my best friend? Do you enjoy tearing scabs from other people's wounds, Prisca?"

Plucking the bottle of wine from his hand, I took a long drink, ignoring his growl. He snatched it back, and I faced him. "I don't see any scab, Marth. I just see a bleeding wound that you refuse to let heal."

He sneered. "You're one to talk. Have you cried yet, Pris?"

"We're not talking about me."

"That's convenient."

I'd known he was in a dark place. So had Lorian. But I hadn't realized just how bad it was.

"Cavis would—"

"*Don't* talk to me about what Cavis would want. Cavis would want to be here right now, with his baby in his arms and his woman by his side. And he's not, because I paid no fucking attention when he told me he was seeing things. When he talked about strange dreams involving *webs.*"

Oh gods.

My mind threw me back to the night at the inn, soon

after Thol had arrived. I'd found Cavis wandering the hall, clearly exhausted. Confused.

Not one of us had paid attention. It had never occurred to us that Regner could have gotten to Cavis.

My throat ached, and I pressed my hands to my eyes.

"You can't blame yourself, Marth. No one else noticed either."

"I spent the most time with him out of everyone," he snarled. "But I was so busy being focused on my next fuck, I didn't listen to him when he told me he was losing time. He'd still be here if I'd paid attention. So don't tell me it's not my fault."

I lifted my head. He'd raised the bottle to his mouth again, and I reached for it. I tugged, and when he let go, I wasn't expecting it.

The bottle slipped out of my hands, smashed against the marble, and splattered both of us.

I stared down at my dress. It looked as if it was covered in blood.

Marth shook his head. "That was your first mistake today, Prisca. Pretty dresses don't belong in your future. The only things either of us have to look forward to are more blood and death."

23

PRISCA

Marth refused to discuss the subject any further. Instead, he'd found another bottle of wine, ignoring me until I left him alone.

Making my way back to my room, I swapped the wine-stained dress for leather leggings and a tunic, Marth's words playing on a loop in my head.

"Pretty dresses don't belong in your future. The only thing either of us has to look forward to is more blood and death."

He was probably right. Pulling my hair into a thick braid, I went in search of the training arena.

A fae woman pointed me in the right direction, and I walked down a winding stone stairwell beneath the castle. The walls seemed to close in on me, but I managed to breathe through the claustrophobia, silently counting the steps until the stairs widened and I emerged into an open cavern.

The arena was illuminated by fae

orbs, along with clusters of glowing crystals. Equipment stations had been set up around the perimeter—balance beams, climbing walls, weapon racks, and archery targets. I was underground, but the ceiling was so high, the space felt expansive.

A steady thud sounded, and I stepped into the arena, crossing the wide space until I found Galon in a hidden corner. He was alone, slamming his hand into a bag filled with sand, over and over. His knuckles were bleeding, leaving streaks on the bag, which had begun leaking sand.

He turned, spotting me. "About time. You haven't trained in days."

"I'm here now."

Galon's eyebrow rose, but he didn't comment on my tone. He seemed to realize I needed a distraction, because he made me run through everything I'd learned so far. Footwork, sword work, wrestling—even shooting with a bow and arrow. By the time we were through, I was dripping sweat, panting, and my muscles trembled from exertion.

"Time to stretch," he said.

I nodded, gratefully falling to the floor. It was made of some kind of springy moss, which was much more pleasant to fall onto than the arena in the hybrid camp. Galon had wrinkled his nose at the moss, muttering something about "precious baby kings."

"You're quiet," Galon said. He'd sat down next to me and was stretching his hamstrings.

I shrugged. He just pinned me with one of his

endlessly patient looks.

"I'm worried about Marth."

"My father once told me that when someone is haunted by guilt, nothing anyone else can do or say will scrub that ache from their soul. They have to plunge into that guilt, sink down in it, let it gnaw at their very core. When they finally rise, they'll either emerge cleansed, having faced and conquered that guilt, or they'll remain forever shacked by it."

I let his words sink in. "You're not worried?"

He let out a low laugh. "Of course I'm worried. I've spent years worrying about every one of those stubborn bastards."

I smiled. Galon just watched me, his expression hardening.

"Lorian has stayed with Conreth because of us, hasn't he?"

It wasn't my place. I opened my mouth, unsure what exactly to say. I didn't want to lie, but—

"That answers that question." Galon let out a low growl. "I'd wondered how Conreth had kept him loyal all these years. It was the one thing Lorian refused to talk about. It seems so fucking obvious now."

"It…it wasn't just you, Marth, Rythos, and…Cavis. You know Lorian loves the fae. He wants what is best for his people."

He nodded, but his expression was grim. "And yet Conreth has been keeping him as far from the generals and the armies and the wardens as possible. Because he wanted him leashed and never a threat."

"Yes." It was true. I might feel sorry for Conreth and the situation he was in, but I would never forgive him for what he had done to Lorian.

Galon had always been difficult to read, but in this moment, it was easy to see the repressed fury in his eyes.

"I'm going to kick his ass."

Despite the situation, I laughed. "He probably deserves it," I admitted.

"He shouldn't have allowed Conreth to use him like this. The rest of us would have been fine."

"Marth almost died."

Galon closed his eyes. "Of course. Conreth had ordered Lorian to put down a wildkin named Krythorx. It was ancient—even to the fae. And far too powerful and clever. Lorian refused to kill it. He said the fae were the ones encroaching on the wildkin's territory. No one else could kill the creature, and Lorian's refusal made Conreth look weak."

And that was the one thing Conreth couldn't tolerate—especially from Lorian. "So Conreth split you up as punishment, and that's when Marth almost died."

"Yes." Galon swept his hand across his face. "I never made the connection. If I had…" His mouth thinned.

Footsteps sounded on stone. I turned. Lorian entered the arena, but for once, my attention didn't linger on him.

No, I was too busy staring at Sybella and Piperia.

Sybella's eyes met mine. There were hollows beneath them, and she looked exhausted. Drained. Piperia had grown, and she let out a soft baby gurgle. Grief swamped me, until it felt as if I'd never be able to take a full breath again.

My gaze jumped to Lorian's. He was watching me, with that stubborn, resolute expression I knew so well.

"Sybella would like to talk to you," he said.

My throat was so tight I couldn't speak. Slowly, I got to my feet. I could feel his gaze lingering on me as I crossed the arena to Sybella and Piperia. Lorian had warned me I was going to have to face what had happened. And clearly, he was deciding it would happen now. I sent him a wrathful look. He tilted his head, his eyes cool, filled with challenge.

"There's a small seating area behind the stairs," Sybella said softly. "Will you come sit with me?"

I nodded, following her behind the stone staircase. The area was tiny, but several armchairs sat surrounding a crystal table.

We both sat, and my heart stuttered as our eyes met once more.

Piperia let out one of her baby sounds, and Sybella bounced her softly in her arms.

I opened my mouth, but everything I wanted to say got stuck in my throat. There was nothing I could say except…

"I'm sorry."

Sybella gave me a faint smile. She was the ghost of the woman who'd jokingly assured me that Piperia would grow into her ears.

"Cavis was always obsessed with helping people, did you know that?"

I nodded, and she sat back in her chair. "He told me once that it probably came from watching his village burn as a child. From knowing all of the most innocent people had been slaughtered."

My nails were digging into the arms of the chair. "Lorian mentioned Cavis had a soft spot for women and children."

Sybella nodded, and her eyes filled with tears. "It was one of the things that made me fall in love with him. He was so gentle. Even with everything he'd seen and done with Lorian and the others, he refused to allow it to make him hard."

"Sybella—"

"He once said you reminded him of what they were fighting for. Our people have a tendency to become jaded. But you reminded him that more than just the fae were at risk. We needed to care about the hybrids and humans too. We owed them that much."

Her grief was soaking into every word. She stared through me, her eyes blank, as if she was lost in the past.

I dropped my gaze to Piperia, who had fallen asleep. "I'm sorry," I said again. "I should have—"

"No." Her voice sharpened. "I don't blame you, Prisca. Cavis wouldn't either. The blame lies entirely with Regner. It would be easier if I *could* blame you. If there were someone close to me whom I could rage against. Perhaps that would help. But you're not that person."

I couldn't speak. The tears I couldn't shed were drowning me, and I was gasping for breath.

But there was something I had to say. A promise I had to keep.

"Cavis asked me to tell you something." My voice trembled, but I would get this out. Cavis deserved nothing less. "He wanted you to know it was always you for him. Ever since the moment he saw you. He said you'd know that, but he wanted to remind you. And he said…he said every second of what he went through in that cell was worth it for the time he got to have with you."

Sybella's eyes flooded, and she let out a tiny, choked sound that cracked my heart.

"Thank you." She got to her feet. And then she was placing Piperia in my arms. The baby was so warm, and she turned her face into me, as if she trusted me.

"Hold Cavis's daughter, Prisca. And make her a promise. Promise her you'll avenge her father."

Walking away, Sybella left me with Piperia. She weighed more than I'd thought she would, the feel of her solid in my arms. Her long lashes lay on her cheek, her tiny features so small and perfect…

Cavis had teased me about holding Piperia. And I'd been too terrified of how small and fragile she was.

Now I was finally holding her, and her father wasn't here to look on with a smile. I could hear him gently teasing me, could see his eyes filled with love as he gazed down at his daughter.

I pressed a kiss to her forehead, and tears began to

roll down my cheeks in a never-ending stream.

All the grief I'd been holding back, all the hurt and sorrow I'd shoved into that box inside me…

It all came pouring out.

I cried and sobbed and rocked, and the baby slept on, even when my tears splashed onto her tiny forehead and I had to wipe them away.

I understood what Lorian meant now. Death was going to come again and again. Not just throughout this war, but throughout our lives. I had two choices—face it and live a rich, full life, or hide from it and never truly experience the joy and happiness of loving with everything in me.

The price of love was loss.

We all paid it eventually.

LORIAN

"Fuck!"

Galon's fist slammed into my face. Thankfully, Prisca, Piperia, and Sybella had left the arena a few moments ago—something Galon had clearly taken as permission.

A spark rose from my own hand, and he frowned. "No power."

"I'm not going to use my fucking power," I muttered. *One time,* I'd lost control. Back when I'd only seen twelve winters. Galon had never let me forget it.

Clearly, he was furious with me. Ducking his next swing, I landed a punch in his gut. Pain swept through my side, and I hissed out a breath. He'd slammed his knee into my kidney. I'd feel that later.

"How many more decades were you going to lie to me, Lorian?"

I sighed. "Prisca told you." I should have known. I'd made her face Sybella, and she was making me face Galon. It wasn't a decision made out of spite or maliciousness. Neither of us seemed to be able to suppress our urge to meddle in each other's lives.

"Your mate merely confirmed what I already suspected," Galon snapped.

"It wasn't relevant."

His backhand was so fast, his arm was a blur. Thankfully, I had just as much experience with his tactics. Catching his wrist, I tripped him, taking him down to the mossy floor. Rolling free before he could turn this into ground fighting, I shot to my feet.

He glowered at me, slowly standing himself. "I thought we were brothers. Thought you knew you could tell me anything."

That wasn't fury in his voice. It was hurt. Tinged with bitterness. And I couldn't blame him.

"We *are* brothers," I said, dropping my guard. Truthfully, Galon was the older brother I'd never had—

more like a father to me. And I would prefer his uppercut to the misery in his eyes. "Brothers protect each other," I said. "So that's what I did."

"And when has Conreth ever protected you?" Galon growled.

I stared at him. Galon had never said a word against my brother. Oh, I'd known his feelings on the matter—the way he ceased talking whenever the subject came up had made that clear. But I'd obviously failed to understand the depth of his rage.

I forced myself to relive one of my worst moments. "When our parents died—"

"Conreth kept you alive and ensured you didn't lose your mind while you battled the grief."

I nodded.

He stepped closer and looked me in the eye. "That's called the bare minimum, Lorian."

Sucking in a breath, I looked away. "You don't understand."

"I do. We've all seen what he has done to you. I'm guilty too. I took the child he sent me and made him cold. Lethal."

"I needed to be both of those things."

"Perhaps. All of us have benefited from your reputation as the Bloodthirsty Prince. Regardless, if you leave, all of us will go with you."

My muscles locked up. "You've spoken to Rythos and Marth."

"I don't need to. You leave, we're with you. Cavis

would…" His voice turned hoarse. "Cavis would want this for you too."

"I can't pull you away from our people. You know the law."

He nodded. "You leave, and Conreth will enforce the boundary."

Grief ripped into me at the thought. It was an old law, but Conreth wouldn't provide any exceptions. There was no chance he *wouldn't* use the Boundary of Blood. Which meant I wouldn't be returning to this kingdom. Conreth had always been concerned that I would take the throne from him. That concern proved that he'd never really known me at all.

Galon sighed. "You were always going to leave. The moment you fell in love with Prisca. But you've been keeping your decision to yourself, because you didn't want to lose us. You won't, Lorian. We won't let that happen."

"We *will* make you pay for thinking you could leave us behind, though," Rythos said from behind me.

Marth let out a humorless chuckle.

I turned, facing all of them. All of us were older. Weathered. Dented from life's blows. Rythos had a faint frown line between his brows, while Marth stank of wine. Galon wiped blood from his mouth.

I want you all to think carefully about this," I said.

Rythos rolled his eyes. Marth just sneered at me.

"Go talk to your brother, Lorian," Galon said. "It's time to make your choice."

I was due to meet Conreth for a strategy session to prepare for the summit. But I could no longer pretend nothing had changed. I didn't bother bathing and changing my clothes, even knowing it would irritate Conreth. Instead, I strode through the castle, finding my brother in the sitting room within his private chambers. The chambers my parents had once shared.

The spacious room was once my mother's favorite place. Plush velvet cushions had adorned the artisan-crafted settees. Drapes made of iridescent silk had hung from the tall windows, pooling on the marble floor. If I inhaled, I could imagine the air still smelling faintly of her favorite roses. If I listened carefully, I could almost hear her laugh echoing in the crystal pendants of the chandelier above my head.

My mother had spent many hours of her days here, taking tea with her favorite courtiers, relaxing with my father, or helping me with my lessons. Her patience was endless, her voice always steady, calm.

I dragged my gaze away from the corner near the wide window overlooking her garden, where she'd loved to sit and admire the flowers.

Prisca had been right. Some part of me had never wanted to admit how much I loved Aranthon—since I spent so little time here. But this castle...

I loathed this castle and all the memories it contained.

"Emara said she likes Nelayra." Conreth kept his back to me, gazing down into the garden.

I stayed silent. Conreth knew my wildcat preferred to

be called Prisca and so had gone out of his way to ignore her wishes—just another way he attempted to put her in her place.

Conreth pivoted to face me, his gaze sweeping over my swollen cheek to the still-fresh bloodstains darkening my shirt and the traces of moss on my boots. One eyebrow arched ever so slightly.

Conreth was shockingly easy to irritate—so easy, that I usually didn't bother poking at him. But now, I had to stifle the urge to punch him in the face.

"I hope you'll dress appropriately for the summit tomorrow," he said.

I just angled my head. "Are my clothes truly what you wish to talk about now?"

He sighed. "No, Lorian. We need to strategize and plan. I've received word that you intend to go to the pirate queen directly after the summit. I can only assume this is yet another half-conceived plan of Nelayra's."

I wasn't surprised Conreth's spies had managed to get that information back to him. We hadn't bothered keeping it quiet. But it was time to address the way he spoke of my mate.

"Prisca has been eyeing Daharak Rostamir's fleet since the moment she learned of it. And since you're no closer to convincing the Arslan to give us their ships, the pirate queen may be our only chance at preventing Regner from entering our waters."

"The pirate queen is a self-serving opportunist who would do anything to hold on to her power."

I gave my brother a slow grin and let my gaze flick indolently up to the crown on his head. "You don't say."

"If you have something you'd like to discuss, now is the time," Conreth said, voice strained with forced tolerance.

"I do. You will watch how you speak about Prisca, or I will ensure that you won't speak for some time."

Conreth's eyes widened, then immediately narrowed. "And now you threaten your king for a woman. Some days, I barely recognize you, Lorian. Let me make myself clear. I gave you three weeks to return. Instead, you killed your way through Eprotha, choosing to ignore my messages. My generals had a strategic plan in place that involved Regner not knowing we were aware of exactly where each of his regiments was, and you blew that plan apart without a second thought."

"And I would do it again. Without hesitation."

A hint of Conreth's power broke free, and a thin layer of ice coated the marble beneath our feet. "I've given you more than enough time, Lorian. You knew this was coming. The hybrid heir will go to the pirate queen, and you will go in search of the third amulet. If the gods are generous, you'll find each other after the war."

Yes, I'd known this was coming. Yet I'd still hoped that this time Conreth might surprise me.

"Where did it all go wrong, Conreth? Once, we were brothers."

"We *are* brothers. And I need you to help me save our people. Together."

And now, he was attempting to manipulate me. Usually, fury would be burning in my gut at his blatant tactics. Now, I just felt empty.

"I'm leaving," I said.

He frowned. "Don't be ridiculous."

"Allow me to make myself excruciatingly clear. I choose Prisca. I will always choose her."

Conreth's eyes had lightened until they were almost white. "You're truly doing this? For a woman?"

"Prisca isn't just a woman."

"She has *ruined* you."

I just laughed. No longer did I seek his approval. Now, the only person I could ever imagine caring about pleasing was Prisca. As long as I could look her in the eye, and know she was proud of me, I would forever be content.

"Prisca is my mate."

It wasn't often that anyone could shock my brother. His mouth dropped open, and he immediately snapped it closed.

Silence stretched between us. Finally, his expression turned to stone.

"Irrelevant," he said. "I walked away from my mate for the good of this kingdom. I know it can be done."

Pity burned in my gut. He could tell himself he'd made the right choice, but we both knew regret would eat at him one day. "Our experiences are not the same."

"And why is that?"

I crossed my arms, staring him down. "You met

your mate and instantly recognized her. The Knowing happened for you, allowing you to flee before you knew her as a person."

His jaw had tightened at the word "flee," but he gestured for me to continue.

"I had been away from the fae lands for some time when I met Prisca. I had been in my human form most of the time and was left with only a hint of my power. Perhaps that is why I had no sudden *knowing* the moment I saw her face. Perhaps it was a different reason entirely. But I fell in love with her over weeks and months. Little by little, against my own will, I found myself desperate to hear the sound of her voice. To see her eyes light up when she looked at me. I wanted to make her *happy.* And when I understood she was my mate…" I shrugged. "It merely complicated things for me because I never wanted her to think that the mating was why I loved her. Even if the fates hadn't tied us together, I would have chosen her every day for the rest of my life."

Something flickered in Conreth's eyes. I didn't fool myself into believing it was understanding. But he was silent for a long moment. Finally, he pinched the bridge of his nose. "If I could change the past, I would make sure you never met her."

I bared my teeth, and the monster inside me evaluated him as a different kind of threat. After everything I'd just told him, he would still take her from me. All so I would be more *useful* to him. "I would put you down before that happened, *brother.*"

Someone knocked on the door.

"Go away," Conreth ordered.

The door opened anyway. Emara stood next to Prisca, who looked exceedingly uncomfortable. Her eyes were red, face swollen, but she smiled at me.

Just a smile, and I wanted to drag her out of this room—out of this castle—and tie her to my bed. She was the most courageous, loyal, beautiful woman I'd ever known, and my brother would take her away from me if he could. A spark of rage began to burn in my gut.

Emara ignored Conreth's frown, giving him a placid smile in return.

"No matter what has happened between you, it's important we are in accord before the summit tomorrow. Surely we can put everything else aside until a later time."

Interest flickered through me. Emara was finally stepping into her role as queen.

Despite Conreth's overall distaste for the situation, he nodded, gesturing to the circular table on the other side of the room. I'd spent hours sitting at that table, gorging myself on sweetbuns while my mother gently teased me.

Prisca slipped her hand into mine and squeezed. Our eyes met before her gaze dropped to the blood on my skin.

I squeezed her hand back, leading her to the table.

Emara took a deep breath as we sat down, clearly unused to such tension. "Shall I call for tea?"

Despite his mood, Conreth managed to eke out a smile for her. "I don't think this will take long." His gaze slid to Prisca's and turned cold. "The day we met, you asked me what it would take for me to ally with you. I told you to show me your people would rally behind you. To make the Gromalian king switch his allegiance from Regner, and to find allies. So far, I cannot see that you have achieved any of this."

Fury blazed through me. "Prisca has been a little busy being *tortured*."

"She had time to find her hourglass. That was where her priorities lay. With her own selfish needs."

My muscles locked up. Prisca squeezed my hand. I knew that look. She wanted to handle this herself.

"Unfortunately, I couldn't trust my new *ally* not to take that hourglass the moment my back was turned," she said softly. The barest hint of a flush rose to Conreth's cheeks. Prisca's eyes gleamed. "We are still working on the Gromalian prince. When he turns on his father, we need it to be completely irrevocable. That takes time."

Conreth opened his mouth. Prisca merely lifted a finger. "I'm not finished."

Emara's eyes widened and met mine.

"You told me to find allies," she said. "And I found perhaps the most important ally of all."

Conreth leaned back in his seat and waved his hand.

"I have a formal alliance with Regner's queen."

If there was one thing my brother was proficient at, it was keeping his thoughts from his face. But I was watching him closely enough to catch the surprise that tightened his lips.

"The human queen has no armies," he said.

"No, but she has given us information that allowed us to take Jamic before Regner could bring down the barrier. That's another thing we have been working on, by the way. Preventing Regner from becoming so bloated with power, he could kill you with a mere thought." She gave him a humorless smile. "You're welcome."

Gods, I loved this woman.

Conreth linked his fingers on the table in front of him. "I told you to make sure your people would fight in your name. Instead, I've learned that your cousin now controls twenty thousand hybrids trained for war. Hybrids who would likely enjoy cutting down *my* people. So, where are the rest of your allies?"

Pain flickered across Prisca's face. "I'm working on it."

"Working on it?"

Prisca angled her head. "Yes. Remind me—while I've been looking for allies, finding my birthright, watching a friend *die*, and freeing Jamic...what exactly have you been doing?"

Conreth's eyes widened. Likely, he was stunned by her sheer audacity.

"Be careful," he breathed.

Slowly, I got to my feet. "Threaten my mate again," I suggested.

Emara held up one hand. "Please," she said, although her voice trembled. "If we are this divided tomorrow, we have no chance of convincing the wardens to help."

"It's a valid question," Prisca said, her tone cool.

"From where I sit, the only thing you've done is judge our actions, all without getting your hands dirty yourself."

"We gave the hybrids a place to hide, and they stayed safe for decades. Perhaps it is time for them to fight their own battles."

Beneath the table, Prisca's hand had fisted. I sat, taking her hand once more.

Prisca gave Conreth a smile. As much as I wanted to rip out his throat, she could handle this. She *was* handling this. And pride burned through me until all I wanted to do was bury my hand in her hair and kiss her until she let out that tiny sound I adored.

"I'm glad you agree," Prisca said. "We will be moving children and elders, along with the weak and sick, out of the hybrid camp. Those who have been training all these years are eager to fight, and they will be moving from the hybrid camp as well. Approximately seven thousand of them are willing and able to meet Regner's forces."

Conreth's eyes met mine. I just lifted one eyebrow. No, I hadn't told him of these plans.

"Fifteen thousand," I said.

Prisca frowned, and I smiled at her before turning back to my brother. "Prisca was unhappy to see the distrust between our people when she visited the hybrid camp. So, the sleeping arrangements were changed. Hybrids and fae have been living together, fighting together, and competing in mixed groups. They've traveled from the camp to conduct various tasks within Eprotha, and hundreds of civilian fae have traveled from elsewhere across the fae lands to train as well. According to Hevdrin, they have vowed to fight shoulder to shoulder with the hybrids."

Prisca's hand shook. I knew she hadn't dared hope for this. Bringing her hand to my lips, I pressed a kiss to her knuckles.

"You've been communicating with Hevdrin," Conreth said tonelessly.

I shrugged. I knew my brother, and I knew he would enforce the Boundary of Blood when I left. Which meant I had nothing left to lose. The fact that I'd received messages from his general was just one more reason for him to distrust me. No matter that I had spent decades communicating directly with Hevdrin before this.

Emara reached for Conreth's hand. He allowed it. "The fact is, we are all in this war, whether we like it or not," she said softly. "Tomorrow, we must put aside our own issues and present a united force. We need their ships. Their soldiers. Their power. Without the wardens' cooperation, we will *lose* this war." Her voice tightened. "Can you do this?"

Prisca nodded. Grinding my teeth, I gave a sharp nod. Conreth released Emara's hand and slowly got to his feet. Meeting my eyes, he nodded. With one last glance at Prisca, he turned and stalked from the room.

24

PRISCA

The next morning, I paced our bedroom, stomach roiling, chest tight. My gown flowed around my feet—a dark purple. The bodice was intricately embroidered with pearls, and I wore the emerald necklace Lorian had gifted me while we were visiting Eryndan's court. Telean had kept the jewels safe for me. She'd advised me to wear the diadem, but I'd refused.

My aunt had sighed, but hadn't argued, handing me a message from Vicer instead.

Prisca

I'd hoped to be with you all by now, to help with your upcoming plans. I know you wanted me back, but I think I'm finally making some progress here. I am, however, attempting to get some more help to you in time.

-Vicer

I'd shaken my head, handing the message back to Telean. She'd scanned it and sighed. "That boy places too much hope in the wrong places."

She wasn't wrong.

Lorian had come to bed late last night after meeting with several officials. When he'd wrapped his arms around me, I'd woken from a strange dream, inhaled his scent, and held him tight, whispering with him until the early hours of the morning.

This summit would determine our exact response to Regner. Even knowing how important it was, I was eager to get to Daharak, and even more eager to bring down the barrier.

The longer we waited, the more time Regner had to make his plans. And those plans always involved blood and death.

Someone knocked on the door. Crossing the room, I opened it, finding Jamic waiting. His eyes met mine. "Madinia told me you wanted to see me."

I stepped aside, opening the door wider. "I was going to come to you. I just wanted to make sure you were feeling all right before I visited."

He nodded. "I'm fine."

I awkwardly held the door open until he finally strode inside.

"I'm sorry about what happened. With the healer," I said. "We promised to keep you safe."

"You did. Madinia killed him."

I nodded. "Listen, Jamic, I want to be clear. We would like you to help us take down the barrier. But it's going to be exceptionally dangerous, especially for you.

If Regner manages to get to you, he'll kill you right there. We'll do everything we can to protect you, but the truth is, it may not be enough."

His eyebrow quirked. "What are you saying?"

"I'm saying, this is your choice. You get to decide."

He frowned at me, clearly unimpressed. "And you'd accept that, would you? You'd let me walk out of here? What would you do if I said no?"

I blew out a breath. "We'd figure something else out. We'd find a way."

"You'd all die." His green eyes were solemn. "You're the hybrid queen."

"Not yet."

"But you will be. Why would you care about what I want?"

"You're a person, Jamic. All of us deserve to have the right to make our own choices. If I start taking away those choices for others, I'm no better than Regner."

He stared at me. "For what it's worth, I think you'll be a good queen."

"Why? You barely know me."

"I watch," he said plainly. "Thank you. For the offer. It...it means more to me than I can say. But I will help you. Even if I were to die, it would be worth it if it would end his grip on this continent."

"I hope...I hope when all this is done, and when you take your own crown, we can be friends."

His eyes widened, and I realized it hadn't occurred to him. That if Regner died, he would be the next in line for the throne. As far as the people of this continent were concerned, he was Regner's son.

A slightly sick look came over his face, but his mouth firmed. "Thank you. I hope the same."

With a nod, he turned and left the room.

Lorian stepped out of the bedroom. He'd known Jamic was here, of course, but he'd given us the illusion of privacy.

He wore black, his tunic adorned with golden thread. His green gaze slid over me, lighting with appreciation. "You look beautiful," he said. "We'll leave as soon as the meeting has concluded. I've already ensured we'll be packed, and I've arranged for a ship to take us to meet Daharak."

"No comment about Jamic?"

He gave me a slow smile. "I fell in love with a woman with a soft heart and a loyal soul."

I blushed, turning to pace some more. I couldn't be distracted by Lorian. I needed to run through all the potential outcomes—both negative and positive—for today…for the third time. He caught my hand as I strode past him, yanking me until I fell into his arms. "Have I mentioned how adorable you are when you're fretting?"

I eyed him. If there was one thing Lorian was particularly adept at, it was distracting me from my thoughts. When he couldn't use sex, his preferred method was to irritate me until I wanted to slap him.

The door opened, and Lorian cut his gaze to Rythos. "I suggest next time, you knock."

Rythos rolled his eyes, stepping into the room with Galon and Marth.

"Everyone ready?" he asked. "After your meeting with Conreth, we need to negotiate like our lives depend on it."

"This is the meeting Emara and I interrupted yesterday? What happened before we arrived?"

"I told Conreth I'm leaving." Lorian's voice was carefully neutral.

"To help me complete my blood vow with the pirate queen?"

"No, wildcat. I told him I was leaving this kingdom and choosing you. If you'll have me."

He grinned, but I glimpsed the barest hint of vulnerability in his eyes. The room had turned silent.

"You..." He'd given it all up. He'd formally separated from his brother. For me. The sheer weight of that decision swamped me.

His grin dropped, and he pinned me with a serious stare. "For months, you thought we were living on borrowed time. That we'd be forced to separate. I did too, at first. And then I realized I would never allow myself to be parted from you. We deserve to be happy."

"You shouldn't have done it." His expression turned blank, and I sighed. "But I'm so fucking glad you did." My voice broke, and I was immediately in his arms.

"You and me, Prisca. Forever."

I willed myself not to think of the seer and her words. To enjoy this moment. "Forever."

Rythos let out a victorious laugh, and I jolted. I'd forgotten the others were there. Galon was grinning at us, and even Marth looked pleased.

"But it's not enough to be your mate," Lorian said, drawing my attention back to him. "Not for me."

I pulled back. "Oh? What is it you want?"

He pulled a marriage bracelet out of his pocket. Precious stones glinted, catching the light.

"Marry me, Prisca. Be mine in the ways of your people, as well as mine."

My throat was too tight to speak. He'd known—how much I'd longed to be married in the future. I'd once told him of the weddings I'd attended. And the words from the woman I'd thought was my mother.

"I'm going to get married one day. Here in the village."

"No, you won't, Prisca. Such things are not for you."

Lorian had remembered. I loved that we were mates, but he wanted me to have a wedding too.

Tears rolled down my cheeks as I nodded.

He kissed them all away, one by one, before dropping his lips to my mouth.

I reached for the bracelet, wanting a closer look, and he shook his head, slipping it back into his pocket. "Not until you're mine in every way."

Stubborn man.

Rythos burst out laughing again, pulling me out of Lorian's arms and kissing me on the cheek.

Galon shoved him out of the way, wrapping me in

a hug. Rythos slapped Lorian on the back, while even Marth gave him a smile.

"Happy for you, Pris." Marth kissed my cheek.

"You'll come with us too, won't you?" I asked hopefully.

Rythos nodded. "Do you think you can find a place for us in the hybrid kingdom if we win this war?" His teeth flashed in a grin, but I knew him well enough to know when he was holding his breath.

I reached out and squeezed his hand. "Of course. We could never leave without you three."

Lorian pulled my hand from Rythos's and pressed a kiss to my palm. I shook my head at him, and he sent me a wicked smirk. Galon just heaved a sigh at Lorian and waved his hand toward the door. "Let's get this done."

PRISCA

According to Lorian, fae nobility were long-lived, often cynical, and almost always bored. So it wasn't entirely surprising to find that before the summit could begin, they first had to bask in the attention of their peers.

According to Galon, the entrance into the room was determined by rank. And so I stood next to Lorian and watched as Conreth's most loyal soldiers entered the hall, followed by his highest-ranked generals and advisers.

Lorian had been stripped of his title, and Conreth refused to formally recognize mine, so we entered next. Lorian was on his best behavior and had only given Conreth a smile that promised consequences at a later date for the slight.

The cavernous hall was the largest enclosed space I'd ever seen. Tiers of seats rose up the sides of the chamber, spiraling upward in a dizzying pattern, most of them full. They'd been carved into the walls, and the sight of so many people made my palms sweat.

But it was the vast round table in front of me that drew my attention. The generals and advisers had already taken their seats—as had Madinia, Rythos, Telean, Galon, and Marth. Lorian steered me over to them, taking his time as he pulled out my chair for me. Madinia and Telean sat on Lorian's right, while Marth sat to on our left, next to Galon. Rythos was currently lounging between me and Galon, eyes hard as he surveyed those seated above us.

When we were seated, the wardens began to enter. The ceremony of it all tried my patience. But I silently watched as they entered one by one, their people gathered around them.

Lorian murmured the name of each warden in my ear. Thanks to our conversation in the early hours of the morning, I knew exactly what we needed from each of them.

Romydan was short and slight for a fae, his frame diminutive but far from frail. His walk was purposeful, his stride as fluid as water spilling from a cup. His white hair had been braided and hung to his waist, contrasting vividly with his ebony robe, silver symbols etched into the fabric. His guards were numerous—so numerous that they were more like a private, well-trained, and highly powerful army.

Thorn's beauty was so cold, I wouldn't have been surprised to learn she could freeze the air in my lungs. Her skin was so pale, it seemed to glow, while her eyes held a chilling blue hue so light, it threatened to fade into the whites. Her gown was long, diaphanous, and a color I had no words for, except that it reminded me of moonlight. According to Lorian, Thorn was the third most powerful person in this kingdom—after Conreth and himself. Her full power had returned as soon as the amulet had been removed from Jamic's neck.

Verdion came next. The pronounced jut of his chin and his long eyelashes clearly marked him as Rythos's father even if I hadn't already known. Tall, even for the fae, Verdion wore a cloak of sapphire velvet that complimented his dark skin, trailing several feet behind him. But where Rythos was quick to grin, his eyes constantly laughing, his father's tight expression seemed etched in stone. Even if we were successful in convincing Daharak to ally with us, I'd seen the power of Verdion's ships firsthand—including the way they could travel beneath the waves. We needed them.

Verdion didn't greet his son. Didn't even bother to nod our way. I couldn't tell if it hurt Rythos or not—his face was carefully blank, his eyes cooler than I'd ever seen them. I wanted to reach over and squeeze his hand, but I buried my hands in my gown instead.

Caliar sauntered, and where Thorn's beauty was cold, he seemed to radiate fire. His skin was a deep tan that seemed to absorb and reflect the light, automatically drawing attention, while his bright-red hair hung freely around his face. His eyes glittered with suppressed mirth. Draped in orange-red robes, he looked as if he might burst into laughter—or flames—at any moment. His family had been responsible for the wards encompassing the fae lands for centuries. According to Lorian, wards were in his family's blood. The kinds of wards that could protect our people from Regner's fae iron.

Finally, Sylvielle appeared, clad in emerald silk that shimmered with her every move. Her territory was known for its deadly predators—predators she wielded at will to guard her own borders. Predators we could use in this war. Of all the wardens, she was the only one to acknowledge Lorian's presence—likely against Conreth's orders. She smiled at him, her full mouth revealing teeth that looked unnervingly sharp, almost predatory. Her yellow-green gaze slid to me, sweeping me with a disdainful look.

"Ah," I muttered under my breath.

Lorian reached out and squeezed my hand. "It was several decades ago, wildcat."

"Uh-huh. I remember what you said about liking dangerous women."

Lorian leaned close. "You'll pay for that remark

later," he whispered in my ear.

I scanned Sylvielle once more. I didn't think it was a coincidence that her dress perfectly matched Lorian's eyes.

On my other side, Rythos let out a low chuckle.

Sylvielle sat down, several well-dressed women claiming their seats next to her. And then everyone rose as Conreth entered, Emara on his arm. She looked breathtaking in a gauzy gold gown.

Conreth sat next to Hevdrin, Emara on his other side. I hadn't seen Hevdrin since the camp, but he appeared as calm as ever. If he was bothered that Conreth hadn't looked at him once, he didn't show it.

"Thank you for your attendance." Conreth nodded at the wardens.

We all sat. The room hummed with power. Now that they had two of their amulets back, the fae were stronger than they had been for some time. Even knowing I was unlikely to need it, I had to clamp down on the urge to caress the hourglass hanging around my neck.

"We gather here to discuss war. For, make no mistake, this is not a battle that will be fought solely in the human kingdoms. The humans will come to our borders. And if we do nothing, they will take down our ward."

Lorian tensed. Likely, it was in surprise. Neither of us had expected Conreth to admit that the fae ward might fail.

"Are you accusing my people of failing the fae?" Caliar asked. He no longer looked amused.

Conreth pinned him with a look. "Since the loss of the first amulet, it was necessary for your people to continually travel to the wards and reinforce them. Has this been happening?"

Caliar kept his gaze on Conreth. "My people couldn't be expected to sacrifice what little power they had left for wards that have stood for centuries."

"They *could* be expected to," Conreth said softly. "Because their king ordered them to. Instead, you chose to disregard orders, just as your father chose not to speak of the loss of the first amulet. Your family has learned *nothing*."

Caliar's cheeks burned, but his eyes burned brighter.

I didn't like to think about the fae wards. Because when I did, all I could see was my people, slamming their hands against them and begging for safety while Regner cut them down. But now, knowing those wards likely wouldn't hold against Regner and his stolen power...

Every muscle in my body locked up. The hybrid camp would be his first target.

If it was Caliar's father who had refused to report the theft of his amulet, then he was the reason the barrier had been created at all. Caliar's father was responsible for all of the "sons" Regner had murdered to keep that barrier in place. All because this man didn't want to fulfill his obligation.

"This once again proves that they should never have been given the responsibility of an amulet," Verdion said. "My people would never have allowed such a thing to happen."

Rythos had once told me Quorith had been considered too small to be worthy of an amulet. Now, it was one of the most important territories in the fae lands—both strategically and based on population. But clearly, Verdion still wasn't willing to forgive the ancient slight.

"We don't have time to linger on our history," Lorian said. "If we are to survive this war, we must work together."

Thorn nodded. But Verdion narrowed his eyes at me. "Yes, and by work together, you mean allow the *hybrid heir* to steal one of the Arslans' ships so she could visit that barren kingdom, ensuring my friend's son bled out on a beach somewhere far from home."

I flinched. And just like that, I was back on that beach, watching Rythos as he knelt next to Fendrel's body.

Next to me, Lorian went still. But it was Rythos who slowly got to his feet. "I suggest you watch your fucking mouth."

Verdion's eyes turned to slits, but Conreth raised his hand. Everyone went silent. Rythos retook his seat, but he was shaking with barely suppressed rage. Fendrel's death had devastated him.

On his other side, Galon murmured something to him. Rythos nodded, turning his attention away from Verdion.

Lorian surveyed the wardens. "As you might have already heard, we have taken Jamic—the boy Regner has been channeling stolen power into for years. With his help, the two amulets we also now have, and the cooperation of all who are gathered here today, we believe we can bring down Regner's barrier before he takes that power for himself and uses it to decimate this continent."

Silence.

I fought to keep my expression blank, even as I studied the wardens. Thorn's pale eyes widened, and she glanced between Lorian and me as if searching for some kind of deception. Neither Caliar nor Verdion reacted, their expressions carefully blank, while Sylvielle angled her head, watching us consideringly. Romydan sneered. "And where is this boy?"

"He had been imprisoned in fae iron and is not yet comfortable with large groups of people. However, he is willing to speak to anyone who wishes to talk to him in smaller groups," Galon said.

"Why should we go to war when we could use that power to reinforce our borders and keep our own people safe?" Caliar asked.

I stared at him. Explaining that he should care about the thousands of lives that would be lost would just be a waste of time. "Because eventually, Regner will have enough power to come for you," I said. "He still has the third amulet, and if he brings down that barrier himself, he will do whatever it takes to invade the fae lands."

"This is all because of that fucking book," Caliar snarled.

"It's a grimoire," Madinia said, her voice dripping with scorn. "And there are two others out there, waiting

440   Stacia Stark

to be used for just as much evil."

Everyone went silent for a long moment, processing that.

Sylvielle shifted. "So far, in this so-called war, has there been any true threat against the fae? All I have seen are losses on the hybrid side."

"Cavis is dead," Lorian said, his voice cold.

Her eyes softened slightly as they met his, then hardened once more as she flicked her gaze to me. "One could argue that was the result of having the misfortune of being taken with the hybrid heir."

"No," Galon said. "One could not argue that. Cavis was one of Regner's spiders."

The room went silent. No one breathed.

"Cavis… That's impossible," Thorn choked.

"I assure you," Lorian said. "It is not. While the fae have been engaged in territorial disputes, refusing to work together over past slights, Regner has been clever and patient. His men plucked Cavis from our kingdom when he had seen just six winters. Cavis allowed his own mind to crack and bleed rather than betray our people. He died protecting my mate."

Cavis's screams echoed in my head. I could feel the ghost of Eadric's hand in my hair, see the glint of his blade next to my face. Across the cell, Cavis gave me that sweet smile.

"Tell them I love them, Prisca."

Someone gripped my hand and squeezed. I jolted, returning to the present, my gaze finding Rythos's. His expression was creased with concern, and I gave him a shaky smile.

Lorian was still talking. "One of the healers tasked with returning our amulet attempted to kill Jamic last night. He had also been twisted by Regner. Who knows how many others are secretly working for the human king while unaware of their own treachery?" He slowly ran his gaze over the face of every person at the table. Murmuring broke out across the hall.

Lorian took his seat. Conreth stared at him, and the brothers had a wordless conversation. Last night, Lorian had told me Conreth hadn't wanted to let Cavis's fate be entirely known. But Sybella had asked Lorian to tell everyone. She wanted them to understand what had happened to Cavis.

"Your *mate*?" Sylvielle snarled, her voice echoing across the table.

She had listened to everything Lorian had just said, and *that* was what she was focusing on?

I met her gaze. "Yes. Move on."

Shocked gasps sounded from the seats above us. Next to me, Lorian shook with laughter. He always found it amusing when I showed any kind of possessiveness toward him. His expression cleared as Caliar let out a disbelieving laugh.

Lorian reached for my hand, found Rythos's, and knocked it aside, shooting him a warning look. Rythos rolled his eyes.

"The fae prince cannot be mated to the hybrid heir."

Caliar scowled at me. "You will need to give up any plans to take that throne."

Conreth rubbed at his temple, giving Lorian a look so cold, I almost shivered. Clearly, he hadn't wanted Lorian to let the others know he was mated to me either.

Lorian sent his brother a wicked grin, which he turned on Caliar.

"No need for that. I will be making my home in the hybrid kingdom after the war."

Romydan's mouth fell open. "You'll give up your title to go and play *consort* in the hybrid kingdom?"

Lorian opened his mouth, but I squeezed his hand. "Lorian will be my husband," I said coolly. "Which will make him the hybrid *king*."

Lorian went still, and I immediately regretted speaking, my stomach fluttering. He'd never wanted a crown. Never wanted to rule. Perhaps I'd overridden his wishes. Just as Conreth had for so long.

"Look at me, wildcat," he murmured.

The others were deep in conversation, and I turned. The look he gave me was all tenderness with a healthy dose of simmering lust. I blew out the breath I was holding, and his eyes darkened.

I knew that look, and I gave him a warning glare before he could do anything stupid like kiss me.

"And will you be enforcing the Boundary of Blood?" Thorn asked.

"Of course," Conreth said casually. Too casually.

Lorian didn't move, but I knew him, and I knew

Conreth's hit had landed. From the hard glint in Conreth's eyes, he knew the same.

"What is the Boundary of Blood?" Madinia asked from her spot next to Galon. I sent her a grateful look.

"When a member of fae royalty chooses to relinquish their title, the reigning monarch may choose to enforce the Boundary of Blood, preventing them from stepping foot in the fae lands for one hundred years," Thorn told her.

I let out a choked noise, and Lorian stroked the back of my hand with his thumb.

One hundred years. An entire century when he wouldn't be able to even visit the kingdom he'd protected and fought for. The kingdom Cavis had *died* for. I gave Lorian a look. He'd failed to mention that little problem when we'd talked.

He just smiled, his eyes darkening as his gaze dropped to my mouth. Then he turned back to Conreth.

"Unless you want to fight this war alone, *brother*, you'll wait to close the borders to us until it is over."

Conreth's mouth hardened, but he nodded, his gaze flicking to Galon.

"It goes without saying that you will no longer lead the Bazinth. That honor will be passed to Talvric."

Galon smiled. "That would make sense, as I will be relocating with Prisca and Lorian."

"As will I," Rythos said.

"And I," Marth nodded.

Even knowing it was coming, I had to swallow

around the lump in my throat.

Verdion looked at his son. Then he looked at me. And all of my muscles tightened at the restrained violence in his eyes.

Romydan laughed. "So the Bloodthirsty Prince has given everything up for a woman."

Next to Galon, Marth let out a low hiss. But Lorian nodded. "Yes, a choice between listening to you bicker about territory disputes for centuries or waking up every day next to the love of my life. It certainly was a difficult decision."

Conreth was now studying me. "Do *you* have anything to say?"

"Yes, actually, I do." My stomach churned, but I forced myself to meet each of their eyes in turn. "We will travel directly from this summit to meet with the pirate queen. Our goal is to convince her to ally with us. Regardless of the outcome, we will then take Jamic to the barrier. Without the book, we're relying on as much power as we can harness. Even if you refuse to join this war in truth, *please* come with us to the barrier. Help us stop Regner from bringing it down and taking all that power."

Caliar folded his hands on the table in front of him. "As far as I'm concerned, there are two separate negotiations happening here. We wardens will negotiate with His Majesty, but we're also negotiating with the hybrid kingdom. And what would an alliance with the hybrid kingdom do for us?" he purred, his gaze flicking to

Madinia. "Perhaps the answer is a more formal alliance?"

Madinia stiffened. But she lifted her chin, her expression carefully blank as her eyes met mine.

She would marry the warden if I believed it would help us win this war. She craved her freedom more than anything else, but she would sacrifice it for us.

Of course, she would likely find a way to kill Caliar at the first opportunity, but she would still do it.

I met his gaze. "My people are not, and will never be, part of these negotiations."

"It seems we are the only ones expected to give something up for these *alliances*," Romydan said. "What exactly are you offering, Hybrid Heir?"

Conreth cleared his throat. "Nelayra has been gathering an army of her own—highly trained hybrids from the hybrid camp in our kingdom. She has also been working to undermine the relationship Eryndan has with his son in the hope Rekja will turn on him."

Thankfully, he'd chosen not to mention that my cousin had taken control of the hybrid army. Although I had no doubt Conreth would use that information at the very moment it could do the most harm.

"So, at this point, you bring almost nothing," Romydan said. He turned his attention to Lorian. "Here's my offer—I will give you my army in exchange for your firstborn daughter. I have no doubt any children created by your…union with the hybrid queen will be powerful in their own right. Your daughter will marry my son."

My entire body went hot, and I reached for the

hourglass around my neck. I would kill him. I would—

Lorian let out a laugh. It was low, unamused, and utterly lethal.

Even Conreth flinched.

The cruel, feral gleam in Lorian's eyes dared anyone to suggest such a thing again.

My heart began to slow. For several long moments, no one spoke. No one even dared look at Lorian—as if afraid to draw his attention.

"As fascinating as this has been, we will return to the subject at hand," Conreth said. "This is not the first the wardens have heard of this threat. I have sent messages for months. Now is not the time for deliberation. It is the time for action. I will join Lorian and the hybrid heir when it is time to break that barrier. Who else will join me?" A tiny seed of hope took up residence in my chest at Conreth's public support.

"I will." Thorn's voice was low but steady. The seed bloomed. Her power was crucial.

"I will not," Caliar said.

Conreth leveled him with an icy look. "While the laws state you have the right to determine the future of your own territory, those territories still fall in *my* lands. If you choose not to join this war, so be it. However, the fae who are currently guarding your borders will be moved to the front, where they can be useful."

Caliar's mouth fell open. "You would leave us to die?"

Conreth's face stayed blank. "According to

everything you've said here today, you don't truly believe Regner presents a threat. Since you haven't found it necessary to reinforce our wards, you will deal with whatever consequences come from that choice."

Caliar bared his teeth. "You're making a mistake, *Your Majesty*."

Conreth ignored him. "Who else?"

"I will join you," Romydan said.

I jolted. After everything he'd said so far, I would never have expected him to agree.

Conreth merely nodded, but I kept my gaze on Romydan. He was looking at Thorn, who gave him a single, heated glance back.

"I will not," Verdion said.

On my left, Marth tensed. Next to him, Rythos let out a bitter laugh. "You're a fucking coward."

Verdion slowly got to his feet. "Excuse me?"

"Did you even take this to your council?" Rythos asked.

"I didn't need to."

Rythos sucked in an audible breath. "You've broken your own laws."

Verdion sneered at his son. Then he turned to Conreth, bowing his head. "With your permission, I take my leave."

Conreth watched him as if he were a poisonous snake that had slithered beneath his bed when he wasn't looking. "You have made a mistake here today, Verdion. I hope your island does not pay the price."

"Just as your people chose to disregard us so long ago, we choose not to engage with your foolish war."

Conreth continued watching Verdion for a long moment, his expression thoughtful. To his credit, Verdion met his gaze. Then Conreth flicked his eyes away, dismissing him. Verdion's jaw clenched, and he stalked out of the summit. Above our heads, others were leaving too. Likely, his people.

I sighed. I'd hoped Verdion would make the better choice. We needed his ships and their capabilities.

Finally, Conreth narrowed his eyes at Sylvielle. "And you?"

"We will not fight side by side with hybrids and humans," she said haughtily. "The creatures in my territory can handle any possible threat from Regner."

Conreth dismissed her with the wave of his hand. Her face flushed, and she looked at Lorian. He simply shook his head, as if he'd expected the worst and yet she'd still managed to surprise him with her stupidity.

"I declare this summit ended," Conreth said. He met Lorian's eyes. "Thorn, Romydan, and I will meet you at the barrier."

25

THE QUEEN

Just when I'd thought I could no longer be surprised by the ignorance, foolishness, and poor judgment of men, they continued to prove me wrong.

The Gromalian king smiled across the dinner table at Sabium, somehow blind to the threat dripping from the slow smile Sabium sent back. Eryndan was clearly unable to see the way Sabium's eyes glinted with suppressed mirth. And if there was one thing I knew about my husband, it was that he was never laughing *with* you.

Next to Eryndan, his son was more reserved, as if lost in thought. Sabium had mostly ignored him, which Rekja seemed perfectly content with.

"So, we are agreed," Sabium said. "Together, we will take back this continent."

"First, I would like to discuss the hybrid camp you insisted I target. Imagine my surprise when I learned that someone had given them an advance warning, and several hundred of my most competent men were dead."

My stomach clenched. Sabium's smile was slow and cold. "I do hope you're not insinuating that *I* had anything to do with that. My goal has always been for every hybrid on this continent to burn."

"I'm *insinuating* that perhaps someone in either your castle or your army has a problem with discretion."

I didn't move. I barely breathed. Rekja's eyes met mine, and I immediately lowered them to my plate, forcing my hand not to shake as I took a tasteless bite.

"The hybrids are cunning, with a network of spies. It's likely that one of them learned of your attack and informed the others."

"You have similar problems on a larger scale," Eryndan said, handing him a piece of parchment. Sabium skimmed it, then casually tossed it aside.

Craning my neck, I caught the last paragraph.

Denial might seem the easier path, brushing aside these truths as mere fabrication. Yet, a moment of reckoning is upon each of us.

Will you rise, defending future generations and guarding the innocent? Or will you allow Sabium's lies to destroy the little goodness left on this continent?

Choose wisely.

"Not a larger scale at all," Sabium said, his tone bored. "The people of this kingdom have spent their lives loathing the corrupt. They won't believe them now."

He spoke with such self-assurance that even with everything I knew to be true, even after everything I'd seen with my own two eyes, I felt myself questioning my own mind.

Eryndan pressed his lips together, his gaze on Sabium. After a long moment, he nodded. "We can discuss strategy at a later date, but I would like to know your plan for the fae on that island so close to *my* kingdom," Eryndan said.

Sabium smiled. "I've already made a deal with the one in power. He blames the fae king's family for not gifting his family one of those amulets so long ago. He has never forgotten the fact that his people were overlooked and has agreed to stay out of the conflict.

Eryndan angled his head, and it was clear he was impressed.

"I've heard rumors about just how fast and agile his ships are," Sabium continued, "and I don't want them in my way. So I approached him before this war even began. And once I've taken the fae lands, I'll blow that island out of the sea."

Rekja's eyes hardened. I filed his reaction away.

"I want the island," Eryndan said.

Sabium waved a hand. "Fine. We'll discuss how to empty it of fae at a later date. For now, we need to prepare for war." His gaze slid to Rekja. "No opinions?"

Eryndan's expression hardened as he glanced at Rekja. "My son has been fucking a commoner. A woman whose only task is to protect us from threats. He can no longer be trusted to have an opinion."

Sabium raised one eyebrow. "I assume she is now lying in an unmarked grave?"

Rekja's jaw clenched, but he didn't say a word. Impeccable self-control.

Eryndan just let out a hiss. "She has since disappeared." He gave his son a blistering look. "But I can assure you that he will fight by my side."

The remainder of the evening crawled by. Finally, I made my excuses, my head pounding. Pelysian could no longer risk sneaking into my rooms—Sabium and his spies were watching too closely. So I was forced to use the mirror.

I would never become used to the absence of sight and sound. For those few moments once I entered the mirror, there was nothing.

This must be what death felt like.

And then someone took my hand. I stepped into the tiny cottage, almost bumping into Pelysian. Thankfully, his mother was nowhere to be seen.

"Sabium's alliance with the Gromalians is fully in place. There will be no severing it."

"Then it is time for you to leave, Your Majesty."

I studied him. He'd cut his hair since I'd seen him just days before. It no longer slid across his shoulders. "Not yet," I said. "Not when I know he still has one amulet."

"Have you sent a message to Madinia with the location?"

I glanced away. "No."

His brow creased, and I strolled toward the rickety table and chairs, changing my mind at the last moment. "Lyrishade is north of the Dytur River. The hybrid heir and her friends are in the fae lands, and it will be too dangerous for them to attempt to make it across Eprotha."

"They have other people they could use for such a dangerous task. Why is it you feel you must do this, Your Majesty?"

I didn't know. It was an emotional choice. After everything Sabium had done to me, to Jamic, something within me refused to slink out of his castle in the dead of the night. I needed this.

"I will help you get out of the castle, out of the city, out of Eprotha, if that is what you want," Pelysian said, his eyes hardening. "But I will not help you throw your life away."

I opened my mouth, but he was already shaking his head. "Your son is free, Your Majesty. If you ever want to see him again, I suggest you leave while you can."

PRISCA

Cavis's body was burned at sunset after the summit. Regner's twisted magic had preserved him, and he looked as if he was merely sleeping. Thankfully, someone had worked some magic of their own, and there were no traces of the damage his body had sustained before he died.

Sybella leaned over, placing one last kiss on his cheek before he was set on the pyre. Piperia was fussy, likely picking up on the pain and rage of everyone around her. I watched Sybella rock her and allowed Lorian to pull me close. I was going to make sure that one day, I could look Sybella in the eye and tell her I had avenged her husband.

Lorian had made sure Sybella was holding the baby, banning anyone else from taking Piperia throughout the ceremony. He'd told me he didn't trust that Sybella wouldn't walk into that pyre otherwise.

That night, we raised a glass to Cavis, but most of us went to bed early. It felt wrong to celebrate his life when we hadn't yet avenged his death.

We were up early the next morning. And despite everything I'd said about refusing to accept the prophecy...

I didn't want Lorian anywhere near the water due to the risk of the "waves being coerced."

He'd been patient soon after we'd arrived and I'd asked for all the mirrors to be removed from our rooms, but the moment I suggested he stay in the Fae Lands, we'd had a vicious argument.

In the end, nothing changed. Not only would he never leave my side during something so dangerous, but we needed him at the barrier. He was the most powerful fae alive.

Still, I couldn't help but analyze the prophecy over

and over again.

Sybella walked us to the courtyard and the waiting carriages, her eyes dazed as she reached for my hand. "After the war, when this is all over, and Lorian and the others go with you to the hybrid kingdom…can Piperia and I come too?"

My chest clenched. "Of course you're welcome. I should have offered. I just assumed you'd want to stay here. But I'd love for you to come." I reached out and hugged her, before pressing a kiss to Piperia's cheek. She chortled, and Rythos wrapped his arm around Sybella.

"So would we," Rythos said. "We should have made that clear. You want out now? We'll take you to the border and arrange for safe passage—"

"No," Sybella said. "Not yet. But when this is over…I want Piperia to grow up with family."

"She will."

Marth's eyes were bleak, but he stepped forward, pulling Sybella to his chest. "We'll see you soon." He kissed Piperia's head and stalked toward the carriages.

Movement flickered in one of the windows. Emara stood and lifted her hand. I waved back. Conreth had refused to speak to Lorian after the meeting, but Emara was at least trying.

Lorian said a few private words to Sybella, who smiled at him, her mouth trembling, eyes filling with tears. When they were done, her chin lifted in what seemed like resolve, and Lorian took Piperia from her arms, nuzzling her tiny head.

Within minutes, we were piling into the waiting carriages and heading toward the dock. As promised, Lorian had a ship waiting, along with a seasickness tonic for me.

And then we were on the open water, and Jamic's eyes were so wide, Rythos was hiding a smile.

If it had been up to Regner, after years of captivity, the only time Jamic would have seen the waves would have been the day he died. I hoped he would get to see more. Hoped he'd get to see everything this world had to offer. But some tiny part of me was convinced we were still taking him to his death.

Madinia stood next to Jamic. This morning, we'd received another message from Vicer. Not only had Vicer used his contacts to distribute Madinia's letter to the Eprothans, but Madinia had somehow convinced Caddaril the Cleaver to utilize his own network. And it was working.

Humans and hidden hybrids were questioning the priestesses. Demanding proof of Regner's deal with the gods. My heart had pounded as Madinia had read the message aloud, and Lorian had silently stroked my back. The first stirrings of rebellion would be put down. We knew that, but guilt twisted my insides all the same. Hopefully, this was just the beginning.

News of what we'd done to Regner's throne room had made it throughout the kingdom—as had the way Madinia had burned the sanctuary. A handful of villages had set their own sanctuaries and chapels on fire. Several of the priestesses had been forced to flee for their lives.

Still more were missing.

Galon leaned against the railing with a faint smile on his face. He'd trained thousands of fae in the Bazinth over the years. The loss of it had to be tearing him apart, even as he attempted to hide it. Making my way over to him, I leaned next to him.

"I'm sorry."

Galon's dark eyebrows lowered. "Sorry for what?"

"About the Bazinth. I know it meant a lot to you."

He sighed. "When you're as long-lived as we are, you learn to let go of things."

I doubted that was true. If anything, the fae I'd met seemed to clasp tighter to the things they loved.

At my silence, Galon gave me a rare grin. "One day, when you've taken back your kingdom, we'll create an elite force of hybrids, humans, and fae. We won't discriminate, except based on skill."

I could almost picture that day in my head. When we would be at peace. It seemed both tantalizingly close and excruciatingly far away.

"Deal."

Leaving him to his thoughts, I studied the horizon. My mind was a more peaceful place than it had been for some time. After the hours I'd spent sobbing, my grief hadn't exactly lessened, but it was no longer tearing me apart. I was able to think of Cavis and Thol and Wila, my parents—all of them—without needing to lock those memories away. I could think of my village with sorrow and rage, but I didn't let it eat into me the way I had been.

Instead, I let it make me stronger.

It was ironic, really—the experiences that came the closest to breaking you were the same experiences that built you into someone new. Surviving one experience meant you were more likely to survive the next. And so it continued, life unfurling in a tapestry of trials.

"How are you, Pris?"

I jolted. The fae moved so quietly sometimes, they were constantly sneaking up on me. Rythos smiled at my reaction, and I nudged him with my elbow. "After everything that happened yesterday, I think I should be the one asking you that question."

His father had been crueler than I could have imagined.

Rythos shrugged. "When I took Fendrel home, I told my father this was just the beginning. I warned him you'd be arriving one day soon, asking for his support. I wanted to give him time to come to terms with it. Time to understand what the repercussions could be if he said no."

"He refused to even consider it."

Rythos nodded. "I'd thought he would at least take it to the council after we were gone. But it's clear from everything he said yesterday that he doesn't think his territory is a target. He believes Regner will aim straight for Aranthon." Misery flickered in Rythos's eyes. A dark, sick kind of misery. A chill slid through me.

"You think he's made some kind of deal with Regner."

"It wouldn't be the first time our people did whatever it took to stay neutral."

No, it wouldn't. Rythos had once told me his people could have helped the hybrids but voted not to. My people had lost by one vote.

"And if the fighting were to get a little too close to Quorith? What would your father do then?"

Rythos frowned. "The island's wards are...different from anything you might have seen before. Quorith will automatically protect itself from any attack—without the need for intervention from my father or anyone else."

Good.

If Verdion thought he could stay neutral in this war, he was wrong. He would either ally with us, or he would formally ally with Regner and turn his back on the fae forever.

But first, I'd attempt to force his hand.

"Are you ready for this?" Rythos asked.

"No," I admitted. "But it has to be now. We can't wait any longer."

We would take the barrier down.

But first, I'd bargain with the pirate queen.

ASINIA

Demos was not happy about being forced to rest in the healer's tent. Thankfully, he was too weak to argue. He'd spent the past few days going in and out of consciousness as Tibris healed him whenever enough of his power had regenerated.

Every time I closed my eyes, I could see those creatures. They'd enjoyed killing us. And they would have continued to tear through the camp, except that we'd managed to kill their leader.

Something told me they would make us pay for that.

I tiptoed close to Demos's tent, peering inside. His eyes cracked open, as if he could sense me. I scowled. I hadn't made a sound.

"Come, Sin."

"You need to rest."

He gave me an impatient, entirely male look. Rolling my eyes, I stepped inside.

"How are you feeling?"

"Fine. I'll be out of bed tomorrow. I would have been up today, but Tibris clucked like a mother hen."

I grinned. Demos's gaze dropped to my mouth.

"You carried me. On your back."

I shrugged. "It wasn't as impressive as it sounds."

"Don't do that. Don't minimize it. You saved my life. You were a warrior."

My chest warmed. A *warrior*.

"I couldn't just leave you there. Besides, you were a hero. That boy's mother has been visiting every day, hoping to thank you."

He waved that away. "You look tired."

I rolled my eyes. "I'm fine."

"Come closer."

His eyes were heavy-lidded. It wouldn't be long

before he fell back asleep, his body desperately needing the rest to recover from his healing.

But it was as if my legs were moving without my control as I stepped next to his bed.

He took my hand. I almost gasped at the heat of his skin. "Are you running a fever?"

"No."

"Demos—"

"Quiet."

I opened my mouth to argue, but he was pulling my hand close to his face. He pressed a gentle kiss to my palm. "Thank you."

My mouth had gone dry, and my heart thundered so hard, I wouldn't have been surprised if he could hear it.

"You're welcome."

"Next time I tell you to run, you run."

And he had to ruin it. I yanked my hand from his. He was still weak enough that he couldn't fight me on it, and his hand dropped to the bed, his eyelids drooping until they were almost closed.

He sighed, losing the battle against sleep. I pressed the back of my hand to his forehead, checking for fever. Despite my best intentions, I found myself gently running my hands through his hair.

His mouth curved. "I knew you wanted me."

He hadn't been asleep. My cheeks blazed, and I pulled my hand away. He let out a rough sound of want, but his eyes remained closed.

Turning, I forced myself to leave him to sleep. He

was alive. That was all that mattered.

Over the next few days, with Demos and Tibris both confined to their tents, I helped with the human healers whenever possible, boiling water, bringing food, and taking orders from just about anyone. Not only did it mean I was actually *doing* something, but it gave me free rein to wander the camp. Every few hours, I'd catch a glimpse of Vynthar, strolling among the training warriors, delicately eating off a plate someone had offered him, or sitting as still as a sleepy house cat while the children petted him with sticky hands.

I'd shaken my head at the sight of him with the children. While several parents watched closely, no one had seemed alarmed by the huge monster in their midst.

I learned the camp's schedule, the times the rebels hunted and where their sentries were stationed. Within days, I could have snuck Demos, Tibris, and myself out of the camp at any time—provided Demos was able to walk.

But that wasn't what I wanted. At least not yet.

I'd received a message from Prisca. They were going to work with the Pirate Queen, before turning their attention to the barrier. I sent a message back—warning them about Regner's creatures and letting them know what had happened with Tibris and Demos.

Just the thought of them all attempting to take down the barrier made my tongue itch, my skin turning chilled. I wanted to be there, helping. But Demos wasn't able to travel, and by the time we reached the front, it would likely be too late.

Still, Herne didn't need to know that.

The camp leader worked from dawn to dusk. I'd expected him to spend his time barking orders, and while he definitely did that, he also checked on the wounded, helped the hunters—many of whom had been wounded in the fight—and even spent time with the children. Each day, when he thought no one was paying attention, he snuck into Tibris's tent and stayed for several long minutes.

It took me an entire day of shadowing him before I was finally able to get close enough to get his attention. Perhaps now, he would be willing to think logically.

"I'd like to talk to you."

He sent me a disinterested look. "I don't have time."

Fury bit at me. He would *make* time. "I've already sent a message to the hybrid queen, informing her of the creatures that attacked this camp. She knows Demos was seriously injured. She also knows Tibris was injured before we arrived. She knows those winged creatures are likely to return to this camp."

He crossed his arms. "You have been busy."

I attempted Madinia's best withering look, combining it with the cool tone Prisca used so well.

"I have. I also received a message from her. They are going to attempt to take down the barrier."

Herne's eyes widened. His mouth opened, and for a long moment, it seemed as if he'd lost the ability to speak. I enjoyed it.

"Impossible."

"No. Not for Prisca. The hybrid queen is my best friend. I know how she thinks. And right now, she's thinking that all you've done is put her family in danger. She's thinking you're too stubborn to see reason. And she's thinking that she doesn't have time or resources to convince you otherwise.

"Prisca is a clever woman. She's also patient—when she sees the benefit of such patience. But that patience is not infinite. There is only one thing she holds more highly than the lives of innocents. And that is the lives of her family. Both have been threatened under your watch."

Herne swallowed. "What exactly are you saying?"

"I'm saying we will *leave*. The moment she tells us to, we will leave you here. Demos would have dragged Tibris out of here already if he hadn't been injured. We are of more use on the front lines, where we can actually help make a difference. And when those creatures come back to kill your people, you'll ask yourself if things might have been different if you'd cooperated with us." I angled my head, sweeping him with the disdainful scowl I'd almost perfected. "The answer, by the way, is yes."

PRISCA

Daharak Rostamir was a small woman with a reputation almost as large as her ego. When I searched her face for any hint of the seer's features, I found none, except for their eyes. The seer's eyes were just as dark and fathomless as her daughter's.

I recognized the man at her side. He was the same man who'd been with her the day we'd met. Daharak gave him a nod, and he cast me one warning look before striding away.

I stepped onto Daharak's ship with Lorian, Madinia, and Rythos, while the others waited on our own ship.

Daharak nodded to the others. She angled her head as her gaze met mine, her long, dark braid swinging with the movement. "You came."

I held up my hand, displaying the thin line of our blood vow.

She laughed. "If you'd wanted to drag this out, you could have waited a while. Could have insisted to yourself that you were planning to fulfill the vow—buying yourself a little more time."

"If only I'd thought of that."

She grinned at me. My mouth trembled, and I gave in, grinning back. Fulfilling this blood vow couldn't come at a more inconvenient time, but a deal was a deal. And despite myself, I *liked* Daharak Rostamir.

"Regner has recently become much more determined to kill me. Almost as determined as he is to kill you." She flipped her hair over her shoulder. "I don't know about you, but I find it more than a little…flattering. Do you think it's his idea of flirting?"

I chuckled, imagining the ruthless human king

flirting. "I don't think so."

"That's a shame." All amusement left her face, and she jerked her head, gesturing for me to follow her into her cabin.

Lorian tensed, and she lifted her chin. "This is a conversation for just us girls."

I glanced at him. "It's fine." Lorian gave her a warning look and stepped away to talk to Rythos.

Daharak's cabin exuded a rugged warmth, and I couldn't help but stare at the eclectic assortment of treasures crammed into shelves, strewn across tables, and tucked into corners. Strange instruments, rolled scrolls, painted masks, an ornate dagger, an alabaster skull, and a sealed bottle decorated with precious gems.

A mahogany desk occupied most of one side of the cabin, its surface littered with maps and ledgers. The lingering traces of foreign spices and spiced rum mingled with salt-soaked wood, giving the cabin a rich, exotic scent.

"Looked your fill?"

"No," I said. "I'd need a few hours for that."

She smirked, grabbed a huge map and sighed as she took in the state of her desk. "We'll use the floor."

Daharak rolled out the map across most of the floor, placing a paperweight on each corner.

Leaning over, I studied it. To the east, a long line ran along the coast of the continent. I didn't understand the scale of her map, but I could tell it was out at sea. "You've mapped the barrier."

"As much as we could. The magic of the barrier urges anyone who comes close to turn around, and most forget they were even close to it. Regner's power may work on the average fisherman or merchant, but my people belong to these waters. And they belong to us. There are still parts of the barrier that are far too strong—even for us. We've mapped at least sixty percent of it and made educated guesses for the rest. But that's not what I want to show you."

Daharak pointed to several islands to the north of Lesdryn. Farther north than even my village. "These are the Frosthaven Isles. I sent my high admiral to retrieve something I needed. He took one hundred of my ships. But I received word that Regner turned some of his own ships north. They're likely to either trap my people or to plan an attack. Usually, I would more than trust that they could handle Regner's soldiers, but I would lose—"

She cut herself off, and I sighed. "You can tell me what it is. I won't try to take it from you."

She sneered at that. I just shrugged. "How can I help you if I don't know what I'm protecting?"

"It's a weapon. That's all you need to know. I wouldn't have attempted to take it now, knowing the seas are teeming with Regner's ships, but I didn't know its whereabouts until now. And I can't risk someone taking it from me and turning it on my people."

"Why couldn't you get to it earlier?"

"The last man who knew where it was died a few weeks ago. He told me its location just moments before he drew his last breath. He was a...rival," she said, but sorrow glittered in her eyes. Sorrow and respect. "But he was honorable, and we made one last deal. I trust his word in this."

I tapped my palm and the mark that sliced through it. "You want me to freeze time long enough for your people to get past Regner's ships."

She nodded.

"How will we make our way north past Regner's fleet?"

Daharak gave me a slow, feline smile. "Regner has been underestimating me for decades. He believes no one can get within a certain distance of the barrier—because his people can't."

She ran her finger along a route close to the barrier. "We travel this way. Regner's men won't know we're there until we're on top of them. You'll use your power, and my trapped ships will sail past Regner's ships. The more time your people spend near the barrier, the less it will affect them as well."

In that case, I needed to convince as many of our people to come along for this little trip as I could.

"You'll need to warn your people, prepare them so they're ready. I can't hold time indefinitely."

"Understood."

"If you can't get your hands on your weapon, the vow is still fulfilled as long as we have done everything in our power to get to it."

She frowned, and I slowly shook my head. "If

something goes wrong on your end, my vow is still fulfilled as long as there were no mistakes on our side."

Her mouth twisted, but Daharak Rostamir had her own code, and after a single stilted moment, she nodded. "You've changed since the day I met you."

I shrugged. "You know, I recently met your mother."

Of all the things I could have said, that was clearly not what Daharak had been expecting. She blinked rapidly several times but recovered quickly, her mouth curving.

"And just what did my mother have to say?"

"When bound by blockade's tightening fist, heed the drifting shadow, else all be lost. To prevail, dance the sails toward the sun."

Daharak closed her eyes, clearly memorizing each word. When she opened them again, I leaned against her desk.

"How accurate are your mother's predictions, usually?" I kept my voice casual. Hopefully she couldn't tell I was holding my breath while I waited for her answer.

Daharak shrugged one shoulder. "I haven't seen her in many years. However…I don't recall her ever being wrong."

I nodded. I didn't tell her I hoped her mother *was* wrong. Didn't tell her I would give almost anything for *her* mother to be parting with her sanity the way the woman I'd called Mama had.

Because if her prophecy was right, then…

No. I refused to even contemplate that. Lorian wasn't going to die. Because I wouldn't let him.

"What is it?" Daharak frowned at me.

I would have preferred to talk to her about the next subject once I'd already succeeded with her weapon. But I couldn't risk rumors from the castle reaching her ears first.

"You know, some people would say that the time and power I will have to spend on this is much, much greater than the time and power you spent finding a hidden cove for Lorian and me to sneak into Gromalia."

Her mouth twisted. "What do you want?"

"I want another blood vow."

Her eyes lit with interest. "And what are you offering me?"

"I know you want that barrier down more than anything else."

"That's not exactly a secret." She pulled a chair from the other side of the cabin and sat down.

"If I bring it down, I want your fleet and your vow to ally with us in this war against Regner."

She laughed. "You really believe you can do it, don't you? You think you can bring down the barrier you've only just learned exists."

I shrugged. "We don't need the barrier down. It's too late for us to get help from any other continent. What we need is a fleet that would rival Regner's and Eryndan's."

"You're forgetting I know how that barrier went up. You would need to pry Regner's son out of his hands and find a way to use him."

If she knew we already had Jamic, she'd know we

were planning to take the barrier down anyway, and I'd lose all my leverage.

It was a good thing Regner would have kept that information to himself. And my people weren't talking.

"Leave that to me."

Her gaze flashed with skepticism. "You're delusional. But…knowing my mother has her hand in this makes me more likely to believe you can accomplish such a thing. If there's the smallest chance you're *not* insane, then yes, I'll make that vow. My fleet in exchange for the barrier down. But I want a time limit."

"I'll bring it down within three weeks."

She burst out laughing. I just smiled at her.

I wouldn't need three weeks. If everything went according to plan, I wouldn't even need one week.

Daharak wiped at her eyes. "Fine, Hybrid Heir. We'll vow."

Just a few minutes later, I felt the vow slide into place, next to the other two marks.

Triumph blazed through me, until it took everything I had to keep my expression blank. I'd gambled on the fact that Daharak wouldn't yet have learned that Regner himself wanted the barrier down. Or that his son had been taken. Likely, she would have learned that information within days. But it was too late now.

The line on my palm proved it.

MADÍNIA

Beneath vast, open skies, the salt-tinged breeze danced across my skin, carrying whispers of faraway lands. If I closed my eyes, I could see almost feel myself walking through crowded spice markets and bustling foreign ports.

This ship was made of endless potential.

It was the closest to peace I'd ever felt.

Finding one of the fae amulets around Jamic's neck had been a stroke of good luck. But there was still one remaining amulet waiting to be found. As much as I ached to yank all that power from beneath Regner's nose, our timeline had moved up significantly. We would need my power when we attempted to bring down the barrier.

According to our spies, Regner was already positioning his troops at the fae border, ready to bring down the ward—likely in an attempt to find Jamic and take him back.

Occasionally, I amused myself imagining Prisca growing up in Regner's court. It would have been like letting a tiny, venomous snake slip in undetected. Her schemes would have turned his court upside down.

There was no doubt that Regner would soon know exactly what we were planning. Unfortunately, the blood vow Prisca had made with Daharak Rostamir couldn't wait. As the summit had proven, we needed allies. Our chances of surviving this war would be greatly improved with the pirate queen's fleet sailing on our side.

Regner likely hadn't anticipated us working with the pirate queen. Jamic was currently sitting on this ship, his expression serene as he watched the horizon. Prisca had ensured he was brought onto the ship separately, with a few fae loyal to Lorian. All of us had agreed to hide exactly who he was from Daharak until Prisca had completed her first blood vow.

Daharak might not react well to learning she had been tricked.

All I knew was I wanted this next part over. Prisca had been practicing with her hourglass and seemed certain she could give the pirate queen's ships enough time to get past Regner's fleet with their weapon in hand. Of course, that depended on nothing going wrong. Just the thought felt as if I were tempting the fates.

A pigeon circled above us, flying down to where Prisca stood, smiling up at Lorian. Her smile disappeared at the pigeon's appearance.

I couldn't blame her. Any messages we received were rarely good news.

She unrolled the parchment, and the color drained from her face. Lorian leaned over her shoulder, his brows furrowing at whatever he read.

Getting to my feet, I made my way over to them.

"What is it?"

Prisca met my eyes. "It's from Asinia. Tibris is okay. But the rebel camp was attacked, and Demos almost died.

He's recovering now. That's not the worst of it, though. The camp was attacked by vicious, winged creatures with fangs and claws. According to Asinia, they showed a high level of intelligence. She described it as a feral malevolence."

Terror thundered through me, my vision spiraled, and my lips turned numb. We'd expected to meet humans wielding iron on the battlefield. This changed everything.

"How?" I asked.

Lorian's expression was dark. "There were rumors of Regner finding fae creatures decades ago. We searched for evidence of such a thing and couldn't find it. But…there are beasts hidden throughout this continent. Remember the stone hags? They'd made their home in the Cursed City—along with creatures that were once solely found in the fae lands. It's possible Regner did find those creatures and that he's been breeding them for just this purpose."

"The best way to kill them is to target their wings and heads. Apparently, burning works as well," Prisca said.

"We need to know how many of these creatures he has," Lorian said. "Now we know for certain that they exist, they would have left a trail on their way to the rebel camp in Gromalia. I'll let Conreth know. And we'll need our spies to search for any traces of them."

Daharak swaggered toward us. She'd demanded that we travel on her ship, so she could "have the best possible view" as Prisca used her power to help her recover her ships…and her weapon.

She glanced between all of us, her brow tightening.

"What happened?"

Prisca glanced at Lorian. But I didn't bother choosing my words carefully. The pirate queen seemed to believe her people would sail out of this war without sacrifice.

"Regner has unleashed vicious beasts with wings," I said.

She met my eyes.

Yes, that's right. They could fly right to your ships at any time.

Prisca sighed. "I'm going to go tell the others."

"Good," Daharak said. She watched Prisca and Lorian walk away before meeting my gaze. "Your friend is very clever."

She clearly meant Prisca. I turned back to watch the ships she'd ordered to sail with us. "I have no friends." But my chest clenched as Prisca's words trickled through my head. *"My people are not for sale."*

Daharak snorted softly. Her dismissal set my teeth on edge.

"A blood vow from the hybrid queen," I mused. "And you used it to find a weapon."

"Your point?"

"I'm merely wondering who it is you plan to kill with that weapon. Is it Regner?"

"No."

Curiosity pricked at me. But her silence made it clear she wouldn't be giving me anything more.

"What is it you want when all this is done?" she asked.

I shrugged. The pirate queen couldn't be trusted. I knew that much. Still, she interested me. Her life interested me. Once the barrier was down, she could go anywhere. See anything. "Why would you care?"

"I see a lot of myself in you."

At that, I turned, facing her. Most people would hunch their shoulders or at least glance away when I turned my disdain on them. Daharak merely laughed.

"I want to be left alone," I said. "When this is done, I want to go somewhere no one knows my name. I want to start a new life. Alone."

"You don't really want that." She shook her head. "But by the time you learn that, you'll be half an ocean away." She tapped her temple. "I like to believe I have a hint of my mother's sight."

I ground my teeth at her patronizing tone, and her eyes lit with humor. "I believe I'll help you with your plans anyway. If we bring down this barrier, find me after the war, and I'll take you with me."

The thought danced along my skin. I could practically taste freedom. "Why would you do that?"

"For the same reason I do everything, of course. My own amusement."

26

LORIAN

My brilliant mate had outmaneuvered the pirate queen.

And when Daharak learned we'd had Jamic for days—and that Regner himself wanted the barrier down, she would be forced to admit just how well she'd been manipulated.

We would see if her ego would allow her to truly be an ally even if she was forced to work with us.

Traveling this close to the barrier had been…interesting. A few times, Prisca and Madinia had both forgotten it existed. As if the knowledge had been entirely wiped from their minds. When reminded, they'd looked haunted.

Even Marth had succumbed to the barrier's magic once, which had put him in an even darker mood. Thankfully, the more time we spent in these waters, the less impact the barrier had. All of us were somewhat immune to it now.

The wind was cool as we stood

on the deck of Daharak's ship, drawing closer to the Frosthaven Isles. Clustered around the inlet's narrow mouth, approximately one hundred of her ships waited, currently being starved by Regner's ships. According to Daharak, her people would have soon needed to resort to drinking seawater. And while she would have gladly attacked Regner's ships from the south, using her blood vow with Prisca would mean as few losses as possible.

Regner's ships had formed an outer ring around the inlet, effectively trapping Daharak's ships inside.

"A blockade," Prisca said when she noticed it, her lips white. I leaned down, rubbing my nose against hers in an attempt to soothe.

I knew what was running through her mind. The prophecy.

When bound by blockade's tightening fist, heed the drifting shadow, else all be lost. To prevail, dance the sails toward the sun.

"Look into the sky, wildcat. There's no hint of a shadow."

Firming her lips, Prisca peered up at the cloudless sky and nodded.

Daharak gestured, and one of her men rang a bell farther down the deck. A stream of fire shot high into the sky—her signal to the ships currently trapped by Regner's soldiers.

Answering fire sparked in the distance, lighting up the sky with flames and smoke.

"They're ready. Are you ready?" Daharak asked

Prisca.

Prisca nodded. "Why is this ship positioned so far right?"

Daharak gestured to the waves on our left. "What do you see?"

"Water," Prisca said.

Daharak smirked. "I see a hidden coral reef. This ship is marking the reef. My people know they can't move any farther east than here."

Daharak moved away to prepare her captain. Before Prisca could pause time, Daharak's ships needed a clear route past Regner's blockade.

Prisca squinted at the water. "Can you see it?"

I shrugged. "No. But I haven't spent my life in these waters."

Daharak sent one last signal back to the ships, and her cannons fired as one. From both sides.

Daharak slammed her weapons into Regner's left flank, just as her ships closest to the inlet did the same. Regner's armada was forced to engage ships from both the north and south at once as Daharak's pirates capitalized on the chaos.

Cannons fired in deafening volleys, setting my teeth on edge. Prisca peered up at me. "Do your sensitive fae ears hurt?"

She said *sensitive fae* as if she really meant *tiny baby*. I pinched her hip, and she smirked.

"If you need a distraction from the violence, I have a few suggestions, wildcat."

Her smirk widened, but she turned back to the carnage. I surveyed the others. Galon stood a few footspans away, his arms crossed.

Strolling over to him, I kept my voice low. "You're not using your power?"

His face clouded over. "I promised Prisca I wouldn't *coerce the waves.*"

Irritation warred with tenderness. Tenderness won. I knew Prisca took the seer's warning seriously. Truthfully, the thought of leaving her alone… It burned a hole in the center of my chest. Wherever I went after this life, I would miss her with everything in me.

Galon glared at me. "Were you going to tell us?"

"About the so-called prophecy?"

"Don't make light of it. We just lost Cavis."

My gut twisted. "I know." I sighed. "I refuse to consider the idea that everything we've been through was meaningless. That I'll ultimately leave Prisca here alone. Because if I let myself dwell on it, I might begin to believe it. And the thought of what my death would do to her…"

Some of the fury drained from his face. "I refuse to believe it either." He turned his gaze to Prisca, who had tightened her hands on the railing, her eyes sharp as she stared into the distance.

"No matter what happens, she'll never be alone, Lorian."

My throat tightened and I nodded.

"You're up, Hybrid King," Daharak said, stalking down the deck toward me. I turned, my gaze finding

Madinia's. She fixed me with a dismissive look.

I preferred when Madinia was afraid of me. Unfortunately, she knew I was far too in love with Prisca to harm any of the people my mate considered hers.

Daharak had created a small gap between Regner's ships on the left flank. Now I would open it up.

Reaching down into the depths of my power, I opened the door I usually kept locked, barred, and hidden.

Lightning jumped from me, cracking through the sky and into the ship Daharak pointed out.

Regner's captains likely hadn't expected power like mine. If Daharak had attacked without us, the humans would have only needed to defend against cannon fire and fae-iron-tipped arrows.

Which meant there was no ward to dampen my blow. I sliced into the first hull, and the ship immediately listed, taking on water. I struck the ships again and again. The larger the gap, the faster Daharak's ships could escape, and the easier it would be for Prisca.

And so, I drowned and burned and destroyed. Tears rolled down Prisca's cheeks at the destruction. Despite the fact that these were our enemies. They were still humans, and she wept for them. Something in my chest wrenched at the misery on her face.

Crew members fell into the sea, weighed down by heavy armor. Masts cracked, sails fell limp, and water poured into gaping holes.

I paused.

"What are you doing?" Daharak demanded.

Slowly, I turned to look at her. Whatever she saw in my eyes made the color drain from her face.

Prisca hiccupped, and I strode to her, clamping her close to my body as I studied the scene in front of us. As I'd hoped, some of Regner's ships were fleeing—cutting through the water to the west.

Not long ago, I might have destroyed every ship, drowned every human—all in the name of expediency. I would have felt nothing, except a sense of grim satisfaction for living up to my name as the Bloodthirsty Prince.

The man I'd been was the same man who had once left the woman in my arms to die without a second thought—a fact that still occasionally made me wake in a cold sweat.

I was a better man now. Because of her.

No longer trapped in the inlet, Daharak's ships unfurled their sails and surged forward as one, racing for the gap opened by the melee. Yet thirty or forty of Regner's ships were hanging back, ready to strike. Prisca would still need to use her power.

"Now!" Daharak roared at us.

Prisca's hand clutched the hourglass, and she focused on Regner's remaining ships.

There was something…disconcerting about the way the hourglass stole a piece of her when she was using it. She went into a kind of trance, occasionally unable to stop using her power without intervention. Some part of me worried that one day she wouldn't come all the way back.

I would smash that hourglass to pieces before I let

that happen.

All sound seemed to pause for a single moment as the pirates surrounding us realized what had happened.

"Time magic," one of them muttered.

"The hybrid heir."

"*Witch*— Ow, what was that for?"

I glanced over my shoulder. Galon had slapped one of Daharak's pirates over the head.

Prisca strained, and I knew she was fighting with the hourglass, which urged her to use all of her power in a single, devastating blow. But she needed to hold time for perhaps the longest she had ever held it.

Daharak had prepared her captains, and they streamed through the gap, sailing past us, all of them avoiding the hidden coral reef Daharak had marked.

Prisca began to shudder. "How much longer?" I asked Daharak.

Daharak's eyes were alight with triumph. "Not long. It will take them a while to recover from the shock when they see my ships disappear and reappear at their backs."

Prisca gasped, the sound filled with pain. My hand found hers. "Let go."

Daharak let out a hiss, and Galon stepped close to her. "I suggest you think carefully," he said.

"Prisca, it's over. I need you," I said.

That did it. She released the hourglass, swaying woozily. I clamped down on the urge to haul her into my arms, well aware that she'd be upset at the thought of appearing weak in front of so many people.

"Did we do it?" Prisca asked.

Daharak let out a wild laugh. "We did. Consider our vow complete."

Prisca smiled down at her palm as the thin line disappeared. When she looked up at me, I couldn't resist lowering my head and taking her mouth. She let out a tiny hum that made me pull her even closer.

"Captain, we have a problem."

I lifted my head as one of Daharak's pirates sprinted in her direction. He pointed at a ship in the distance.

"It's not part of the original blockade," he said. "It must have been nearby."

Daharak reached for a spyglass. "The *Sea Shadow*." She frowned.

In my arms, Prisca stiffened, immediately wriggling free. "What did you say?"

"The *Sea Shadow*. The captain is one of Regner's best. I was pleased when I heard this ship hadn't been seen in the area. Obviously, we celebrated early." Her frown deepened. "What is he doing?"

"He's going to ram us," someone screamed.

The ship barreled toward us, the wind pushing it forward. I lifted my hand, but Prisca grabbed it. "Dance the sails toward the sun," she said.

"What?"

"The prophecy. It's the shadow. Dance the sails toward the sun."

I had no idea what that meant, but I grabbed Daharak as she ran past. "Lift anchor and dance the sails toward the sun."

"What?"

"Just do it."

"We need to—"

"Do it, or you're on your own."

Daharak glared at me through slitted eyes. "Pushy fae bastard." Realization slid over her face. "My mother's prophecy."

She screamed something to her captain, who spun the wheel, angling the ship. Our sails caught the wind. The *Sea Shadow* was so close, I could make out the faces of the crew. Grabbing Prisca, I pulled her into me, covering as much of her as I could.

Our ship lurched, leaning to the left.

Slam.

The *Sea Shadow's* prow sliced through the water, smashing into the stern of our ship. Someone screamed. Wood splintered as the two ships collided violently. Daharak's captain continued turning the ship out of the *Sea Shadow's* path...

And then the *Sea Shadow* smashed into the coral reef so close to us, its rear deck instantly reduced to a mess of broken planks and railing. Crew members were thrown from the ship, while jagged fissures arched through the shattered bow, tilting the deck precariously.

Daharak's crew were already rushing to patch our damaged ship. In my arms, Prisca shuddered. I knew it wasn't from watching the ships sink.

No, it was because the seer's prophecy had been

correct. The last-second turn had saved us and ensured the *Sea Shadow* would never hound Daharak again.

We spent the next several hours sitting on the stern while the others gave us some privacy. Prisca didn't seem to want to talk about the prophecy, and I couldn't blame her. So I held her tightly as she laid her head on my chest, napping occasionally, until Madinia appeared, her eyes wild.

She held up a message. "The queen's spies have reported both Eprothan and Gromalian ships leaving their docks in the hundreds. Regner knows what we're planning."

Prisca lifted her head. Her eyes were hard. Focused. "Send every message that needs to be sent. We're taking the barrier down now."

PRISCA

Daharak was livid. She didn't rage, didn't snarl, didn't even say a single sharp word. But her silence ate at the air between us.

I had thought *I* liked to pace, but she had stalked back and forth between the walls in her cabin so many times, it was making me dizzy.

She stopped moving long enough to glower at me. "You knew Regner was going to bring the barrier down."

"Yes."

"And how long have you had the boy?"

"Jamic? Since the attack at Lesdryn."

"That was you."

"Yes."

She paced. "You used me."

"Yes." There was no point denying it. All I could do was hope Daharak would appreciate honesty.

Silence stretched between us, Daharak's expression colder than I'd ever seen it. If I wasn't careful, I would make a dangerous enemy today.

I sighed. "Regner wasn't just going to bring the barrier down and let you sail away to more profitable waters," I said. "The only reason he wanted to bring it down was to take all of that power for himself. What do you think would happen to your fleet—to your people—if he was that powerful?"

"And what happens when Jamic does the same? Will he take that power for himself?"

"He says it will return to the people it was stolen from."

"And you believe him?"

I would be lying if I said some part of me wasn't worried about the strange, silent boy who radiated enough power that Galon was almost always by his side, wards ready. But...

"We don't have any other options. Either we use Jamic, along with the most powerful people we have, or Regner ends this war within the next couple of days—and all of us die. We freed Jamic, and he has agreed to help."

She shook her head. "Since you outmaneuvered me, I have no choice but to work with you. But if that boy turns on my people, I will make you pay."

If Jamic turned on us, I would have much, much bigger problems than Daharak. "He won't," I said.

She just shook her head. But some of the ire had drained from her expression. "Regner's ships are moving this way. Eryndan and his son are with him, bringing ships from their own fleet."

I nodded. Thanks to the queen's warning, we were prepared for Eryndan and Rekja. All I could do was hope Rekja was willing to listen.

At the very least, with his lover missing, some part of him must wonder if we knew where she was. I was betting he wouldn't want us killed until he was sure we didn't know her location.

I met Daharak's eyes. "Ally with us. Not just because of the vow, but because this is your opportunity to create a better future for everyone. Help us take down Regner with full cooperation, and I'll make sure your name is spread across my kingdom. Every hybrid will know the pirate queen helped save our people."

She gave me a slow, feline smile. "Thanks to your scheming, I *have* to work with you. But I must admit, I like the sound of that, Hybrid Heir."

"Then let's get to work."

Opening the door, I stepped aside so Lorian could enter. I had no doubt he'd heard everything with his fae hearing, but he kept his expression neutral as he tucked a curl behind my ear.

Within a few minutes, he'd gathered Galon and Jamic. Daharak watched Jamic as if he were a poisonous scorpion.

I gave her a warning look and turned to Jamic. "Let's talk about the barrier. How close do we need to be in order to take it down?"

"It depends on how much power we can gather. The more power we have, the farther we can position ourselves from it."

I pointed to the map. "We bring it down here."

Daharak narrowed her eyes at me. "Why?"

"You'll see. We need to buy ourselves some time," I said. "Can we send some ships to another part of the barrier? Make it look as if that's where we're about to bring it down?"

Daharak tilted her head. "We can. It will mean splitting our forces, but if time is what you need…"

"It is," Jamic said. "Without the book, the only way to bring the barrier down is with time and sheer power."

"The moment Regner realizes what we're doing, he will do anything he can to prevent that from happening," Lorian said. "And he'll do everything he can to get to Jamic so he can kill him there."

I glanced at Jamic, but his expression remained neutral. If the discussion about his potential death bothered him, he didn't show it.

"We need to further split our own forces," Lorian

continued. "Half of us on the front, dealing with Regner's and Eryndan's ships, and the other half pouring their power into the barrier."

We discussed the details into the early hours of the morning. Conreth, Thorn, and Romydan were on their way, traveling with as many high-powered fae as they could gather. Vicer had also reached out to his contacts, ensuring that any hybrids who wished to fight would travel to our meeting spot.

Finally, there were only small details left to discuss—all of which would be figured out tomorrow. Lorian led me to our cabin, pulled me onto our bed, and curled his body around mine.

I was shaking, I realized. My chest ached, my throat burned, and I felt as if I could climb out of my skin.

"Are you ready to let go, Prisca?"

Lip trembling, I nodded. And then I told him everything. I told him what Eadric had done to me—the details I'd never spoken of. I repeated every word Eadric had said, which sometimes played in my mind on a loop. I explained how Cavis had looked at me, and how often I saw that expression when I closed my own eyes. I told him what happened during my nightmares, and how all of the people I loved replaced Cavis each night, and I could save none of them.

I cried and I raged and I howled. And through it all, Lorian held me, his own eyes wet, his body shuddering with barely suppressed fury.

THE QUEEN

My horse danced restlessly beneath me, and I shivered, terror curdling in my gut.

I had listened to Pelysian's warnings.

I had even forced myself to picture my ending if I were discovered. I'd lived my own death so many times, I'd woken over and over these past nights, certain Sabium's guards were about to burst into my rooms and arrest me.

And yet...

Sabium had left. Even my spies hadn't been able to learn where he was going or what he was doing. Pelysian had been entirely useless when it came to obtaining Sabium's plans too. The bastard had stayed away, refusing to engage with me until I agreed to leave.

Sabium's spies continued to watch my every move. I could feel their intent, suspicious gazes on me constantly. While Tymedes had traveled with his king, there was no shortage of others to report my actions back to him.

And yet...

Nelia hadn't refused to help me. No, Nelia had understood why I must do this. She was a woman as trapped in the castle as I was—her husband drinking his days away and fucking Sabium's maids until even the lowliest servant sniggered as she walked past. Together, we'd considered my options.

As much as I wanted Sabium to know I had been the one to outmaneuver him, it was not the only reason I was considering such a dangerous move. If I could find the third amulet, could see exactly what monsters Sabium was breeding within Lyrishade, I would have a way to bargain with the fae and the hybrids.

Pelysian had assured me he would keep me safe if I fled the castle. He may be related to Daharak Rostamir, may benefit from his mother's link to the fates, but he was just a man—little more than a servant, despite his network of spies.

So, together with Nelia, we'd arranged for a visit to the market—one I often took with my ladies. They'd seemed relieved at the return to normalcy, although all of them had remained quiet while we'd traveled by carriage, the guards behind us.

The acrid scent of smoke had been the first sign that Nelia's distraction had begun. It had quickly replaced the scent of meat skewers and honeyed almonds.

Commoners had begun to scream, scrambling for safety. My guards had reacted instantly, closing tightly around me. As I'd known they would.

"What are you waiting for?" I'd hissed. "Put the fire out."

"Your Majesty?"

"How do you think my reputation would fare if word spread that I had ignored such a calamity when my guards have more than enough power at their disposal? I will wait here. Go."

Three guards had left. Two of them had remained. When someone had released the animals from their pens, the market had turned to chaos. It had been a simple matter to drop beneath the closest stall, sweep up the ragged cloak left for me, and slip away, my gown and hair covered with gray homespun.

A woman had slammed into me, her face wet with blood. I'd known there would be injuries. Perhaps even deaths. But sacrifices needed to be made.

It had been easier than I'd imagined to board our waiting ship. Nelia's documentation was so meticulously forged, it was impeccable. So impeccable, I'd wondered if she had been planning to flee Eprotha for some time.

I'd held my breath while our papers were checked. Nelia had provided me with the kinds of clothes a commoner might wear—the fabric rough and thin, cold at night and too hot during the day. She'd also tied my hair back in a messy braid—the type several of the fishermen's wives had been wearing. The guard had barely scanned us, the harbor master busy managing several of Sabium's ships, which were departing minutes before us.

"Your Majesty?"

Nelia's voice shook me from my thoughts, and I gazed at her. We'd docked past Mistrun. Not far from the village Sabium had ordered razed. Nelia had ensured our horses were waiting, but it had still taken two days for us to reach the granite mine.

She rode terribly, bouncing around in the saddle until

I'd winced for her poor horse. "You've done well, Nelia. You must go now."

By now, Sabium would know I was gone. Every guard in Eprotha would be searching for me. My stomach clenched with a new, unwelcome feeling.

It wasn't fear. No, I knew the feeling of terror intimately. I was used to it choking my throat and burrowing deep into my bones.

No. This was something else. Something that might have been regret. This plan had seemed so simple, so…necessary from the safety of the castle. Now, I was entirely alone.

At least, I would be. As soon as Nelia removed herself from the vicinity.

Nelia's mouth went slack. "And leave you here?" Her gaze flicked to the yawning mouth of Lyrishade, waiting below us.

It stretched wide, an imposing abyss cut into the base of the mountain like a gaping black wound. The guards had changed shifts since we arrived, and they strolled the perimeter of the mine, expressions bored.

If I hadn't already known that Lyrishade was where the final amulet was hidden, the glaring lack of workers coming and going from this mine would have roused my suspicions.

"Listen to me," I said. "My power is weak. I must be fiercely focused in order to use it, and I have only ever been able to hide my own presence."

That was more explanation than I would have given most people, but Nelia had greatly sacrificed for me.

Her face drained of color. "Then I will wait for you," she said.

"You will not. Go, Nelia." I handed her a purse, filled with enough coin to make her a rich woman in any kingdom.

Her hand shook as she took it. "Please, Your Majesty."

"I won't tell you again."

Her eyes flickered with pain and what looked like betrayal. But she firmed her lips and nodded. "May the gods be with you."

She turned her horse, her head held high. And I returned my attention to the mine entrance.

That same feeling burned through me. This decision was stupid. Reckless. Pelysian had been right.

And yet, I couldn't stop myself. Sabium would never expect me to come here. This was perhaps the one possibility he hadn't prepared for.

Tying my horse's lead rope to a low branch, I slipped back through the forest and down the bank. It took several long minutes before I could even risk using my power. The more guards I had to keep track of, the more eyes I needed to turn from my presence, the quicker my power would drain.

I couldn't risk being trapped inside the mine.

Finally, as the sun began its slow descent, it was time. My power came to me quickly for once, and the location of each guard appeared in my mind.

Now.

I kept my pace purposeful without running. Running drew attention that would cost me more power to hide.

And I would need to sprint from the edge of the forest into the entrance of the mine. Slipping between trees, I waited until the guard closest to the entrance turned his back.

Another guard was approaching, but my gut told me it had to be now.

I sprinted, stumbling over the uneven ground. I hadn't run since I was a child, and my form was poor.

I was footspans from the entrance when the guard began to turn.

I leaped, crashing through the open entrance and into the darkness beyond.

Hitting the ground with my entire body, I stifled a groan, attempting to catch my breath.

It was cold within the mine, the chill sliding beneath my clothes, stroking along my skin. Light orbs flickered soft illumination against the imposing dark, casting feeble glows every few footspans. The ground beneath me was a mosaic of fragmented stone and compressed dirt, and I dragged myself to my feet, forcing myself to continue.

Scaffolding lingered on the peripheries, once used to aid miners in their relentless excavation. Now, there was nothing but this strange emptiness.

Ahead, dimly lit passageways forked. I turned right, then left, carefully memorizing my choices. The rock ceiling turned jagged, pressing down as if to entomb me here.

At the next turn, a stench assaulted me, and I gagged at the sudden foul scent. It coated the inside of my throat with each shallow breath, an indescribable, nauseating reek.

The dim glow from the light orbs began to mesh with

a different kind of luminescence. A sinister green glow. A symphony of distant growls, whimpers, roars, and the clinking of metal pricked my ears.

Pelysian had once told me of the creatures Sabium was breeding here.

"Long ago, before the fae and humans were truly at war, Sabium's ancestor attacked a fae settlement. The winged, monstrous creatures had left their young to go hunt, never imagining they would be attacked. The king had the young taken and hidden so our people could experiment on them. Those creatures are still alive. But Sabium has been using the amulet to manipulate them. To make them not only more powerful, but loyal only to him."

I wasn't afraid of Sabium's monsters breaking free. He would never allow such a thing to happen. No, he would likely wait until the very moment the hybrids and fae thought victory was within their grasp and unleash hundreds of those monsters among them.

The stench became thicker the farther I traveled. I focused, using my power to search for any guards ahead of or behind me. Nothing. The first stirrings of dread trickled down my spine.

The dirt beneath my feet became a slick, slightly tacky surface. The green light grew brighter. I took a deep, steadying breath and stepped into the expansive cavern.

Terror exploded through my chest. Monsters. Not hundreds of them. Not even thousands. Tens of thousands of them, snapping and snarling at one another, thick chains—no doubt made of fae iron—around their necks.

On one side of the vast space, winged creatures stretched and snarled, those chains allowing them to stretch their wings enough to lift several footspans into the air at most. Their claws were as long as my hands, and they scraped against the ground as they attempted to fly again and again.

On the other side, kept carefully away from their winged brethren, more creatures paced and growled. Dark, sleek fur coated their bodies, showcasing powerful haunches that held the latent energy of a coiled spring. Their heads were low and angular, their jaws lined with razor sharp teeth. No wings graced their backs. These were beasts evolved not for the skies, but for ruthlessly chasing prey across unforgiving terrain.

There were enough monsters in this cavern to decimate an army.

This was impossible. Even with the centuries Sabium had devoted to breeding the fae creatures, there were far too many.

Perhaps they had a faster incubation period for their young.

This was why Sabium had radiated that calm confidence throughout most of the last few weeks—even with Jamic gone.

He was waiting to unleash these creatures on his enemies..

Scuffing sounded behind me, and I froze, casting out my power.

Too late. I'd allowed myself to become distracted.

I turned, and a huge hand clamped over my mouth.

27

PRISCA

Less than two days later, I stood at
the prow of our ship as it sliced
through the cerulean water,
sunlight dancing on the surrounding
swells. Overhead, gulls screamed
viciously at one another.

Just how high did the barrier
span? Could those gulls fly to distant
lands? Or were they as trapped as
everyone else on this continent?

The deck creaked beneath my
feet, and I forced myself to keep my
expression blank. The healer had
given me a tonic for the seasickness,
but it was up to me to ensure my
natural...disconcertment of the open
water wasn't obvious. With this many
eyes on me, I could show nothing but
hope, fearlessness, and grim resolve.

After the way I'd broken down in
Lorian's arms, I felt...steadier. Just as
he'd assured me I would.

We were positioned with the
boundary to our right, the Gromalian
coast to our left. Conreth's ship
floated astern of us, her hull and

sails gleaming in the sunlight. Ahead of us, a formidable flotilla of several hundred of Daharak's ships held their positions, preparing to engage Regner's and Eryndan's ships. Surprising no one, the pirate queen herself had insisted on positioning herself adjacent to us. The last time I'd glanced at her, she'd been issuing commands unflinchingly, her eyes sparking with vicious promise as Regner's fleet approached.

Madinia had been standing by her side, practically glowing with suppressed magic. Several ships away, Galon had gathered the best warders from both Conreth's fae and our hybrids, and he was currently deep in discussion with a group of them, explaining our tactics.

We had one purpose—to form a defensive line to shield the five ships behind us, all of which were currently facing the barrier. I peered into the spyglass, finding Jamic's hand lit with golden light as he aimed his power at the barrier, his expression once again placid, almost peaceful. He'd taught some of the strongest fae how to channel their power and direct it into the barrier. Together, the fae struck the barrier from a distance, hundreds of them pouring every drop of power they had into it.

Next to Jamic, Thorn and Romydan were doing the same. Meanwhile, Rythos was on a ship of his own, accompanied by Daharak's pirates. Each ship held some of our most powerful people—anyone who could be spared from defensive magic or with power strong enough to help us keep Regner's army at bay.

We didn't have the grimoire that had created the

barrier. But Jamic seemed convinced that with enough time and power, we could bring the barrier down without it. If we couldn't, Marth's one task would be to get Jamic as far away from here as possible—so Regner couldn't use him.

I was holding on to one fact—it was always much easier to destroy something than it was to build it in the first place.

A shout rang out from the crow's nest, and I snapped my gaze to the left. At first, it was just a blemish on the horizon. A disturbance in the seamless merging of sea and sky. I shaded my eyes, peering into the distance. Billowing sails unfurled like opening claws. The armada took shape, carving through the waves, growing larger by the moment. Sunlight glinted off weapons and armor, but it was the gold etched into the ships that made my breath catch.

These were warships, yet Regner hadn't been able to resist gilding them. Intricate swirls and patterns decorated the hulls, the gold gleaming even at this distance. The wasteful opulence made my stomach churn. I'd walked through the slums in his kingdom. I'd seen how his people suffered.

"All that gold is going to end up in the bottom of the ocean one day," Lorian said softly from behind me.

I nodded, but I couldn't take my eyes off the fleet cutting through the waves toward us. Regner had designed the ships to inspire awe and terror. But they symbolized all the reasons *he* was corrupt. His lust for power and wealth was sickening.

I'd thought we would have more time. I turned to glance at Daharak. From the sick look on her face, so had she. It was the pirate queen's people who'd been sent north as a distraction.

I squeezed the trowth stone in my hand until I thought it might crack. These had been Galon's idea and would allow all of us to communicate, as long as no one moved out of range—a few hundred footspans or so.

Regner's ships closed in, and my gaze locked on the weapons fitted to the side of the ships. "Lorian?"

"I'm not sure what they are," he said, stepping closer with a frown as he gazed at the ships. Unlike us hybrids, the fae didn't need spyglasses to be able to see that far into the distance.

We'd prepared for Regner's cannons. But these were much longer, and they gleamed silver—clearly new.

I lifted the trowth stone. "What are they, Daharak?"

"I don't know," she replied, her voice tight. "And that isn't a good sign. I'll ask my fleet commanders if they've seen anything similar before."

A few minutes later, her voice echoed from the stone.

"One of my fleet commanders believes they're elemental cannons."

"What does that mean for us?"

"They'll be loaded with something that would channel magic—likely something similar to an oceartus stone. And then a human with an elemental power like Madinia's or Galon's would pour their magic into that something. When they fire, it'll be as if a powerful hybrid or fae has unleashed their full power mere footspans away from our ships."

My heart leaped into my throat. I was willing to bet Rothnic had helped create those cannons.

Lorian watched the ships contemplatively. As much as I knew he wanted to let his power roar free, there was a chance we might need it later for the barrier if the others were unable to bring it down.

"How long will our wards last?" I asked him.

"It depends on how powerful each warder is. Galon can hold his ward for hours when not under constant attack. But Regner has likely been preparing these cannons in advance. We need to get this done quickly."

Someone tapped my shoulder. I turned. If Telean was at all concerned, it wasn't evident on her face. I'd begged her not to come, but she'd merely patted my cheek, insisting that I might need her when I wielded my power.

"Are you ready?" she asked.

I nodded. "You promised you'd stay away from the fighting."

"I will. But first, I have something for you."

"What is it?"

She handed me a glass vial. "A healer in Gromalia owed me a favor." She frowned. "And yet he still attempted to empty my purse."

"What is it?"

"It's a tonic. For your vision. You may not have time to use spyglasses and such. This will enhance it, allowing you to see across long distances when you focus. You may feel a little dizzy and nauseous when you first begin, but it will fade."

"This is unbelievable. I'll have eyes like the fae. Thank you."

She patted my shoulder. "You can do this, Nelayra. Your parents and grandmother are watching."

My eyes stung, and I leaned down, kissing her cheek. She smiled, turning and walking back to the pirate I'd convinced to stay with her.

Taking a deep breath, I lifted the stone. The first part of our plan would be up to me. "Tell them to fire everything they have."

"You better make sure this works." Daharak's voice came over the stone. "If my people die because you can't wield your power…"

"They won't."

My stomach twisted. This would require perfect timing. If I couldn't freeze time for long enough, all the people currently standing on the deck of one of our ships were dead.

"Good, because I ensured your friend Marth is on that ship."

My blood froze. "You—"

"Just making sure you have enough motivation to hold time in place."

"Do you want war between *us*, Daharak?"

"I'm merely playing the game you began, Your Majesty."

Grinding my teeth, I gently placed the stone down, suppressing the urge to throw it.

"You can do this," Lorian said. "You've done it before."

"They won't have a ward in place." If they did, our plan wouldn't work.

"Every person on that ship volunteered. They know how important this is. Even Marth."

"You knew about this?"

He shook his head. "No, but I know him. Now is not the time to question yourself, wildcat. That's not the woman you are."

I snorted. Sometimes it felt like all I did was question myself. But he was right.

"Fine. Tell them to begin."

LORIAN

The plan was simple. Simple enough that I'd only requested a few minor changes when Prisca had come up with it. Thankfully, it hadn't taken much to convince Daharak to attack the barrier this far south. It helped that this location meant we were closer for Conreth and the others to reach.

Marth's ship broke away from our line, moving southwest and aiming at the ship Regner had positioned closest to the coast. I squinted, watching as Marth stood next to the ship's captain, hands on his hips as the ship fired again and again.

It slowly moved into position, until it was within range of the blurred, shadowed island of Quorith.

Positioned between the ship Regner was on and the island, Marth's attack was relentless. Again and again, they fired, giving Regner's ship—the ship positioned the farthest west—no chance to escape.

"What's happening?" Prisca asked. Her lips were white, and she focused on the ships close to us, likely concerned their weapons would make it through Galon's ward.

"Regner's captain is screaming orders. He has broken away from Regner's lines, assuming that will help. The ship is turning."

Her breath hitched. "Tell me when."

The elemental cannon—which had previously been aimed at our front lines, was now almost aimed at Marth's ship. I could see its captain, his teeth bared as he spat orders.

One of his men stepped forward, loading a long, oval object into the cannon.

Prisca stepped up close to me, focusing on Marth's ship.

"Almost," I said, picking up the trowth stone. I silently cursed Rostamir. If something went wrong and Marth died here today, Prisca would never forgive herself. And I would make Daharak regret her games.

Regner's captain said one word. The elemental cannon sparked.

I lifted the trowth stone closer to my mouth. "Now," I roared.

Marth glanced down at the stone in his hand and smiled.

Prisca reached for me, and I wrapped my arms around her. She clamped her hand on to her hourglass, and everything froze. It took so much power for her to freeze such a large area, the only way for me to not be trapped within that power was to hold on tight.

She strained, panting, her eyes slamming closed. Marth's ship was the only movement. It was eerie. The birds above us were poised mid-flight. The breeze had disappeared. And yet the captain of Marth's ship screamed his orders, the oars heaved, and I focused my power into a steady gust of wind to help. They would only have moments, but they knew exactly what to do.

Our ship slid out of the path of the elemental cannon. But Prisca kept holding tight to her power until the ship was at least a hundred footspans away.

"They're clear," I told her. "Let it go."

Her breath hitched, and my hand found hers on the hourglass. I gently stroked her wrist, lowering my head to press a kiss to her cheek. "You did it, wildcat. Let go and celebrate with me."

With a broken gasp, she managed to release the hourglass. My breath shuddered out of my lungs as she turned to watch.

Regner's ship had fired, the elemental cannon's projectile already hurtling through the air.

I watched the dull realization sweep across the captain's face. To him, it would appear as if Marth's ship had disappeared and then immediately reappeared out of range.

With the ship gone, there was only one target for the elemental cannon to hit.

Quorith.

The projectile hit Quorith's ward, and Prisca squeezed my hand. For a moment, the ward was visible—a color somewhere between gold and silver, encompassing the entire island like a bubble.

Fire exploded into the ward.

But the ward didn't buckle. Instead, it reflected that fire straight back from where it had come.

Their ship imploded. Warm relief slid through my tense muscles, loosening them.

Prisca shuddered, but her eyes gleamed with suppressed victory.

My gaze turned to Regner, standing on the deck of his ship. His expression was cold. I smiled.

"Regner was watching. He won't know how the ward works. All he will know is that Quorith fired on his fleet. Verdion is no longer neutral. You did it, wildcat. Quorith and their ships are in this war whether Verdion likes it or not."

Rythos had managed to contact his cousins, who'd evacuated civilians from that side of the island. We'd known the wards would hold—unlike the remaining fae wards, Verdion had ensured Quorith's wards were continually bolstered every few months. Besides, Quorith's wards were created with an ancient sea magic. The island had always been a little…different. Not quite sentient, but not entirely normal. Still, we'd both refused to risk innocent lives.

We'd made the first move—one that would hopefully pay off throughout the rest of the war.

Daharak whooped, her voice spilling from the trowth stone. "That was beautiful. How did you know that island was going to reflect their magic?" She suddenly let out a hiss. "Prepare for attack!"

Regner lifted his hand, and one by one, those elemental cannons began to fire.

PRISCA

"Wards!" Galon's voice screamed from the stone. Our warders raised their hands as one, and my lungs constricted as the elemental cannons spat fire and ice.

The wards held. Our people cheered.

And the cannons were loaded once more.

But it wasn't just the cannons we had to contend with. Regner wielded his stolen power—power he had given his most trusted generals, along with those he had plucked from obscurity simply because he'd learned of their gifts. Now, they aimed that power at us.

"Fire!" Lorian roared, and our archers aimed at Regner's ships.

Regner sent arrows of his own. Arrows made of fae iron. And from the way Galon flinched, I could tell it hurt when they hit his ward.

Daharak's people rallied, her ships providing enough cover that Regner couldn't yet get through to Jamic and the others. Without the pirate queen, we would have died here today. That knowledge sank into me like a stone dropped into a pool of water.

My power was best used here, on the battlefield. But I had to pick and choose my moments. Eventually, that power would be drained, and I would have nothing left. It killed a piece of me when several wards buckled farther down the line—and one of Regner's ships took full advantage, blowing one of our own ships out of the water. But I couldn't think of all those lives lost in this moment. I had to stay focused.

Regner had the wind. And his ships slammed into our front lines.

Lorian struck.

Conreth let loose with his power.

Madinia's fire arched through the air, aiming for the masts, sails, and rigging.

The perfect distraction while Rythos attempted to board Rekja's ship, a tiny, frail woman at his side.

MADÎNIA

When I'd asked where Rythos had disappeared to yesterday, Lorian had told me he was busy *making friends*. Galon had walked in with Jamic and interrupted before I could clarify exactly what that meant.

Now I understood.

Rythos had been busy using his magic on Rekja's crew. So when his ship approached, the crew merely waved at him, gesturing for him to board. I watched through the spyglass as the Gromalian prince's mouth dropped open. Color swept up his cheeks, and he yelled something—likely ordering them to fire.

They ignored him, extending a gangplank instead—all while Rekja's captain nodded, a wide smile on his face.

Rekja snarled, lifting his own hand in warning as he said something to Rythos. Rythos gestured to one of the pirates, who guided a woman toward him. She was so thin, she looked like she might snap, and she clutched the man's arm with both of her hands. When Rekja saw her, his face drained of color.

Telean had done it. She'd found the evidence we needed. The proof that Eryndan had killed Rekja's mother.

She'd located his aunt.

Rythos helped her walk across the gangplank, his steps graceful. When he was just a few foot spans from Rekja, he held out a message.

Rekja took it.

His aunt stepped forward, and Rekja's hand dropped to the sword at his side. My heart jumped into my throat. When we'd discussed this plan weeks ago, Prisca had been certain he was reasonable. That he would listen. Yet the prince was clearly enraged, his face tight as he snarled something.

Slowly, his aunt slipped her hand beneath the neckline of her dress.

I barely breathed.

Rekja's mouth was frozen in a snarl, but his face turned blank and the air shuddered from my lungs. The necklace his aunt was holding was clearly familiar to him.

He snapped some words that made his guards melt away. Then he stepped closer to his aunt, examining the necklace.

Tears were rolling down her cheeks now. Dropping the necklace, she held out her hand. Rekja took her hand, bowing his head. She spoke for several long moments, replying to his questions. Finally, he dropped her hand and stalked to the other side of his ship, his hands gripping the railing.

I felt a presence to my right and turned. Daharak was watching through a spyglass of her own.

"How long has this plan been in place?" she asked.

"Prisca has been attempting to turn Rekja since the

moment she met the Gromalian king and realized he would never ally with us."

"And she thinks this woman will change that?"

I turned my attention back to the spyglass, watching as Rekja's shoulders shook.

"The Gromalian prince has just learned that everything he knows is a lie. His father killed his mother. Not to mention, the moment he learned Rekja was in love with a guard, Eryndan directly threatened her life. Rekja may not ally with *us*, but I'm betting he won't ally with his father anymore either."

Rekja shouted something to his crew.

His ship was turning, until he faced Eryndan, who was speaking to one of his guards.

Rekja lifted his hand. Eryndan's senses must have screamed at him, because he whirled, but it was too late.

Rekja speared him with his power and blew his father apart.

PRISCA

Eryndan's ship *exploded*. Even from this far away, the heat bathed me, and I felt Galon reinforce his wards as the others continued to fight.

I'd expected Rekja to turn on Eryndan. To demand the crown. To perhaps kill him at a later date.

I hadn't dared to hope for this.

Rekja's ship was now turning northwest, back toward the Gromalian capital. The Gromalian fleet was in tatters—their captains clearly confused. Several other ships followed Rekja's, while others seemed to be waiting for further orders.

I turned to Regner's ship. He stood at the helm, hands on his hips as he barked orders of his own. The invisible chain around my lungs began to unravel. Perhaps this battle was turning in our favor. Perhaps—

I caught movement next to Regner. My heart seized.

My cousin stood next to the Eprothan king, his gaze on our ships.

Zathrian and Regner were working together.

And next to my cousin…

Eadric.

Fury burned through my body, incinerating every thought other than "kill." If we could just get close enough, we *could* kill them. But along with Regner's own wards, he'd surrounded his ship with what were likely the best human warders in his kingdom, his ship floating among so many others, I kept losing sight of him.

Just footspans away, Lorian was fighting, teeth bared, his lightning cracking again and again. He'd told me to wait until the next opportunity to use my power. The next time I could do the most damage.

Daharak's soldiers were highly trained. As were Conreth's. But Regner's and Eryndan's outnumbered us five-to-one. And with so much of our power being directed at the barrier instead of right here against our enemies…

We were on the defensive.

Conreth's power tunneled through our enemies' wards like an icy spear. He was aiming for what he'd called high-value targets—Regner's generals, advisers, and anyone else who seemed critical to the human king's army.

As I watched, Conreth's power slammed into a ship on Regner's front lines. Six men stood on the deck. Their ward shimmered, and Conreth's ice arrowed through it, driving into all six men. Ice swept up their bodies, along their legs, their torsos, until their faces were frozen. And then they shattered. Nausea swept through me. Nausea and reluctant admiration. But…had the ward surrounding their ship faltered moments *before* Conreth struck?

My instincts screamed at me.

I was missing something.

"Prisca." A voice came from the trowth stone.

I picked it up. "What is it?"

Daharak's voice was a rough growl. "Tell me you know the people in that piss-poor excuse for a ship before one of my captains blows it out of the water."

What was she…

I whirled. Daharak was right. The ship that approached from the east could hardly be called seaworthy. Patched sails billowed with holes, the mast leaned slightly askew, and the rigging was as tangled as uncombed hair.

It was an old merchant ship, likely procured illegally. And its passengers…

My lungs turned to stone and then expanded, my heart soaring.

"What is it?" Lorian asked.

"It's…" My throat was too tight to speak.

Lorian studied my face and lifted the trowth stone. "They're here to help," he said. "Don't touch them."

Daharak said something, but I was too busy watching Natan and what had to be a hundred other humans— dressed in mismatched armor and wielding old crossbows and dulled swords, a clearly stolen cannon listing off the side of their ship.

Somehow…somehow, Natan had survived the massacre of our village. And he'd found others willing to fight.

I am, however, attempting to get some more help to you in time. Vicer had written. And this was what he'd been working on.

We might all die here today, and yet they'd come anyway.

Our ship rocked beneath us. Something had slipped through our ward.

"Now, Prisca!" Lorian yelled. And then he enveloped me in his arms, and I reached for my hourglass, pulling at the threads of my power. It was difficult. So difficult to only stop time for Regner's men. It had drained me when I'd done it just days ago at the Frosthaven Isles, where there had been far fewer ships to manage.

Our people jumped into action, taking advantage of the brief respite. Arrows slammed into Regner's front lines. Madinia was aiming her fire at the ship closest to hers, while Lorian lifted one hand from my body and aimed at several ships at once. Just a moment later, he closed that hand over mine.

"Let go."

It was easier this time. Just as it had been easier to focus on what was happening around me, instead of becoming lost in my power. Perhaps I was getting better. Or maybe it was that I was becoming drained and could no longer hold time for as long.

Several of Regner's ships exploded, their wards faltering beneath our attack. Fire swamped the one Madinia had hit, and Regner's soldiers jumped overboard, braving the ocean. Lorian was using his power like a spike, keeping it narrow and drilling it through the hulls of the ships on the front lines.

Our people were channeling as much power as they could into the barrier. But even with Conreth's and Galon's best warders protecting our ships, they couldn't hold against all the elemental cannons continually firing fire and ice—and iron arrows shooting through the sky toward us. Our wards buckled in places and were instantly shored up. But some of those elemental cannons sent our ships to the bottom of the sea, while those vicious fae-iron arrows slammed into fae and hybrid and human.

Turning, I surveyed our people, then Regner's and Eryndan's.

We were losing. If Verdion, Sylvielle, and Caliar had joined us, perhaps we would have taken down the barrier and slaughtered Regner's most powerful people. But the human king only had to keep us from bringing down the barrier. We had to kill them *and* find a way to smash the barrier without the grimoire.

Every single decision I'd made began to flash in front of my eyes. Sending Demos and Asinia after Tibris. Allowing Vicer to go back to the hybrid camp. Choosing to strike now, rather than waiting. My eyes met Lorian's. His expression was grim, but his eyes blazed with fury.

One of Regner's ships was circling us, attempting to get to Jamic and the others. Lorian's lightning torched the hull, and it went up in flames. But another ship was ready to take its place.

We were out of tricks. I had no more plans.

Their ships just kept coming.

If we dropped the wards, we would have enough power to take down the barrier. But the loss of life would be immeasurable.

Watching our people aim their power at the barrier, I understood. The fae could attack it from a distance, their power awe-inspiring. But there were others with power too. Immense power, even drained as they were. The problem was the distance. The hybrids and humans had to be much closer. Right now, their power was a weak stream compared to the fae.

Sweeping my gaze over our warship, I pointed at the small boat on one side of the deck. "What is that?"

Lorian aimed his power at the ship closest to Regner. He ignored my question, his lips curled in a vicious snarl. "When were you going to tell me your cousin was here?"

"Just as soon as we were close enough to kill him," I said.

"And I suppose the man standing next to him is *Eadric?*"

"Yes."

Lightning flashed through his eyes.

I'd threatened Eadric with Lorian. But this vengeance was mine to take. *I* was the one he should be afraid of.

"If we get the chance to kill them, we take it. But this is important, Lorian. We need to get anyone with enough power left into those small boats and as close to the barrier as possible. Now."

His brow creased further, but after a moment of deliberation, he nodded. "It's dangerous. If it goes wrong, anyone in the skiffs will be dead."

My stomach churned, and I forced myself to breathe through the instant nausea at the thought.

"I know. Make sure everyone knows how dangerous it is. I don't want anyone volunteering without full understanding. Can we hide them somehow?"

"If we create enough smoke, I can blow it toward them. But it won't last for long."

"It's our only chance."

He picked up the trowth stone. "Let's do it."

28

MADÎNIA

My hands ached as I clutched at the side of the skiff. It felt fragile, as if it could break apart at any moment.

So did I.

When Prisca's message had come, I hadn't hesitated. She needed one of us to lead the others, and I'd volunteered.

The gods had given me a power that simmered through my veins— urging me to burn and destroy whenever my rage took over. Perhaps all those years clamping down on that urge had been worth it. Perhaps every moment I'd spent wrestling with that power had been leading up to this.

Thankfully, Daharak's pirates lowered us quickly over the side of the ship. At least thirty of us were in the small boat, all of us tense, some trembling. On the ship, we'd been surrounded by weapons and shielded by wards. While the warders would protect us for as long as they could, once we slipped into place, all we could do was hope we could take the barrier down before one of Regner's ships spotted us and killed us all.

More boats joined us, all of them filled with anyone who'd volunteered. One of them looked as if it might sink before it made it to the barrier, drowning those inside. My gaze caught on their homespun tunics, their flimsy armor.

Villagers. These were humans. I didn't understand how they'd gotten here, but they were here all the same.

The wind changed, sending us all floating toward the barrier. Lorian. How the fae prince still had any power left was inexplicable in itself, but Prisca would use the hourglass while Lorian and Galon used their elemental powers to get us closer and hide us from Regner. If this didn't work…

No. I refused to even entertain that thought.

Wrapping my scarf around my face, I gestured for the others to do the same. Someone had created smoke, and Lorian's wind sent it straight toward Regner's ships, thick and black and choking.

On and on, we rowed, all of us grappling with oars, moving with the current.

It would be up to us. Fae with unremarkable magic and hybrids without the ability to attack from a distance. Humans who were willing to give what little they had. What little Regner hadn't taken.

They weren't the most powerful. The power they did have wasn't spectacular. But in the absence of great power, they had courage. And even though my heart had been hardened for years…my eyes still burned at the sight of fae and hybrids and humans joining together to risk their lives in one last attempt at bringing the barrier down.

Or perhaps my stinging eyes were due to all the smoke.

We glided toward the barrier, stifling our coughs, peering into the distance. The skiffs slowed, and it was evident Lorian knew exactly where that barrier was.

Either we succeeded today, or we died.

I wasn't ready to die.

"Madinia," a voice called.

I turned to see Jamic in the skiff next to mine, Thorn next to him. "Don't be afraid," Jamic said.

My teeth were chattering with fear, but I forced a smile. If there was one person here who should be afraid, it was him. Yet he smiled back at me.

Our skiffs began to turn, until we faced Regner's fleet, all of us maneuvering until we were directly next to the barrier. I could feel it alongside me, seething with its own power. It seemed to hum with *life*.

"Hands up," Jamic called.

We raised our hands, calling our power forth.

"Now!"

As one, every fae and hybrid and human slammed their hands—and their magic—into the barrier.

PRISCA

In the distance, the skiffs lined up, filled with some of the bravest people on this continent.

Madinia's red hair stood out, her dye almost completely faded. She lifted one arm, channeling her fire into the barrier. Everyone in her skiff did the same. Two boats over, Natan lifted his own hand, along with what had to be one hundred other fae, hybrids, and humans.

My throat tightened. Lorian had moved to the other side of the ship and was aiming the last of his power at the barrier. I could feel him weakening, exhausted.

Everyone was weakening.

I wished I had an attack power. Wished I could funnel everything I had into bringing the barrier down.

I turned toward Daharak. Her expression was victorious, as if there was no way this plan wouldn't work.

And her words rang in my head.

"That was beautiful. How did you know that island was going to reflect their magic?"

Reflect. Another word for "repel."

"Oh gods. Oh gods, oh gods."

Trembling, I looked up. The cloud of smoke Lorian had sent toward our enemies had drifted higher.

Blocking out the sun.

When the land itself repels war…

And unnatural clouds obscure the sun…

I whirled. Just as one of Regner's men raised his hand, creating a whirlpool of water in an attempt to drag the skiffs away from the barrier.

When the waves are coerced...

Where was the threat?

Urgency burned through me, until I panted, my gaze shifting from ship to ship.

My legs moved of their own accord, and I sprinted toward Lorian, still craning my neck, desperately searching.

One man wasn't using his power to take down the barrier. No, Conreth was staring at Regner himself, who was now standing on the upper deck of his ship, staring at the barrier, screaming at his soldiers.

Boom!

The sky cracked. It seemed as if the world had torn in two. The ship rolled, until I dropped to my knees, sliding on the deck.

The barrier had fallen.

I grabbed the nearest rope and clawed my way to my feet. Lifting my head, I saw the moment Conreth decided to risk it. His power hurtled across the waves, directly for Regner's ship. My heart stopped. Regner had some of his most important people on that ship. Including my cousin. Regenr may not die, but Conreth could end the others and cripple Regner's armies.

But my instincts were still screaming.

I stumbled toward my mate.

"Lorian!" I roared.

He'd thrown back his head in a victorious laugh. Gradually, as if in slow motion, he turned toward me.

I pointed at Regner's ship.

Regner ducked, and together, Regner, Zathrian, and Eadric lifted an object they'd kept carefully hidden.

A mirror.

When the waves are coerced...

And reflection deceives...

Dread exploded through my gut. I grabbed my hourglass and hauled my own power to me.

It didn't work.

Time didn't stop.

My lungs seized. I pulled harder. Nothing.

What was happening? I wasn't out. I still had power left.

On the ship, standing next to Regner, my cousin smiled at me, his hands high in the air, aimed at us.

He'd *neutralized* me.

That was why he was here. He'd saved his power just for this.

Conreth's power hit the glass. But instead of freezing and exploding, that mirror reflected his power.

A trick. Regner had sacrificed some of his most important people earlier, making sure his wards appeared weak, ensuring Conreth couldn't help but use his power...

That power was heading back toward our lines. But instead of Conreth, it was aimed at...

No.

The ship rocked again. Someone slammed into me.

One of Daharak's men. He fumbled an apology, but I was already pushing him aside as I tripped forward.

I launched myself at Lorian

Just as his brother's power hit him in the chest.

Lorian looked at me, and realization flashed across his beautiful face.

I saw him forming the words.

"In another life."

He was turning to ice, eyes blank. Gone.

For a single moment, I felt him next to me, his soul caressing mine.

I love you.

The ice exploded into thousands of pieces.

Conreth screamed his brother's name.

Everyone was shouting, ducking for cover.

But the sound dimmed.

No.

No, Lorian wasn't gone.

He'd promised.

"I want you to feel how much I love you. I'll always be with you, Prisca. It's you and me."

My hand snapped to the hourglass. Behind me, Telean was screaming.

"No, Nelayra, don't! It will *kill* you!"

I stopped time with a mere thought. I could feel Zathrian attempting to neutralize me, and I ignored him. He'd used all of his power to neutralize me once.

And one day, he would pay and pay and pay…

It was rage that drove me now, thundering through

my body. Through my soul.

I'd frozen time, but it wasn't enough.

No, if time restarted now, Lorian would still be gone.

Telean's voice seemed to echo through my mind.

"The world must be balanced."

I didn't care about the world.

The warnings I'd received pounded over and over in my ears.

Ysara, sympathy flickering through her eyes. *"Enjoy your time with your fae prince. But know this—you cannot keep him."*

The queen's seer, her voice matter-of-fact. *"The Bloodthirsty Prince will die."*

The gods may have demanded his death. They'd gotten what they wanted. But I would bring him back.

I didn't care that it was impossible. That, at the very least, it was forbidden. That if I succeeded, the gods might just smite me for my audacity.

Throwing back my head, I screamed, pulling every drop of power to me. I had so little left, and yet I took it from every part of my soul. And when there was nothing left, I took more.

Agony raged through me. And for the barest moment, Lorian's presence was next to me once more.

"Let go," he whispered. And there was so much love in those two words that it suddenly felt as if my chest was being crushed.

I didn't let go. I dug deeper. I pulled harder.

I pictured Lorian's soul reentering his body. Pictured

the tiny, shattered pieces of him reforming.

The hourglass heated, as if even the ancient artifact were screaming at me to stop. Pain burst through my head, dropping me to my knees. Gritting my teeth, I held on. He didn't get to leave me. He didn't—

Blood poured from my nose, leaked from my ears. It wasn't working.

Still, I held on.

"In every life, wildcat. No matter what happens, you hold on to that. It's you and me in every life."

I bared my teeth and shoved everything I had into defying the laws of nature and the gods.

In every life, Lorian.

THE END.

Thank you for reading a Crown This Cold and Heavy! I hope you enjoyed it! The next book is called A Queen This Fierce and Deadly, and it is the final book in this series.

Acknowledgments

Phew, this book was a rollercoaster, huh? I fully admit that there were times I sobbed like a baby while writing it. But Prisca had lessons to learn. Life isn't just about the people who surround you at your best. It's about the people who will pick you up off the ground when you're at your worst. When you're so heartbroken, you don't know how to keep going.

Thank you to my family and friends, who put up with me when I cancel plans last minute because I'm on deadline, or suddenly begin daydreaming as the perfect scene comes to me.

To my brother, Adam: thank you for being so invested and listening so intently when I tell you all the tiny details about publishing. Your excitement and enthusiasm mean you're always one of my first calls when something great happens.

To my incredible agent Kimberly: thank you for your patience, counsel, enthusiasm, and general kickass-ness. You're amazing.

Thank you to my amazing editors. Dawn and Lisa for being so flexible, even with last-minute changes. I promise to extend my deadline next time. ;)

To Fay, Elli, Angela, and Deb, I couldn't do this without you.

Thank you to Bianca from Moonpress, for my amazing covers, Amy for formatting, and Stella Colorado

(@petit_kitsune) for the gorgeous character art.

And last but never least, thank you to my readers. Thank you for every TikTok, Instagram post, review, comment, share, and email. Thank you for your enthusiasm, your support, and for every single page you read.

Stacia x